SPEAK OF THE DEVIL

SPEAK OF THE DEVIL

KARLA M. JAY

First Hedgehog & Fox Edition, May 2016

Library of Congress has catalogued the Hedgehog & Fox edition as
follows:
Jay, Karla M.
Speak of the Devil / Karla M. Jay. – 1st ed.
p. cm.
1. Humor — Fiction. 2. Thriller & Suspense — Fiction 3. Romance —
Fiction 4. Language — Fiction.

Cover design by Frances Parker.

More information can be learned about Hedgehog & Fox at
warnerliterarygroup.com

Printed in the United States of America.

ISBN 978-0-9961950-7-2 (original paperback)
ISBN 978-0-9961950-8-9 (ebook)

This is for all of my fellow speech and language pathologists. You understand what it takes.

"You have to stay in shape. My grandmother, she started walking five miles a day when she was 60. She's 97 today and we don't know where the hell she is."

—Ellen DeGeneres

Can I Buy A Verb?

As body parts go, I'm fascinated with mouths. I'm sure most speech therapists are. The King of Mouths, Mick Jaggar, happened to be belting out his lyrics on the radio, reminding me I couldn't always get what I want. Oh, the prophecy. This pretty much sums up the last three weeks at my new job in Tungs.

Mick reassured though that if I tried, I might just get what I need. There was hope.

At the moment I needed to find the home of Tinsel Tabbish, purported Chia Pet collector and a new patient in my whopping caseload of six. I turned off the radio and concentrated on Beaver Hollow Road where the instructions from my home-health agency, Therapy on Wheels, said a lane would veer off to the right "close to where the trees thinned."

The only thing thinning was my patience. I hated being late, but that's what was happening. I had no GPS, no access to a boy scout, and when I called my new patient, she tried to guide me to her house by saying, "By the forest for the dirt trail to car on."

This broken-down speech had me salivating to get started on this recovery, if only I could find her. Repairing tangled words and tormented language was another obsession, right up there with watching mouths. I loved words and always had, so when words become trapped behind stalled nerve fibers, I'd nearly die along with the person who couldn't say even the simplest of them. I dropped the driving instructions onto the seat of my aging silver Accord and did the only thing I could think to do—I phoned a friend.

"Marleigh?" Elyk Ash shouted over a clattering, roaring racket.

His mother, Ivory Ash, had been a patient of mine until a few days earlier when she miraculously recovered from a horrible voice condition. Thirty years earlier, she'd named her son Kyle after one last contraction shot him into the arms of a waiting nurse. Once the drugs wore off, she decided "Kyle" was boring, so she reversed his name. Elyk Ash. Unintended, but it sounded like a skin disease. *Well, looks like you broke out with a bad case of Elyk Ash."*

I shouted, "Elyk?" The loud buzzing revved up and backed off like a huge mosquito with Tourette's. "I can barely hear you."

He recently compared himself to the Michelangelo of Northern Pennsylvania, his sculpting tool a chainsaw and medium of choice not marble but a stump of wood. He carved overpriced yard ornaments to sell at his market, The Ash Country Store and Souvenirs.

When I first arrived in Tungston, I stopped at his store to ask directions. That's when I discovered the locals called the town "Tungs" for short, and right on cue, the jokes started about a speech therapist working in Tungs. Over the last few weeks, I met Elyk's girlfriend, Dottie, who was twenty-four, exactly my age, but a Little Person. Not that I was tall at five foot three inches. She was fondly called "a shorty" as she liked to call herself. Elyk and I had developed an oddball bond, which grew stronger when we helped each other overcome our deepest fears. He'd shown me how to catch a rattlesnake and I'd taken him clothes shopping at the big man's store.

The chainsaw stopped but he still shouted, "If you're calling to solve the puzzle, I already got the last answer. 'Chimera. A figment of the imagination'... You wouldn't have figured it out anyway."

Elyk had entered a sixty-day crossword puzzle contest to try to win $60,000. Each day by 5 p.m., the solution to forty-six clues needed to be emailed to puzzle headquarters, or the players were disqualified. If I counted correctly, this was day nineteen and he'd solved exactly five on his own.

I snorted. "That's an easy one." I moved the phone to my left ear, and rooted in my purse for a pen. "Which by the way, I have an address that is a chimera right now. I'm lost."

"You've been lost since you got here." He chuckled, more amused than seemed necessary.

"Not *this* lost." I sounded a bit whiny. I'd had a rough start on this job when I alienated one of my patients on my first visit to his home. Just recently, I was able to convince him to work with me again. Now I had a new patient in my caseload and being late wasn't going to help.

"Do you even have a clue what town you're near?"

He wasn't a guy who liked to chat, so impatience was already riding high in his voice.

"I went through Proxy and past that little church I like, then about two miles farther, I turned left on Beaver Hollow Road. There's supposed to be a lane—"

"I know where you are. Did you go over the old covered bridge?"

"A million times." I sighed. "I'm about a quarter mile from there now."

"Which side?" When I didn't answer right away, he said, "Just drive and tell me what you see." He cleared his throat and I knew he was about done being helpful.

I put the car in gear and pulled back onto the two-lane road, the tarmac veined with long runners of filler tar. I didn't believe her driveway was along here at all. I'd gone down this narrow pavement twenty times, and the forest on either side still looked as solid as green tapestry.

"Okay. There are trees on the left, a deer crossing sign, trees, a dead opossum. Oh, and here's something."

"What?"

"A sign for a school bus stop." With no houses in sight, I couldn't imagine why it was there.

"That's not helpful," he growled. "The road you want should be right there but it's gonna be one lane and hard to spot."

"Like flea lice?"

He paused, then said, "I *will* hang up on you."

"I know you will. Sorry."

I rolled along the asphalt, cutting my eyes from side to side. Cool air-conditioning lifted my hair off my neck as I leaned toward the windshield, squinting. "I'm just passing a crappy pickup...looks like it was abandoned before Kennedy got shot, and there is nothing ahead but—"

"Is anyone in the truck?"

He obviously wasn't listening any longer. "I just said it's been rotting here for about four decades. So, no."

Elyk didn't answer for a moment and I thought he'd hung up. "That's your stop. Your person parks at the end of their lane."

I studied the tree line behind the vehicle and spied the narrow opening. "Uh, you're right."

"Get a GPS," Elyk snapped, and then hung up.

Although this was a great idea, I didn't see that happening on my slim salary.

Fresh from my life in San Francisco, I'd underestimated the effects that hundreds of miles of pressing forest would have on me. I hadn't completely shaken the notion that all mass murderers got their start in rural places. They'd practiced by killing chipmunks, then beavers, and worked their way up to burly truck drivers. I'd recently lost fifty percent of my fear of the thick woods, but common sense grasped the other half and *me* at the moment. With the thought of heading down that tiny lane, the skin on my arms had gone all goose-bumpy.

Edging my car off road into the tall grass, the weeds ticked softly as they brushed the undercarriage. I pulled in behind the truck and turned off the engine.

The instant I opened the door, heavy humidity, pungent with scents green and fertile, enveloped me like sauna steam. Acclimated to the cooler, foggy climate of home, my system still caught a jolt each time I stepped out of air conditioning into the thick blanket of hot, heavy, wet air.

I popped the trunk, grabbed my therapy bag, and tossed my ID lanyard around my neck. The picture showed a startled version of me, taken at the very moment I'd found out that part of my job involved plastering large magnets to each side of my car, which read: *Therapy on Wheels—Wheely Good Care in Your Home.*

I was almost over the humiliation. Almost.

Easing my way past thistle and burdock bushes, I headed on foot toward the narrow road, moving alongside the rusting white truck. I stopped in front of the side mirror, and pulled it toward me. It hung loose, having lost a bolt. I pushed a blonde wave of hair off my forehead and studied the hard line of midnight blue, lining my eyes. Trying for a softer look, I ran my finger back and forth across the line, smudging it, making a mess in the end. Dottie had given me this eyeliner, saying it matched my eyes. I should have known better than to experiment. For now, I was stuck with clownish smears under my pale lashes. Pushing the old mirror back toward the window, the mirror completely snapped off and bounced to the ground.

"Crap!" I looked around. I was alone. Breaking my client's vehicle was a terrible first impression.

And it was probably my imagination, but the croaking and buzzing in the woods suddenly stopped like they'd been shushed, the quiet now louder than the previous sounds. I really needed to get over this claustrophobia, or *verdophobia* as I'd dubbed it—my fear of thick green places. I'd be here another ten weeks, finishing out my summer contract. I was also looking for my birthparents who, twenty-two years ago, gave me up for adoption from a town near here. Last week I learned they were dead. But there was still so much I needed to know, questions I needed to have answered.

Why was I given up at age two? Where had they lived or worked? How much did I look like them?

I reached for the broken mirror with remorse and put it into my therapy bag. In that same instant, I heard the hard click of a cartridge shell jacked into a gun chamber behind me. I might be a city girl and light years from being a hunter, but I was a moviegoer and this noise had no other twin in the sound universe.

I turned around very slowly and staring at me was a tall, raw-boned man pushing middle age. His face pockmarked around his black goatee. His mouth set tight. His eyes a squirmy brown.

My heart banged around in my chest, pushing short bursts of air out of my lungs. I was about to be shot by a man, perhaps one of those little-creature-killing mass murderers, but uglier than I'd imagined.

A few seconds bounced back and forth between us. I think my mouth opened and closed a few times, but the words refused to leave. My worst nightmare: I'd become aphasic.

"You busted off Frank's mirror," he said, spitting a streamer of blackish-brown liquid sideways onto the dirt path.

"I'm sorry." My voice was a traitor and I hardly recognized it. It sounded so off-key. "I bumped it as I was scooting by."

He shrugged. "Why'd you put it in your bag?"

I saw his point.

"I was taking it to the owner. To Tinsel." He'd mentioned a man. "And to Frank. I wanted to let them know what happened."

His black eyebrows bunched. "What're you doin' out here in the first place?"

Though he'd lowered the gun, I didn't like the way he stroked the barrel. And his question was valid. The same question I asked myself every other day since the contract had started. Why the hell was I here? There were genealogy databases online. I could search for the Kingstons from my apartment in San Francisco. But I had come here to feel part of *them*, to take in the air they breathed, to meet the people they surrounded themselves with. I raised my chin. "I'm Marleigh Benning, a speech therapist." I tapped my ID tag. "I work for Therapy on Wheels, out of Wellsfield. The woman who lives here is a patient of mine."

He stepped toward me and I recoiled, my back pressed to the heated metal of the truck's door. He shifted the gun and stuck out his hand. "Well, howdy then. You're seeing my ma."

There was no way around it. I reached for his hand, his skin dry and crusty. "You're her son?"

"Sure as shit ain't her daughter." If sarcasm had a face, he was wearing it. He caressed the gunstock and waggled his eyebrows. "Couldn't resist cocking my gun...it is an attention-getter, ain't it? Oh, and sorry about my truck blocking the road. I didn't know you were coming."

His truck? He'd said it was Frank's. I took a guess. "So *you* are Frank?"

Relaxing, I switched out the image of serial killer with that of just a weird relative. I could deal with weird, and I'd gotten pretty good at surfing and drowning in these dam-busting waves of fear.

He chuckled and spat another foul streamer into the weeds. "Let me be *frank* with you."

No. Tell me he isn't trying to be clever after nearly scaring the pee out of me! Don't think I would be too far off the mark in assuming Frank was single and ran in inebriated crowds.

"I called your mom, so she knows we have an appointment."

"A big thank you, then." He scratched his goatee as he studied me. "I've been taking care of the place while she was in the hospital. S'pose I'll be seeing you around."

Perhaps without pointing a gun at me? What was it around here about mothers and their curious sons? Maybe his name was Knarf. Did they know Elyk and his mother Ivory and her fascination for backward words? "Yes. Your mom's in my schedule three times a week."

His mouth did a strange twist that could have been a smile. "When's that?"

I wasn't proud of this but I had recently mastered the art of lying without hesitating. From begging off the chance to go squirrel hunting, to learning how to bottle venison. I added another lie now. "My company keeps me on a random-ized schedule, so I'm not sure when I'm here." I shrugged to validate the statement.

"Hhnn," was all he said. "Well, whatever. I got a pile of dead animals waiting on me."

Those words hung in the air like a foul ribbon of rotting meat. I reached into my bag. "Here." Then I handed him the mirror.

He tossed it into the open truck bed. "I'll send you the bill." His laugh was as corroded as his truck. He yanked open the door and a long, rusty scream of tortured metal ripped the air.

A shiver moved up my spine. When he pulled away, I turned and walked down the hard-packed dirt track toward Tinsel's house. Under the leafy canopy, butterflies fanned their bright wings, legs hooked on fading lilac clusters, the middle of June signifying the lilac's final days.

I tried to picture Frank's mom based on my impres-sion of him. I hoped she wasn't packing heat when I got to the house. What I knew about her was this: Tinsel was born on Christmas, which explained her name, and last month at age seventy-two, she'd had a stroke. She'd just returned home a few days ago from the hospital with a diagnosis of Anomia, which consisted of word-finding difficulties.

The lane opened up and I saw a pale green home in the center of a bright clearing, its brick patio loaded with blooming flowerpots. Neater than I'd pictured. A one-car garage and plenty of turnaround room made me question why Frank parked by the road.

I knocked on the aluminum door and waited. When it opened, a slender woman with short gray hair stood there. She was dressed in a blue-flowered blouse and navy polyester slacks, smiling widely. "In my house." She swept her arm toward the interior.

I catalogued her speech errors: short phrase, no verb.

"Sorry, I'm late, Mrs. Tabbish." Even though all my patients were considered homebound in the eyes of Medicare, it didn't mean I could wander in and out of their lives without a schedule. They had things to do. "I'll know right where to find you next time."

"No problem." She pointed to a dining room table just beyond the living room, all in gold tones. She nodded. "We chair at the table."

The house held a clean, lime scent. The wall to my right was lined with mismatched shelving, displaying dozens of greenish-gray pottery pieces.

"My pride," Tinsel said, indicating the aged Chia Pets.

"That's quite a collection." I reached the dining area, silently celebrating the clean house, having learned anything was possible once I crossed a patient's stoop.

I spotted a Chia Hans Solo in the middle of the kitchen counter, his grinning face topped by a full head of green sprouts. "You're up-to-date." While I unloaded a few books from my bag, I asked, "How long have you been collecting these?"

"Many, many years."

"Well, it shows." I wanted to get the subject of Frank out of the way. "I met your son."

"My boy." She crossed her hands on her chest and smiled. "A good boy."

"He said he does something with dead animals? I have to say I'm curious." I was going with the idea Frank could be any one of these three—a glue-maker, pet cemetery worker, or just damned strange.

"Taxidermist," Tinsel said. There was a mother's pride in her answer.

"That makes sense." Much better than the roadkill scenario playing in my head.

She shrugged. "Number one place for his job products. Some days, high in back of truck."

If the animals are dead, why carry a gun? Maybe Frank was a poacher. I wasn't going to ask. I'd have to talk to Lawyer Hunt about Frank Tabbish. Oh, his first name's Lawyer. He's not in any legal field, but he should be arrested for the way he kissed.

The hot fire chief in the nearby town of Mapleton, Lawyer seemed to know everyone within a tank-of-gas drive. With toffee-colored eyes and a body I imagined in only suspenders and briefs, he had been a pleasant surprise when I arrived. I'd been in his arms exactly four times, only one romantic. All the others were under emergency conditions. I was now aiming for more romance and fewer if any emergencies. But I didn't have a good record.

A hairless miniature dog stumbled into the room, ending my reverie of Lawyer. The dog looked older than moss and less alive than the clay collectables on the shelves.

"Here, Lovey," Tinsel cooed to the dog. It growled. She scooped up the animal, cuddling it.

Tinsel's chart made no mention of a dog. I turned to her. "I didn't know you had any pets." Since my first few days on the job, I'd gotten better at reading every detail about my patients after I accidentally let a man's dog out. That dog decided it was a jailbreak and had covered more countryside than the game warden before it finally returned home.

"Two months ago," Tinsel replied. "Frank from other town, Lovey in road, empty dog, sad. In car for here."

I got the gist. Frank had brought her a discarded dog. But I withheld judgment. I offered my advice only when it concerned a patient's speech and language, so my opinion of adopting a dog rescued from euthanasia didn't fall into that category. Tinsel set the dog back on the floor and it veered toward the wall.

"Lovey is probably good company." I patted Tinsel's back as we moved to the table to work. "Now, let's see what I can do for you."

We'd established she'd had ten sessions of speech therapy at the hospital. "Much better words out now," she bragged.

"I'm glad. But did you notice that you aren't using any action words? All your verbs are gone."

She appeared startled. "Really?" Then her shoulders slumped.

I didn't want to make her feel bad since she'd obviously progressed a great deal up to this point. "You're doing fine but let's explore this." I took out a data collection form to map out her utterances. "Tell me about your morning routine...like what you do every day."

She smiled. "I water and soap in the tub, percolator the coffee, and frying pan some eggs." She shrugged. "The usual."

"Ah. Did you hear that you said 'frying pan the eggs' instead of fry the eggs?"

Sadness changed her face as she shook her head 'no.' From her dangling earrings—tiny steepled churches—rang a jingle.

I pointed to her ear, hoping to lift her spirits. "Those are cute."

It worked. She touched them and said, "From my Church in the Pines up the road."

I'd been by this church a lot, especially when I used to visit Elyk's mother in Proxy. "I know right where it is. And the marquee in front has some pretty creative messages."

Her face lit up and I knew I'd found the common ground, the *in topic* we could always fall back on if therapy became too hard. She said, "My favorite one so far...When you under water, God a lifeguard that shoe on water."

I smiled. I'd seen this message just last week:

If you're drowning, get the lifeguard who walks on water.

Tinsel clasped her hands in front of her chest. "Pastor Betts the best man in the world." She got a dreamy look in her eyes. I imagined a clean-cut, white-haired pastor, charming the stretch pants off the members of the women's organization, joking with the youth if there actually were any young people attending, and trying to keep his worshipping minions tithing and baking noodle casseroles.

Elyk said the pastor had turned the church around by allowing casual dress attire and better community activities. "He's new here, isn't he?"

"Yes. Three months ago."

"Sounds like a nice guy." I reached for my therapy bag and pulled out pictures of people involved in daily activities. "Okay, let's resurrect a few of your missing verbs."

I placed a card on the table. "Repeat this after me. 'Feeding the baby.'"

"Spoon the baby." She crumbled at her awareness of the words.

I smiled. "Don't be upset. You'll be verbing all over the place soon. Honestly. It'll just get better with practice."

Her eyes held a rim of wetness but nothing spilled down her powdered cheeks.

"Just say, 'feeding,' when I say it." I drew out the 'F' and said the word slowly.

She repeated it along with me. I said, "See? It's going to work."

We practiced talking about the twenty pictures I laid out on the table, and after forty minutes, we reached the point where she could repeat the words much more quickly. This was the part of my job I loved. I could watch the dams break, the words and expressions form and flow freely.

Lovey wobbled her way toward us and snuck under the long, lacy tablecloth. A warm, sandpapery tongue licked the top of my foot and I jumped. "Oh! She's licking me." I lifted the white cloth and looked under. The dog's head was resting on my foot. I lifted my shoe and tried to ease her away gently.

Rejected, Lovey turned on me.

"No, Lovey!" Tinsel shouted. "No teeth in foot!"

I will lose it if this dog bites me.

The dog lunged onto my foot and bit into my canvas shoe. Shoes I had just purchased after another pair had been ruined. Jumping to my feet, I pushed the chair backward against the wall. I heard pottery pieces knock together and prayed nothing broke.

As Lovey emerged from under the table, Tinsel rushed to pick up her dog. As if at the circus, the animal keeled over, mid-snarl, like she'd been shot.

I'd read about this before but had never seen it. "Is she narcoleptic?" I asked.

"No," Tinsel said. "Miniature poodle."

I covered up my laughter by clearing my throat, and quickly packed my things. Then I set up our next appointment, and left pictures and sentences for her to practice.

"I'm very excited to be working with you."

"Happy with you, too." She reached for a dusty Chia Pet of Porky Pig. "You in your house." She pushed it into my hands.

"Oh, I couldn't. I can't accept any gifts, Mrs. Tabbish."

She took the Chia pig back.

My gaze dropped to Lovey, who hadn't moved, and I hoped she wasn't dead. "Will she be all right?"

"Little nap, then good."

"Okay." I closed the door. On the way to my car, the scene with Frank, pointing a rifle at my back, replayed in my mind. Everyone around here seemed to own weapons. I needed to get used to it. Besides, Tinsel seemed normal enough. How bad could Frank actually be?

The bright warm sun felt good, and I smiled when I saw that my car was the only vehicle in sight. Then I spotted something. Propped up against my windshield was that freshly dead opossum, I'd seen on the road, with Frank's side mirror clasped between its paws.

Frank *was* a whacko.

My eyes shot in every direction. Was he watching from the woods in order to see my reaction? I dropped my therapy bag in the trunk and grabbed the tire iron. I tried not to look too closely at the sad, lifeless furball. I lifted the animal with the tire iron and walked toward the trees. I gave the iron an arm flip and the poor creature somersaulted from the force into the bush, still holding the mirror!

Frank had wired the mirror to its tiny paws. My breakfast began to rise in my stomach, so I had to do some deep breathing to keep it down.

Once in the car, I locked the doors, blasted the air conditioner, and flooded the windshield with wiper fluid, letting the wipers clear the view *and* my mind. I couldn't wrap my head around taking the time to wire a car part to a dead animal, just for the sake of a bad joke. It danced the line between criminal and crazy.

Putting the car in gear, I sped away, kicking up gravel.

Then Lawyer and his lips came to mind. His mouth was currently at the top of my list, especially when he wasn't talking. Or smirking.

We had a date scheduled for tomorrow night. I planned to show him what the four muscles of the tongue could do beside produce speech.

HOME AWAY FROM HOME

Tinsel was my only visit today, so I headed toward Tungs and to the safety of the Pfoltz's (that's pronounced *Foltz-ez*) Bed & Breakfast where I was renting for the summer. Richard and Rose Pfoltz were spry, both in their seventies, with more energy than most forty-year-olds. Their Victorian house was busy from May to October as visitors to the Little Grand Canyon chose it over the hotels in Wellsfield. They advertised a well-earned five-star rating with many guests returning each year.

I parked in the driveway of the red brick Victorian. Rising out of the thickly wooded hillside, the B&B now felt like home. It reminded me of the houses terracing the hills at home in San Francisco, and after losing my parents, I received such a warm welcome from Richard and Rose when I arrived. You could name a line of soft flannel pajamas after these two. They maintain this huge house, which was a busy funeral home and mortuary in the late 1800s. The large, welcoming home softened the finality for families of the men who died in the lumber profession, the industry that built this area. One book in the B&B library, *The Ghost Towns of Northern Pennsylvania*, revealed these were originally logging camps that lost their rush, leaving behind desiccated buildings and dried-up hope. A few of the towns were said to be haunted. Whether the rumors were true or stirred to attract tourists, I chose to steer clear of creepy empty logging camps, having already fulfilled my quota of fainting spells, hospital visits, and near-death experiences.

I parked the car and pulled my therapy bag from the back seat. I was surprised that Milt, Richard's father, wasn't in his usual seat on the wide front porch. Milt was close to ninety but looked twenty years older, and at times, seemed utterly lifeless. However, he proved he was no one's fool. Stuck in a body that had declined and wilted around him, he was sharp, and on several occasions had beaten me at a hand of twenty-one. I'd taken him on as my private client, trading my speech therapy services for a phone on the Pfoltzes' plan. Until last week, Milt hadn't spoken for years. I'd coaxed an eight-word vocabulary from him and now this elfish man in a bow tie desperately needed to expand his word pool. He had the word "hate" down pat and the guests at the inn were often the targets of his finger-pointing and "I hate you," "I hate the man," or "The man is a wolf." Since he started talking again, he looked like someone had connected a tire pump and inflated him a few PSIs. I wondered where he was and then thumped up the thickly carpeted steps to my lavender-colored room.

The small room with a double bed, desk, and rocking chair had one big personal advantage—a walk-in closet. While some people buy clothes because of the way the material feels, my purchases were based on the way they smelled. Silk could be earthy with almost a dirt smell or even a hint of coriander, but the fishy and metallic silks I couldn't deal with. To avoid looking like a pervert in stores, I'd haul armfuls into the dressing room and emerge with the clothes that met my olfactory needs. In times of stress, which really covered the last three months of my life, a closet full of the entwined scents of cloth, canvas, and leather had been a lifesaver.

Voices pulled me to the window overlooking the expansive backyard. A creek bubbled along the right side of the lawn, and a Koi pond was off to the left under a trellis. There he was. Milt was on a bench, head lolled back, enjoying one of a half-dozen naps he fits into his day. I raised my eyes to the hillside and the woods at the back of the property where Milt's wife, Miriam, had been laid to rest in the two hundred-year-old private cemetery. I'll take Milt up there again and hope he'll have more to say to his wife, who had been gone three years now. But we would have to drive the short distance. Milt moves slower than a cold caterpillar.

Laughter floated up from below where Rose was teaching four B&B guests how to turn antique plates into wall decorations embellished with decals, spelling out uplifting thoughts like HOPE and LAUGHTER. Rose is petite, wears her gray hair short, and can cook like no one I know. Granted, I arrived here stressed, emaciated, and hungry, but I've gained ten pounds from her delicious gourmet meals and desserts. Which explained why my clothes were a little tight. I peeled off my work outfit and pulled on my running gear.

Once I was out the front door, I headed down the long narrow drive that met up with the two-lane road. This eventually reached a highway deemed busy enough to warrant painting dashes down its center. I had a three-mile route but today I wanted to add more miles. During my last two months of grad school at San Francisco State University, I had increased my distance to twelve miles in an effort to keep myself from thinking about my parents' death. My *adoptive* parents. How long would it take me to start thinking of Marc and Janette Benning as my adoptive parents? I had to reverse twenty-four years of the opposite belief.

Picking up my pace, I let my mind lose its thoughts and drew in the scents of warm greenery and the humid marsh. Cicadas buzzed above and a netting of gnats hovered steady in front of my face. By the time I reached the intersection, I was swatting bugs and sweating, my heart pounding to the beat of my footfalls.

I slowed as I neared Elyk's store and spotted the sheriff's cruiser parked at one of the two gas pumps. Printed along the car doors were the words, Moose Run, a town about three doors over from Tungston.

A memory, just a flash, pulled me to a stop: the police at my apartment door last March. *"Terribly sorry. Marc and Janette were killed immediately... at the John Wayne airport. A Malaysian jumbo jet rolled over their Cessna 170."* And that shock was still deep when, only a few weeks later, I found adoption papers in their safe. I was two when someone in Butterfield, Pennsylvania, signed me over to them. Even as I had pushed my legs up the steep streets of Nob Hill, raced across the Golden Gate Bridge in the foggy cold dawn, or wound through the hillside trails in the Presidio, one thing remained a constant. Always there. Taunting. "My parents didn't want me."

I crunched across the gravel lot, heading for the hose Elyk kept to the side of the building, wondering if he was in trouble with the law. He liked to hunt whenever he wanted. In other (legal) words, he liked poaching. He'd told me about his out-of-season "procurements" in confidence, and since I didn't need a 300-pound guy built like a black bear angry with me, I'd told no one else.

Being too thirsty to care, I drank from the hose and headed into the store. The buzzer on the screen door sounded when I pulled it open.

Elyk stood behind the counter drinking a Rolling Rock beer. He wore his customary work uniform. Black jeans and a plaid shirt with the sleeves cut off at the shoulder. His dark hair was cut shorter on the sidewalls, and rose into long gelled spikes that swept back from his forehead, conjuring what Paul Bunyan would look like in a porcupine hat.

The Sheriff leaned against the counter with his arms folded, his leather belt loaded with cop gear and then some. He turned and stopped talking when I entered, but he'd been saying something about the mud in Mexico. He was tanned with wavy blond hair and a thick mustache.

"Hey, Marleigh," Elyk said. "This here's Jaxson Mills. He's a running fool, like you."

"Nice to meet you." Jaxson dropped his hands to rest on his belt, the leather creaking as it shifted. "You're looking ratchet."

I hated that word. It was big back home, as in, "That outfit is so ratchet." Funny, the same slang had drifted to this rural area. I stuck out my hand and walked toward him. "Thanks. Nice to meet you."

He had an overly exuberant handshake, sending a sharp pain through my palm. Why squeeze someone's hand like wringing juice from a lemon? The words *small dick* popped into my head. I forced a smile. "Elyk doesn't understand the whole running deal."

Elyk shrugged. "I understand lots of things...black holes, why cows face north or south while grazing, chicken barbequed in Coke. Running for fun is unfathomable."

I laughed. "You do not eat Coke-covered chicken."

Elyk took a slug from his beer. "I'll bake it for you when you have a makeup party for Dottie."

His girlfriend was a Mary Kay representative in one of the remotest parts of the U.S. Enthusiastic enough, I couldn't imagine there were enough women in the area to keep her sales up. "I'll talk to her but I don't know who I'd invite."

Jaxson moved closer, a supportive look on his face. "I have lots of female tweeps. I could contact the local ones."

"Tweeps?"

He stood a bit taller. "My Twitter Peeps."

"Oh." I saw Elyk smile behind Jaxson's back.

"Also belong to a local running club if you're interested." He cracked his knuckles. His gun was holstered in his belt and he swung his arm wide around it, drawing attention to it more than anything.

A running club might be fun. "How far do you run?"

"We try to put in a decade, sometimes we boss up more."

I hate slang. This guy is butchering words all over the place. Were the words *ten miles* too much? He was waiting for my answer. I tried for an equally indirect answer. Holding to his analogy of a decade, I quickly did the math and said, "My goal is to reach a one twentieth of a year."

Elyk laughed but Jaxson's look screamed math wasn't in his skill set. Or was that in his "sket"?

"About eighteen miles," I said.

Jaxson cleared his throat and ducked his head as he fumbled with his wallet. "Here." He handed a business card my way. "Give me a call, if you want to lay some tread with us."

I accepted the card. "Thanks, I'll let you know." Running alone was preferable to listening to him slaughter the English language for one more second. I tried to think of a place to carry his card but since I was without pockets, I slid it into my running bra.

He seemed to be waiting for something else. I remembered he and Elyk had been talking about Mexico when I walked in. "Were you on vacation?"

"Nope. Too busy with crime to fold away the old badge."
He tapped his chest.

Who was he kidding? Petty theft and drunk-driving stories made the news in the local paper. "There's not much crime around here, is there? And I heard you mention Mexico so I thought—"

"Mexican Mud. Skag, H, Black Tar, Birdie Powder."

My eyebrows rose into half moons.

Elyk rescued me. "Heroin. A farmer's kid keeled over in the feed store this morning. OD'd."

"Ah." I nodded. "Hadn't heard all those other names before."

Jaxson adjusted his hat and pulled a set of keys from his pocket. "Seems we got a big problem here now. Kids used to get high or drink too much. Now they gotta ride the horse or get skagged."

I looked to Elyk. "Heroin?"

He grinned and said, "Yup."

"I'm busting outta here." Jaxson slapped a palm on the countertop and swaggered from the store.

I noticed Elyk was watching me. "What?" I asked.

"He likes you."

I squinted at him and blinked. "Too much work. He hardly speaks English."

He finished off the beer and dropped the can into a recycle bin. "You still have the hunky fireman chasing you?"

I tightened the hair tie on my ponytail. "Yeah. Hope he catches me soon."

Elyk cut open a box and started unloading jars of pickled beets. "I'll tell Dottie you'll have a makeup party at the Bed and Breakfast next Wednesday."

"I have to ask Rose first." My eyes danced around in their sockets while my brain tried to come up with someone else to invite. "And seriously, who would I invite?"

"The guests might think it's fun. My mom would come. And aren't you seeing any new people for therapy?"

I'd be fired for inviting my patients. "I'll see what I can do." I headed for the door. "Talk to you later."

I was nearly out of the parking lot when Elyk yelled, "Invite the fireman's old girlfriend." I didn't turn but I knew he'd be smiling.

Veronica. Jealousy sent a ripple through my chest. Although I wanted to trust Lawyer when he said he and Veronica were only friends and no longer involved, I was reminded of the way I first saw them together. Her arm hooked around his, both of them laughing. And she lived in his mother's home, where he also lived. I pushed my legs harder and aimed for a long uphill climb that would take me in a new direction. I stuck to the side of the road, my feet crunching the small stones there. The thick woods on each side of me, pulsing out scents of something fungal, yet freshly grown and woodsy. A crow took flight from the weeds ahead and I flinched. When I reached the spot the sheriff had vacated, a garter snake squirmed in the dirt, half of its body crushed by a car but still trying to make an escape.

I empathized. I'd been half smashed by the loss of my parents in California and now I was looking for an escape from the pain of being alone. When I learned I might have relatives in northern Pennsylvania, I grabbed the job at Therapy on Wheels, reaching for a new lifeline.

My legs were burning, but I leaned into the hill and modulated my breathing. The trick to surviving a steep incline was not to look up. You watch the road just in front of your next step and you keep doing that until the surface levels out. Running hills and living life are a lot alike.

Lawyer promised to help me find more information about my birthparents—the Kingstons. That was the hill I was currently climbing, taking several small steps forward, looking for relatives, hoping I wasn't completely alone. I had never thought about wanting brothers and sisters but when my parents died, I wandered their house alone, needing someone to talk to, someone to go over the details of planning their funerals and burying them. Instead, I huddled in the recesses of my apartment's closet, and came out for important events, like finishing my thesis, graduating, signing the legal papers to change ownership of their property to me.

I crested the hill and headed down the long slope into the next valley.

When the dust of the legal matters cleared, I inherited a trust fund that included their too-big house outside of San Francisco, investments, and a good chunk of cash. I'd get it all in six years when I turned thirty. Currently, I had under $2,000 to my name and a burning need to *belong* someplace.

Thirty minutes later I was back at the home, I mean the B&B, pushing through the beveled-glass front doors on an endorphin high. The antique furnishings looked brighter around the edges. The lilacs in a vase on the entry table filled my nasal passages all the way to my brain, and I was feeling no pain. I showered and headed to the spacious kitchen decorated in deep green and maroon tones with dark wooden ceiling beams, and hanging copper pots and pans.

Rose hummed as she cut cooked chicken breasts into chunks. A satisfied smile stretched across her face. She was in her element, preparing another fancy meal.

"Can I help you?" I moved to her side.

She smiled. "It's an easy recipe this time. I'll be okay." She washed her hands and pulled long skewers from a drawer.

"What are we having?" In twenty days, we had not eaten the same thing twice.

"Balsamic chicken and fig skewers, a watermelon, tomato, and mozzarella salad, and I just popped blueberry tarts in the oven."

"Honestly, Rose...do you know how that's not even remotely considered an easy meal?" I rolled my eyes. "It smells wonderful already."

She threaded chicken and figs on the long metal sticks. "Was it a good run?"

"It was." I leaned over the sink and filled a glass with water. "I'm going to be sore tomorrow because I added miles."

"I envy you. Do it while you can."

We both turned at the sound of someone entering the room.

Rose said, "Marleigh. These are our newest guests, Betty and Earl Wilson from Maine."

I stuck out my hand and greeted the couple who looked more like brother and sister than husband and wife. Round faces, jack-o-lantern smiles, with wild gray hair and comfortable slouches. "It's nice to meet you. I promise, you'll love your stay. This is THE best Bed and Breakfast on earth."

Earl spoke. "We saw the reviews online." His voice ended with a questioning lilt.

Betty leaned over the food preparations. "And not just breakfast. Three meals a day." She turned to me. "How long are you staying?"

"I have a summer job in the area. I'll be here through August."

Honestly, both of them seemed a little high. They were smiling a little too widely, their cheeks next to their ears. Earl asked, "What do you do?"

"I'm a speech pathologist, working for a home-health company."

Rose raised a loaded chicken skewer in the air. "She has already helped my father-in-law speak again and he's been mute for years."

Betty dropped a hand on my back, the force pushing me ahead a step. "That's wonderful. You know, my grandmother lost her speech and it was just horrible."

"I'm sorry. It's so hard not being able to talk." I hesitated then asked, "Did she get any speech back?"

She shrugged. "Not really. But the horrible part wasn't the lack of speech, it was when she would spit on the glass table and write out words in it." *They had to be stoned or drunk on their own cider.*

Earl added, "And she wasn't much of a speller either, so it wasn't all that helpful." The couple bobbed their heads in tandem.

Yup. Stoned. "Well, we have better training techniques these days. Spit therapy has pretty much gone the way of the spittoon," I said.

They smiled, obviously missing my sarcasm. I changed the subject. "How long are you in the area?"

Betty pulled out a chair and sat at the small kitchen nook area where Rose and Richard took their private meals. She planted her palms flat on the table and leaned forward. "A few days. We're floating the Piney Creek River and we want to visit the Lumber Museum. Mostly, we just needed a break from our apple cider business."

Earl had his wallet out and was handing me a card. "That's us. Betty and I started this about ten years ago."

I studied the card. "Did you design this?" An apple orchard was hand-drawn across the bottom with the words *All Things Apple Cider!* written above it.

Earl stuck his hands into the waistband of his pants and I hoped he was a frequent hand washer. "Sure did."

I put his card in my back pocket. "It must be nice to be entrepreneurs."

Betty said, "We grew this company from a few scraggly apple trees."

Rose wiped her hands on her apron. "Outside of apple cider, what else do you sell?"

Earl moved to the table to stand by his lookalike wife. "Cider donuts, cider cake, gum, tobacco, hair spray, deodorant, foot powder."

"Wow." I smiled. "You weren't kidding with that slogan, *All things apple cider*, were you?" *Did people really want an apple cider scent covering up their underarm BO? I couldn't decide if it would be an improvement.*

Betty held up her hands. "We may give up the donut part. We make them on conveyor belts with these sweeping glazers. We have to take the hot donut off the belt by hand while it's still got the scalding glaze on it. I actually have no feeling left in my hands." She turned them back and forth in the air, then smacked them together hard as if that clarified it for me.

Her extra hard pat on my back made sense now. "That's bad." I paused and thought for a moment. "How about some gloves?"

Earl tapped his T-shirt. "You are reading our minds. We're heading into an apple cider infused clothing line, and gloves are a good idea."

I felt my brows bunch and noticed that Rose's face matched mine. "I meant, could you use gloves to get the donuts off the belt?"

"Not the way it's done, Marleigh." Betty waggled her index finger from side to side.

When Richard pushed through the back door, I was saved. He reminded me of my grandfather, who'd been the biggest tease. That was before his laryngectomy left him with a fake buzzing voice. Like Richard, my grandfather was a whistler, always with a nameless tune on his lips.

Richard placed a bowl of red cherries on the counter and turned toward me. "I see you've met the Wilsons. They're convincing me to put in an apple orchard."

Rose opened the oven to check the dessert.

"With your giant chess set, you are already the coolest B and B around," I said.

The twelve-foot square playing area was laid out on a cement pad near the maple shack off the back patio. The giant chess game recently arrived and was a hit with the guests. The lightweight pieces were life-size and intricately painted.

"Yes, but an orchard will take years to grow..." Richard washed his hands in the sink, talking over his shoulder. "People will be tired of giant chessmen by then."

Rose nudged him out of the way with her hip, her hands full of greens. "Okay, big dreamer. Can you set the table?"

I left them with Earl and Betty, talking about the medical benefits of apple cider. I didn't need to hear the word hemorrhoid twice to know it was time to go find Milt.

Milt leaned to the left, where he sat on the bench next to the Koi pond. Over his head, green tendrils of the flowering orange trumpet vine and blue morning glories interwove across the trellis, tempering the sunlight to create a lacy umbrella overhead.

"Hi, handsome." He didn't move. I sat next to him and watched the dozen marbled fish, cutting leisurely below the surface. Rose had them trained, so they would come to her at the side of the pond to get their morning serving of dried bug pellets. They also seemed to know that when people took the bench, it wasn't worth the energy to swim toward them. "I started work again today."

Milt slowly raised his eyes my way. His powder blue shirt made his eyes startling sapphires set in folded layers of skin. While his eyes announced his depth, they also betrayed his prison. He cleared his throat then wiped his palms down his gray slacks. He had something to say.

Like a pressure cooker, he needed time to build up—o be ready—to release his few words. I waited. A large Monarch butterfly landed on the edge of the stone bird-bath just beyond the pond. I jumped when I felt Milt's bony hand touch my arm. His eyes were boring into mine and he started to shake.

"You can say it." I leaned in closer. "I'm not in a hurry."

His lips quivered, then he said, "I hate..." His voice was oxidized, disuse making it almost scary.

This was how he started most phrases. "Try to just breathe out the next words, Milt. Smooth and easy."

"I hate..."

I could finish this easily in my mind—*being mute, being treated like I don't count, having my hair oiled so it looks like white frosting.* Okay, that last one was my own personal objection. It wasn't like his hair fell into his eyes and needed to be greased back. I just thought Milt looked happier when Richard let his hair hang loose and lift a little on a breeze.

"I hate no..."

I leaned closer, waiting for new words to come from him.

"I hate no...jokes."

I smiled. "Jokes" was a new word. "Do you mean you want to hear jokes?" I imagined his day was pretty dull, being moved from area to area, catching a nap wherever he was parked.

Milt slowly shook his head. "Joker."

"You miss telling the jokes?"

He sagged into his shirt collar and I knew I was right on the money. "That's what we can work on, Milt. We'll practice some jokes you can tell." It was a thousand percent better than running around the inn telling everyone they were hated. One of my clients had been using a word board to point to words instead of speaking. This might be the answer for Milt as well. I tapped his leg. "I'll be right back."

I headed to my room. I had some leftover pictures from making the word board, so I grabbed those and a notebook. Once seated next to Milt, I spread eight pictures of common items out on the cover of the notebook. I headed to my room. I had some leftover pictures from making the word board. "I want to see if you can point to pictures."

He studied the black and white drawings and then looked at my face.

"If you were hungry, which picture would you point to?"

Milt didn't move. I waited and smiled, and nudged the pictures a bit closer. Then he reached for the notebook. This would work! I'd get him pointing to pictures, then he would be able to make sentences and we'd write jokes together.

He put both hands on the edges of the notebook and leaned forward, studying the pictures. Since he never did anything fast, I was startled when he flipped the notebook in the air and the white pieces of paper took flight, most of them landing on the surface of the pond.

Fish churned to the top of the water, their mouths opening and closing at the edges of the floating debris, and I knew they would all be dead if I didn't get the paper out fast. I dropped to the ground, lying on my stomach, the stones bordering the pond digging into my ribs as I grabbed the closest floaters. Others were out of reach, so I stuck my hand in and swirled the water, circling them toward me. Finally, I had all eight pieces. Pulling myself to an upright sitting position, I glanced at Milt. His mouth was pulled into something I had never seen. "Are you smiling?"

He wiped his hands on his pants. "I joke."

"Ah. You did surprise me with that little prank." I stood next to him and dropped my hand on his shoulder. "You don't want to point to pictures. You want to be able to joke around."

He rubbed his arm. "I joke."

"Okay. We can work on that." I extended my hand. "Let's head in for lunch."

We slowly crossed the lawn, his arm hooked through mine. The day's backdrop consisted of chirping birds and a far-off chainsaw. Could be Elyk for all I knew. As we neared the back stoop, I paused and said, "Prepare yourself for a bunch of high apple cider mania."

He looked at me and then back to the door.

"Just warning you." I pulled the door open and Milt went in first.

Everyone was gathered around the long dining table while Rose put out the food. I helped Milt into his chair and put his napkin on his lap.

Earl leaned toward Milt and said, "You've enjoyed a cool glass of apple cider, haven't you?"

Milt rubbed his hands on his legs, then blinked his eyes and said, "I hate you."

The couple gasped. I left Richard and Rose to explain as I hurried to the bathroom to wash off the pond water. I knew I was smiling but couldn't help it. Milt used a new word today. "Jokes." It really was a breakthrough. Plus, I only needed to teach him one new joke since the guests turned over regularly.

Dinner was a loud affair with Betty and Earl describing every apple known to exist, including the one Adam and Eve shared. I helped Rose do the dishes and headed to my room to get ready for the next day.

I had just pulled out the files when my phone rang. My heart raced at the caller ID: Lawyer. I would be a mess by tomorrow night if he was already having this effect on me. "Hi, there," I said. My voice sounded high with a trace of insanity.

"You okay?" His voice was deep, sounding like he was on the verge of laughing.

I cleared my throat. "I'm fine. Are we still getting together tomorrow?"

"We are. I'm taking you some place cool."

"Cool sounds good. Do you mean cool as in chilly? What's the dress code?"

"Your running clothes are fine. We'll be walking about a mile."

Running clothes? Not exactly the romantic evening I imagined; me, willingly pressed against a wall by him with a smoldering fire binding our bodies was better. Running clothes sounded like a workout but not the kind I wanted. "All right. I'm intrigued."

"And don't eat. I'm bringing food."

Uh-oh. "Sloppy Joes?" I asked. He had told me it was the only meal he and the other firemen cooked when they were at the firehouse.

"No, not Sloppy Joes. I have skills you have yet to see."

"That's for sure." Every time we got close to a full exploration of his talents, something interrupted us. "Well, I'm more than willing to judge them, so don't hold back."

"This is what I like about you," he said laughing, "those unfiltered thoughts." Then he paused. "Speaking of skills. Have you been practicing your woodhicking abilities?"

The annual Bark Peelers' Convention was in a few weeks in the town of Fenton, Pennsylvania, thirty-six miles away and one hundred twenty years in the past. "No, I haven't. I'm a little confused as to what I should be practicing."

"Well, you could throw an axe, but that seems dangerous given your recent past."

"Not fair." Sure I'd had some trouble in the last couple weeks, but none of it was my fault. "What else?"

"Log rolling, birling, sawing." He cleared his throat and laughed, adding, "There's always greased pole climbing."

I snorted and said, "No comment."

He laughed. "We'll talk about it when I see you. I'll pick you up at six-thirty. Come hungry."

"Okay, got it. See you then."

I lay back on the pillows and thought about those words. I was hungry. Hungry to be connected to someone. I needed to find out more about the Kingstons, to find their relatives. Even meeting distant family members would do. It was weird to suddenly have no one to position my dreams, desires, and thoughts around. Even though my parents in San Francisco hadn't always agreed with me, I was safe sharing my deepest thoughts. They knew my fears, what I loved, what made me laugh. That kind of sharing wasn't something I could instantly do with a friend, a new lover, or a colleague. My family knew me before I knew myself. They'd seen me in panoramic view while others saw me in the snapshots I allowed.

I put away my files and changed for bed.

Maybe that was where I was going wrong. Maybe I needed to be more open.

I sunk into the pillow-top bed and switched off the light, which plunged the room into darkness. The frogs and crickets took over, assuming their nightly role of lulling me to sleep.

Scrambled Plans

I awoke to scurrying sounds and whispers before morning had fully arrived. When I heard Rose mention "getting things put away," I knew Milt had had another restless night. Although he moved through most of his day with sloth-like speed, he could rearrange a house in a matter of hours. I threw on sweats and a T-shirt and found Richard in the library.

"How bad is it?" I asked.

He held a slice of cheese he'd picked up from the arm of an overstuffed chair where the now-missing crocheted doily had been. "Perhaps the missing doily is in the cheese drawer?" he said, shaking his head.

I wonder what sets Milt off. A week had passed and nothing, then one night he's on the move again. Was this his idea of a joke?

I followed Richard to the hallway. "Was your dad much of a prankster?"

Richard rearranged a stack of books on the table in front of the bay window. He seemed to think about that. "He liked a good joke now and then. And he loved gag gifts, like a pen that would squirt water, or handing someone a piece of wasabi candy. Once, he drove across the country wearing a fake arm with a hook. When people asked, he told a tale about cheating at poker in Montana."

I listened, then added, "I think he's still doing the same thing. He simply has fewer resources to work with." We walked toward the kitchen and I grabbed the fork sticking out of the ficus plant. "Seems like harmless humor. It is kind of funny to find a toilet paper roll in the bread box."

Richard touched my elbow to stop me. "Marleigh, remember, he started a toxic reaction and a fire at his nursing home. That's why he's here during the rebuild."

"Oh, yeah. That's not good." I put the fork in the sink and opened the refrigerator. The chair's doily wasn't in the cheese drawer, so I kept looking. "Oh, look at that. He'd balled it up and put it into an empty spot in the egg carton." I could see it through the transparent plastic. "I'll put this in the wash. What rooms haven't you checked?"

"We got the upstairs, but the half bath and front sitting area need a once-over."

I headed in that direction. The more I thought about Milt and his need to joke, the more determined I was to help him with this. I knew the frustration. A six-week study abroad in Germany, during high school, left me at the fringes of conversations. My limited German never allowed me more than the most basic of thoughts—a limited vocabulary of travel words, food, and emergency questions. I had funny comments, insights, philosophical ideas to express with the locals, but I was reduced to pointing and smiling, and became almost as mute as Milt when the conversation got any deeper.

Minutes later, I removed a glass angel figurine from the toilet brush holder and found the toilet brush, sticking out of the inkwell in an antique rolltop desk.

I met Rose in the kitchen and gave her the all clear. She handed me a mug of coffee with a hint of cinnamon floating in the steam. I stared longingly at the breakfast she was laying out, but I was going to be late if I didn't hustle. I grabbed a food bar from the pantry and headed upstairs.

Betty and Earl were barely stirring behind their closed door, so we averted undue questions. However, tonight two more sets of guests would arrive, and all it would take was one guest to be up early to see the disorder and wonder if those rave reviews were legitimate. Not to mention whether they should call the health or elderly welfare department.

I was showered, dressed, and on the road in twenty minutes. A mauve dawn had spilled across the sky and was quickly changing to warm buttercup hues. The green hills were fat and looked soft, like sleeping animals as I crossed over a hilltop with views in all directions.

The town of Milepost consisted of a smattering of houses separated from each other by thick woods, acres of green lawn or swampy lowland. From what I learned, the population was one hundred and eighty-two, although I'd only met one resident, who also was one of my patients. Beryl Holmes. Unfortunately, our few sessions together hadn't involved any speech therapy to help with his swallowing problem. On every visit to his house, a new disaster took place and we got sidetracked. Today, we'd get down to the point of why I was here.

I smiled as I passed the area where I first ran into Lawyer, or rather where he nearly ran me over with his truck. An auspicious near-death experience on my first day of work here. Lawyer certainly knows how to make an impression. Or maybe I do.

A moment later, I turned into Beryl's drive and my heart leapt into my throat. Beryl's Malamute dog was outside, a very bad idea since it had a history of being a runner. I was not in the mood to sprint around his massive yard again, trying to catch it. Just as I was opening my door, Beryl appeared from around the side of his garage. His hair was a closely shorn brush cut, his stance straight and tall, a military retiree who'd never succumb to slouch. His walker was folded by the steps, and I was glad to see he was walking steadier now.

I closed the car door and pointed to his dog. "Aren't you worried that he's outside?"

"Naw. I fixed the problem."

I walked toward the pet he had named "The Dog," and scratched his neck through his thick fur. He was wearing a collar with a small metal box attached. "What's this do?" The Dog leaned into me and panted as he let me scratch him.

Beryl reached for a walkie-talkie shaped device lying beside the steps and moved it to his mouth. "Come!" he said loudly.

The Dog's neck device vibrated and he brushed me away as he hurried back to Beryl's side, his tailed swishing back and forth so fast I swear I heard the air part.

The Dog hadn't actually heard his loud command; he's completely deaf. I laughed. "You built that?" I shouldn't be too surprised. He recently built a Segway out of old motor parts and scraps from his garage.

"Yup. Got him trained in four days." His face shifted into a sideways sneer I learned was his smile.

"You're amazing. Now we can finally concentrate on solving your swallowing problem." I turned to my car to get my therapy bag when he spoke to my back.

"We'll work on it in your car." He led The Dog my way, and before I knew it, he had the back door open and the dog hopped inside. He went back for his folded walker and put that in before closing the door.

"Wait! What's going on?" He was bossy but never this pushy. "We aren't going anyplace."

He opened the passenger door and slid into the seat and closed it behind him.

I pulled the driver's side door open and leaned inside. The Dog was going crazy sniffing the back seat. Beryl hooked his thumb over his shoulder. "What's he smelling?"

"Chicken." I shrugged. "The real question is what are *we* doing?"

"You're driving us to The Gray Roof Inn to check out a playmate for my boy. I got to thinking he could use some company." He looked straight ahead. "It's not far. Hop in."

I folded my arms and forced refusal into my stance. "It's against the home-health rules."

"Well, so was letting me drink booze in your car when you took me to the optometrist, but we got over that, didn't we?"

He was infuriating! That day, he whipped out a flask and started drinking before I could stop him. "*That* is unfair."

"Let's go." He chuckled and fastened his seatbelt. "I've got a guy waiting on me. Then we'll do what you want."

"It's not what I want. It's what you need."

He didn't move.

"You're eating pureed food."

He swatted away my remark. "Mashed-up food. I'll live. Get in." He paused. "Please."

I didn't think he knew that word. My sigh was loud and purposely long as I slid behind the wheel. A big part of therapy *is* bonding with a patient. "You should lock your house."

"I already did. Was just killing time 'til you got here."

I slowly exhaled, then turned the key, and waited. "Where're we going?"

He laughed and then gave me directions.

I concentrated on driving. We rolled up and down thickly wooded back roads before reaching low, marshy flatlands with high skies. A flutter of large birds rose from the surface of greenish murk, flying as a single beating organism, circling to a grassy island farther away from the road. Breaking my resolve not to speak, I pointed. "What were those?"

"American wigeons." Beryl leaned toward the side window. "You're lucky. Don't often see that many together."

I nodded. "They're beautiful. Was there something blue on them?"

"Their pale blue beaks."

Another minute passed. I glanced at The Dog. He had sprawled out along the seat and looked content, like he did this all the time.

Beryl was watching me so I asked, "You take him for drives?"

"Before I wrecked the car, we went everywhere together. Just glad he wasn't with me the night I had the accident."

I shot a look his way. He was chattier, more open than when I'd first met him. "Where had you been?"

"Poker night. Over in Wellsfield. Pea soup fog coming home on the back roads. Thought I saw a deer, so I swerved, caught the edge of the road and rolled."

His chart said he was drunk that night. "How soon before you get your license back?"

"Another few months, give or take." He sucked on a tooth. "But, I've got you to help me out."

"I could lose my job." I bunched my brows together to let him know I meant it. "Seriously. I'm not supposed to be driving my clients around. You're homebound, remember?"

"Sure am." He was nonchalant, detached. "Just keep writing that in your notes." He paused. "And this job is not the reason you're here."

"What do you mean?" He knew nothing about me other than I came from California.

"I heard the nurse at the hospital say you were looking for some local folks."

"Why am I not surprised you know that?" I paused a few moments. "A couple in Butterfield put me up for adoption when I was two. I just discovered they're dead." I didn't expect the tightness in my chest that came with those words, but there it was.

Beryl drew in a long breath. "If you need help looking through records, I could do that."

The glance I shot his way must have held confusion.

He cleared his throat. "I have connections. Sheriff's department, government. From my time in the military."

"You said you built tanks out of chewing gum and chicken wire."

"Doesn't mean I wasn't in intelligence."

That stopped me. Maybe he did have connections. "My birthparents were in the witness protection program before they died. Those records are kept secret for a reason."

"Here we are." He pointed to a building along the road and I pulled the car next to a half-dozen pickup trucks and parked.

He unclipped his seatbelt. "You get me their names and I'll see what I can do."

I smiled. "Okay. Thanks."

I studied the The Gray Roof Inn and discovered it was a bar. A large wooden structure painted white with a neon announcement over the door, and of course, a gray roof. Beryl was halfway out of the car when I asked, "This is where we're meeting a dog?"

He laughed as he walked toward the front steps, using the hood of my Honda for support. "We aren't just meeting it. We're bringing it back."

I sputtered and tried to protest, but ended up lowering the windows halfway so his dog didn't overheat. I followed Beryl into the inn.

The place was dim with weird colored lighting, pushing pinks and ambers into the main area, but leaving the dark sections running off on both sides of the room. Several stools were taken at the bar area, the colorful bottles on the wall in front of them lit like carnival candy. Calling cards for the depressed. Everyone seemed strangely serene, even after we stepped inside. A few heads turned, but the people drinking alone stared straight ahead, their posture warning against approaching.

From someplace indiscernible, came a booming voice. "Holmes, you old bastard."

At the same time I flinched, Beryl laughed.

A man floated out of the gloom, his hand outstretched. He was pudgy, wearing plaid Bermuda shorts, and a yellow fishing hat with hooks and lures stuck around the outside band.

"Chester." Beryl took the man's hand and a bit of hearty backslapping ensued. They broke apart and Beryl pointed toward me. "Chester Morgan, meet Marleigh Benning. She offered to give me a lift since my car's in the shop."

It occurred to me that Beryl might not want people to know he'd lost his license. I stuck out my hand. "Glad to meet you." Chester's hand was soft, his palm damp and hot.

Chester eyed me up and down without pretense. "You from this area, darlin'?"

"I'm not." Without breaking any HIPPA rules by saying I was Beryl's speech therapist, I went with the other reason I was there. "I'm doing genealogy, trying to locate family members."

Chester moved in fast and hugged me, too tightly and for too long. "We're probably related," he said a little too close to my ear and a little too delicately.

I broke away and prayed that my family tree had never branched in his direction. He was drunk. The scent of sour booze oozed from every pore, and the silly grin on his face looked like a kindergartener crayoned it there.

Beryl saved me. "Let's go see this dog you want to sell."

When I met Beryl's eyes, I whispered, "Thank you."

We followed Chester. He used a chair to first steady and then propel himself forward. He didn't exactly stumble across the room but he didn't walk either. We went through the tiny kitchen area and out the back door. A black lab mixed with something in the sheepdog family sat obediently in a shaded area, a small rope hooked to his collar. Chester pointed. "Here's Jack."

Beryl patted the dog's head and Jack swished his tail, but seemed to stare off into the distance.

I stood back, not wanting to alarm the animal with too many new greeters at once. I said, "Jack's a nice name."

Chester shrugged. "He wandered into my yard about a week ago and that's when I named him. As in, I don't know Jack Shit about where you came from." He laughed, but it quickly grew phlegmy and he choked. Without apology, he leaned off to the side and spit something the size of a peach pit into the grass.

Beryl picked up the rope and asked his friend, "You say he doesn't see too great?"

Chester parked his hands under his armpits. "He's got some issue. Bumps into shit…missed a step on the back porch. Not sure how much he can make out."

Beryl shrugged. "Sounds fine. Let's find out how he plays with my dog."

I stood behind for a moment, impressed with Beryl. First, he had a deaf dog and now he was taking on a nearly blind one.

We walked around the side of the building past decades of rusting appliances, a huge upright gas tank, and a broken toilet. This side of the building wasn't visible to guests. A cinderblock wall with a wooden gate separated the nice upfront exterior from the *I'll-get-around-to-hauling-that-crap-away-someday* side. Beryl kept Jack on a short leash, touching the side of his leg, so the dog could feel the direction they were moving.

When we arrived at my car, Beryl let out The Dog. The animals circled and sniffed each other, tails moving in cautious wags, and then Jack playfully lunged in the direction of The Dog. The Dog was all in at that point. As they played, I watched Beryl's face. I'd never seen him content, but that was what he appeared to be. I was glad I'd driven him here today.

Chester moved to my side, studying my license plates. "You thinking of leaving California and settling here?"

I thought about that before answering. "No, not really. It's beautiful for sure but I have to go back in about ten weeks."

"Well, you just wait. This place does get a grip on you and you won't want to leave. I can trace my family's roots seven generations back. Original woodsmen, my ancestors."

I thought of Lawyer. He had returned after a few years of being a high school history teacher near Philadelphia. His was different from my situation, though. Although I was born here, I had no memory of it. Sure, I was really young, but some people had memories before they were two, so it was frustrating that I didn't have any recall. Maybe when I finally found pictures of the Kingstons, some feeling of a connection would be there.

"Let's go." Beryl touched my back and moved me toward the driver's side. He circled the car and coaxed Jack into the back seat, and The Dog followed. I slid into the driver's seat and started the car. The dogs jockeyed for places to settle and the smell of overheated dog filled the air. Beryl pulled out his wallet and handed Chester some folded bills.

Chester waved, the movement making him sway on his feet. He turned and climbed the front stairs in a few lunging movements.

I pulled out of the tavern's parking lot and turned left. "Is he always this smashed during the day?"

"Mostly. He's lost a lot...a wife, a son." He was silent for a moment. "His ten-year AA pin."

I pointed toward the back seat. "Then he should have kept Jack for company. And you had to pay him? He said the dog wandered into his yard."

Beryl chuckled. "He got the dog some shots, and I know he could use the money."

I smiled. "You're a softy under all that armor."

He snorted. "Don't be spreading that around."

We headed back to Milepost, the drive quiet except for the heavy breathing coming from the back seat.

We reached an open stretch of road. Ahead of me an advancing storm of dust approached, and as it neared, it then became a pickup truck passing by. Hell-bent for possibly the tavern, spraying my car with rocks and gravel projectiles. I flinched as they hit the car sides and the windshield, leaving me adrift in a cloud of dust.

My heart was racing and I realized I'd almost come to a complete stop. Beryl was looking my way, his eyebrows raised. "What?" I asked.

"You're a jumpy sort, aren't you?"

"I didn't know what was coming. It looked like it was taking up the whole road."

"Jumpy's good."

"It's how narrow everything is. The roads are as wide as sidewalks." My voice held a challenging bite I didn't like hearing.

"You'll get used to them. And, I'm going to teach you another self-defense move so nothing scares you."

I cringed remembering his safety lesson. He used a Show-Don't-Tell method to teach me a straight-finger poke to the windpipe. "I'll just use the last moves you showed me." I hated to admit it, but that self-defense move actually had proven to be useful already.

"Nope. You're going to learn more if you're staying all summer."

I gripped the wheel tighter. "It's not a war zone. I'm acclimating just fine."

We were nearing his house. He undid his seatbelt even before we came to his driveway. "You always have to be thinking ahead. What if something happened right now? What would I do?"

"Like if we hit a pole and you weren't wearing your seatbelt?"

Muscles in his jawline flexed several times. "We're going twenty." He turned away, staring out the window.

I turned right, crunching into his drive. "I'm supposed to be helping you, not trying to get you more injured. So don't be mad at me."

He was out of the car and had the dogs released before I could get out on my side. He grabbed his walker and slowly worked it in front of him across the uneven ground until he reached the steps.

The dogs were running figure eights around the bushes across his lawn. Jack stayed hooked to the side of The Dog.

I smiled. "This was a good idea. Jack's going to be a good companion for The Dog."

"Looks like it. But I'm going to change his name. Jack's no good."

I knew we were out of time for today. "Tell me what you come up with when I see you in two days. When we actually start doing therapy."

He chuckled and picked up his walkie-talkie device and called The Dog to him. Jack bounded along behind. I waved and he raised a hand over his head in a parting gesture, his back already turned to me as he held the screen door open for the dogs. I'd be curious to see what name he came up with. Two Dog? Thine Dog? D.O.G? Could get very Dr. Seussy.

A mosquito buzzed my cheek and I slapped at it, quickly rolling up the window. Why had I chosen my aging Honda to drive when I could have driven my parents' Audi? It was parked in the garage and would stay there forevermore until I decided what to do with it. At this point, I couldn't bring myself to drive it. I'd never been behind the wheel while they were alive and I couldn't deal with taking ownership just yet. That would mean they were really gone.

I backed out and hit the road. The town of Milepost soon fell away in the rearview mirror and I lost radio reception, heading east toward my next client's house. Glad to be free of the constant commercials for fiberglass fly rods, heavy duty bug zappers, and local church picnics. The first two items I couldn't care less about, but I actually wanted to go to a church picnic. Most of the towns I passed through germinated a church spire rising above the tree line and marquee, or wooden signs announcing events. I wanted to sit on sagging benches with yawning bowls of German potato salad, baskets of homemade bread with apple butter, and something called Shoo Fly Pie. I didn't believe a bug zapper was involved in its production but I wasn't one hundred percent certain.

I wanted people to say, "Gee willikers. All the way from California, huh?" Or they could *Gesundheit* me if I sneezed. Or ask, "Djeetyet?" I'd nod and say, "Yes, I did just eat."

Maybe Chester was right. Northern Pennsylvania might actually be in my blood and calling me back home.

I was miles away before I realized I hadn't given Beryl the name of my birthparents. I'd take him up on his offer to help find them. He probably had been some sort of super spy. That gruff demeanor, although it no longer bothered me, was surely hiding something.

THANKS FOR THE MEMORIES

My next stop was a small burg named Cussler Glen. When I reached the blinking light at the one and only crossroad, I turned left and found the home of another new client—the mayor's wife, Sofie Dougan. Their home was three stories tall, painted white with black shutters, and two bay windows.

I knocked and waited on the painted wooden porch. A rusty wheelbarrow, overflowing with sprawling annuals, took up one end while a two-seater swing creaked slightly in the breeze on the other. Even with houses on either side of the Dougans, the small town steeped in a dead silence. The kind that makes you wonder if everyone had died the night before. The silence caused a keen level of unrealistic panic, one I never possessed in San Francisco. Street sounds meant life was going on around you, and there was safety in numbers. Such quiet implied the opposite. I was alone and on my own if the unthinkable happened.

I'd barely rung the bell when Jon Dougan welcomed me into their foyer, a beautiful area with polished wooden floors and a blue and maroon oriental runner stretching down the hallway. He offered his hand. "Hi there. I'm Mayor Dougan. Welcome to our home."

"Dapper" was the word I'd use to describe Jon with his thick gray hair, well-trimmed mustache. He was dressed country-club casual in pleated dark gray slacks and a blue button-down shirt.

"Thank you," I said. "I'm glad to be here."

He pointed toward the living room to the left. "My lovely wife, Sofie, is waiting for you."

Following him, I turned the corner to see an attractive woman in her late seventies, who wore her dark hair in a fashionable cut. Dressed in a peach silk blouse and white slacks, she looked like she was ready for a tea party.

I took the matching, maroon plaid chair next to her. A dainty table on spindly legs separated us. Sofie's chart stated she had dementia from the onset of Alzheimer's. My job wasn't to improve her communication skills, but to do the opposite. I needed to teach Jon what's known as Validation Therapy: No matter what off-the-wall thing his wife said, he and others in her life needed to validate it as truth. It was a simple yet effective way to keep his wife from becoming upset as those around her told her the things she believed to be happening were not real.

"Hi, Mrs. Dougan." I leaned closer to her, and she met my gaze with startling green eyes. "May I call you Sofie?"

She smiled, her peach lipstick looked like she may have applied it without the benefit of a mirror. "Yes, Sofie Fritz." She leaned closer to me. "But I can't stay long. Gramps and I need to get the mail out to the camps."

Jon cleared his throat as he stood by the white brick fireplace. "She is talking about the days when she and her grandfather delivered the newspaper and mail to all the lumber camps and towns back in the forties."

Although he fought it, his eyes were sad. His wife had used her maiden name, Fritz, meaning she most likely had no memory of being married to him. I touched Sofie's hand. "Do you have children?"

"My Lands, no. I'm barely out of grade school." Her look said I had to be completely off my rocker.

"Marleigh, we have a son and a daughter." Jon brought a framed photo to me from the fireplace mantel. "Cindy and Jon, Jr."

The Christmas photo showed the four of them, perhaps twenty years earlier, everyone in semi-matching red and green sweaters. "Very nice." I started to hand it back to Jon when Sofie took it from my hands and studied it. A scowl slowly bloomed on her forehead. "Are these the Zeiglers from Garrison Knob?"

Jon knelt beside Sofie's chair. "That's us, honey. Remember?"

She studied the photo then pushed it away. With ease, she stood from her chair and began pacing the living room. "I have to finish making Evan Faust's suit, or he isn't going into town Saturday night. And the apple pie contest... the bake-off is coming up." She whirled to face me. "Thank you for the cookies. It was lovely of you to have me in your home but I have so many things to do."

She headed for the front door but Jon hurried to block her way. He whispered to me, "She's fast, so I can't let her be outside alone." He took her elbow and steered her to the chair she had exited, but she fought him and slapped his hand away once she was seated. In a tone of surrender, Jon said, "I'm lost when she gets this way." He patted his shirt pocket and pulled out a cigarette pack. He had the lighter out and the cigarette lit—a magician's trick. Drawing in an impossibly long breath, he asked, "Do you mind?" The words were encapsulated in the smoke curling from his mouth, each puff a separate signal of pain, frustration, and worry.

It was his house, how could I mind? "I want to talk to you about the therapy we're going to try. Can we sit somewhere and chat while keeping an eye on your wife?"

"Sure." He motioned to the couch at the far end of the living room. He turned on a radio near Sofie's chair and she relaxed in her seat, her head tilted toward the broadcast.

But it wasn't music coming from the radio. A woman's monotone voice crackled from the device, "We have a report of a man threatening his neighbor with an axe. Route thirty-five near Hammerston Dam. Requesting two cars to investigate."

Jon sat a few feet from me. "Police scanner." He shrugged. "For some reason, listening to these emergencies calms her down. I don't know. She was such a classy lady, on all of the local charity boards. If we can just get her memory back."

I let some time tick by, giving it a moment before responding with the truth, information he had already heard from doctors but didn't want to believe. "Her memory isn't going to get any better, Mayor. I'm sorry about that."

He dropped his head and ran his hand along the back of his neck.

I continued, "But, we can help her through this period in her life. It's frightening to not remember what people around you insist you used to know. The memories truly are gone, erased as if they never had happened."

"But she remembers happenings from her childhood up until she was about twenty. What happened to everything we've done since then? I married her when she was twenty-one."

"Picture her walking backward along her timeline. As the road falls away behind her, so does her memory of that time period. It's a winding road, and she may circle back to some more recent memory, but overall, the lights will continue to wink out as the disease progresses."

His brows bunched together. "Can't some of this be attributed to old age? It can be such a prankster at times. I mean, even I can get confused over the slightest change."

"I wish that was it. The good news is that although this is so devastating for you and your kids, it doesn't have to be for her. And this approach will, over time, help you adjust to who she is now."

He picked at a button on his shirt and didn't speak for a few moments. "Okay. What do we do?"

I smiled. "Not to sound like a lecture, but let me explain why we have new techniques about dementia and therapy. Reawakening a person to the fact that he or she has dementia used to be the social norm, even for caregivers. It was even considered a 'gentle reminder' or 'correction.' However, we know better now."

"She gets so angry or sad. It breaks my heart," he said.

"Exactly. These reminders shatter that person's reality, and repeated experiences can be psychologically damaging. Dementia affects Sofie's brain, but she retains her humanness. She still has a mind, an ego, and feelings that need to be respected. And it's cruel to force her to accept aspects of reality she can't comprehend."

Jon looked toward his wife. "That makes sense."

"Validation therapy is based on the idea that a person with dementia may be sorting through past issues in the present time. You know...all of the things we'd like to forget, and we push out of our mind as we age? Well, those become current issues when we regress. Validation therapy allows Sofie some measure of control, even over her old issues. It helps her self-worth and reduces the occurrence of negative behaviors." After that lengthy explanation, I drew in a much-needed breath and exhaled.

Jon understood. He turned his wrist to see the face of his silver wristwatch. "As far as I know, she had no childhood issues or trauma in her life. But do you have time to show me what I should say?"

"Of course. And I'll be back again in a few days."

We moved to the chairs next to Sofie. The scanner squelched. "We have a missing teen in Mansboro. The family said he didn't come home last night. Who's in the area that can take this call?"

Jon spun the dial lower and the dispatcher's voice faded away.

I smiled at Sofie and asked, "What would you like to do today?"

She looked from me to Jon and back. "I have to get ready for deliveries with Gramps. We missed Fox Trot Run last week 'cause the water was too high in Turning Creek."

I leaned closer. "What's your favorite thing about the deliveries?"

Sofie smiled and relaxed. "I like how all the men at the lumber camps look at me."

In my peripheral vision, I caught Jon flinching but I raised a finger his way, indicating he shouldn't react to this. I smiled. "You are an attractive young lady. I'm sure they all like seeing a pretty woman in camp."

"I sew and cook for them, too. I'm sure I'll find a husband there soon." Her eyes gleamed with desire and young hope, nullifying years of being in a stable marriage.

Jon stood and stammered, "I can't encourage her to talk about stuff like this."

"I know. Just change the subject, redirect her." I touched Sofie's arm. "If you're going to be ready for a day of deliveries, you'll need to have a big breakfast first. What would you like?"

She smoothed down her blouse, which for John was probably seductive. "Good idea. I'd like two eggs and bacon and toast."

I looked toward Jon and asked, "Can you cook?"

He cleared his throat with a nod. "Sure can. I'll get right on it."

We followed him to the kitchen and sat at the table while he pulled together pans and food from different cupboards. The room was open to a glassed-in porch with a large manicured yard beyond.

I pointed outside. "You have a beautiful backyard, Sofie. Do you like yardwork?"

Her forehead wrinkled and a thoughtful expression etched her face. "My mother usually takes care of all of that but I like to dabble."

"Well, dabbling or not, it shows."

She leaned toward the window and said, "Oh my, that's a beautiful peacock right there. Isn't that just gorgeous?"

"Dear, that's our statue—" Jon blurted. Then I saw him shift gears, and he started again. "Yes, isn't that the finest bird you've ever seen?"

We both waited, studying Sofie's face.

She smiled and said, "It sure is."

I chimed in hoping to keep the conversation going. "Have you named him?"

Sofie thought for a moment and said, "We call him Mr. Proud Feathers."

"Fitting," I said. "And what does he eat?"

"Probably whatever my dad will make for him." She pointed to her husband and waggled her finger. "We are tired of runny soup and Raisin Squares, Dad."

I watched Jon shrink at the counter.

Our gazes met and I said, barely above a whisper, "Sometimes it's okay to not say anything ... as hard as that is."

He nodded—his mouth set in a straight line—but he seemed to appreciate that I understood his pain.

Before I left, they had food on the table and Jon was doing a great job of validating the incongruent realities from Sofie's mind. For a moment, they both seemed happy and relaxed. I encouraged Jon to keep track of any conversations that seemed to upset his wife, and those would be the ones I would explore and try to create peace with on my next visit.

Back in my car, I paused to write up the therapy notes: Sofie seems to be in the third stage of Alzheimer's or very close to it. Current events were not reality. She doesn't recognize Jon as her husband but she seems to like having "a dad and a grandfather" around. She's fixed at roughly age sixteen. Had no episodes of anger and her husband caught on quickly to Validation Therapy.

I pulled out of the driveway and recalled one of the books in the B&B's library, one full of pictures of the lumber history in the towns and camps of Northern Pennsylvania. I'd bring that next time. Going through that book might stimulate old memories, provide added comfort, and give Sofie and Jon more to talk about. It would be interesting if she had stories from some of the local camps. Sofie was searching for her past, like I was.

One Hot Fireman

I studied Lawyer's profile from the passenger seat as we bounced along a narrow trail in his white pickup, heading uphill through thick-swelling hills of pine, creeping laurel, and hardwoods.

His wavy brown hair was a bit long, stopping just above the collar of his green polo shirt. Could I just take him by it and bring his mouth my way? Distracted by his mouth—chiseled jawline and cheekbones, slight five o'clock shadow, and eyes the color of warm caramel—I was not listening to his lesson on how this area led the states in the production of hemlock and white pine. Okay, I was half listening and showing interest just so he would keep moving his mouth.

I guess I wasn't shocked at my immediate attraction to him. I had been alone for three months before arriving in Tungston, and before that, managed an on-off relationship with an adjunct professor in our department. It was his first year and probably his last at San Francisco University. His emphasis of study was autism and speech disorders, but what he really excelled in was egotism and narcissism. I was admittedly dazzled at first by the attention of a professor. However, it wasn't long before his self-important stories, his at-the-ready selfie stick, and how *it* measured up in the locker room, drove me into my closet to clear my head and see him for what he was. Not worth it.

Lawyer tapped my leg. "...and that's why unicorns don't eat peanut butter."

"What?" How had he gotten from lumbering to unicorns?

"You're not listening to me." It seemed like he tried to make a joke of it but he looked hurt.

I said, "White pine, biggest wood production in the world, floating logs down the Piney River to the Susquepatchie."

"Susquehanna. The only thing patchy is your attention." Then he pulled the truck to a stop in a wide spot in the road and put it in park. Leaning my way, he pressed his mouth to mine, pinning me gently but firmly against the seat. *Finally.*

What started as a tingle of excitement when his lips connected to mine soon turned into a snapping electrical charge. As we explored with our tongues, we were nose breathing fast, in no hurry to part.

He sat back and smiled. "Now I have your attention."

I laughed. "Yes, you do. All systems are on alert."

"Okay, let's go."

I waited for him to lean my way once more, but instead he opened his door and hopped out. He glanced into the cab and stopped moving when he saw I hadn't moved. "Can you pause those thoughts you're having right now for fifteen minutes? We can pick up where we left off once we're there."

I hoped my expression didn't look as let down as my mind.

He closed his door and walked around to my side just as I reached the ground. "We have a mile climb but I promise it will be worth it."

Pushing a smile onto my lips, I said, "I have no doubt." Then he held out the blanket and asked, "Would you carry this?"

"Sure," I said, and watched him shrug the backpack straps over his broad shoulders.

He picked up the picnic basket. "Here we go."

We followed a road, well, a set of dirt tire tracks with grass and weeds growing in the center. I heard waterfalls before we approached a bridge made from cut logs, spanning a boulder-strewn creek. Water foamed on the crests wrestling down the twelve-foot-wide creek, the sound exhilarating. Its wildness stirring inside me, connecting with dormant places. A ray of sunlight caught in a shallow pool, painting the bottom in an illuminated mosaic of orange, tan, and gold.

I drew in a long, slow breath.

Lawyer turned back to study me. "You okay?"

"This is spectacular. I want to bottle this air. It's so ... so leafy, with a hint of timelessness thrown in." I breathed deeply again.

"It is great, isn't it?" he said then paused. "I thought you had fallen."

I held the blanket to my chest in a protective move. "You think I'm completely inept."

His eyebrows rose. "I think you are very ept." A sideways smirk played on his lips. "At many things."

"That's not a word." I readjusted the blanket in my arms. "That's like me saying you are kempt."

He tilted his head to the side. "Thank you. And I'm also feeling very gruntled."

I laughed. "Okay. We could play this unword game all day, but exactly where are we heading?"

"You'll see. We're almost there." He turned to lead the way. "You won't be disappointed."

"Please, lead the way so I can be *appointed*."

He chuckled but pushed forward. The sound of fluttering leaves filled the spaces between the trees as we climbed higher along a ridge. The forest thinned and soon a tall steel tower loomed ahead.

"You ready for the hardest part?" he asked.

I studied the tower, which had steep stairs, leading to an enclosed structure on top. "Exactly how tall is that?"

"Sixty feet. Balding Knob Fire Station. Built in nineteen twenty. But this time you lead the way."

Annoyance rose in my chest. "Because you think I'll fall?"

"Hell, no. I want to watch your cute butt climb those stairs," he said and smiled.

I jogged toward the steps, hoping to stay ahead of him but he soon caught me on the climb, taking two steps at a time. We raced the last few steps and arrived at the top out of breath.

The enclosure had four large windows, one in each wall in order to see in all directions. Wooden planks made up the walls and roof. A bunk bed was against one wall, and built-in shelves ran across another with an old rotary phone attached to the third wall.

Lawyer set the backpack and basket on the floor and took the blanket from my arms, tossing it on the bunk. He pulled me to his chest and pressed his mouth to mine.

I was pretty sure I felt the structure sway.

He kept me wrapped in his embrace. Warm. Soft. Yet strong. A place I could possibly stay for days.

"I've always wanted to get high and kiss a girl. I can check that one off my list now."

I pushed away so I could see his face. "You've never brought anyone else up here before? I don't know if I believe that."

He shrugged. "I've been here dozens of times with others."

"But you didn't kiss them?"

"I did not. We use this tower to train the rookies on how to spot a fire. I swear I have yet to kiss one of those guys."

I laughed. "Then I'm flattered."

He took my hand and led me to a window. In panoramic view, lay an endless sea of undulating green hills that rippled off before they disappeared into the distant blue haze. Next he pointed to another area. "More than one hundred thousand acres of woodlands can be seen from here." He pointed to a cut in a valley far to the right. "Tungston is over there, and at the bottom of that ravine is Piney Creek."

"It's amazing. No wonder I get lost all the time."

"Well…" He shot me a devilish grin.

"Hey. I'm doing a lot better than I was a few weeks ago."

"Agreed."

I wandered to a metal plaque on the wall.

September 24, 1920: "Arrangements were made for erecting this sixty-foot steel tower, with a direct telephone connection with the Gleason Knob Forestry Department and the nearby homes of the fire wardens. These towers had a primary objective of reducing the forest fire damage, but they also furnished a period of pleasure to visitors, those who were well repaid for the climb in exchange for the wonderful view obtained." (The Wellsfield Agitator)

Lawyer came up behind me, and wrapped his arms around my waist. He whispered into my neck, "Did you read that line about a period of pleasure?"

I turned to face him. "I did. Do you know when that begins?"

"Yes." He crossed to the picnic basket, flipped open the wicker top, and brought out a bottle of wine. Then he filled two red Solo cups half way. "I know. Fancier than you imagined."

I accepted the drink and tapped the plastic rim to his cup. "To getting tipsy in high places."

He raised his cup. "To that and more."

My heart pounded and I knew he had to see the pulse beating in my neck. Suddenly self-conscious about the thoughts I was having about him, I put the cup to my lips, swallowing most of the wine.

He held my gaze. "You in a hurry?"

I felt the blush take over my face. I decided to go with the truth. "Just nervous."

He touched my arm and pulled me closer again. "Me, too." He released me, and pulled out a red tablecloth that he spread on the linoleum floor. Then he unpacked food onto it. Plates of cheese, salami, fruit, and crackers, and a chicken salad sandwich on a croissant appeared. "See? No Sloppy Joes." He knelt down on the cloth and tapped the spot next to him. "Get your cute butt over here."

I dropped down next to him. "This is impressive." I held out my drink. "How about a splash more?"

He filled it halfway again, even as I tried to protest and pull it away. "Whoa. Remember, I have to make it back down those steps."

"I'm not worried. I carry people out of burning buildings. I'm certified to handle twice your weight." He leaned in to kiss my nose, and my stomach hatched a kaleidoscope of butterflies.

I laughed, though it sounded too high-pitched, clueing I was right on the verge of catching a buzz. "I like a guy that comes with a certification."

Within a few minutes of picking at the food and making small talk, it was obvious we weren't really hungry. We poured the rest of the wine and sipped it as I helped him put some of the food away.

He tugged me to my feet and enfolded me in his arms. The kiss he delivered was no nonsense and I wanted him right there and then. Slowly, he guided me backwards until we reached the bunk. He pulled away for a moment to spread the blanket on the top bunk, and then nudged me toward the four-step ladder. "Better view from up there."

View? I didn't give a darn about those hundreds of miles outside the window. My focus was narrowed to the wonders just a few inches from me. As I stretched out on the bunk, a small puff of dust floated up from the edges. I waved it away and laughed. Once Lawyer reached the bed, he crawled on top of me. His clean scent overpowering everything. His weight pinning me to a place I'd been looking forward to for weeks.

The room glowed with a hazy pink as the sun settled lower. He stared into my eyes and spoke softly, his voice husky. "Hi, bunkmate."

"Hi, you."

"I have to confess something."

I pulled my head back a few inches, studying him. "You actually kissed a rookie fireman?"

"Right." He drew out the word as he pushed the hair away from my forehead, his fingertips hot against my skin. "No. I confess that I've been obsessed with the thought of getting together with you."

"Me, too," I said, smiling. The temperature was climbing where our bodies touched. I wrapped one leg around his. "And here we are."

"And I left my phone and pager in the truck. No fireman equipment, no interruptions."

I raised my hips and ground against his hardness. "You're *not* carrying a flashlight?"

He groaned and pressed back, but raised his head and bumped the ceiling. He rubbed the spot with his hand, wincing a bit. "Not a flashlight."

"Then I like your personal equipment."

We kissed and time slipped away. I ran my hands up under his shirt. His back was smooth, and his muscles rippled as he moved his hands under my clothes. I'd worn workout clothes as he'd suggested—a jogging bra that hooked in the front under a T-shirt, and nylon shorts. Now I wondered if this wasn't for convenience sake rather than for the walk to the tower.

With one hand, he unlatched my sports bra and cupped my breast. I stifled a gasp and pushed my hands down his shorts, and squeezed his butt. With our mouths interlocked, we explored. Our breathing was fast, coming in steady bursts.

He pulled off my shirt and dropped his mouth over my nipple. This time I gulped, unable to suppress the electricity that passed through my chest, and I writhed under his weight, silently begging him to let me have everything he had.

"Your shirt," I gasped.

He pulled it off and tossed it to the floor. When he eased back down onto me and our skin met, I knew it rated as one of the best things I had experienced in my life. The warm and complete connection ran heated charges along inner pathways I didn't know I possessed. I moaned and he did, too.

We rolled to our sides, both of us trying to pull off each other's shorts first and this time I hit my head on the ceiling boards. "Ow." I rubbed the spot but the pain melted away.

"I want you so bad," he muttered in my neck. He raised himself up and I prepared myself for ecstasy. "No room here," he said. "Let's move to the floor."

I giggled and leaned over the edge of the bed. "I thought we were bunkmates."

"We're debunking now."

"That's not what that means."

"It will be when we're through." His wide grin and tousled hair made him irresistible.

"I like new words," I said as he eased me over the side of the bed and lowered me to the floor. I wobbled a bit. The wine. My blood flow not exactly in my legs any longer.

Then he straightened. "Dammit!" The groan that escaped his lips was animalistic, pained, as he gently placed me on both feet.

"Wha... what's wrong?" I was dizzy. The change in direction from what we were doing to just standing there was giving me whiplash. "What happened?"

Taking my face in his hands, he turned my head to the window.

This was about the view again? Screw the view! What the heck was he thinking? All I noticed in the dusk was a distant ridgeline caught in the final orange and red highlights from the sun, clouds billowing up behind it. But in another second, it all came together just as he was reaching for the rotary phone and a pair of binoculars on the shelf.

The hills were on fire.

He rattled off a few lines of directions and yelled about calling in another fire company before hanging up. When he turned to me, his face was all business, the passion gone. "We need to go."

I didn't move. "But, you're off-duty. Can't the other guys take care of this?"

He gently took me by my arms and leaned in close. "I'm sorry to say, I'm never off-duty unless I'm out of town. And that's not a bad idea. We can go away." He handed me my shirt and pulled his over his head. "We can go to the Poconos."

I followed his frantic actions and dressed, but my mind was having a hard time processing that we were leaving.

He muttered cuss words under his breath and I could tell he was just as upset as I was.

Once we gathered everything, he said, "Keep a hand on my shoulder as we go down."

We descended rapidly and all but jogged to the truck, his arm steadying me against the wine buzz. We were on the road and moving fast.

"Um, maybe you can slow down some. I'm sure the other guys are taking care of it. They must be used to forests catching fire all of the time."

"Oh, they are the best and I'm sure they are hard at work. But the fire isn't in a forest. It's on the outskirts of Cussler Glen."

The town Mayor Dougan and Sofie lived in.

LATE NIGHT HANGOUT

Back at the Bed & Breakfast, I pushed through the front door and tried to decide what kind of mood I was in. I could join the new guests in the dining room for the evening dessert hour, which was always a spread of inventive pastries and fruits. Or I could take an ice cold shower and clear my head of another disappointing date. Laughter burst from the kitchen and I made up my mind—I headed to my room.

I walked by Milt's door and it was partially open. He sat in a recliner beside his bed, watching a tiny TV on a tray table in front of him. His eyes were closed and I realized he must be bushed from last night, busily rearranging the items in the inn.

I tiptoed to my room, flipped on the bedside lamp, and within moments, was in my walk-in closet, sitting up against the wall with the door closed. Recent events in my life felt magnified. I closed my eyes and tried to rein in the fear that my world would always stay gloomy, especially if I studied my most recent forecast: Dating a fireman called for more rain.

He'd apologized, saying he would plan a weekend away within the next few weeks. I couldn't be angry with him. I was equally worried about the fire being in a town with my newest clients. But the dull ache and raw nerves were from more than sexual frustration.

I touched the necklace at my throat, which held my parents' wedding rings. When the funeral director handed them to me, I wasn't sure what I'd do with them. I put my mother's large diamond in the safe and their gold bands on a simple chain. I wondered for the hundredth time why they hadn't told me I was adopted. Had they personally known the Kingstons? How had they found out about a young couple in Pennsylvania who was in trouble and ready to disappear, but first had a daughter to give away? They must have had good reason to keep this from me all these years. If the Kingstons were in danger, then I probably was, too. I was not a gloomy person. But there were times when hope seemed entirely clouded over. When looking for the light in my dark circumstances felt like trying to catch a glimpse of the sun from inside a crypt.

The door to the closet slowly opened. My heart jumped into my throat, the thoughts of a crypt a fresh image. Then Milt's outline filled the space in front of me. "Come on in, Milt. You probably need some closet time, too."

He shuffled forward and pulled the door closed. I helped lower him next to me, and the scent of spicy shaving cream perfumed the closet, as the hangers scraped and settled on the metal pole above our heads.

Seconds passed. Maybe they were minutes. Having a nearly mute closet companion was not a bad thing. Milt quietly, slowly hummed a song—something old, a tune I knew I should recognize but I couldn't place.

I drew in a big breath. "It's nice in here, isn't it?"

He didn't answer but he stopped humming.

"I was a bit down but now I'm feeling better. I had a date with the fireman I told you about," I said and paused. "We can't seem to have a complete evening together without an interruption."

Milt's body vibrated next to me. He was getting ready to say something. I waited.

He croaked out a word but it was broken and unclear. I nudged him. "Did you say 'math'?" I didn't really care if he made sense. It was another new word.

He cleared his throat. "Moth."

"Moth?" I asked. "Do you think there are moths in the closet?"

He vibrated again, like a restaurant device letting me know my table was ready. "You moth," he said.

"I'm a moth? As in I like dark places, kind of moth?"

He became still, sitting in the comfortable gray hue created by the tiny ribbon of light under the door.

"You know why I appreciate closets?" I asked.

I gave him a chance to answer.

"They are positive, hopeful." I moved the clothes above me. They swayed against our shoulders. "With all of my favorite clothes hanging here, it seems like an irrefutable argument that my life is meant to go on. Why own all of these things if nothing good will happen while wearing them? Does that make sense? My outer coverings give me hope, even when my insides are sad or lost."

Milt's arm began to shake. He attempted a few false starts with random sounds, then went still.

"Are you okay?'

His bony hand reached my leg and squeezed. "Moths," he said.

I took his hand and held it. "I agree."

I pulled him to a standing position and we left the closet. Squinting against the light, I wished him a good night. He shuffled out of my room and down the hallway.

A dull rain had started. I hoped it was downpouring in Cussler Glen where there was that fire that pulled Lawyer from me. I crawled under the covers and tried to sleep, but not before listing the things I needed to get done for work and making a note to find jokes for Milt. *What did he mean by "moth"?* I wondered.

I thought of the heat Lawyer and I shared. The phrase "a moth to the flame" went through my mind. I smiled. That summed up our relationship so far. I hoped getting burned was not the next step.

SMALL TALK

A fuzzy, hot morning greeted me as I headed out to see my patients. Later in the afternoon, I was planning to head to the courthouse where I would dig as deep as possible into the Kingstons' history. I debated whether to recruit Beryl's help with my search, but was starting to think that was against home-health rules.

Casey Lester was the only child in my caseload. He was five years old, the son of Honey and Karl. Karl was a long-haul truck driver and Honey was an overwrought mom, who pacified her daily nerves with a tumbler of gin and TV soaps.

On the way, I passed by the Mapleton firehouse. I couldn't help but take a peek toward the building, wondering if Lawyer would be there. Richard mentioned the Cussler Glen fire and said it had taken three fire departments all night to knock it down. They suspected arson. I wondered if Sofie had had the police scanner on the whole time, enthralled yet calmed by the urgent messages. I'd have to ask Jon. Lawyer's truck wasn't there, so I supposed he was home sleeping.

Vixonville was to the northwest, about fifteen miles into a heavily forested area past Mapleton. Its main street was prosperous and tidy. The surrounding avenues were filled with mostly large old homes sitting on ample lawns.

Three miles outside of town, I turned onto Collard Street, and after a few more miles, I bumped along Rutabaga Drive. An aspiring dirt road. A quarter of a mile later, I parked in front of the Lesters' two-story house with chipped gray paint and patches of shingles missing from the steep roof.

I grabbed my therapy bag and headed for the house. The steps creaked as I climbed them and the planks of the wooden porch sagged in the middle. I stood on a new door-mat. This one read: "WOW! Nice underwear!" Despite the obvious, I smoothed down my walking shorts.

Footsteps quickly thumped down some stairs and the door flew open. Casey was a chunky boy with thick blond hair and big blue eyes. Today, he looked like he'd had a run-in with live wires, his hair all shocked out and uncombed. He jumped up and down, and then flung his arms around my legs, nearly knocking me off my feet. I grabbed the doorframe for balance. "Hey, there, Casey. I'm glad to see you, too."

He was wearing a light tan T-shirt stained with some-thing that resembled a red Rorschach test plate, and *camo* shorts with bulging pockets on each side of his sturdy legs.

He pointed to his ears. "I hah new ears."

I smiled, realizing he wasn't talking so loudly now that he had hearing aids. "You do have new ears."

He was mostly unintelligible when I first met him, when no one had realized it was his hearing that needed to be addressed and improved before we could focus on his speech. These hearing aids would help him drastically improve the clarity of his speech.

He turned his head and laughed. "Thah a bohd." He jumped up and down again, pointing to a tree where a bird trilled.

I looked in that direction. The poor kid hadn't heard a bird before. He was in for auditory overload with all the new sounds in his world.

Honey appeared at the door. She was twenty-seven, but deep lines on her face said she'd carried heavier emotional loads than I ever had. She motioned me inside. I stepped into the high-ceilinged foyer where a dusty chandelier hung in the center. Casey and I worked at a card table in the living room to the right, except when Karl was home. On those rare occasions, we worked on the porch. He had an obsession with newspapers, hoarding thousands, stacks of them throughout his house.

Despite his obsession, he disliked admitting to it, or having people in the house where they could nose about and discover this obsession.

"Hey, Marleigh. Good to have you back." Honey wore her lanky copper hair down today. Her freckled cleavage fought a tight, hot pink tank top.

I pointed to Casey's hair. "What's going on there?"

She waved a hand his way. "He discovered that hair gel makes a funny sound coming out of the tube so he went nuts. He's a real sound scientist now that he can hear."

I laughed and said, "I like that. Sound scientist." Casey walked around, tapping furniture with his hands. "Any meltdowns?"

She shrugged. "Yeah, yesterday. I thought it was noisy around here *before* with his yelling, but now he's making noises *nonstop*. So I had a talk with my old friend, Tanqueray, and things smoothed out." She moved her hand slowly in front of her like she was evening out the horizon.

I paused and said, "I meant has *he* had any meltdowns? All of this new stimulation can be overwhelming."

She looked puzzled for a beat. "Hell, no. He's doing fine. I'm the one that needs help."

I turned into the living room. Casey hopped onto the edge of the couch, watching the lava lamp on the end table burp up globules of orange goo. "That's new," I remarked.

"Oh, yeah. Since he's such a little nerd now, I got that for him. Keeps him quiet, and that's my goal."

"Well, we actually do want him talking so he can practice his articulation."

"Yep. He can talk when you're here."

I bit back a remark about how only a few sessions a week would not change anything. I said, "Could you get him building blocks or Legos?"

"Karl doesn't want him exposed to expensive toys. I've got a woodburning kit and Creepy Crawler Thingmaker in the basement from when I was little."

Karl was an idiot. Those toys were taken off the market in the '70s for good reasons. I held my tongue. "Well, I need to get working with him." I sat on the couch while Casey took a folding chair next to me. He seemed happy enough, and safe. But it was hard to keep from lecturing Honey on everything she did with him.

I pulled out pictures of common objects, words that began with sounds he couldn't yet pronounce.

Honey remained in the doorway. Usually, she hurried off to enjoy forty minutes of alone time. I shrugged, smiled, and said, "I'll let you know when we're done."

She nudged the carpet edge with her toe. "I thought I'd sit in today."

I would have been less surprised if her hair had ignited. I stammered, "Sure, I mean, yes. That's a wonderful idea."

She came over and actually sat next to me on the couch. So, I began. I started with the /f/ sound, a phoneme that is impossible to hear if a person has a severe hearing loss. I showed Casey a picture of a fork and said the name of it. He repeated back twenty pictures, ending with "Fan, Face, Farm, and Fox." I turned to Honey. "He's doing great today. Remember how he couldn't say the F sound at all?"

She was studying the reverse side of the cards. The names of the pictures were printed on the back of each. "Huh? Oh, yeah. He was the shits," she said. She held up the cards and asked, "Hey, can we keep these?"

I felt my eyebrows push together and fought to put them back where they belonged. It was then I realized why she wanted to sit in on therapy. Honey had a lot of things going for her and pride was one of them. She didn't want to ask for help and I wasn't going to point out something she had already told me in confidence. "Sure. I'll bring more if you'd like."

Her shoulders slumped. I could tell she was grateful I hadn't brought up the reason she wanted the cards. "Do you have any interesting books I can read to him? You know, something around fifth grade."

I didn't have the cruelty to acknowledge they were for her, or the other obvious truth that Casey would be reading kindergarten books. So I smiled and said, "I'll bring a variety." I could help two people at once, a bonus for the therapist in me. Casey would learn to talk and Honey to read.

By the time I walked to my car, Honey held every picture card I had with me that day.

As I backed out to turn around, Casey was beating out a rhythm on the porch railing. He was no longer running around and acting like a dog, which had been his old way of getting attention. Honey would be in for it when Casey moved beyond experimenting with the sound world and the noises he could make. I hoped she would be able to handle her son once he really started talking, especially when he started launching curious, often awkward five-year-old boy questions.

He Swears, It's Ivory

I reached Ruttsford twenty minutes later. Melvin and Sandy Carlisle lived in a large, yellow home that was all about being regal with its bay windows and wisteria vines as thick as an arm, pretending to support the sides.

Melvin had had his second stroke six months earlier and developed word-finding problems. He'd been the pastor's assistant at the Presbyterian Church, a very devout man, until he was left with a narrow bandwidth of vocabulary.

Sandy, a petite woman with close-cropped white hair greeted me at the front door. "You know where to find Mel." She pointed down the hall. "And Ivory is here. I'll be heading to the store for a while."

I walked to the den. Ivory was Elyk's mother. She had been in my caseload for a brief period of time until she was found not to be homebound in any sense of the Medicare definition. Needing a job, I got her set up through Therapy on Wheels as a respite care worker, directing her to Melvin and Sandy's house.

The den was more of a library with wall-to-wall bookshelves, and furnishings in rich green and gold plaid colors. The heavy scent of old books was satisfying, an invitation to sit and relax.

Melvin was nearly bald with a sprig of gray combed across his shiny crown. He reclined in a chair, sipping lemonade. He smiled and said, "Amazon bitches alive."

I gasped and scanned the room for his word board. He could point to entire sentences now but when left on his own, he was Picasso at creating these warped cuss word patterns. I pulled it from under a stack of newspapers beside his chair and dropped it on his lap. "Okay. What were you saying?" I asked.

He studied the board and slowly pointed to the words—Big, Woman, Help, Me.

"Ivory," I said. "She's a very nice woman."

As the words left my mouth, I saw movement in the doorway. Ivory stood there. She was a plus-size woman, close to 300 pounds. She wore a floral muumuu-style dress and purple Crocs. Her dark hair was swept up into a beehive cone, lacquered into a shiny funnel. A thermometer stuck out from the side like a bamboo stick in a geisha's hair, but this one full of mercury. Gabriel Fahrenheit couldn't have foreseen where his invention would end up these four hundred years later.

"Don't lie to the man," she said with a laugh deep and hearty. "I'm not sure he's that fond of me." She came to his side and dropped a hand on his shoulder. "Do you like having me here?"

"Twitter tits and horse's shit." He smiled pleasantly and patted her hand.

She laughed. "He's a regular Dr. Seuss."

I sent a scowl her way. "Ivory. That's how he talks to everyone. You need to use the word board I made him." I tapped the cardboard chart with pictures and words taped to it. "Melvin, tell Ivory how you feel."

He pointed to Help, My, Sandy, Good.

"See? He *is* happy that you're here."

Ivory turned to go. "He's got a mouth on him. I thought I'd heard it all while I was in the military. Nuh uh." She smiled. "He's a blast to be around." Then she turned and left.

Not exactly the idea of what should be happening here. The goal was to make him swear less, not more. He'd cussed most of their church friends right out of their house; he and Sandy felt like untouchables. No one came to visit anymore, according to Sandy.

The good news was Melvin had made progress. By pointing to words, they surfaced in his mind when he wanted to speak, so occasionally the words showed up in his conversation. I also discovered he could sing lyrics without any problems. Every chance he got to practice words, even if it meant singing them, would benefit him.

Today, I brought a handheld device that showed a printed sentence as a man's voice read it. Because the words stayed on the screen, our goal was to repeat it after the voice.

I explained what we were going to do then I loaded the first card. The mechanical voice read, "The man put gas in his car," as the words were individually highlighted.

"Our turn," I said. I slowed the word speed down and hit replay. "The ... man ... put ... gas ... in ... his ... car."

Melvin smiled and nodded his satisfaction. "Boogers ass."

I shook my head. "Well, not exactly. Try it again." I pushed replay again and he managed to repeat the sentence. This was very good. He'd never been able to say anything without someone in chorus speaking at the same time.

We had practiced for thirty minutes when Ivory popped her hairdo and head inside the door and asked, "Do you two need anything?"

I waved her in. "Did you know Melvin can sing without swearing?"

She tilted her head and studied Melvin. Then she broke into the opening lines of *New York, New York*. She even threw in some Frank Sinatra swagger, almost clearing off an end table with her girth.

Melvin sang along, his face suddenly lit up like a surprised child, as tears came to my eyes.

When the song ended, I applauded. Ivory had a beautiful voice, and in years past, had sung in musicals at the Clemmens Center in Elmira, New York, just a twenty-minute drive north of Tungston.

I packed my therapy supplies. "Ivory. Can you sing with him while you're here? It's the perfect therapy."

Melvin pointed his finger her way. "Pudgy whores alive."

Ivory scowled. "Did he just call me fat?"

I snorted and asked, "*That* was the word that upset you?... There is not a mean bone in his body, so don't take *anything* he says personally."

Melvin and I made eye contact. "Use your word board, Melvin. I'll be back in a few days."

He raised his hand in a farewell. "Dammit to goodness," he said happily.

The lyrics to *Send in the Clowns* pushed me to the front door. I couldn't stop smiling as I sat in my car, writing notes in his chart. Melvin's prognosis was looking better and better. And it seems Ivory had found her calling.

Passing through a hamlet on the way back to Tungs, a church bell tolled as a firehouse whistle announced noon almost at the same time. Such simple charms.

My phone rang and I grabbed it without looking at the caller ID.

"How are you today?" Lawyer's voice was deep, but with a hint of raggedness. Perhaps overuse from shouting, or worse yet, sucking in smoke.

"I'm fine, but the question is, how about you? You sound tired."

"I dropped into bed sometime around five this morning." He cleared his throat. "Sorry about yesterday. Can we try that again?"

"Debunking in a fire tower? There may have been only one shot at that." I tried to keep the tension out of my voice but it was there anyway. "But I'm still willing to get together."

"Okay, then. Where will you be in about thirty minutes?"

Now he was talking. I pushed dusky and sexy into my voice. "What do you have planned?"

He paused. "Well, maybe not what we were hoping. But, I made an appointment for you with a U.S. Marshal. A guy who knows about the witness protection agency, and possibly your birthparents."

Uncovering the Past

I tried to restrain my excitement as we sat with Scott Schumer, a U.S. Marshal for twenty years. He'd known Lawyer's dad, Huck Hunt, who passed away last year. Lawyer and I sat across the table from him at The Lazy Steak Diner on the outskirts of Williamsport. The building had been around since World War II. It permeated with the welcoming, yet artery-clogging scents of grease, fried meat, and all things slathered in gravy. Scott was tall and lanky, and dressed casually in dark jeans creased down the front, and an olive-colored, button-down shirt.

The waitress was on us in seconds, holding a clear glass coffee pot with thin brown liquid in one hand and menus in the other, her white uniform hiked up a few inches in the back.

Lawyer smiled at her as he accepted the laminated menus. "Could you give us a few minutes?"

"Take your time, hon." She went off to somewhere just beyond our line of sight, possibly counted to five and came back. "Are you ready to order?" Her blouse had been unbuttoned with pushed-up cleavage to greet us this time.

I felt my eyes roll. Scott was a good-looking guy with short dark hair, greenish eyes, and a hard chin line, but my bet was she was looking at Lawyer. I met his gaze and he sent me a wide smile and winked.

He looked from me to Scott. "Are we ready?"

Nervous and not all that hungry, I ordered the Cobb salad. The waitress scribbled on a pad and leaned toward Lawyer. "The name's Bitsy if you need me. For *anything*."

He sent her away with his smoking-hot smile and a thank you. Then he looked my way. "What?"

"Bitsy," I whispered, my voice husky and sexy. "Wait until she finds out you're a fireman. She'll self-combust."

"Just being neighborly."

Scott watched all of this with an amused smile. Then he narrowed his eyes toward Lawyer. "You came back to the area to take over your dad's job, didn't you?"

"My mom's lost her vision, macular degeneration. I came back to live with her. And since my dad had just died, the fire chief job was open so I applied and got it."

Something he wasn't saying played along his jawline. He must have felt my eyes on him. He continued, "And a friend of mine from Philly is here now and she's helping out with mom. Veronica. She's heading back down state next week, though."

I hardly knew Veronica, but I was happy to hear she was leaving. I mean, who has an old girlfriend living in their house?

Our meals came and Bitsy rested a breast on Lawyer's shoulder as she slowly set his Rueben sandwich in front of him. He didn't pull away and a smile tugged at his lips.

Good Lord.

Once she was gone, Scott ate a few bites from his roast beef platter, wiped his mouth on a napkin, pulled a spiral notebook and pen from a briefcase, and started talking. "I know you're hoping to find information about your birth-parents." He glanced at the notebook. "Aliases Daryl and Amber Kingston." He steepled his hands and squinted my way. "Here's the problem. Witness protection is only for people who need to disappear, not just anyone wanting a new start. The Kingstons were in danger... they'd witnessed a federal crime and needed to testify. Their lives were at risk."

I sighed. "But not any more. They're dead. Which seems wrong, doesn't it? If the Kingstons had been protected, what got them killed in the end?"

He took another bite and swallowed. "I'm going to check into that. They'd been here a year. I think you already heard they were from the Pittsburgh area... and car accidents happen all the time on these back roads."

"You're saying they just had horrible luck?" I leaned closer. "That doesn't feel right, especially since they'd just put me up for adoption. Something else was going on."

Scott shrugged. "Maybe it was hard, continuing in their new life with a kid. No connection to any relatives. Who do you trust to babysit?"

That stopped me. *Had I been a burden?*

Lawyer squeezed my thigh, obviously seeing my reaction to Scott's words.

I said, "They're dead now. They couldn't talk about anything they saw. Is there any way to trace backward and learn who they were before they entered the program?"

Scott said, "They would have testified against someone big, like drug traffickers, organized crime, that sort of thing."

I put down my fork. "Wait. There's organized crime here?"

Scott talked around a mouthful of food. "Sure. The mob loves rural areas, especially when they're built on moneymakers like lumber, coal or aluminum. Started with bootlegging in the twenties. Ethnic groups. The Irish or Sicilians got powerful, especially in the Pittsburgh area."

My eyebrows shot up. "The Kingstons might have been killed by the mob?"

Lawyer dropped his hand to my knee to stop my leg from bouncing. "You okay?" he asked.

"Yeah. This is all more complicated than I hoped," I said.

Scott held his fork in the air. "Not complicated. Dangerous. Witnesses go away but not the criminals."

"Well, the criminals don't need to know. You *could* get into the records and look up their original names. But like you said, they *are* dead."

"Highly unlikely that a judge will allow that." He shrugged.

I could hear my optimistic brain cells disappearing with little popping sounds. I don't know what I hoped, but I didn't like hearing the word "unlikely."

"I will ask around. You do have a point that the need for the protective order should be over, but I won't know until I hear what they were hiding from." Scott glanced at his watch. "I'm going to look up the criminal cases that occurred around the years your parents went into WITSEC. And you need to ask yourself... maybe the criminals knew the Kingstons had a little girl at the time." He raised his eyebrows, forming a challenging look. "And if that little girl starts getting nosy, do the original criminals get worried about her?"

My heart beat faster. I hadn't considered the upshot of anything like that. I let out a long breath. The day had changed somehow. There was one thing I didn't want to drag back with me when I returned to California in August and that was doubt. But from what Scott said, I might be doing just that.

We said our goodbyes but not before Scott said, "If I learn anything you are allowed to know, I'll call."

Not very encouraging.

Once we were back in Lawyer's truck and on the road, I asked, "Do you think I should leave this alone? I mean, is it too dangerous?"

He stared ahead for a few moments. "Hell yes, it's dangerous. Your parents saw something or learned something and they were put in the WITSEC program, and...despite that, they were discovered and killed." He took a breath. "But let's see what Scott finds out first."

We crossed a metal bridge, a glistening smear of dark gray going off in two directions over a wide river. He was taking back roads I didn't recognize until I saw the white, steepled church Tinsel attended, the one with the ever-changing slogan on its marquee. Today it read:

Cars aren't the only thing recalled by their maker—
are you ready?

I pointed. "Have you seen these? So creative."

He snorted. "New guy took over a few months back. Nobody else wanted the job after the last preacher died."

The sign above the front steps read, The Little Church in the Pines. I asked, "Is this guy single?"

From the corner of my eye, I saw Lawyer's head swivel my way. I raised my eyebrows in what I hoped was an interested look. I wasn't sure why I was teasing him.

"Yeah. I hear he fills the pews on Sunday, and if you stand real still as he takes the pulpit, you can feel the earth move as all the ladies swoon," he said.

"Might be worth seeing." I laughed, then teased him this time by touching his thigh and heat radiated through his jeans. "Want to take me to church?"

He grinned. "Only if it's after hours and we're alone."

I gently side-slapped his arm and let out a fake gasp. "You would *defile* the sanctity of a house of worship?"

"No, I'd leave the church alone and completely defile *you.*" His wide smile heated up several parts of my body, and I felt dizzy. Talk about swooning.

He turned onto another crumbling road of sparsely laid out houses with huge stacks of graying firewood piled against them.

I regained my senses. "Threats, threats, empty threats. With our luck, you're not even going to *file* me."

He slowed the truck as we rounded a corner, and then pulled off to the side of the road under a cool island of trees in an ocean of fields and patchwork forest. He turned toward me. Expectation lit his face. "Oh, it's not a threat."

Bugs hummed an electrical static sound from the depths of the forest, but blood pounding in my ears drowned out everything else. Was I this adventurous? In broad daylight in a truck? I was contemplating my answer when he reached over and grabbed my head and pulled me into a long kiss. All my senses went on alert, wanting to feel everything.

A horn beeped and our eyes flew open, each of us startled. A car idled next to Lawyer's side of the truck. "Crap," he muttered as he dropped back into his seat and buzzed the window down. "Hey, there," he said. "What's going on?"

Sitting in a dark green SUV was a young guy with thick black hair in a messy self-assured cut, a watch gleaming on his wrist, his elbow resting on the open window frame. "Just wondering if you'd broken down."

"Nope. Thought we saw a deer."

The guy stalled, looking as if he was rolling that idea around. "Long way from Mapleton." He pointed to the fire company's name emblazoned on Lawyer's truck. Then he turned his gaze toward me and I squirmed, suddenly feeling like a speaker pushed on stage, naked.

Lawyer shrugged. "You're a long way from Jersey. How are you adjusting?"

Lawyer knew this guy?

The guy let a slow smile take over his face. "I guess you know who I am then. And who are you two?"

"Lawyer Hunt and this is Marleigh Benning. Marleigh, meet Christian Betts. The pastor of that church we just passed." Lawyer's face was tight and I wondered why.

I leaned forward. "Nice to meet you."

Christian smiled. Not only was he handsome, but now he poured on the charm. "Come on by and see what we are all about this Sunday. We're having a picnic right after."

"Okay." I bobbed my head. "Thank you."

Lawyer did that chin jerk thing that meant something just between guys. In this case, it must have meant goodbye because he started the truck and we pulled away.

I waited a few moments, letting the cornfields zip by. "He seems nice."

Lawyer didn't answer right away. We let the silence hover around in the truck before he said, "I don't like him."

"Why not?"

"I ask myself why a single, good-looking guy leaves a much better paying job to come to a rural area." He shrugged.

Was he jealous? "If you're worried about me, he's not my type."

He shot a look my way. "It's his congregation I worry about. He's tripled the number of people attending."

"And that's a bad thing? Sounds like people needed someone to take over that church."

"He insists on a twenty percent tithe, has a whole list of causes, like Bibles for Babies or some made-up shit like that."

I laughed. We had almost reached Tungston, my hamlet in the hills. "You know this how?"

"Nothing is a secret here." He worked the truck up the long road to the Bed & Breakfast. "I wish he'd have come by and found us ten minutes later though." He chuckled. "Like to see his sanctimonious face then."

I hadn't seen this side of Lawyer. He had never seemed annoyed with anyone. Of course, he had the right to have these feelings. "I might go to the picnic. It sounds like a must-do while I'm here. Lots of local foods I haven't tried yet. You want to come?"

Lawyer pulled to a stop outside of the inn. "I have a better idea. Come to my house Saturday night for dinner. My mom is THE best cook in the area." His shoulders relaxed. He was back to his carefree self.

I pushed my door open but didn't get out. "Okay. And thanks for setting me up with the Marshals Service. I have a good feeling about that."

He took my hand and tugged me his way to kiss me, and then pulled me into a hug. "Outside of achieving no afternoon delight, I had fun today."

I squeezed him tight, pressing him as close as I could in our awkward position. I whispered, "There's always tonight?"

He hesitated. "I promised to fix some things around the house. Since my dad has been gone, the property is falling apart. Then I have a two-day training in Buffalo with the guys. But Saturday night, right?"

I agreed, although waiting three days seemed like a long time. I hopped out of the truck and watched him turn and pull away. The day was still hot and the heat came off the road in waves, such that the farther away he got, the blurrier he became. I tried to convince myself it had been a good day. I needed to stop expecting heated passion from our time together. Then I'd be less disappointed.

Ash's County Store and Souvenirs

An hour later, I happily agreed to make the run to the store for whipped cream. Two new families had shown up at the inn, one with a ten-year-old daughter who was a little bit creepy. It seemed like no matter where I was in the B&B, she was there. Silent. Her head dipped, so her stare came from the top of her eyes with an aura that made me want to point her toward the nearest cornfield, where—like in a B movie—she could start her killing spree. She was unnerving and her name didn't help. Wisteria. Really?

I pushed through the screen door of Elyk's store, setting off the buzzer. Elyk was seated on a stool, stocking a shelf, his back to me. I forced my voice into a high falsetto. "I need some pickled squirrel parts."

He didn't turn, but his ears moved backward so I knew he'd smiled. "You're in luck. I'll even feed them to you."

"Oh, gag me." I walked to his side. He was labeling cans of Pork Brains and stacking them on the bottom shelf. "No way. People do not buy brains." My stomach rejected the idea and something rolled around inside.

"Yup, they do. They're in milk gravy, after all."

I leaned closer to read the can and it sure was. "Stop talking about it." I brushed away the image as he laughed. "I need whipped cream."

"You've come to the right place." He stood and I followed him to the refrigerator case. With two cans in hand, we headed for the register.

A crossword puzzle lay on the gray speckled Formica, and a sheet next to it was full of words, all crossed out. I leaned toward the page. "How's the puzzle contest going?"

"Day twenty-two." He tucked his hands in the back pockets of his black jeans. "Since you're here, I'll let you look at tomorrow's puzzle."

"You mean you're stuck?"

He shrugged.

I pulled the paper around and studied the last blank. I read, "Negotiated, haggled, to get a better price." I laughed. "Oh, geez. This one must have you all flustered."

He scowled and his Mohawk haircut moved forward on his head. "Sounds dirty, and look at the letters I already have. D I C K _ _ _ _."

I snorted. "Oh, my gosh. That's funny." I turned the paper back to him.

"Wait. You don't have any ideas?" Panic stained his voice.

"Oh, I do. I really want to hear what you're thinking."

"It's gotta be 'DICKHEAD.'"

I pulled out money and paid for the whipped cream. "It's not. But I won't *dicker* with you."

He squinted hard, looked at the puzzle and then picked up the pen. "Dickered." He wrote letters in the tiny boxes. "Thanks." He handed me change. Then he reached under the counter and brought out a card. "And as a reward, I have this for you."

My insides slumped. Without looking, I assumed this was the invitation to host a Mary Kay party for his girlfriend, Dottie. I waited for a few moments and drew in a slow breath. "I'll call her and get something scheduled."

He cocked his head to the side. "It's from that cop, Jaxson. He was smitten with you."

"Oh? Weird." I didn't know if I was relieved or not. Officer Mills, the slinger of slang.

"And you *do* need to call Dottie." The phone rang and he reached for it, moving his hand in a sweeping motion, brushing me toward the door.

I sat in the car and read the note. He'd invited me to run with his group in the morning. It gave a location in Wellsfield and meeting time. I'd consider the idea. Running alone was hard, and meeting jogger friends would be nice.

Back at the inn, I helped Rose get nightly desserts ready. We were side by side at the prep table in the kitchen. I whispered, "Does that girl seem a bit odd to you?"

Rose looked over her shoulder then leaned closer. "Her mom said they are letting her experiment with her individuality. The dad is a psychiatrist and believes in children directing their own personalities."

I dabbed piles of whipped cream on the berry chocolate streusel bars while Rose arranged caramel dipped pears on a plate. "Someone is going to guide her to an exorcist if she stays this creepy."

Rose laughed and gently nudged me. "I love having you here. I wish the summer would slow down because I'll miss you."

Warmth spread through my chest and I fought back tears. "I love being here. You've made me feel at home." I moved the plate aside and started cutting brownies into bite-sized pieces. "And, since it's only mid-June, let's not think about summer's end just yet."

A moment later, I grabbed the silverware to take to the other room. I turned and Wisteria the Mysteria was standing right behind me. I let out a little scream before sucking air. My heart hammered as I slowly walked around her, almost afraid to have her at my back. I returned for plates but she was gone. "How long are they staying?" I asked Rose.

"Two nights." She looked toward the doorway. "But it might feel longer."

I finished setting the table. "Rose. Unless you need me, I'll skip the witching...I mean, dessert hour. I have some paperwork to do."

"Go ahead. Sleep tight..." she said, giving me a hug, "and thanks for the help."

When I got to my room, I changed into my pajamas and needed a few extra minutes in the closet, drawing calm slow breaths before sitting at my desk. I pulled out my clients' charts and made sure I completed my daily notes. They're due every Friday at Therapy on Wheels with my billing sheets. Once I finished adding to Casey's file, I packed the charts away and remembered Jaxson's note. I decided I would meet his group for a run, but hoped he was a texter because I didn't want to encourage nightly chats on the phone. I put his number in my phone and typed, "See you in the morning. Thanks for the invite."

I crawled into bed, relishing the cool sheets, and the bliss of rest.

My phone pinged. Jaxson responded, "Hope U R chillaxing. Will be good to have a noob in the group. See you on the flip side."

This was going to be terrible. I would voluntarily pop my eardrums before listening to this for ten miles. I sighed. I needed sex and didn't want to wait three more nights to see

Lawyer. Now that I committed to running, maybe I could burn off my sexual frustration that way.

I slid lower under the down comforter. I was still surprised by my new life. It was a mere four months ago I was sitting down to lunch with my parents at Nob Hill Grille for my mother's sixtieth birthday. Tomato bisque, lobster salad, crème brûlée. They toasted my approaching graduation, offered a "hear, hear!" to my earning a master's degree, and to all things possible. Two weeks later they were dead. The most ordinary thing in the world, lunch with my parents, made extraordinary because it would never happen again.

It drove a hole right through my life, one I was here trying to recover from. It had never occurred to me that my adoptive parents had been forty and forty-five when they brought me home. But what if they knew the Kingstons, or whatever my birthparents' names really were, before the WITSEC program? Could there have been a family connection all along, like my adoptive parents were actually my grandparents? I got excited. That happened all the time, right? Grandparents stepped in to raise a child. I listened to the blind softly flapping on the windowpane in the breeze, pushing from the outside. I did the math and realized Daryl Kingston would be fifty-one now and Amber would be forty-nine, while the Bennings were only sixty and sixty-two. It didn't add up.

I was tired. My mind was unable to deal with anything on this scale just now, so I let the damp scent of earthworms and flowers lull me into sleep.

RUNNING ON EMPTY

The next morning as I drove toward Wellsfield, my head-lights cast jumping beams of brightness through the maples. I questioned my decision to run so early. Even the sun had the sense not to show itself yet. And something was brewing with the weather. The wind beat against the window, bugs exploded in a variety of colors against the windshield, garishly backlit by my headlights.

I passed through tiny towns, all dark, surrounded by bristly forests and meandering roads. It felt like I was the only person alive, pulled along a lush course to the unknown.

Fifteen minutes later, I rolled into the park along Main Street and stopped next to a sheriff's cruiser. Someone was a few feet away, stretching under one of the town's gaslights. I locked my car, tucked the key into the pocket of my running shorts, and walked in that direction.

Jaxson wore a gray T-shirt and blue sweats. He was whistling something almost identifiable, but it escaped me. He had the beginnings of both a mustache and sideburns, something he didn't have just days before.

"Good morning," I said, searching the park for the other runners. The shadows of trees, dancing on the sidewalk and grass below the streetlights, were the only movements around us.

"Morning, glory," he said, and hopped to his feet from a sideways backbend, more limber than I expected. "Glad you came."

"Me, too. Where's everyone else?"

"About two miles out." He pointed in an indeterminate direction. "Hard to find the place and I knew you couldn't nav your way there. Didn't want to put you in a skid trying."

He planned this so we would be alone? *I should get in my car and leave, and get a run in at the B&B the second the sun showed itself.* He threw himself into a high stepping move—knees to his chest—warming up, swinging his arms back and forth in wide arcs.

I felt my teeth tighten. It would've been rude to leave. And it was just running, not a date. "Okay, I'm ready."

We fell into stride, side by side, the streets quiet. Wellsfield was the county seat, trim and prosperous, no graffiti. From any street in the town, it was a short and pleasant stroll to the library, or a diner. I liked the companionship of running, but preferred the sounds of footfalls and regulated breathing to conversation. It's not what I got. Jaxson was a talker.

"There's a mountain trail race coming up at the end of the month that our club is training for. I think you'd like it."

"Okay."

He rattled on about different races, his running schedule, and his training diet of Chia seeds and coffee. I thought of Tinsel's Chia Pets and the "hair" that grew from the same Chia seeds spread on the pottery. I focused on the edge of the road, as the sidewalks disappeared at the outskirts of town. Faint sunlight was rising along the horizon, blushing the sky with pale streaks of pink around low and shapeless clouds. The wind had stopped; the day seemed to be holding its breath for the next weather display.

He brought up the heroin problem again. "We haven't had anything like this here before, but I guess small town America is dealing with 'H' now. Cheap and deadster."

Why couldn't he use real words? "What's your plan? To go after all of the known drug dealers in the area?"

"Different this time. Not local."

He was breathing harder now because I kicked it up a notch. If faster meant less chatter, that was good.

"Coming in ... New York ... Ohio ... some border."

"I heard a farmer's son died."

"Got four dead now ... all under thirty."

"Terrible." Up ahead I saw a group of joggers, running in place, looking our way. Relief washed over me. "There they are." My voice was high, and I couldn't contain my excitement.

We slowed to a stop in front of them. Jaxson introduced me to the nine other runners—four women and five guys. There were too many names to stick, but I moved closer to the group of women, planning to run with them the rest of the way.

Jaxson spread his arms wide. "Welcome to Got the Runs."

I choked on the name. "Really?" I looked to the others for confirmation.

One woman with a bright pink headband spoke. "We let Jaxson name us. He's got a way with words."

I laughed. "He sure does."

"Leggo," Jaxson said, and we paired up, staying to the left side of the road, the crunch of eleven sets of running shoes drumming the gravel. A soothing yet powerful sound.

The countryside was unfolding with farms running in all directions. Within minutes, though, a warm morning drizzle started, the day now holding a dreary hand over us. We turned around and headed back along a different road as the rain picked up. A short, compact girl named Tiffany had been at my side most of the way. She had two kids and a new divorce under her belt. She explained her reason for running. "My husband left me for a skinny stick of a thing...seriously, she has no boobs...so I'm reinventing my old self."

I said, "Good plan. And running *is* therapeutic."

"It'll keep me out of jail. On most days, I still want to kill him."

"I'll bet." I changed the subject, telling her how running got me through my parents' deaths and kept me calm in my new job. I omitted the part about discovering I'd been adopted.

She vaulted a dead crow. "How long have you and Jaxson been together?"

What? "We aren't together."

She laughed. "Not what he's saying."

I fumed, watching his back. He was in the front, arms pumping, back straight, leading the group. I was surprised he didn't carry a backpack of rocks to prove his wonderfulness. "I'll have to clear that up."

The rain increased again when we reached their start and the group began peeling off to their cars. With another few miles to go, by the time Jaxson and I reached town, spinning tires were splashing up fans of water and we were soaked.

"This is good for the soul," he said, holding his face up to the rain. "Cleansing."

I couldn't fault his positive attitude. "It was a good run," I said.

Once at our cars, I had to bring up the dating subject. "You know I'm dating Lawyer Hunt, right?"

He stepped back, the look on his face saying I must be completely completely delusional. "No. I didn't since he's got that girlfriend living with him."

A dull weight dropped into my stomach. I hated that feeling. "They're just friends."

"Not what the rumor mill says." He laughed. "Have you been out with him?"

I dug my keys out of my shorts. "We've had several dates. One just the other night in the Balding Knob Fire Tower."

He stiffened. "Wait. Lawyer got to storm the cotton gin already?"

I burst out laughing. "Where do you get these sayings? And no, not quite. But we, in your words, we got the rollers moving."

He looked defeated, then he brightened. "Well, if you ever want a taste of some real horizontal refreshment, you know where to find me." He beeped his car open. "I'll show you what's the haps in the private dance department," he said and shut his door before I could respond.

I slid into my seat, wishing I had a towel. I'd have to pack one plus a jacket next time. Next time? I had to admit, compared to a still afternoon in my darkened room with a migraine, being with Jaxson and Got the Runs wasn't half bad. I'd probably do it again.

CHICKEN FOR LUNCH

An hour later, showered and awake, I arrived in the town of Swell, so small it was only hinted at on the map with a tiny dot. Luella Bledsoe lived with her sister, Margritte, between a rock quarry on the right and a swamp of dead trees on the left. Their mobile home sat on several rolling acres. I started seeing Luella after she'd had six rounds of aspiration pneumonia. She was lucky to be alive. We worked on strengthening her swallowing ability and showing her how to thicken drinks, so she wouldn't choke on faster moving fluids, and also confronted a little trouble with her fondness for Jack Daniels.

When I stepped away from the car, a feathery flood of chickens surged out from under the trailer skirt. As always, the hens fought each other, taking random stabs at my therapy bag and jabbing at my shoes.

"Go on," I said, gently sweeping one leg in front of the other—an effective chicken dance I learned.

Margritte pulled open the door. She resembled a short popsicle on two sticks, comfortably pushing the outer limits of her fuchsia-colored Spandex pants. Bright red hair flamed out around her head, but today there was no toothy smile. In fact, she looked sad.

"Come in," she said, her voice matching her face. Dejected.

I walked past her as she stepped aside. "What's the matter? Is it Luella?"

"She's the same. Mad at you because you won't let her drink." She swiped at a nonexistent tear. "We're all sideways about our chickens. We have to get rid of them."

I crossed the room to the table where Luella sat. Unlike her bulbous sister, she was bony and looked like an old leather strap. She sat hunched over the table, peering hawk-like at her nails. I said, "You can have a drink if you thicken it. And who said you have to get rid of them?" I studied three sets of chickens, roosting around the room—in a rocker, on the couch, and under a coffee table.

"Someone turned us in to the Health Department." Margritte scowled my way. "Did you do that?"

I had thought about it but never made the call. I concentrated, trying to remember if I had mentioned the chickens in my therapy notes. "I haven't said a thing. How about the nurse that comes by?"

Luella and Margritte exchanged a look that said, *Ah ha!* Luella slapped the table and I jumped. "I bet it was her. She's the one that hardly stays, all hoity-toity and wouldn't sit down."

Margritte picked up a brown-speckled chicken from the sofa and nuzzled it against her chest. "Rats and mice are worse pets. Besides, I clean every day."

My gaze dropped to the burnt umber carpet dotted with splotches of chicken crap. It always smelled fetid and musty in here, closed off like no breeze had blown through in a while.

Margritte must have seen my gaze. She cleared her throat. "Been busy this morning though. Vacuuming is on my *afternoon* list of chores."

Luella said, "They gave us only a few days to get them out of the house." She sagged in the oak dining chair.

"Can't they just live with the others outside?" I wasn't sure what the problem was.

Margritte gasped and grabbed her chest. "We raised them in here from chicks. They would get murdered out there."

"You have that back porch. Maybe they can live out there." Was I really helping them? The chickens were a health hazard.

They seemed to consider this idea.

I turned to Luella. "Are you still doing the swallowing exercises?"

"I can do two of them dry swallow thingies in a row now." She stuck her tongue tip between her teeth, bit down, and showed me how she could swallow twice.

I grinned. "That's impressive ... and not easy to do." I made a note in her chart. "Three in a row is the goal, but you're almost there." I pulled out a list of other exercises to strengthen the tongue and throat muscles. "Let's go through these."

She followed my example from initiating a strong cough which slams the throat muscles and vocal cords together, making them stronger, to saying glottal sounds like /g/ and /k/ really fast. I saw her only once a week now, down from twice that. "You're doing great. Seriously. What an improvement from just a few visits ago."

I glanced at the clock. I was always surprised at how fast forty minutes flew by. I packed up my belongings just as Margritte, covered in a sheen of sweat, came in from the porch area.

She pointed to an overstuffed chair and said, "Now you can help me move this to the back porch."

I stalled in the middle of the room. Speechless.

"Marleigh ..." She swiped a meaty wrist across her forehead. "We're grateful you're helping us with the babies. You know what they mean to us."

"Move the furniture? How about just the chickens," I said a little short as I had another appointment to get to.

"You get so angry at the fly of a hat," Margritte clucked at me and her face flushed. "What in the world would they sit on? Of course, we're moving the furniture."

Luella stood and touched my back, nudging me toward the chair. "We have no one else, you know."

I let out an exasperated breath. "I'm not angry." My eyes shifted back and forth between them. Side by side they looked like the number ten. I set my bag on a chair. "Okay. Let's do this." I forced cheeriness into my voice.

I had to crab walk the chair across the carpet on its stubby legs since Margritte couldn't lift the other side. Once on the porch, she pointed out a space she'd cleared by the canning shelf. I wiggled the chair into place and stood back. The room had not been used for a long time. Cracked pottery sat on sagging shelves, and under a bench were men's shoes and boots. To my knowledge, Luella's husband had died years earlier.

Margritte turned and headed back in. "Let's go get that couch."

"I can't move the couch." It came out whiny.

"Fine. I'll help you."

Once I had my hands under the edge and had lifted one side, Luella let out a tiny scream and I almost dropped the couch.

"There's eggs under there," she said and hurried toward me. "Lift it again." Holding up my end, she gathered both blue eggs and held them up like they were gold nuggets. Then I remembered the sisters made money selling them.

"Good eyes," I said. "I could have stepped on them." I tugged the herringbone couch a few inches at a time, with

Margritte pushing from the other end. After the morning run and this manual labor, my muscles were burning.

With the couch in place, I said a hasty goodbye, knowing I would be late arriving at Tinsel's house. Again.

I passed The Little Church in the Pines that Christian Betts was in charge of. The new message on the marquee had changed:

I wish Noah had swatted at least one of those mosquitoes.

Christian was not only handsome but had a sense of humor as well.

On Beaver Hill Road, I found the lane to Tinsel's house on my first try. Two bits of good news came with that— Frank's truck wasn't there and I was only seven minutes late.

I pulled down the long lane and parked in front of the garage. After I pushed the doorbell, I heard her open the sliding-glass door in the back of the house and call for Lovey. Moments later, she opened the front door.

"Lovey for back bedroom. No teeth on foot today." She backed away and I entered.

"Thank you." I smiled and waited for her to take the lead as to where she wanted us to sit. The shades were pulled, the room a blend of diffused grays, and the Chia pieces were nearly invisible on their shelves. When she didn't move, I said, "Where do you want to work?"

"On the kitchen table."

"Perfect." I unloaded her file as she sat down. The cards I had left her were in a stack beside a cup of coffee.

She lifted her cup. "I pot you a cup of coffee?"

"Let's practice that phrase." I grabbed a piece of paper and wrote out a sentence. "I'll say this first and then you repeat it with me." I dragged my finger along the words as I read them. "May I make you a cup of coffee?"

She said the sentence several times with me. "Okay. Now you ask me again."

She paused, then pointed to her cup. "May I bake you a coffee?"

"Good." She had two verbs in there, even if they weren't perfect. "Say, make. Make you coffee."

"Make you coffee."

I smiled. "I think I *will* have a cup." This would be the focus of our therapy. "I want you to tell me all the things you are doing as you get that ready."

"Good idea." She stood and started for the cup holder under a cupboard.

"Stop. You have to tell me every movement you do."

She sat back in the chair and slowly stood. "I up from the chair."

"I stand up from the chair." She repeated it.

She took deliberate measured steps toward the cups, and cracked me up with her slow-motion actions.

"I shoe to the cup."

"Walk. Use that word."

"I shoe-walk to the cup."

I laughed. "Okay. Close enough. What's next?"

She put the cup on the counter and reached for a metal pot that looked like it had been brewing coffee since World War II. "I handle the coffee." She lifted the pot.

Although "handle" was technically a verb, I knew she hadn't used it that way.

We talked through the process of pouring, stirring, and offering a cookie.

Raspy barking came from the back room, just as the doorbell rang. Tinsel said, "My eyes at the door," as she walked that way. We were making progress but I couldn't expect complete changes in just one session.

When Tinsel arrived back at the kitchen doorway, she looked ten years younger, her face flushed and beaming. Behind her stood Christian Betts. He wore a yellow golf shirt, dark jeans, and Jesus sandals. "Pastor Betts chair with us." She slid the coffee she had made for me across the table and parked it in front of an empty chair. Then she moved the plate of cookies closer. She motioned for him to sit.

"How nice, Mrs. Tabbish." His gaze met mine. His eyes were light green with a dark black outline. Mesmerizing this close up. "And, it's Marleigh, right?"

"Yes. Nice to see you again." I smiled. "The messages on your sign are very funny."

"Glad you noticed. They're a kick to write." He glanced at the therapy materials. "Don't let me stop you. I'm intrigued by what a speech therapist does."

I swallowed quickly, nervous under his scrutiny. It had to be because he was much younger than I first expected, perhaps early thirties, only ten years older than me. "We were just wrapping up our session. I can't share what we're working on, since it violates Mrs. Tabbish's privacy."

He tipped his head to the side. "Preachers are exempt from most rules, you know." He looked like he was fighting a smile. "But I understand."

Tinsel took the chair next to him. "I words better now."

He dropped his hand over hers in a comforting gesture. "I can tell Marleigh with her secret bag of tricks is helping you." He winked at me and turned back toward her. "Why don't you bring Marleigh to church with you?"

I stood and quickly packed the cards away. I had thought about going to his church but now I wasn't sure. Maybe Lawyer was right; this guy seemed too slick for these hills. I touched Tinsel's back. "I'll see you next week. You did great today."

"Car to church with me?" Her drawn-on eyebrows raised into half moons on her face, expectant and needy.

"I'll think about it and let you know." I wasn't supposed to socialize with my patients outside their homes, so I have a good reason for not going. "Enjoy your day," I said and let myself out.

I let my shoulders drop, unaware they had climbed toward my ears. What was it about him that made me so nervous? I didn't think I was attracted to him, although he was very easy to look at. And nice. I was a sucker for nice which was why I'd fallen for Lawyer. Maybe because Christian seemed so available. The preacher arrived here unattached, something I wasn't completely sure about with the fireman in my life.

Since it was only early afternoon and I didn't need to be back to help at the B&B for a few hours, I pulled off the road at a trailhead and parked. I needed some quiet time. A rectangular sign pointed down a dirt trail with the words "Finley Creek 1 mile" etched into it. I locked the car and stuffed my phone in my Capri pants pocket. I wandered through the woods and across an open field, a light wind rippling the long grass like an invisible hand trailing across their tips. Through another forest, the path dropped lower and the creek came into view. I sat cross-legged on a rock the size of a buffalo and breathed deeply, closing my eyes.

Something about the breeze and the water reminded me of the first time I had been to the ocean. I must have been three or four when my parents had taken me to Coronado Beach. I remember the loud rush of waves was comforting, secluding almost, even though the beach with its huge expanse of sand and bright sun was packed with people. When I thought back to those days, I remembered my parents as being very protective, never letting me run to the edge of the water alone, shielding me from other kids and their families. What did I know as a four-year-old? Had they looked over their shoulders whenever we were in public? What secrets did they keep from me beyond that I was adopted? Did they know those people were in trouble? That I could be in trouble if they, as new parents, weren't vigilant?

I felt an immediate ache, a need as basic as thirst, to know exactly what had transpired all those years ago.

I needed answers.

You Must Be Joking

Our front porch rockers creaked as Milt and I rocked them slowly back and forth. We overlooked the front yard, the only quiet area since the five guests booked the place full for the night. Wisteria the Mysteria went on a rafting trip with her parents, and Richard just returned with her exhausted family in the B&B van.

Milt wore a pale yellow dress shirt, a darker yellow and black polka-dot tie, and black slacks. He was as animated as I had ever seen him, sitting upright, eyes bright, almost wearing out his pants with so much hand rubbing before he spoke. We had been practicing a joke he would tell during dinner. As a near mute, Milt had become like a family pet. Talked at but no one expected an answer from. "Dad, let's go sit in the library," they would say as they moved him there for a few hours. Why he didn't protest, I don't know.

But being able to contribute, even in the slightest way to a conversation, would change things for him.

"Let's try it one more time. What do you get when you cross an elephant with a rhino?"

He paused, rubbed his knees, and answered the joke perfectly.

I laughed and said, "You could tell a new joke every day."

He sagged into the padding, rocking the chair with a contented look on his face. "I joke," he said quietly.

Rose pushed the screen open. She looked back and forth between us. "You two look like you are up to something."

I grinned. "We might be."

"Okay, then. Dinner is in ten. Do you want to help Milt to the table?"

"My pleasure."

Moments later, Milt was seated in a chair next to my usual seat at the dinner table. I helped Rose carry the large bowls of spaghetti mixed with mascarpone, lemon, spinach, and pine nuts to the table. The smell was intoxicating and for a moment I felt dizzy. An appetizer of zucchini and Swiss cheese stuffed mushrooms, and a basket of braided bread-sticks were already on the table. Apple dumplings with vanilla ice cream would be dessert. The area attractions around the inn drew people to stay at the Pfoltzes' B&B, but it was mostly Rose's cooking that brought Richard and Rose their high ratings online.

The newest guests were from Iowa, Brittani and Steven Howard. With a generational history of dairy farming in their lineage, their occupation shouldn't have surprised me.

"We make waterbeds for cows."

Everyone's utensils stalled, mid-action, except for Mysteria who was building something in the center of her plate with her food. Her mother stroked Wisteria's hair signaling her approval after her daughter tapped her arm to show her the masterpiece.

Richard saved us after dabbing his mouth with a napkin. "That's quite interesting. Why do cows need waterbeds?"

Steven set his fork down and pushed his plate forward, setting his elbows on the table. "When a cow is lactating, she's lying down for twelve to fourteen hours a day."

Brittani corrected, "It's not twelve hours in a row... they get up and go eat, get a drink, get milked, and spend time with their friends. Yes, cows actually have friends and hang out in groups." When she smiled, her nose wrinkled and the freckles on her face arranged themselves into new constellations.

I noticed we were all nodding, so the story continued with Steven taking the lead again. "They need to rest in between their activities to conserve energy for making milk. If their beds aren't comfortable, they can get bedsores from lying around all that time." He smiled and looked around the table. "We're here to let local farmers know it's uber-important to ensure cows are protecting their pressure points."

Wisteria looked up and said, "Cows stink. They uber-poop everywhere."

The kid had a point. Maybe she wasn't that strange.

Rose changed the subject, turning the conversation to the available activities in the house as well as the sites to see in the area.

Milt ate steadily but he seemed nervous as his big moment got closer. I put my hand on his arm and squeezed.

Rose and I cleared the dinner dishes and we brought out the dessert. Once it was served, I cleared my throat and everyone looked my way. "You have all met Milt, and you probably think of him as a quiet guy when in fact, he's really quite funny. Due to some circumstance we won't go into, he is just learning to speak again and he has a joke he would like to tell you."

Richard's eyebrows shot up, and he sent me a wary glance. When I smiled back, I hoped it conveyed reassurance this would be okay.

I smiled again, and said, "Okay, here we go, Milt. What do you get when you cross an elephant with a rhino?"

All eyes turned to Milt. His hands moved back and forth on his thighs, his way of building up to his response. My pulse thumped in my neck, I was so excited. He'd been silent for too long.

His lips moved just as Wisteria shouted out, "Elephino!"

I gasped and Milt sunk into his shirt collar, his gaze returning to his plate, deflating so visibly I thought I heard a hissing sound.

The table went completely quiet, the kind that said everyone was thinking carefully about how to respond. I held back a whole string of adult swearing. What a letdown. And the way the girl was smiling, I was pretty sure she knew what this had done to Milt.

Silverware clinked again and someone cleared his throat. I glanced at Rose and our eyes met as she slowly shook her head, a subtle reminder these people were our guests. And the guests were always right.

I pushed back my chair, clamping my jaws together. "All right, then." I tapped Milt's shoulder. "Let's go learn a harder joke."

I got him to his feet where he wavered, then we slowly moved off. I steered him toward the library. He sat on his usual settee and I took the matching winged chair. "I'm sorry." I leaned toward him. "That girl is mean." He studied the crown molding, his blue eyes bright. "We can learn a joke no one knows. She'll also be gone tomorrow."

He didn't move and I felt his defeat. We sat that way for several minutes. "Milt. What do you get when you cross a mean girl with a sense of regret?"

He slowly turned his gaze my way and studied my face. Then he grew excited and slowly built to, "Elephino."

I laughed. "You're right. I don't know either," I said while standing. "We'll work on it again tomorrow. You're doing great."

Heading to my room, I arranged my therapy bag for the four patients I would see the next day. Being a Friday, I had to stop at Therapy on Wheels to drop off the notes and hand in my hours after seeing my four patients.

I checked my phone and found a text from Lawyer. "Buffalo is boring. I'm tired of looking at men in yellow gear. Rather look at you in, well, you know. Are we still on for dinner Saturday?"

Smiling, I typed, "Funny. I was just sitting here in my 'you know.' Sorry you missed it. And, yes. Looking forward to Sat. night. What can I bring?"

No answer immediately came back, so I changed for bed. Then the phone *pinged.* I read, "Looking forward to that mouth of yours."

A gusty wind hit against the side of the house as I pulled the covers up and then mashed the down pillows into the right position. I thought I'd have to lie awake for hours mulling over Milt's defeat but to my surprise, the Sandman quickly shut me down.

GONE TO THE DOGS

The next morning I called Beryl to let him know I would be late. From my bedroom window, I watched the fog drooping and rolling over everything below. Me, hovering above as if in a hot air balloon, looking down on the murky gray soup. San Francisco was known for its fog, so again I felt right at home.

Despite my comfort with fog, I had a hard enough time navigating the back roads with visibility. I was betting with no good sense of direction and no clear line of sight.

I left my room and tiptoed down the hall to check on Milt. He hadn't been at breakfast and Rose said he was still sleeping. Or perhaps depressed. I knocked lightly on his door, my ears overhearing continued chatter from downstairs about bovine beds.

I slowly turned the knob and pushed Milt's door open, peeking in. The shades were pulled and the room dark and quiet. Cocooned in the center of the bed, Milt lay wrapped in a quilt. He lifted his head to see who it was.

"Good morning, sleepyhead." I slowly crossed the floor to his bedside, following the light beam from the hallway. "You can get up now. Wisteria and her family have left the premises."

He watched me, then his lips trembled.

Oh, my God. Was he about to cry?

"I joke," he said, his voice froggy, unused.

I swallowed a lump. "I found some new jokes. You can look them over today and we can practice them when I get back. Let me go get them."

Back in my room, I grabbed the sheet I printed earlier in the morning from a website that had one-liners. I had circled five I thought he could easily learn. When I got back to his room, he had the window shade up and was sitting on the edge of the bed, gaunt and frail in his blue pajamas. "Here you go." I handed the sheet to him and glanced out the window. The fog was tearing itself into long entrails, pulling back toward the fringes of the trees. I could get on the road. "I'll be back later and we'll talk."

I left Milt studying the page like it was a secret.

Purse over a shoulder and therapy bag in hand, I thumped down the stairs, listening long enough just out-side the dining room to catch another cow tidbit from Steven. "There are more than eight million dairy cows in the U.S. They each make around seventy-five to a hundred pounds of milk per day, and some of them have nutrition-ists, some have chiropractors, all of them get pedicures, you know...."

In the distance, the rain fell in pale gray curtains while I drove into a sun, peeking out intermittently behind banks of clouds like a shy young neighbor kid.

When I pulled into Beryl's drive, he was outside dressed in a black rain slicker and Pittsburgh Steelers' cap, relaxing in a lawn chair and watching his dogs play.

I stepped from the car and grabbed my bag. "They look happy," I said.

"Doing good together," he said. As he moved in the lawn chair, his plastic raincoat crackled. "The other dog fits right in. Glad I got him."

The Dog seemed to understand his new companion couldn't see well. He nudged the ball toward his new friend, waiting for him to grab it before he chased him.

I approached Beryl, hoping he was in a therapy mood. "What did you name him?" I asked.

Beryl stood and reached for his folded walker. "The other dog."

"Yeah. What did you name him?"

"The. Other. Dog." He gave each word a placeholder all its own.

"Of course you did." I slowly smiled. "But since The Dog can't hear, you could have just given the new guy the same name."

"You need to stop thinking on your own," he said and motioned me toward the door. "Let's get to work so you don't have a cow."

"Did you know some dairy cows sleep on waterbeds and get pedicures?"

He scowled. "Is that a liberal California thing?"

"Nope. Midwestern idea." I waited for the dogs to bumble in the door ahead of me and I followed.

He said, "Whole world's going into the dumper."

We took seats at his scarred kitchenette table, old but solid. The room was neat and the dishes had been recently washed.

The sun lost its fight with a new bank of clouds and the room became dim. Beryl reached the wall switch and flipped on the lights. I squinted until my eyes adjusted. Why do fluorescent lights make everyone appear like they are dying? Beryl aged instantly, and I assumed the green hue wasn't doing much for me either.

I pulled Beryl's chart from my therapy bag. "We're actually going to get to work on you now."

He shrugged. "I've been managing."

"You can't eat a steak. Or bread." I tapped a paper. "These are strengthening exercises so you'll be able to swallow everything once again, without choking."

He made a dismissive sound but seemed to be waiting for my next move.

"Okay. Good. We need to concentrate on the muscles at the back of your throat and your esophagus. They were cut during your surgery and are weak."

"So you are saying I have a good malpractice case against the surgeon."

"I'm saying no such thing." There was a touch of panic in my voice. I was already breaking home health rules all over the place. I didn't need him to get me involved in a legal battle.

He smirked, but I knew it was a smile. "It's easy to get you all rattled."

I let out an exasperated sigh. "And you love doing that. Now let's just do these exercises."

"Ready when you are."

"Okay. We are going to start with chin dips." I stood and walked to the sink and opened a few cupboards before choosing a plastic cup. I filled it halfway with water. "These exercises strengthen the esophagus at the top of the throat which helps you when you're swallowing." I handed him the glass. "Take a sip and before you swallow, tuck your chin."

He complied.

"Do three more, please."

He finished the swallows and set the glass down. "You get paid just to watch people drink?"

"I do. Now we are going to do airway exercises. You will be holding your breath and then I want you to put both hands under the table and try to lift."

He slowly followed the instructions.

"Just a few seconds more. Now let your breath out when you stop pushing upward."

He waited expectantly.

"Do five more sets. What you should notice are your throat muscles contracting."

When he completed them, he said, "Harder than you'd think." He brushed dog hair from his pants.

"Very hard." I turned to study the view out the kitchen window. Through gauzy drapes, the farm fields loped off to the edge of thick woods where they were consumed by a distant mist. I slid the list of exercises in front of him. "But you're getting it. Practice all weekend and I'll see you next week."

"Okay." He stood and once again reached into the drawer that seemed to hold everything, and pulled out tape. He stuck a piece to the sheet and then attached it to the closest cupboard. "Won't miss it here." He remained standing as if all that needed to be said, had been.

"Okay, then." I gathered my things. "You have a nice weekend."

He raised his hand, and graced me with a departing wave when I turned one last time at the door.

Working with Beryl had more ups and downs than the local roads. But he was doing great, and was almost ready to be discharged. I wondered what the work policy was for visiting past patients because I knew in this case, I'd miss Beryl.

PAST INTERESTS

"We had some excitement three nights ago," said Jon Dougan. "An old building a few blocks away caught fire."

Yeah, I was having some excitement too when that all happened. I set my bag down. "I heard about it and that it took all night to put out."

Jon crossed his arms. "I was half asleep in front of the news when the sirens went off and I couldn't find Sofie. That was a good scare." His gaze went to their covered patio beyond the kitchen. Sofie appeared relaxed, reading a paper.

"Where was she?"

"At the end of the block, heading toward the fire, like a kid drawn to the circus."

A few doors away, a lawn mower sputtered then caught and buzzed to life.

"That's frightening. She must have heard it on the scanner."

"That's what I thought, although the scanner was turned off when we got back." He pointed to a pot of coffee. "Would you like some?"

"Oh, no thanks," I said.

He filled a mug and sagged against the stove. "Now she is obsessed with fires. That's all she's talking about. I've been doing the validation thing, but that just keeps her going on and on. I don't know."

He looked tired. I touched his elbow. "Why don't you go rest or run an errand while I'm here. I can actually stay a bit longer if you need me to."

"I do have to run to the store. If you could stay about fifty minutes."

"Go. I'll see you then." I headed to the back porch. Sofie looked my way when I took the chair next to her. "How are you today, Sofie?" I had to remind myself not to call her Mrs. Dougan since she didn't remember being married.

She wore a white silky blouse with black piping, black slacks, and gold sandals. "I keep waiting for my fireman to come."

Yeah. Join the club. "Which fireman is that?"

She smiled and her gaze shifted to a far-off place. "Roger Kline. He's in charge of the whole battalion."

I explored that idea for a few minutes before moving her to a new topic. "Where did you meet Roger?"

She clutched her fists to her chest. "When I deliver suits to the men at West Trout Run. He's a log driver but when a fire breaks out, he has that to take on, too."

I reached in my bag and pulled out the book I'd found in the Pfoltzes' library and opened to the index. "This book has stories about some of the lumber towns in Northern Pennsylvania. Let's see if West Trout Run is in here."

She perked up and moved her chair closer. The metal legs squealed against the cement.

I found a listing for the camp and turned to those pages. One grainy picture showed about sixty men standing, some squatting, against a long wooden building. All in overalls with torn ragged bottoms, hanging loose above their boots. A good mix of men with and without facial hair dressed in undershirts, some holding tin cups, others leaning on axes. A smaller group stood off to the side, showing a game of horseshoes in play.

"Do you recognize these men?" I turned the book toward Sofie. She leaned closer. A smile grew on her face as she scanned the picture, moving her finger from man to man.

After a few moments, she looked at me. "Roger must be out on the rafts. He rides them down the west branch of the Susquehanna to the mill in Williamsport and catches a lift back. That's how Gramps and I know him. We pick him up every now and again when we deliver papers."

I noted the present tense she used. None of this was in the past for her. "That's right. Your grandfather delivers newspapers to several lumber camps."

She returned to the picture. "He does. And I sew tailor-made suits for some of these guys." She dropped a crooked finger to a guy in the back row. "That man right there pays me forty bucks for a new suit so he can go into Wellsfield Friday nights." Then she laughed and said, "But he always gets drunk and into fights and when he gets back on Sunday, that suit is only fit for everyday wear."

"That must keep you busy."

She blushed and ducked her head, the bashful look of a young woman brightening her face. "Well, it's just until I get married." She smoothed her hair back. "I won't work after that."

I thought about the direction in which I should steer our therapy. She was happiest as a late teenager, a young woman with her whole life in front of her. "Do you like to write?"

She considered the question. "Yes, I do. I write letters to my sister in Yorktown. She got married last year." Then she looked from side to side and dropped her voice to a whisper. "She's not so happy."

"She's not?" I matched her conspiratorial tone.

Sofie widened her eyes. "She said her husband's baloney pony isn't worth the ride."

I couldn't control the laugh that burst from me. *Baloney pony?* I had to remember that one. "That's not good." I touched the book. "I was asking because I think you should keep a diary of what you are doing. You know, write down all these stories from the logging camps. They're very interesting."

"I guess I could. When I'm not sewing, that is."

"Oh. You sew every day?"

Her face contorted and she aged in an instant. "I think my dad took away my sewing machine." She studied her nails. "He doesn't want me to leave home."

I went with an easy lie. "No. Your sewing machine is in the shop. And let me ask you something. Why were you outside the other night heading to the fire? Did it have something to do with Roger?"

"Oh, yes. He said he would meet me as soon as the fire was out." She looked confused. "But he never showed up."

I wonder what had happened to Roger all those years ago. I planned to ask Jon if he knew of him, if Roger had played a big part in her life. Studies show that no one remembers their life in its entirety. Most people remember parts of their life that evoke an emotional response. Whether the feeling was happy or sad, it didn't matter. The event got catalogued as a photo stored in the *my life* file. If Sofie could write out her daily thoughts, we'd get started on her own *my life* file.

Jon returned and I explained. He had never heard his wife mention a Roger Kline, leaving me to assume the infatuation with that fireman may have been one-sided.

As I pulled away, I wondered if I was following the same course with Lawyer.

Honey Bunches of Goats

I'd barely parked at Casey's house when he came bounding down the steps, arms and legs flying, before he disappeared around the side of the house. I reached the porch as Honey stepped out. "I don't care if he couldn't hear before, he sure isn't listening now."

"Uh-oh. What happened?" I asked.

"He spilled macaroni all over the place. So much for those expensive hearing aids."

I raised my hand to stop her. "Just remember he hasn't had any reason to listen like we do. Speech was a low-level hum when we were all talking to him before." I noticed she held a glass half full of ice cubes.

She opened the door and kept it open by bouncing it on her hip. "Well, you're going to hear a high-level scream if we don't get this place cleaned up before Karl gets here in fifteen." She disappeared inside while my mind bossed me around, mainly telling me to leave and come back another day. Karl and I had not seen eye to eye about paper products after he accused me of "violating" a piece of paper when I tore it from a notebook. He'd gone psycho, as if wood pulp products were his god and I had torn off the deity's clothes.

I opened the door and stepped into the house, leaving my therapy bag by the door in case I needed to make a fast exit. I followed the meandering path through the newsprint maze to the kitchen where Honey was on her knees, using her arm against the floor to sweep together dried pasta. "The kid took my broom. Rode it someplace out back and I can't find it."

"I'll help you." I left for a moment and returned with a clipboard from my bag. "Let's use this." I bent down and crab walked around the kitchen, pushing and pulling the elbow macaroni into the center pile Honey had started. She looked like she was about to cry.

"How big was this bag?" I asked. "Looks like it could have fed a football team."

"Big. Karl likes to buy at Costco or Sam's Club when he gets near one."

We swept the rest of the pasta into the trash and I stood at the sink to wash.

"Why is Karl coming home so soon? Didn't he just head out to Texas?"

Honey twisted open a cap on the gin bottle and poured more than a state-regulated amount into the glass. The room grew quiet and the ice cubes popped, cracked, and settled down in the liquid. Then she added a splash of club soda to it and took a long pull before speaking. "We got a notice about the newspapers...the city wants to condemn our house."

This was bound to happen. The word must have gotten out about the accumulation of so many papers. People worry about the fire danger. My thoughts stalled. *I* had been the one who brought the focus to their house. Karl never let anyone else in. I met Honey's gaze. "Oh, no. Karl is probably furious with me," I said.

She slowly nodded. "He's pretty mad."

"Does he know I'm here? Is that why he's coming?"

She swirled the ice around in the glass. "No. I didn't dare tell him. He just said he has an idea that will solve the problem."

Maybe he would haul them away in his big rig. "What's he planning?"

"I was hoping for a large trash barrel and a bunch of matches, but he mentioned goats."

Karl spent a lot of time alone in his truck with only himself to bounce around ideas. When I met Karl, he told me he knew Casey had speech problems because "he only used five percent of his brain, half of what an adult uses." When I mentioned neuroscience had shown the idea of ten percent usage to be false and the brain is highly activated in MRI scans, he said, "You probably think people in the medical field tell the truth."

I shrugged. "Goats? I'm not sure why that is a solution."

She leaned against the counter, now more relaxed, younger-looking. "From what he said, goats are herbi... hebbismores..."

"Herbivores?"

She shrugged. "Yeah, that kind of animal. They eat plants, grass, and even things made from wood. Like paper. Karl said that since it smells like wood, the goat thinks that it is also one of the plants."

I stood still, wondering where the closest Humane Society was located. Karl had a ton of paper in this house, true, but it was covered in ink, newsprint. And it wasn't soy ink. "I'm not sure that will be good for them. There's ink in the paper, you know?"

Honey scowled. "Paper is a vegetable fiber. Besides, you need to stick to all the shit you know about speech and leave us problem-solvers alone." Her phone pinged and she glanced at the text. "You need to get set up on the porch right now. Karl is five minutes away."

My heart picked up its pace and I looked at her drink, suddenly wanting one of my own. I also wanted to leave but I needed to see Casey one more time this week. I went to the living room and took three trips to the porch to set up the card table and the folding chairs, and then spread out my therapy pictures. We found Casey tossing pebbles into a full water barrel beneath a downspout, imitating the *ploob* sound as the stones broke the surface. "Okay, Casey. Let's get to work," I said.

"Ploob, ploob, ploob," he echoed as he ran ahead of me to the porch.

Jumping right into therapy, I had Casey repeat the lists of words I prepared for today, hoping that if we were completely engrossed in therapy, Karl would ignore us.

Moments later, the diesel truck's growl reverberated through the thick trees surrounding the property, then the black cab and trailer appeared on the road.

My voice caught in my throat and I stopped talking. Why was I feeling like this? Karl wasn't dangerous; he was just full of ideas that made no sense to most human beings. I tried to get Casey's attention back to our therapy, but he had bolted out of his chair, knocking it over, and was down the steps before I could call his name.

I got the chair back in place as Karl pulled the truck to the right of the house, the cab stopping fifteen feet away. Casey ran to the truck, yelling, "Dahee, dahee" and lots of other words which were not clear.

Karl stepped from the truck and scooped up Casey in one arm. Karl must have shopped at Redneck Central— dressed in a plaid shirt, the sleeves cut off at the shoulders, and a cap that looked like it had real pieces of bark stuck to it with stitching of a deer front and center. The words "Buck off!" were written across it. In his other hand, he held a green camo beer koozie, the top of a can of Bud visible. He hadn't shaved in days and he had the kind of eyebrows that shaded his eyes like a set of brown bangs.

We faced each other for a moment before he spoke. "Thanks for figuring out the kid couldn't hear."

"You're welcome." I smiled. Maybe he had changed his mind about me.

"And thanks so much for bringing the law to my house and ruining my privacy." Apparently, he could do sarcasm.

"I'm sorry about that," I stammered. "It wasn't planned."

He set Casey inside the cab and turned back to me. "Being killed by having a vending machine fall on you isn't planned but it happens about thirteen times a year."

What's he insinuating? I wondered.

Another sound reached my ears. The muffled bleating of goats.

I couldn't ignore Karl. As I needed to see Casey many more times this summer, I had to connect with him. I pointed to his trailer and said, "I heard you bought goats."

He scowled, then walked to the back of the trailer. He called out, "Don't even think about turning me in for owning a few goats." He worked the latch and the sliding bar on the door.

I shrugged. "Didn't even cross my mind." Adding a smile, I jogged down the steps, showing interest in his new pets. I helped Casey climb down out of the cab and set him on the ground where he hurried toward his father. Honey pushed through the front door, wearing a pink summery dress—high-school short—and strappy sandals. She'd combed her hair and found some makeup.

"Hi, babe." Karl said, smiling, transforming his look into that of a kind but weary woodsman. Maybe he'd change his mind about feeding all those newspapers to a couple of goats, and the animals could instead help manicure the yard he had no time for.

Honey reached my side just as Karl raised the door, and a brown and white speckled goat hopped to the ground and blinked in the sunlight.

Casey yelled, "Fuhing Dote," and rubbed his hands all over the animal.

Honey flinched beside me. "Where has he learned that kind of language?" She leveled her eyes my way.

I stammered, "Don't look at me."

Casey jumped around imitating the first goat as three more jumped from the trailer. He yelled, "Fuhing Dote," each time one landed.

Karl growled, a sound similar to a rabid dog, "What the hell is my kid saying?"

I held up my hands to say calm down. "Not what you think. He's saying, 'jumping goats.'" I held my breath as two more goats reached the ground.

Honey laughed and said, "Silly kid."

Karl begrudgingly relaxed, probably unhappy he'd lost his excuse to fire me.

I drew in a long breath, calmed my racing heart, and watched him unload thirty-five goats. Thirty-five. The yard soon swarmed with dazed looks. Some with bells tied to their collars. Others with jangling keys or old metal pieces.

Honey looked back just as dazed. "Um, Karl. Where are we going to keep them?"

He pointed to the property. "We have five acres surrounded by woods. They aren't going anywhere."

One of the goats butted Casey and he nearly lost his footing. I moved in and pulled him to my side, away from the curious animals. "I think Casey and I'll get back to work. As you can tell, we have lots of sounds to address."

Casey followed me without a problem. He seemed over-whelmed with all the bleating and bells, walking with his hands over his ears. It was quieter on the porch and I placed his chair so his back was to all the commotion in the yard. We worked through the pictures I brought, but I left the books Honey requested in my bag. They were called Hi-Lo Readers, meaning the interest level of the subject matter was that of an older grade, but the words were easier to read for several grades lower. Honey had told me she read at a fifth-grade level. So for her I'd brought *The Hobbit* and *Lord of The Flies*, both junior high books, but for someone with a lower reading level.

Casey was able to correctly repeat thirty phrases about seventy percent of the time with the /f/ and /v/ phonemes, nearly the same sound except the /v/ was voiced when said. I reviewed the /b/ and /p/ sounds and they were much bet-ter, probably because they were easy to hear and see on the lips. I tried the /k/ sound. "Say 'car' and hump the back of your tongue up to the roof of your mouth."

"Tar," he said while driving the picture of the car around the tabletop.

"Okay. Do this." I put my finger on the tip of my tongue to hold it down and showed him how the back of my tongue touched the roof of my mouth on "K, K."

When he put his finger in his mouth, I regretted asking him to do it since it was dirty.

"No, Casey. Wait a minute." I pulled out a package of tongue depressors. "Open up." I gently held the tip of his tongue down. "Okay, now say, K, K."

He did it and then seemed surprised by the sound.

"That was perfect! Now I'm going to hold your tongue down as we say more words." We ran through twenty words that started with the /k/ sound, like "kite, corn, cup, and cold." He did fine as long as I kept his tongue in place. Once he could put the /k/ at the beginning, we would move to the /k/ at the middle and then the /k/ at the end of words, since these were harder.

Shouting rose from the yard and I glanced up to see Karl, trying to pull his pants up from his knees where a goat was still hooked to them. His beer gut saved the day, hanging down over the private bits, to my relief. But his cussing! Every other word was the F-bomb with Honey's laughter in between. The goats scattered to the recesses of the yard and some ventured into the woods. Before Karl's theory that the goats would stay in the yard could be tested, I packed up my supplies and let Casey choose a candy.

Honey moved my way when she saw me stand. "You're done?"

No. I'm trying to get a better view of your husband. I forced patience into my voice. "He did great today. Do you want me to leave some of the lists of words we practiced?"

She looked like I'd offered her a dead rat. "Heck, no. We're going to be busy with this mess."

I smiled. "Karl does like to overindulge, doesn't he? But, the good news is you won't get evicted, so that's good, right?"

She pushed her hair off her neck. "Sometimes your positive-Polly attitude pisses me off, but this time you're right."

I laughed at her frankness. "Good to know. And as far as working with Casey, just try to get him to say the words more slowly, but have him look at your mouth first."

"When are you coming back?" She folded down the legs of the card table.

"Monday." I quickly glanced behind me and then back to her. "Will Karl still be home?"

"Nope. And if this fiasco doesn't work out, I'll have goat stew ready for you."

I knew she wasn't kidding.

Once in the car, I slowly eased it out of the driveway, parting the goats as I reversed. With acres of grass to eat, would the animals even touch the newspapers? Guess I'd see next week.

I had one more stop to make before I ended my week— drop off my paperwork at Therapy on Wheels. One of the nice things about this job was I was quite independent. I could set my own schedule, and unless something went wrong, I didn't have to check in every day. I hadn't even checked in all week.

My phone pinged and I glanced at the message. Lawyer had written, "Miss me?"

I slowed my car along the empty road and stopped, then texted, "Maybe. A tiny bit. What are you doing?"

"Watching videos of burning wood and buildings coming down. Thinking about you."

"Burning wood reminds you of me?"

"You and collapsing asphalt. Your ass-fault, my wood..."

"I like a man in yellow rubber who can talk dirty. What time am I arriving for dinner tomorrow?"

I waited but he didn't answer right away. Why does liking someone make us so insecure? When his answer didn't come right back, my first thought was he was figuring out how to uninvite me. *I made a mistake. I have to stay home and brush Veronica's long, shiny hair. Maybe another time?*

"7:00 works. Gotta go. A dumbass fell off a ladder."

I texted a sad face and pulled back onto the road.

Dinner at his house was going to be interesting. My main goal was to figure out what Veronica thought about her "just friends" relationship with Lawyer. I know he insisted he felt that way about Veronica but was that feeling reciprocal? Somehow I doubted it. I mean, he did score high on the irresistible chart.

Marching Songs

Sandy met me at the door and offered me a warm chocolate chip cookie from the oven. Couldn't say no to that, so I started eating after I asked her if Ivory was helpful or not.

"She's very bawdy, isn't she?"

I swallowed. "I hope I didn't make a mistake in suggesting she help you."

She smiled. "Oh, no. She's saved me. Sometimes I just drive around and do absolutely nothing. It can be so energizing to speak to no one for hours."

My mind flashed to Milt. He'd give anything to just be able to get a full sentence out, to be able to make people laugh.

"I'm glad you're getting a break. And the fact that Ivory can sing is such good practice for Melvin." I ate the last bite of cookie. "That was delicious. Thank you." I looked toward the den. "I'll head in now."

Sandy smiled. "I think Mel learned a few new words but I don't know what he's saying."

"Like what?"

"He's saying 'something that sounds like 'drat sab' and 'chib rowe.'"

I tried unsuccessfully to make those words have meaning "Wow. I don't know. I'll have to hear them to understand how he is using them."

"He's also learned some military songs. At least I think that's what I was hearing the end of when I came home an hour ago."

Why hadn't I thought of that? He had been in the military and the songs of the '40s and '50s were very popular.

I stopped at the door and watched Melvin as he thumbed through a book. Reading was the one thing he could do well, which was why the word board worked.

"Hi, Melvin," I said, bracing for the colorful possibilities.

"My talk more lady."

I laughed at first then my throat clenched. My voice was off when I said, "That is the first clean thing you have ever said to me."

"Marching army anuses." He pointed to the book of what appeared to be song lyrics. "Goober peas on Johnny."

A snort flew from me at the possible double meaning. I smiled. "Military songs, huh? Let's see what you know." I leaned over the book. The page was open to *When Johnny Comes Marching Home Again.* "This is a good one. Sing this."

He ran his finger along the words as we sang, "When Johnny comes marching home again, Hurrah! Hurrah! We'll give him a hearty welcome then, Hurrah! Hurrah! The men will take their peckers out, the—"

"What the heck!" I snatched the book from his lap and turned it over. The gold lettering across the front read, *The Bawdy Side of Every Song.* I slumped into the chair next to Melvin and looked his way.

He looked surprised, like I'd hurt him.

"Did Ivory give you this?" I would kill her when I saw her next. He already had a potty mouth. This family was very devout.

He nodded. "Big hair bollocks."

"I knew it."

"Knew what?" Sandy stood in the doorway with a large glass of iced tea.

Turning the book upside down, I searched for a lie. "I knew...that all of this singing would make his voice hoarse, so we're stopping for now."

"Oh, dear. I was hoping to hear a good old marching tune. Mel loved those songs." She pushed back his hair. "Do you need a drink?"

He reached for the iced tea and I was relieved it would keep him from talking.

"You said he sang in the choir. Does he have favorite hymns?" I asked. "I'd like to point him in the direction of singing in church again."

Sandy swallowed hard. She was on the verge of crying. "That would be the best thing for him. He misses it, I know."

I had set up the sentence reader on the table to his side. "Sandy, these sentences are all about requesting common things. Besides singing, it's important to give him everyday speech ability."

Melvin handed the glass to Sandy, and started humming the tune to the Johnny song again.

I pointed to the card reader. "Melvin. Let's give the songs a rest, okay? Will you listen to this sentence and then repeat it?"

Sandy waved and left as we launched into the structured therapy. He was about sixty percent accurate if I said the sentences with him. I was sixty percent distracted by the idea that Ivory thought this was hilarious. Melvin and Sandy were very religious. I considered reporting Ivory to Jake when I got there later today. She was causing more harm than good.

On the hour, I packed my supplies, including Ivory's book, and asked Melvin to say the phrase we'd been practicing.

"Goodbye, Marleigh." He tilted his head, waiting to see my reaction.

"Perfect, Melvin. Just perfect." I patted his hand. "See you next week."

"Shitastic God smacker," he called out happily. "Drat sab."

There were those unclear words. "What's that again?"

He smiled and said cheerily, "Drat sab."

I had no idea so I smiled and left. Sandy was at the kitchenette table, looking at a headline in the paper. When she saw me she tapped the paper. "Another young person died from drugs last night. What has happened to our nice little cluster of towns?"

"A policeman I know said the drug problem has always been here but now it's worse."

"This article said the heroin in this boy was full of other weird chemicals." She ran her finger down the page. "Formalin. Is that like that crack stuff they're always talking about?"

I felt an internal flinch, but said, "No. I think that's different." I tried to be casual, scratching an imaginary itch while I was picturing my no-verb client, Tinsel Tabbish's son, Frank. He was a taxidermist; Formalin was his friend. And he travelled all over the county. And he possessed a sick sense of humor. And the *ands* went on and on. I'd come to the earlier conclusion he was harmless, but now I wasn't so sure.

As I pulled away, it occurred to me what Melvin had been saying and I swore. Ivory's penchant for liking how words could go backwards produced "dratsab" and "chib rowe" or when reversed, "bastard" and "bitch whore." I swore again, my words clearly going in the right direction. I'd made a mistake suggesting Ivory help out. I needed to get her out of there right away.

THERAPY ON WHEELS

After parking in front of the Ace Hardware store that shared the building with Therapy on Wheels, I carried my files inside. Jake Griffin was on the phone when I entered. At six feet, he was on the chunky side of healthy with dark hair cut short, retro glasses reflecting small golden orbs in the overhead lights, and an easygoing smile.

I waved and walked into the charting room where I make copies of my daily logs and two-hole punched them to fit in the main files.

"You've had a good week?" Jake asked, leaning against the doorframe with his arms crossed. He wore a white knit shirt with the Therapy on Wheels logo stitched on the right side of his chest. Thank goodness we weren't all required to dress in a uniform or wear that shirt; the magnets on the car were enough.

"A good week, yes, maybe even great." I spread out my files, replaying the progress at each house. "Nobody wants to fire me." I smiled.

"Hmm."

I turned to see if he was joking, but his face said he wasn't and he had more to say. *Now what?* "Did I do something wrong?"

He rocked his head from side to side, a "maybe, maybe not" motion. "The nurse said you told the Bledsoe sisters that it was fine to keep the chickens inside. You even moved their furniture?"

Oh, crap.

He moved closer to stand beside the worktable. "The county health department gave that order to get the chickens outside. You do know they overrule us in cases like this?"

"The chickens are on a back porch now that's closed off from the house." I waited but he continued to study me. "Jake, I'm sorry. I felt like I was helping them."

He studied me hard. "Just stick with the speech thing, okay? I mean, you did help Melvin and Sandy by getting Ivory in there as a respite worker. Sandy called to thank me again."

It was not the time to bring up my complaint against Ivory. "Good. Sandy is a lot less stressed."

Jake tapped the table as if that was all there was to say and returned to his office. I worked for forty minutes, making copies and filling out Medicare forms for all my patients, except Casey who had private insurance.

Jake was filing a stack of forms when I knocked on the open door of his olive-green, '70s-styled office. He had a huge metal desk, probably designed during the Cold War as duck-and-cover protection. "Come in. I have something for you," he said.

Hopefully not a warning letter for my file.

"I see you aren't wearing your lanyard," he said.

"It's in the car. I always wear it in my clients' homes." *He couldn't ding me on this one.*

He opened a box and pulled out a small bag, and began laying items out on the table. "Well, good. You need to attach these to it. We decided that everyone would be safer after what happened to you last week."

A violent fugitive had been caught in the area, one deemed worthy of a statewide manhunt. I had come face to face with him at Casey's house, and it was the reason Karl was in trouble with the law for newspaper hoarding.

"Okay. And speaking of that, Karl Lester is solving his newspaper problem," I said.

"He is?" He handed me a mini spray can of Mace® and a flashlight, both with clips.

My lanyard was going to be crowded. I already had a whistle and my ID tag. "Yup. He's going to be getting rid of them all, slowly."

"I'm surprised because hoarders usually can't do that." He pulled a three-inch long mini fire extinguisher from another bag. "This won't put out much, but it could buy you time until you get to a bigger extinguisher."

I turned it over in my hand. It was very cute. "No pin to pull?"

"Naw. Works like the Mace® can. Point and spray."

I was going to sound like Karl's goats with all this metal clanging around my neck. "Can't I just carry some of these in my purse?"

"We need to make the statement that our therapists and nurses are safe."

"Danger *will* hear us coming." I didn't want to give him any other reason to be angry. "No, really. Thanks for thinking about us."

He smiled for the first time and said, "I've called your patients. They're all happy with you."

"Good news!" I said, and picked up my new paraphernalia and charts and headed for the door. "I'll see you next Friday."

"Not if I see you first." He shrugged. "We are also doing random supervisory visits."

I left the building. I needed to keep Beryl home, Ivory from singing dirty ditties, Karl from storing any more papers, Luella from letting the chickens back in the house, and Sofie from running away. I slid into the car and attached the new trinkets to my lanyard. Basically, Tinsel's home would be the ideal place for Jake's surprise visit. Perfect. I had a one-in-six chance of looking good when Jake supervised me. But not even that if her son, Frank, showed up with his roadkill humor and pistol in hand.

I took a new route toward Tungston, meaning I got lost. I hadn't seen a town for fifteen minutes and the roads were mostly without sign posts, because they led from nowhere to nowhere. Just unrecorded back roads. But for some reason, they had all kinds of other signage up: "No Overnight Parking On The Dam," "Low Flying Geese In Spring," or "Unfenced Farm Area, Livestock On Road."

Finally, I saw a smattering of houses. The sign before the town announced "Brook Falls, Pop. 378." The business side of town started right away with a small post office, a gas station and an ice cream/pizza stand combo. Twenty-five miles an hour was too slow. I got too much of a long look at the people. They were sitting at wooden picnic tables eating pizzas the size of truck hubcaps. For a second, we made eye contact. Me, the voyeur.

After Brook Falls, I hit a crossroads and knew where I was again. Eureka! I headed back to Tungs.

Pfoltz Bed & Breakfast

"Yeah," Jaxson said through the phone to me. "Another one bit the dust on his Jenny Crack diet last night. This kid was in college, though, played football and seemed to have a lot going for him."

I pushed myself in a rocker on the wide front porch. Milt was sleeping on the settee in the library and everyone else was on a tour, or grocery shopping. "Are you any closer to figuring out where the drugs come from?"

"No, the sitch hasn't changed. We can't find a link between the deaths so we have no sus'pees."

I cringed and rolled my eyes. *Who reinforces his slang?* The light wind played with my shirt and my hair lifted in the soft breeze. For mid-June, the temperature was perfect. "I wanted to tell you something but it has to stay our secret," I said.

"You want to go out with me tonight." His voice betrayed a smile.

"Uh, no."

"It's Friday. Your pretend boyfriend is gone. Why not have some fun?"

"How do you know Lawyer is gone?"

"Hashtag, half of the fire department is out of state training, hashtag, he's the fire chief, and hashtag, you are calling me."

Hashtag, I'd never date you. "Oh. Anyway, I know some-one you should check out for this drug problem. He seems squirrelly to me and the fact that Formalin was in this last batch of heroin, makes me suspicious."

"I should deputize you. Who is it?"

"He's a local taxidermist. Frank Tabbish. And the rea-son you can't tell anyone is I see his mother in therapy."

He laughed and said, "And didn't you just break HIPPA policy by telling me that?"

Dammit. "You're a cop. You don't count."

"If you have a beer with me tonight, I'll keep the mums," he pressured.

My next words came out too fast, heated with annoy-ance. "You'll do this because it's your job."

He let out a long whistle and said, "Calm down. Take a joke."

Silence ran back and forth along the airwaves, then I said, "I have a bad feeling about this guy."

"Thanks for the tell. I'll check him out... Try not to miss me." Then he hung up.

I really hoped that wasn't a mistake.

Tires crunched in the B&B driveway. I expected to see Rose pulling in, back from the store. I promised to help her cook dinner, although I wasn't sure I was anything more than company during the process. But a taxi arrived, not something I'd seen since leaving San Francisco. The side of the car said ROC Airport, so these people had come two hours from Rochester, a hefty price for a ride. Doors popped open and people, bags, and three bikes spilled out. Since no one noticed me, I studied the group. The father was a tall forty-something with graying sidewalls on his dark hair. The mother was fit with arms that clearly pressed weights, and wiry red hair pulled back in a ponytail. The son, in his late teens, had long dark red hair, an angry slouch, and wore headphones. He grudgingly took one bike and followed his parents to the front door.

I stood up from my rocking chair and said, "Welcome to The Pfoltz Bed and Breakfast."

"Hi there, we're checking in today. The Diffleys. I'm James, my wife, Marti and our son, Beers."

"I'm Marleigh," I said and shook hands all around, then asked the son, "What was your name?"

"Beers, as in do you have one?"

Marti laughed, lightly punching her son on the arm. "Sixteen's not legal."

Beers pulled away. "It could be. Make it one of your stupid experiments," he said and looked my way. "Where's my room?"

I showed them where they could store their bikes and helped carry the bags through the front door, stopping at the stairway. "You have the first two rooms at the top of the stairs. You share a bathroom between the rooms."

Beers snapped his headphones into place and took the steps two at a time. His parents offered sheepish grins, as if to say *we know he's rude.* James spoke. "We're researchers, so that crack he made was about us experimenting. And his given name is Clifford Beers, named after a famous researcher."

"In the field of psychology," Marti added. She looked up the steps. "We'll just get settled in. Is dinner at a certain time?"

"Yes. Six o'clock. Let me know if you need anything."

Why did they arrive in a taxi? And Clifford? Parents can be so cruel with names. No wonder the redhead chose to stick with Beers and drop "Clifford the Big Red Dog" reference. Did they even realize?

When I turned, I let out a little scream. Milt was standing two feet behind me. "Did you hear any of that?"

He stared my way, not moving a muscle.

I whispered, "We have researchers in the house. Arrived by taxi. Who does that?"

His lips jittered, then he said, "Elephino."

I laughed. "That's perfect!" I took his elbow. "We have a few hours before dinner. Want to go for a ride?

The Roseburg Cemetery sloped downhill in three directions from where Milt and I sat on a bench in a patch of shade from a large maple tree. Rows and rows of empty dreams, encased under marble, dotted the green grass. Some with fresh flowers, others with patriotic memorabilia, or like my biological parents' grave, nothing. Guarding our backs was a thick forest, and the caretaker's buildings just at the edge.

From here, I could see their headstone and the inscription below their names: *October 6, 1992*. Each time I looked at the stone—their names, that date—they floated further away from my comprehending them. They gave their two-year-old up for adoption, and four days later, they died in a car accident. The police report said it had been a single car accident, a rollover. Had they been fleeing from someone? I needed to ask Marshal Schumer if he could discover more details about that day.

Milt seemed content, alert, taking in the view. Then he suddenly sniffed the air and I looked to see if he was okay. A second later, the smell of a skunk in the distance reached my nose.

"Hope it stays away...You ever been sprayed by one?"

He raised his eyebrows, saying nothing.

"Me either." I pointed to the Kingston grave. "Those are my birthparents right there. The Kingstons."

He slowly turned his head in that direction. I thought about coming here alone, but Milt is good company. A great listener.

"You know, the idea of family, until a few months ago, eluded me. Like when you're a kid. You get dragged around to the nursing home to visit a relative. For me it was Grandma Benning. She was nice enough, always gave me stale mints. She had a tiny room we all crowded into that smelled like face powder and chicken soup. It always seemed a lot like sitting in church, hoping the adults would stop talking. Now, with everyone gone, I understand the importance of having *some* family. I mean, anybody."

I remembered who I was talking to. Milt's wife had died three years earlier and he *did* live in a nursing home. He was only staying at the inn until his place was fixed after a chemical fire. I glanced his way, and to my relief, he seemed unaffected by my sad soliloquy.

I changed subjects. "I thought of a new joke you can tell."

He rubbed his thighs, starting out slowly but then with more rapid movements. His face trembled. "Good joke."

"Well, I have two of them. And 'good' is a new word for you. Nice."

He waited.

"Okay. First one. What is Forrest Gump's email password?"

I gave it a few seconds then said, "One Forrest One."

His face sagged.

"Okay. Too techie. Second one. Why did the guy get fired from the calendar factory?" I held my hands in the air and waited before offering, "Because he took a day off."

He chuffed air; he was excited.

"Okay. That's the one we'll practice later. Let's save it for the weekend crowd, though. There's yet another cranky teenager under our roof tonight."

The next few moments were peaceful. The day was sultry. The top leaves on the trees remained still while the inner leaves and branches twitched and flapped. From the forest, a warm concert of chirping, buzzing, and croaking pushed from the trees, and I closed my eyes and a breathed deeply. There were healing properties here, a wholesomeness hard to find while walking on concrete. Was Beryl's friend Chester right? Would I find that I could live here?

My phone buzzed. It was the main line at the inn. We needed to get back so I could help cook. I answered, but to my surprise it was Richard on the line.

"Are you on your way back?"

"Sure. We can be." I took Milt's hand and pulled him slowly to his feet. "What's up?" We started walking toward the car. No more than thirty feet away, it would take us five minutes to get there.

"We need you to serve the guests tonight. Another family arrived. Their information is in our study. I'm taking Rose to the hospital."

"What happened?" The rush of worry that flooded my legs stopped me. Milt's face pulled together in a puzzled look.

"Well, I'll explain more, but Beers the teenager who arrived today pushed Rose down. Something has happened to her back."

"Oh, my gosh. We'll be there in fifteen minutes." We both hung up at the same time.

I took Milt's arm and started walking. "Rose is going to the hospital. We need to get back." Milt moved at a pace I'd never seen before.

We were on the road before I thought to ask if the Diffley family was still at the inn. I'd find out soon enough.

TAP DANCING IN BIG SHOES

Injuring a proprietor had to be a good reason for finding a new place, but James and Marti Diffley stood in the kitchen, sheepish, wringing their hands. Clifford the big red bully was locked in his room.

James cleared his throat. "Would you like us to leave?"

I wanted to scream, "Hell, yeah. You injured the kindest woman on earth, the only mom-like person in my life." But I didn't. I left Milt on the porch in a rocking chair, where his agitation showed as he pushed the chair back and forth, his flinty stare a laser beam toward the tree line.

I looked from James to Marti and back. We each leaned against a kitchen counter, our arms folded in defense mode. The groceries were spread around, many of them unpacked, something I needed to get to work on. "What happened here?"

"Beers was talking to Rose about our last research project. You see, we studied how people fall down."

Cuss words flew through my head.

Marti nodded, a motion that begged to be understood. "We knock people over for a living."

"You're serious? Where would you study such a thing?"

James reached for a spoon. "Our degrees are in biomechanical engineering. That's the background for this field of research. We did the study at Mount Sinai because they got funding from a government grant to study fall prevention." He tapped the spoon against his leg as he spoke.

Marti moved closer to her husband. "I recruited the subjects, did data analysis, fitted people with the equipment for collecting the data. James ran the tests, so basically he knocked the people over."

James held up a hand in defense. "You understand, I didn't physically push them down. They stood on a floor that moved backwards, forward, left, or right, unpredictably, so that the subject could not anticipate the movement. Like the feeling you get standing in a subway car that abruptly stops. We would distract them by telling them to count down by sevens, things like that, and then shift the floor."

I let some time go by. "I understand that you talked about this to Rose and Richard, but why would he push Rose down?"

"Well, in our defense, Mrs. Pfoltz asked Beers how this was achieved and he pushed her a bit too hard." James paused a minute before continuing. "We actually never let him try this before so ... you know. He went too far."

"I need to make a call. Then I need to make dinner. Would you excuse me?" I closed the office door behind me and called Richard's cell. I had my questions ready when he answered. "Do you want them to stay or should I drive them into Wellsfield?"

"Marleigh, they can stay. They'll leave in the morning."

"How's Rose?"

"A strained back muscle. She'll need ice packs and Ibuprofen, but we're leaving here in about twenty minutes."

"Good. That's a relief. I'm going to make dinner so don't worry about that." My shoulders dropped down from their tense state. "Do you know where Rose keeps the arsenic?"

Richard laughed. "Check the little cabinet by the spices. And, thanks for holding down the fort."

"No problem."

I shooed the Diffley family out of the kitchen just as the new couple, Nathan Gallagher and Rachael Proust wandered in. After our introductions, I knew enough about them. They'd just gotten married, were from Detroit, and had come to raft the Piney Creek River.

As I unpacked the groceries, I said, "Dinner will be in forty minutes but in the meantime, you might like to walk the property. It's gorgeous."

They left and I had the big kitchen to myself. I had no idea what Rose had planned for dinner, but I studied the grocery items and got to work.

An hour later, I carried a plate of food to Milt in his room. He had refused to come to the table, muttering, "Hate man," over and over. Beers had stayed in his room, too, which was fine with me. The two couples and I passed the chicken curry, rice, and the steamed vegetables around the large wooden table. There were blueberry tarts for dessert Rose had made earlier in the day. The four had a lot of questions about the attractions in the area, but I only had three weeks of knowledge to share. I know they were disappointed in my ability to direct them to points of interest outside of the famous Pennsylvania Grand Canyon, twenty miles from Wellsfield. I was relieved when I heard the back door open and Rose and Richard's return.

They entered, smiling with a kind of patience and ease I probably would never possess. Not a trace of anger on their faces as they took their seats and joined the conversation.

Rose's gaze met mine and she smiled. "What a lovely dinner, Marleigh. Thanks for stepping in."

"I didn't know what you'd planned so I hope this is fine."

"It's great."

She was being kind. Thank goodness for the curry paste already in the fridge. My concoctions were typically bland. I stood and cleared some plates. "I'll get the dishes. You just relax."

Rose joined me in the kitchen twenty minutes later after Richard had carried the rest of the plates to the sink. She stood stiffly, like she didn't dare move fast.

"How are you feeling?" I asked.

"I'm going to be fine. I was more startled than hurt."

"I'm free all weekend, so let me do as much as I can around here." I paused and said, "Except for tomorrow night. I'm going to Lawyer Hunt's for dinner. I'll get everything ready before I leave."

Rose's face brightened. "Oh, we were meaning to tell you. We saw Lawyer at the hospital just now."

How could that be? He was supposed to be in Buffalo. "Really? Did you talk to him?"

"No. He didn't see us. He was with that young woman who stays with them. She was under some kind of duress, it seemed."

"Oh, okay." I fought a circus of emotions but tried to keep my face calm. He said he'd be back tomorrow morning, so why lie to me? In giving him the benefit of the doubt, Veronica may have had an emergency issue. But he still could have called. My vision blurred; the tears hung back, but they were close to falling. I leaned over the pans in the soapy water and scrubbed for all I was worth. Maybe I was *very* free tomorrow night to help Rose. It suddenly seemed more appealing.

THE QUESTION OF FAMILY

B reakfast the next morning was a spread of Pennsylvanian Dutch dishes. I'd been up since six thirty, helping Rose get ready. Although she said she was fine, I saw her wince more than once as she lifted a pot or turned too quickly. I insisted on preparing the whole meal with her explicit directions, of course, but she couldn't be completely stopped. Rain, the big and loud kind, had been hammering the house since early morning and the temperature outside dropped to the low sixties. Cool for mid-June. The growl of faraway thunder occasionally masked the quiet sounds from the radio she had on low. It was an oldies station, and not from the 80s. Rose hummed along to Big Band era songs, and at one point while Richard grabbed another cup of coffee, he announced these songs were popular when he and Rose had been dating. I wanted to absorb that sensation of a warm kitchen, of family, of happiness in every pore of my being, so much so I dreaded the appearance of the other guests.

We set out platters of pure comfort food. Bacon and cheese dumplings, chicken and waffles, pickled red beet eggs, and warm cornbread with homemade apple butter. When the Diffley family took seats around the table, I worked very hard to be nice to them. Rachael and Nate arrived and we all sat to eat. Richard wasn't his usual chatty self and he seemed to be keeping an eye out for any fast movements Beers might make.

Rose asked the newlyweds what they had planned since the daylong rainstorm had cancelled their river float.

"We're going to drive out to see a few abandoned lumber towns and probably that lumber museum."

Since Sofie and I had spent time researching the old days of lumbering, I asked, "Which towns are you going to?"

Nate set his fork and knife across the plate. "The closest one is on Kettle Creek, a place called West Trout Run. Most of the buildings are still standing."

Richard reached for the basket of cornbread. "That's a good one. Used to have about sixty houses, two general stores, a hotel, a school and even a Methodist church."

Rachael nodded. "We hear the town could be haunted." She looked at her husband. "Seems perfect to go exploring on a gloomy day."

Laughing, Richard said, "I don't know about that, but the old church, hotel, and a few houses are still standing. Maybe head to the church if things get creepy."

Beers perked up. He looked to his parents. "Why don't we go there instead of this stupid survival trip?"

Silence filled the room as everyone looked to the Diffley parents. Marti answered, "Because that's not what we are here to do, son." She smiled quickly, but it looked pained. "We are exploring ourselves these next two weeks. Testing out how well we can live off the land and solve our own problems."

Richard looked confused. "Is there a program in this area for that sort of thing?"

James quickly swallowed, then answered, "Well, in a way. We will need a ride to the drop off point today." He cut a dumpling in half. "We've located the most remote spot in Pennsylvania and that's where we're headed."

Beers crossed his arms, his face red. "Tell my parents that we are going to die out there."

James jumped in. "We are not going to die. Besides, this is research. During the time we spend out there, we will record quantitative data on direct or indirect human presence and absence. We will observe sights, sounds, and smells of anything of human origin, then we will identify it, estimate its distance, and record the compass bearing of the data."

Richard frowned. "Which remote place are you talking about?"

"Hammersley Wild Area," Marti said. "Do you know it?"

Richard paused, almost like he was waiting to see if it were a joke. "I've hunted there."

"So, actually we're going to be murdered," Beers said holding up his hands.

Richard said, "Well, I'm sure your parents have safely planned it all out. But just know, that's black bear country. If you hear any sounds like woofing, growling or jaw-popping, that's the male. He'll be six feet tall and over five hundred pounds. I assume you have a gun."

James smiled. "As you can see, Beers is angry because we've brought him along. The judge in juvenile court recommended it. We're following her orders."

Beers had been in juvie? He looked so uncomfortable at the moment, I felt a new empathy for him. My gaze met Rose's across the table. Her raised eyebrows said, *Are we even surprised?*

Beers grumbled, "Thanks for that, Dad. And the judge said I should *get outside more*, not that we should become the summer version of The Donner Party and end up eating each other."

I quickly looked down, afraid I had a smile on my face. The kid had a point. These woods were thick, went on for hundreds of miles, and were full of all kinds of hazards.

Nate and Rachael excused themselves at that point, saying they had to get going and they'd be back later to report on any ghost sightings.

James pushed back from his plate, smiled and said, "We're going to be fine. And we have no weapons other than a knife and that's to build shelter. Also a handheld GPS and whatever we can carry in our backpacks. This is an experiment on how well we can live off the land, and how we adapt when we're out of our element. What a feeling of satisfaction and accomplishment, something like this can bring."

Rose stood and gathered empty dishes but paused before going into the kitchen. "You'll have your bikes with you. The trails might be fairly easy to navigate up to a point."

Marti stacked her plate on top of Beers' plate. "We wondered if you could store them until we get back. We will need them later when we ride the Rail Trail to New Jersey from here."

"I might just find another way to Jersey," Beers mumbled, but his parents ignored him.

"Oh. You are the adventuresome ones." Rose shrugged. "We can store your bikes. When will you be back?"

"July fifth." James stood. "Could someone drive us out to our adventure in an hour?"

Richard looked my way. I *had* agreed to run all their errands today. "I'll do it," I said.

After they left, I started on the dishes while Rose put food away. I turned to Richard, who was studying the rain through the window. "Do you actually believe I can find where they need to be dropped off?"

"Sure. It's right off a main road but I'll get a map." He thought for a moment. "And I'm going to let the Sheriff's Department know that we've got some urban warriors up on that ridge. It wouldn't hurt to check in on them without them knowing about it."

With an hour to kill, I planned to work with Milt on his jokes, but my phone rang while I was in my room. Ten zeros showed up for caller ID. I had no idea what that could mean, so I almost didn't answer it.

"Hello?"

Static buzzed my ear for a second, then Marshal Schumer came on. "How are you, Marleigh?"

"Good. And you?" My heart sped up. Was he about to tell me he'd found some relatives in the area? I pictured being at their dining room table, listening to stories of my parents, leafing through yellowing photo albums, me saying, "Ah, that's where my blonde hair came from."

"I have a question for you... What did your parents do for a living? Not your biological parents."

I slumped. He was just gathering more data. "They owned downtown storage units in big cities."

"Hmmm. Which ones?"

"Houston, Boston, LA, Denver, Chicago..." I kept going until I'd named all twelve locations.

"Nothing in Pittsburgh?"

I thought for a moment. "No. It would have been too small. They only opened in cities bigger than that."

"Okay. Just trying to come up with a connection to the Kingstons."

"Have you learned anything new about them?"

"No. But I've got feelers out to other law enforcement agencies here so something might break loose. Let me ask you something else..." I heard papers being flipped and shuffled. "Who runs the storage company now?"

"There's a board of directors, of course, but Dean Kennedy is the CFO. He's been with the company as long as I can remember."

"Do you have a number for him?"

Although I wouldn't be at any dining room table as soon as I'd hoped to be, I was happy Scott was actively working on my request. I gave him the number and waited for him to repeat it back.

An office phone rang on Scott's end. "I'll call you."

"Okay. Thanks for everything."

"Don't thank me yet. I might just end up being as useful as a screen door on a submarine."

Although that was funny, I was sad at the same time. Would I ever get enough answers to feel satisfied?

DRIVING ME MAD

Half an hour later, with the rain still filming the windshield, I drove the Diffleys toward their new family experiment into what James explained was one of the remotest spots in the U.S. He and Marti were in high spirits while Beers seemed lifeless in the back seat of the van slumped toward the window with his hoodie cinched so tight only his nose stuck out.

Now that James had me captive, he seemed compelled to explain their experiment with pushing people over. "We were studying ways of preventing falls in older people."

They obviously failed the prevention part. I was still angry about Beers pushing Rose.

"Elderly reaction times during a fall are different than in younger people," he said.

Words formed in my head and I tried not to say them but these popped out: "Did you keep track of how many broke a hip? I hear that's different in older versus younger people, too."

Beers snorted from the back seat but James and Marti were unfazed.

Marti leaned forward and tapped my shoulder. "There was a harness suspended from the ceiling in the middle of the room. The rope supporting it was loose when the subject stood still. They could stumble quite a bit before it supported them, but no one actually fell flat on their face or anything."

I shot a look back toward Marti. "Well, that's good." They insisted on sitting behind me, leaving my passenger seat open—the "death seat" as they called it—spouting car accident statistics.

James added, "We put goggles on them that limited their vision as soon as the floor moved. Then we measured what visual information people used to restore their balance. Our eyesight really does matter in balancing. If you distract the eyes, you can easily push someone over."

"This is all very interesting." I understood and sympathized with Beers' frustration with his parents. His daily life most likely went from one experiment to the next. I flicked my turn signal on to make a left turn up the final road before I dropped them off. When we arrived and I saw how isolated they'd be, I worried they would soon become an unfortunate news story. "Do you have a plan in case things get too rough out here?" The steering wheel jerked and bucked under my hands on the washboard dirt trail, and Beers sat up and rubbed the side of his head after bouncing against the window. "Any emergency numbers?"

James laughed. "We have no phones with us. No connection to the world. A perfect situation to test us."

Or a perfect storm. They were heading into the woods, an incredible tangle of growth without fixed reference points, and apparently bear country.

The road ended in a small, cleared area and I parked. By the time they'd shrugged on their backpacks and turned toward a small opening in the trees, we were all wet. I wasn't sure if I admired or pitied them. I called out, "See you in two weeks." James waved and then they disappeared into the blurry green wash of trees and rain, ill-equipped in an unknown landscape.

I executed a fifteen-point turn to get the van pointing back down the road, regretting I let them go. My only solace was that Richard said he would inform the local authorities about the Diffleys' plan, so I assumed they'd be monitored, somehow.

When I reached the main road, I headed in a different direction, needing to run some errands. First, a post office then Elyk's store.

I dropped into a town, but missed seeing the name. It consisted of a half-dozen vacant lots with patchy grass, some houses in sad shape, steeped in poverty, one step above living out of a plastic sack. For a moment, I thought it was an abandoned town. But bib overalls and shirts hung limply on one laundry line, waiting for the sun. Another home had a newly painted sign above a fruit stand advertising "Fresh Scrapple."

I'd heard that scrapple was a must-try, but decided I could wait. To me, "scrapple" didn't sound like something anyone should eat.

The next town had a stoplight at its four corners and a post office. It was a tiny building painted cerulean blue with burgundy trim, so small I almost missed it. The rain had eased up but I still dashed to the entrance, hunkered over my mail and small package to keep them dry. The interior smelled like paper and glue and was a little overheated. With one window and a short wall of combination lock mailboxes, it wasn't anything like my multifunctional post office back home. There I could get a tax form, apply for social security, get a passport picture snapped, or buy package wrapping supplies. This joint was hyper-focused on envelope matters.

When I stepped up to the window I heard music coming from the back.

Chair legs scraped the wooden floor before a man appeared. "Howdy," he said. "Can I help you with something?" He chewed the corners of his white handlebar mustache, and his eyes blinked constantly behind a pair of reading glasses. With long silver hair and rosy cheeks, he was radiating a Santa Claus vibe.

"Just postage, please." I dropped the letters and package on the wooden counter.

As he busied himself with an antique scale, opening and closing drawers for stamps and labels, I asked, "So, exactly what is scrapple? I saw a sign in the last town and wondered if I was missing out."

His eyebrows knotted. "You talking about Buddy Samson's place back in Mossburg?"

I shrugged and pointed from the direction I'd come. "That way about eight miles."

"That's him. I wouldn't buy anything from that dumb bastard. He couldn't pour piss out of a boot with the instructions written on the heel, so he sure as hell isn't making scrapple the right way."

My image of Santa dissolved. "All right then." I guess I'd have to wait to find out what scrapple was.

While Postman Potty Mouth finished the transaction, my phone buzzed. I pulled it from my pocket and saw Lawyer's name. I debated answering it as I slid money across the counter. He had a lot of explaining to do and I wasn't sure I was in the mood. I let it go to voicemail.

The postman stared my way as if to say, *Why are you still here?*

"Thank you." I left the building. The rain had stopped and layers of clouds were racing each other, parting sporadically for the sun to reach through and then disappear.

I was on the road and steering the car around wavering pools of water when my phone buzzed again. Lawyer. I'd have to talk to him sometime. "Hi. When did you get back?"

"Hi." His voice was on guard, maybe sensing something was up. "I actually had to come back last night. For an emergency."

Part of me wanted to set him up and see how long it would take him to say Veronica's name, but the other part didn't want to play games. "How is Veronica doing?"

He didn't respond and I wondered if I'd lost the signal as the road dipped and rolled. I passed huge fireworks signs, realizing we were just weeks from the 4th of July.

You'll get the biggest bang out of Wally's Works—Five miles ahead

"You still there?" I'd caught him off guard.

"She's fine, thanks." He had regained his usual self-assuredness. "We can talk about it when you come for dinner tonight."

Now it was my turn to pause. Did I want any part of this "she's just a friend" deal?

"My mom eats early. I know I said six o'clock but does five thirty work?" he asked.

I sighed. Resistance was futile. But I had to get answers so would get them in person. "That's fine. Are you sure I can't bring anything?" *Like a one-way plane ticket for Veronica?*

"Just you. That's all I need." He sounded relieved there'd been no more discussion.

We hung up and I drove to The Ash Country Store and Souvenirs. I needed a dose of Elyk, of his no nonsense logic. And scrapple? I needed to know what the heck that was.

I passed The Little Church in the Pines. The marquee asked the question:

What is missing from Ch__ Ch?
U R

I thought of Christian Betts, of his invite to church for tomorrow. I wondered how Tinsel Tabbish even got to church. She wasn't driving at the moment and I didn't see her son, Frank, making the effort to take her there, especially with all the countywide roadkill that needed scraping up. And doing whatever else he did while he was out there.

By the time I reached Elyk's store I'd made a decision. I would offer to drive Tinsel to church tomorrow. Although I wasn't supposed to socialize with my patients, my defense was that this was just being helpful, neighborly.

Agreeing to Disagree

I took a bite of the sandwich Elyk had made from deli meats and cheeses. "What did you call this?" He insisted we sit outside on a bench, the rain never having reached his store. A strong, humid wind was moving dirt and dust across the gravel parking lot. I had my sunglasses on to keep it out of my eyes.

His sandwich was almost gone. "It's a hoagie."

"You're making that up."

He scowled. "No, Miss West Coast, I am not. You ask anyone, it's a hoagie."

I smiled. "I'm going to do that." We watched a large tractor-trailer roll by, and as it shifted gears to head up the approaching hill, its grumble echoed off the store and back. Once it disappeared, the hiss of the wind returned as we both finished eating. I crumbled my wax paper wrapper into a ball and stood. "That was very good. What do I owe you?"

Elyk smiled and his face took on a friendly demeanor. "Just that makeup party you're having for Dottie."

I groaned. *Not this again.*

He had his phone open and was dialing, raising his finger in a *wait-a-minute* gesture. "Hi, hon. Marleigh wants to know if Tuesday or Wednesday works best for your party."

My mouth dropped open and I wiggled my fingers toward the phone. "Let me talk to her." I reached for his phone but he headed for the store. I followed in his footsteps, trying to reach around his arm to get the phone away from him.

"Okay. I'll let her know. See you later." He pushed the end button and shoved it in his pocket as he opened the door for me. "She chose Wednesday night. Seven PM, your place."

"I. Don't. Have. A. Place," I said with emphasis on each word.

"You made her very happy, Marleigh. She has so few friends."

I started to protest then realized that was most likely true. Dottie was a "little person." She'd told me that until she met Elyk, she'd been lonely. I threw the balled up wrapper at him but he caught it midair.

"Fine. But I'm mad at you."

"Here." He pushed a crossword puzzle my way. "Get unmad and help me with this word."

I squinted his way but said nothing. Turning the puzzle page I read the clue, "able to be set on fire." Eleven spaces. _ _ _ LA _ M_B _ E.

The word "me" went through my head and I thought of Lawyer. He certainly had set me on fire several times.

Elyk continued to hover. "It should be flammable, but that's nine letters."

I hesitated and said, "Actually, you're right. It's 'inflammable.'"

He snorted and crossed his arms. "No. That means the opposite, to not set on fire."

"Well, once in a while the language gods have a cruel streak. In this case, 'in' does not function as a negative prefix. It's an intensifier."

He turned to his computer and rapidly tapped on the keyboard, then leaned closer before looking my way. "Well, whoop-de-doo. We're both right." He wrote the word "inflammable" in the puzzle.

It was always like that with him, so I didn't try to argue with his logic. I pulled a rickety cart from a line of four. "I have groceries to buy." I pushed it to the far aisle and started matching items on my list to those on his shelves. Someone opened the door at my back, a guy, and he and Elyk exchanged comments about the weather. When I had everything, I returned to the front and stopped in my tracks. Frank Tabbish stood at the counter. In front of him lay a large rattlesnake, thankfully not moving.

Frank flicked his chin upward. "How ya doing?"

Elyk spoke. "Marleigh this is Frank Tabbish. Frank, Marleigh, our local speech therapist on wheels."

Frank's mouth moved into a sneer.

"We've met," I said and pushed my cart toward them. "He tied a dead opossum to a car part and left it on my windshield."

Elyk's eyes shot up to Frank's face. "You did that?"

Frank laughed a gravelly sound. "Yeah. I did." He turned to me. "You overreacted." He snorted. "You gotta remember, don't sweat the petty things and don't pet the sweaty things."

Elyk had a huge grin on his face. He shrugged then said, "Seems like good advice." He opened his huge cash register and handed Frank two twenty-dollar bills. "Thanks. This is a real nice tail."

Elyk caught rattlesnakes and then made their tails into key fobs or souvenirs he encased in a small glass container. I had one in my glove compartment, a welcome gesture when I first arrived which turned into an unexpected lifesaver.

Frank raised two fingers and whipped them away from his forehead in a military salute. "See ya around."

Elyk lifted the droopy four-foot snake and handed it my way. "Hold this so I can ring you up."

"Ask me again and you will get an earful."

He laughed, turned, and carried the snake through the back door to a small shed and dropped it inside.

I moved closer. Seeing no blood on the counter, I started stacking my groceries there.

He rang them up, still fighting a smile. I ignored him and packed the supplies in paper bags and then paid him. He finally spoke. "Your boyfriend was asking about you."

"Who?"

"Jaxson. He's convinced he's going to win you away from Lawyer."

"Oh, God." There may be no *winning away* after tonight. It would depend on what Lawyer had to say. "Maybe if he pistol whips me."

He laughed again. Then his face relaxed and he touched my arm. "Thank you for having the party. I owe you."

He was a softy inside. I liked how he cared so much about keeping Dottie happy. "You do owe me. Big time." He grabbed the groceries and walked me to the van, loading them in the back. I reached for the door handle and screamed, yanking my hand back. A huge black beetle, the size of a walnut, was balanced there.

Elyk picked up a stick and nudged it, but the bug didn't even flicker its shiny black wings. He leaned in closer and prodded it again. "It's dead." He reached over and plucked it off the door handle and tossed it aside. A sticky goo hung in strings from its underside where it had been glued to the metal. "What did you do to piss off Frank?"

"Nothing! Something's not right about him, Elyk."

"Kind of a loner, I know." He opened the door for me. "Maybe that's how you get when you spend your day picking up animals pasted to the road."

"Maybe. But maybe not." I climbed into the van. Before closing the door, I asked something that I had been wondering. "Do you think your mom likes volunteering at my patient's house?" Teaching Melvin to sing dirty songs wasn't right. If I told on her, she'd be let go from the volunteer program.

"She loves it." He scratched his neck. "Says it's the most fulfilling thing she has ever done. So thank you for setting her up with the contract."

"Oh, okay. Well, great then." I closed the door and waved as I backed out. I'd have to talk to Ivory, carefully, and see if she could change her ways.

At the Bed & Breakfast, I unpacked the groceries and went looking for Rose. She was in their private den, the recliner kicked back, her feet up, something I'd rarely seen her do. "Are you okay?"

"Yes, I am. Just taking a breather. You missed lunch. Can I get something for you?"

"No, thanks. I had a sandwich, I mean a hoagie, with mustard and a mouthful of dust. So I'm good."

She studied me, then laughed. "Okay."

"Where's Milt?" I asked.

"Richard drove him to the store. He kept talking about a calendar, so Richard is going to buy him one." She shrugged. "If it makes him happy."

"Calendar" was in the joke we had practiced. Maybe Milt wanted a visual aid to go with the punch line—*taking a day off*. "I'm going to be gone for dinner tonight, but let me help you get your meal ready before I leave."

"I already have it ready. Warm chicken and butter bean salad, curried carrots in a honey glaze, and Asiago cheese-stuffed rolls. And the two new couples arrived and they are, well, let's just say they're a breath of fresh air after this week's unique visitors. School teachers and the other couple works in accounting."

"You are amazing, Rose. Really. And I'm glad the new guests are normal. But do you think the Diffleys will be fine out there? I felt bad leaving them out in the rain and wilderness with no phone, nothing."

"Richard called the state police and the forest service after you left." She smiled. "They'll keep an eye on them. Where are you going for dinner?"

"To Lawyer's house. His mom's cooking."

She hesitated. "I thought I heard Ginny had lost her eyesight."

"She has. That's why they have Lawyer's friend staying there." I wasn't so sure about the truth of those words.

"That's right." She snapped her fingers. "I almost forgot. You're popular. A guy named Christian wants you to call him back." She reached for a slip of paper and handed it to me. "Very charming man."

"So I hear." I flapped the piece of paper. "I'll be in my room, getting charmed."

COMPETITION

Christian and I were on the phone, catching up on how we'd both found ourselves in northern Pennsylvania from opposite sides of the country. He wanted to get away from home in Jersey City, where his large family "was overbearing in that old school Italian way" while I was looking for mine. "How did you know I was coming to church?" I asked.

"Mrs. Tabbish called to say, 'My Marleigh car me to church.' That was pretty clear."

"What do you think about her son?" Maybe I shouldn't be telling him my concerns, but I assumed he was safe in that he must know about everyone's dirty laundry by now.

"I haven't met him. But you sound like you aren't sure about him."

Silence hung in the air for a few seconds. "He's just odd. I don't know. I get a weird vibe around him."

"Is Tinsel in any danger?" Christian sounded truly concerned.

"No. Frank seems devoted to her. Very kind. Forget it, I shouldn't have said anything."

"Well, I'll keep an eye out for him. And the reason I called earlier was to see if you wanted to come back after church."

Was he asking me out? Maybe I was just overthinking Christian's invite. "What do you have in mind?"

"I'm running out of pithy sayings for the marquee. I assume a speech pathologist might be of some help."

I laughed. "Okay. I'll get working on it but I don't know how good I am at pithy."

"We'll put our heads together. See you tomorrow."

I milled around impatiently, changing my clothes twice before leaving for Lawyer's, not sure if I should go for an "I'm-casual-and-cool" look, or heat up the summer evening with something low-cut. Perhaps a challenge to Veronica's looks. I compromised with a flirty black skirt and baby blue strappy top a store clerk told me made the color of my eyes pop. Maybe it will make Lawyer's eyes do the same.

The liquor store in Wellsfield was on the way to the Hunt home outside of Mansboro. I grabbed one bottle of white and red, unsure of what they'd be serving. Chewing a thumbnail as I drove, I was nervous about what the evening would hold. Discovering what Lawyer and Veronica's relationship really was made me edgy. Not that he wasn't a nice guy. He seemed like he was, showing kindness time after time with his mother, people in emergency situations, with me. I was jealous and irritated at the same time. Not a great way to arrive.

I rounded a bend to find myself, suddenly and breathtakingly, looking out over a glassy lake full of boats. Some anchored, others cutting the surface, leaving long white Vs behind them as they motored across the dark blue waters. A stirring view with hours of light left until the evening sky shut down.

Memories washed over me, fast and hard, and I pulled my car to the overlook and parked, letting the panorama sink in. My dad loved to go boating, although I don't remember him doing it much after I hit middle school. But I couldn't forget those predawn mornings in California, motoring on gorgeous Lake Loch Lomond set in a redwood canyon somewhere in the Santa Cruz Mountains. We pretended to fish and birdwatch, but we rarely caught fish, and although my dad spent a lot of time with the binoculars to his face, I honestly didn't see any birds. Our time away seemed more about being miles from everyone, and in that boat with just my dad, we were at the center of this universe, alone, yet together. I wondered now why we'd stopped going. Had I switched interests as a teenager from the only dad I knew to friends, movies, and silly gossip? Probably.

Now, as I studied this Pennsylvania lake full of the same time-old summer activities—smelling the motor oil and gas, the slightly swampy lake water, watching twirling gray spires of barbeque smoke heading skyward—I missed my parents fiercely.

I backed out and pointed my car toward Lawyer's, trying not to feel guilty about brushing off my dad all those years ago. Guilt seemed to be my default setting. Magnified in the last three months since my parents, who took the time to adopt me and raise me, were so suddenly ripped from my life. I hoped I was worth the trouble they went through to get me. The image of my dad and his binoculars flashed into my mind. Was he really birdwatching? Now that I had a new perspective on the Kingstons and their need for a protection program, maybe my dad needed to be cautious.

My heart pounded as I stood on the front steps of Lawyer's home, a modern log cabin style ranch house, sitting on a small hill above acres of green lawn and woods at the back. Bird feeders in different colors and shapes hung from a branch of a tall, old Eastern Hemlock just off the wide porch. Rockers and a padded swing took up most of the wooden floor space.

When Veronica opened the door, my pulse increased even more. I'd forgotten how pretty she was. Flowing black hair right out of a shampoo commercial, perfectly even-toned skin, a dancer's body, and offering a genuine smile. "Marleigh. It's so wonderful to see you again. Come in."

"Thank you." Even my voice sounded dowdy, matching how I felt. "I hope you are feeling better."

She studied me and slowly smiled, verging on a smirk. "I'm better." She pointed to the room past the entryway. "We're in the kitchen."

I followed her, trying to imitate her walk, movements more like floating than stepping. Until I saw myself in the hall mirror. My hips didn't seem to move that way.

Turning the corner, I had just a few seconds to study Lawyer and his mom before they knew I was there. They were side by side bent over the table. Ginny was arranging vegetables on a tray while he transferred barbequed chicken and ribs from a grilling rack to a serving platter. They were laughing about something.

"Marleigh brought wine," Veronica said, taking the bottles from my hands. She held them up as Lawyer turned toward me.

"Hi." I walked forward and touched Ginny's arm and gave it a squeeze. "Thanks for having me."

"You're welcome." She dropped her hand over mine and squeezed back. "It's our pleasure."

Lawyer walked up to me and gave me a peck on the cheek before pulling me into one of his world-class hugs. He put his mouth by my ear. "I'd like to have you." Then louder for everyone else, he said, "Glad you found us. And thanks for the wine."

"I'll pour everyone a glass," Veronica said, disappearing through a doorway.

I calmed down and drew in a long breath. It was going to be fine. The house smelled like something I couldn't quite place. Not unpleasant—a hint of cherry pipe tobacco maybe, homemade bread—but something on the edge of a memory from long ago. Of course, I wondered had my parents' house smelled like this. Smells. Straight to the heart.

Lawyer took my hand. "Let me show you around."

As he led me from the kitchen, a police scanner mounted above a desk was turned to low, reporting a possible home burglary. I pointed toward the device. "One of my patients is glued to her scanner. Poor thing has early dementia and believes she's still a young woman with a crush on a fireman." I stopped speaking, hearing the words that described myself.

"Probably a bad choice." He laughed. "And, almost everyone in the county has a police scanner. Makes it hard to stay ahead of the bad guys sometimes." I wondered if Lawyer's dad would have known Sofie's old boyfriend. They'd have been about the same age. I'd ask later. We moved from room to room as he explained, "My dad built this house for my mom when he got back from the Korean War. But these antiques..." and he pointed to a huge dining room table and a china cabinet, "came from my grandmother, who brought them over from England after World War II."

"They're beautiful. This house should be in a magazine. It's gorgeous."

"All my mom's doing." We continued down a hallway but I suddenly stopped before an entire wall of pictures, studying one.

"Oh, no." He pretended to pull me away as I leaned closer. "Don't look at those."

"Aw, that's you."

He examined the photo of himself with rueful fondness, a skinny kid of about eight, holding a basketball. "Sure is. I still had hopes of making the NBA in that picture."

Another photo had him wearing a green suit and tie, clothes stylish two decades ago, but always a question of fashion sense in hindsight.

I stood back and studied his face. "Did you ever try out for the NBA?"

"Heck no. Not when you're only five eleven and second string on your high school team." He pulled me away from the photos and pointed down the hall. "There's the bathroom and those are the bedrooms."

I smiled. "Let's see yours."

He cocked his head. "Really? My childhood bedroom? Or are you talking about something else?"

He pressed me to the wall opposite the photos and kissed me long and deep. My hands slid up under his shirt and found hot skin. My plan was to skip dinner completely if there was any way to do that.

"There you two are." Veronica stood in the hallway, holding our glasses of wine.

I felt my face flame, knowing she'd been kissed like this before. Her smile gave nothing away, and as she handed the drinks to us, she winked at Lawyer. "Dinner's ready."

The meal was less awkward than I'd expected. Lawyer and I sat on one side of the table while Ginny and Veronica faced us. His leg pressing against mine was exciting but also reassuring, a connection that kept me aware of his feelings.

Ginny kept us all laughing with stories about Lawyer's dad, Huck, when he first became a fireman. One less serious mishap in his career was when Huck found a naked couple walking along the road. "They were holding big maple leaves, trying to cover up their special parts," Ginny said giggling.

Lawyer pressed his leg harder to mine when she said those last words. Ginny's giggle was infectious.

Veronica spoke next after the giggles passed. "I wished I'd known him. He sounds like he was a good man."

Ginny's face held a faraway smile. "He was the best." Then she directed her gaze to Lawyer. "Not much different than Lawyer."

"Right." Lawyer drew the word out, pretending he was uncomfortable rather than proud. He changed the subject by offering to get us more wine.

Veronica leaned closer to me. "He has unnecessary guilt for what happened to me."

Maybe he was uncomfortable? I waited to see if she would continue but she stopped there. She must have assumed I knew her story when all Lawyer ever said was she was taking a break from Broadway.

He returned with the wine and divided it between our glasses. Studying the silence, he asked, "What did I miss?"

Veronica stood and replied, "Nothing. I'm going to get the dessert ready for later but for now, are we all up for a game of Scrabble?"

"Sounds great," I said and stood as well. "I'll help clear the plates."

When we were all seated at a round table in the den, I wondered how Ginny would be able to see the tiles—that is, until the box was opened. The letters were raised. As she chose seven from the box, she traced each of them with her fingers before lining them up on her letter holder.

I won the first game (Elyk would have been proud!) and we were well into the second game when the town fire whistle blared. Lawyer jumped out of his chair and raced toward the scanner where he'd also placed his phone and truck keys.

He listened to the scanner then jogged toward us, kissed his mom and Veronica on the foreheads before planting a soft one on my lips. "Sorry everyone. Cussler Glen has another fire." At the door he turned. "You two." He pointed to his mom and Veronica. "Don't wait up." He looked my way. "I'll call you tomorrow."

We sat in silence for a few minutes as we slowly put the game away, perhaps all thinking about his job, the dangers involved. I spoke first. "Ginny. You must have gotten used to this during all the years you were married to Huck."

She sighed. "It never gets any less nerve-racking."

Then I remembered Sofie's old boyfriend. "Did you ever know a fireman named Roger Kline? He might have been close to your husband's age."

She thought for a few moments. "That name doesn't sound familiar. Why?"

I explained Sofie's situation without offering her name. "I thought showing her some pictures of him would calm her down."

Veronica put the game away and moved to an overstuffed chair. Kicking her sandals off, she folded her long legs into the chair. Her arms and legs, even the tops of her feet, were tanned.

"Huck has dozens of photo albums in the basement. I could look through them for you," offered Ginny.

"Oh, no." I waved away the idea. "That's too much to ask, but thank you." I looked at my watch. "I really should be going anyway."

I thanked them both and turned to leave. Veronica spoke. "I'll walk you out like Lawyer would have done. But I'm not going to kiss you."

I laughed. "Deal."

We stood in a circle of light from the porch as I dug my keys out of my purse. "Thanks, again."

She laughed gently, and then her eyes narrowed. "Don't be too sure about that." She stared at me, and I saw a battle take place behind her eyes. "You need to know that I love Lawyer."

I shrugged. "I'm fine with that. You seem to have a great friendship and I know he cares a great deal about you. It's nice."

She set her lips in a straight line, a serious look. "No. I mean, I love him and if I have my way, I will have him back again. Soon." She waited a couple of seconds as if to let that sink in. "Seriously. This infatuation he has for you is temporary." Then she smiled. "And, my emergency last night? I can keep making those up all day long. Or shall I say, all night long?"

Her words forced me to take a few steps back and I was unable to speak. Had I been so wrong about him? Misread his interest as something more than temporary? She seemed so confident. I felt these words as if Lawyer had said them, not Veronica.

Revving up my own self-confidence, I stared her down. "Lawyer will speak for himself, thank you. And he's made it pretty clear to me that I matter to him and that I'm not some *leftover* responsibility. But it's sure been lovely to see you again." At those words, I flashed a fake smile and closed the door gently behind me. Once in the car, I turned over the engine. I could see her in the review mirror, standing ominously in the window watching me as I drove away.

Between the buzz from the wine and the idea she was desperate to get him back, my mind was fuzzy and I had to focus all my energy on staying on the road. I was ten miles into my drive back to the inn when the long bleat of a train horn startled me. I didn't realize the track ran parallel to the road. The engine and its cars emerged from a tunnel, seemingly out of nowhere.

What was it about a night train that made you feel like the loneliest person on earth? The pull of air tugging at you long after it was already running away, leaving you behind?

However I thought this evening would end, it wasn't with me fighting away tears and questioning my relationship with Lawyer. And it had somehow turned into a competition, something I hated. I wanted to call him right then to get his opinion about what Veronica had said. But he would be unreachable until the fire was out, which now sounded more like a metaphor than I would like to admit.

A Religious Experience

Christian stood at the front of the church, wearing a white shirt, a navy blue sports coat, and blue jeans. "Going to church doesn't make you a Christian any more than standing in a garage makes you a mechanic." It was obvious why he was popular and why this church was gaining members. Comfortable in front of the congregation, he easily switched from being a comedian to telling a poignant story.

Tinsel and I sat on the front row, a seat I wouldn't have chosen unless a plague of locusts filled the back pews. When we arrived, she pulled me to the front saying, "I ears better up here." Far be it from me to get in the way of her "earing" what he had to say.

His message was that each person is in charge of him or herself when it comes to following the right path. Life is not a passive route.

The church had fifteen rows of wooden pews on each side of the center aisle, deep windowsills, and tall stained-glass windows, changing the morning sun into soft beams of color which did lift the spirit. The building was old but well-maintained; the wood shined with polish. A dozen choir members sat against a backdrop of maroon velvet in the raised quire, its ornate façade decorated with intricate spindles. A young woman from the choir took the pulpit to sing the final hymn, *How Great Thou Art*. Tinsel leaned my way. "She word the best."

I whispered. "Her voice is amazing."

Christian offered the final prayer and encouraged the congregation to greet any newcomers. Within seconds I faced a long line of people, strangers to me but not to Tinsel. I tried to say I was a *friend* of Tinsel's but she blew my cover with, "This my teacher for mouth and word."

Several people seemed to know there was a new speech therapist in the area, so I stopped trying to protect Tinsel's medical privacy. After reassuring everyone I was settling in fine—that, yes, it was beautiful here and, no, I'd never been in an earthquake in California and, no, I didn't believe the state would crack off anytime soon and slide into the ocean—I made it through the introductions.

Finally at the front door, Christian took my hand in both of his, his smile hypnotic. "Thanks for coming. Looks like you've been amply and warmly welcomed by this congregation."

"Yes, what a great group."

He placed one hand on my lower back, moving me off to the side. "You're still coming back for lunch, I hope."

"Yes. I just need to drop Mrs. Tabbish off and I'll be back. What can I bring?"

"Your creative mind." He smiled. "The rest I've got covered."

As I helped Tinsel down the steps, I wondered why Christian, who was kind and radiated an undeniable sexual energy, appeared to be single. I realized I was looking forward to lunch and could ask him then.

Once I had Tinsel seated at her kitchen table with a half turkey sandwich, macaroni salad, and a cantaloupe wedge, I said, "I'll be back in the morning. Thanks for asking me to attend church with you. I enjoyed it."

She smiled and touched her chest and sighed, saying, "Revered Betts. Good church now."

"Looks like he's doing a great job. Wasn't the pastor before him older?"

"Reverend McCallister," she said shaking her head, her mouth turned down in a sad clown expression. "Old man. Dead in parsonage last winter."

"I heard he died in the church. How long was it before Reverend Betts took over the church?"

"Three months. No preacher to bible verse there, then he car here." She smiled. "Better now."

"Seems like it." I touched her shoulder. "I'll see you tomorrow."

On the drive back to the church, I wondered what Lawyer was doing. The fire may have kept him out all night, so he would be sleeping. But maybe not. I could call him, could ask if he knew about Veronica's plans, about her *emergency*. I didn't. I'd wait to see what he does.

The cars were all gone in front of the church and Christian's dark green SUV was next to the parsonage. I locked my car and then felt foolish. There was no one around for miles. As I started up the few steps to the door, Christian pulled it open. He'd taken off the suit coat and rolled up the sleeves of his dress shirt, leaving the shirttails casually out over his jeans. "Hi. Come on in." He ran his fingers through his thick black hair, leaving it in that messy, but fashionably tousled look.

I studied the parsonage, a small home. The small dining room ran up against the kitchen, which was open but architecturally stuck in the 1960s. White steel cabinets with sideways "V" handles, and spring green-colored appliances broke up the Formica countertops. The porcelain sink was deep enough to launch a ship, and the white and black tiled floor made me momentarily dizzy. The living room in red tones had flowered carpet, matching the drapes and wallpaper. It reminded me of my grandparents' old house in Loma Linda. "Very retro," I said.

"I like it. Anything newer would have been wrong." He stuffed his hands in his back pockets and flashed a charming smile. "I'll give you the tour."

I followed him down a dark hallway with paneling on both sides, containing pullout drawers as we neared a bedroom. I peeked in. Spartan with a double bed, a quilt over one rocking chair, and one bedside table. Monkish without the candle or hair shirt. When we passed a tiny office, he said, "We'll work in there after lunch."

A few steps later, we reached the sagging back porch. Beyond the screened-in windows was a huge backyard broken up with clusters of weeping willow trees, their lacy green skirts looking like dancers poised, waiting for the signal to begin a waltz.

"Peaceful," I said. "Must be quite the change after Jersey City."

He thought a moment then said, "I've had some moments of rural-itis."

I raised my eyebrow. "Sounds painful."

He laughed, a warm and genuine sound. "Initially, the emptiness would get to me. You would have thought I would embrace the sound of no emergency vehicles, but some nights the only cure was a generous bourbon."

"Isn't it a job requirement to be a wino?" I asked.

He laughed again.

Then I offered, "I have Verdophobia."

His eyebrows rose. "Go on."

"The fear of pressing greenery. For me, all the thick trees and heavy humidity verge on too much."

"Does alcohol solve it?"

I scanned the yard and smiled. "At times. Mostly I've been running, trying to appreciate all the nature up close. But that doesn't mean I'm against assessing alcohol's ability to ease my fear."

He squeezed my arm. "I am in fact a wino...and I've been saving a bottle of Cabernet Sauvignon for a special occasion. Did you know my church has a wine cellar? I'll be right back."

What special occasion? Did making up funny church slogans count? I wiped my newly damp palms on my dress, now completely unsure of his intentions. I wandered back through the small home, stopping at his bedroom door. The narrow, cracked closet door begged me to look inside. I glanced into the vacancy and obvious stillness behind me, and crossed to the closet door and pulled it open. Typical of an older home, the closet was small with one horizontal metal pole and a small shelf area overhead. On one side hung three suits, and below them, two pair of expensive-looking shoes. *Didn't buy those here.* I stepped in and scrunched down, pulling the door nearly closed behind me. Breathing deeply I asked myself what I smelled. The age of the closet came through, mustiness mixed with old lumber painted fifty times. But the clothes themselves had a different scent—good wools, rich cotton, and new leather. They smelled like youth, something edgy. But nothing comfortable. I wouldn't spend time in here even if I could fit.

I had just stepped from the closet to cross the bedroom when a floorboard creaked in the house. I froze, hoping the sound came from the kitchen since that would give me time to get back into the hallway. A moment later, Christian stood in the doorway, a quizzical look on his face. "Find anything interesting?"

Embarrassed, I wanted to say, *What're you reading?* Then my eyes scanned the bedside table: The Holy Bible. Of course.

He was waiting for an answer so I told him the truth: "I have a thing for closets." His gaze slid to the closet door and back to me, but he didn't say anything. I pressed on. "It started in childhood. I, um, it calms me down when I'm nervous. Er, something about the scent of clothes." I held up my hands. "I'm sorry for snooping."

His face brightened from one of dark concentration to simple understanding. "I get it. For me, it was my mother's canning shelves in our huge basement. When the family got too loud, I'd crawl in there and lay out flat. It was dark. The smell of metal from the canning lids, a slight hint of vinegar from the pickles...that was my calming scent."

I relaxed. What had I been thinking? He invited me over and I became a spy. "Thanks for understanding."

He held up the bottle. "Like-minded people need to share a drink. And I set up on the patio if you're ready to eat."

I was ready for almost anything to get out of this situation. "More than ready."

A large walnut tree to the side of the house, away from any view from the road, shaded the stone patio. The square metal table had four chairs. He had set up two place settings side by side. A large serving plate in the center had strips of grilled chicken, several varieties of green and black olives, squares of goat cheese, and bunches of grapes.

I took a seat as he helped scoot the chair closer. "How elegant."

"Actually, you should be thinking 'How Italian.'" He poured the red wine into our glasses. "It's about all I know how to make."

"It's perfect for a summer's day."

When he was seated, he raised his glass and I followed suit. He smiled. "To new friends with quirky habits." We tapped the glasses together and drank.

I swallowed and then smiled. "This is nice."

"Good." He spun his glass slowly at eye level. "I like a good Cabernet Sauvignon. Something about it being impermeable to the light suits me. Dark, with the scent of oak. You know Sauvignon means savage, right?"

"I didn't." I sipped again and studied him. I had enough trouble keeping one guy in my life. Why tempt this one's savage side? "You're a bit of a poet, aren't you?"

He remained silent as he reached for my plate, and began selecting food from the platter. "Not really. I work hard to be creative, to shake off the notion that all preachers are boring."

"I see no danger there. You replaced an older pastor, I heard. He may have fallen more into that boring category."

He shrugged. "McCallister was almost eighty, dementing. I heard he slept a lot, which does serve me well, stepping into his shoes."

The afternoon breeze moved the branches above us, warm patches of sunlight danced on the table, and the talk turned to our lives before Pennsylvania.

Forty-five minutes later, the food was half eaten but the wine was gone and our conversation had moved from formal to flirting, from past dates to recent interests. His arm draped across the back of my chair. "Your fireman, Lawyer, whose weird name is that of another profession, is really into you. I saw the way he looks at you." He smiled. "'Course, I don't blame him."

I tilted my head and watched the world follow. I should know my drinking limits and three glasses of savage were too many. "I'm not sure what's going to happen." I didn't want to talk about Lawyer right now. "And you. You've been here three months or something. No one has caught your eye?"

He studied the table and then lifted his eyes. "Let's just say, your boyfriend had better realize what he has. I can be very persuasive." He held up the empty wine bottle. "I'll grab another."

Holding up my hands, I waved the idea away. "I'll walk you to the cellar but I'm done. Especially if you want church sayings, not religious slurrings."

I followed him along the connecting hallway and into the back door of the church. The air grew cooler as we descended the cement steps. He pulled a chain and a bare bulb lit the bottom portion of the stairs. A five-foot wine rack stood off to the right, next to a huge boiler full of bottles. "McCallister left you this wine?"

He laughed. "No, it's mine. There was nothing down here but dead mice and spiders."

I wandered the room, breathing in the basement's combined scent of musty earth and cold stone. To the left were stacks of flattened shipping boxes and other boxes full of bibles. Lawyer had made a joke about Bibles for Babies, but it looked like the pastor did ship the Word of God somewhere. Next to it were other cartons with "Bee a Honey" stamped on the sides. The smaller print said, "4, sixteen pound slabs of pure beeswax." I pointed. "What's all of this for?"

Christian slowly stood from the rack when he saw what I was pointing to. His eyes flattened and something crossed his face. "Wax. I make the candles for the church."

"You do not."

His face hadn't changed, and I realized I had probably embarrassed the macho Italian side of him. I quickly added, "But very prudent. And cool. Let me know if you ever need help."

I walked to where he stood and he slowly smiled. "I will." He touched my back and directed me toward the steps. "I think I've had enough to drink, as well. Let's go write some soul-altering lines for my marquee."

Moments later, we were settled in his office and soon I had him laughing. "What? You don't like that one?" I acted insulted.

"When you read about the evils of drinking, you should give up reading?" He snorted, leaned back in his chair, and interlocked his fingers behind his head. "I'll get fired for that."

We came up with a few good ones that he wrote down, then we started making up absurd sayings. I said, "Okay. Let's get serious. We need something about not worrying."

It was quiet for a moment, both of us lost in thought. He spoke, but when his lips twitched I knew he'd come up with something absurd. "How about, 'Don't let worry kill you, our church can help'?"

I laughed. "That's it." The smile remained stuck on my face and I realized I was having a really good time. Playing with words, sitting across from a handsome witty guy, laughing. If he was trying to win me over, it was working.

He tapped the pen on the paper. "I really needed this help, Marleigh. I was down to lines like, 'Come inside. Let us change hell into hello.'"

I laughed. "That's pretty bad ... but we did make up some great lines. Which one are you putting up first?"

He dragged his finger down the list, stopping halfway. "I like this one. 'Stop, drop, and roll doesn't work in Hell.'"

That one was mine. "Divine ..." I said, drawing in a long breath and standing, "I should be going."

He stood and came around the desk. "Well, I've had about as much fun as one preacher is legally allowed in one given day." His smile was wide, and his eyes drilled into mine. "But, promise me we'll do this again soon."

"Yes, let's do that." I stood. "Thanks for everything."

He stood in the same position as he had at the door hours earlier. Hands in his back pockets, casually sexy, not looking the slightest bit like a man of the cloth.

Sauvignon man.

I began driving. I meant to ask how he found the job opening all the way from Jersey. Was the position advertised all over the country in some ministry magazine?

My phone rang. It was Lawyer. I let it go to voicemail. I needed to be in a completely different mindset to talk to him about Veronica. And that wasn't going to happen with Christian's wine still fresh on my palate.

The roads meandered but surprisingly I knew where I was. What had been so confusing just a few weeks ago was now making sense. Most of the time. Something else was new. Being alone out in the wilderness like this with miles between towns wasn't *as* frightening now. This quiet time felt like the only space that was truly mine. It had somehow changed for me.

I passed a county worker mowing the sides of the road and I kept looking until he disappeared in my rearview mirror in the green heat haze. Did he wonder who I was as much as I wondered who he was? Unlikely.

The roads rolled away behind me and I knew the real question was: Who am I? What would I become if I found out I had no remaining family tree to hang my name on? A possibility I both feared and suspected.

Abandonment Issues

Rachael and Nate held our attention during dinner. That evening, they were the only guests and I could tell Richard and Rose liked not having to keep several conversations going, which was the norm with more people. The Diffleys had not come running back to civilization, so they must have survived their first night. Or not. Rachael and Nate couldn't say enough about West Trout Run. They recounted the history they learned about the town and whole area.

"We learned that when the bigger cities called people to factories, whole farms were left behind here. People just left. The villages slowly sank into the ground."

"We have a lot of lost villages in New England," Richard said, serving another helping of salmon in dill sauce to Milt, who seemed extra alert tonight as he followed the conversation from person to person. We would try out his joke as soon as we got a chance. "You walk in many of these woods and you'll find stone walls, foundations of abandoned barns and houses."

Rachael interjected, "We saw an open well with ferns and trees growing up through it."

Taking Sofie to West Trout Run might be something that would make her happy. Her mind was stuck in the time period before the lumber town was abandoned. I'd see her in two days and could discuss it with her husband. Transporting my patients anywhere was against the agency's rules but if her husband Jon went, too, it could be considered more of a fact-finding drive. Actualization therapy. Perhaps she would stop obsessing about her crush on Roger Kline, the once-upon-a-time fireman in her life.

Speaking of firemen, I didn't call Lawyer back yet but texted I'd call after dinner. With that time approaching, I realized I had no idea what I would say. Did I want to come right out and present Veronica as the manipulative person she revealed, or should I wait to see what he says about the hospital visit on Friday night when he was supposed to have been away?

As Rose set out smaller dishes for her Moravian sugar cake and vanilla bean ice cream, I touched Milt's arm. "Are you ready for your line?"

He rubbed his hands on his thighs; his powder blue dress pants wrinkled and unwrinkled under the movement. I leaned closer and whispered, "Your line is, 'He took a day off.'"

I cleared my throat and waited for everyone to look my way. "Milt and I would like to share a joke with you."

Richard looked concerned while Rose's eyebrows arched up into the middle of her forehead.

"Sure," Nate said. "We love a good joke." He and Rachael waited with eager smiles.

Milt looked ready. I asked, "Why did the man get fired from the calendar factory?"

He chuffed a few breaths out and I raised my finger, signaling the audience to give him a minute. His face moved rusty muscles around.

"He took off."

I was surprised no one heard my internal groan. Why had I given him such a long answer when he hardly puts two words together?

Nate slowly bobbed his head. "That most certainly will get you fired. Good one."

Milt's uncertain eyes met mine and I smiled. "That's right, Milt. He took a day off."

Everyone laughed and Richard leaned over and clamped his hand on his dad's shoulder. "It's nice to hear you talk, Dad." I thought I saw tears brighten Richard's eyes.

I squeezed Milt's hand under the table. He slowly turned his eyes toward me. "I joke," he said. My eyes blurred with emotion, and I fought to keep tears from spilling. We'd practice more jokes later. If this was the path to helping his speech return, it'd be the most fun therapy I'd ever done.

After cleaning up dishes, Rachael and Nate went outside to play a game with the giant chess set near the maple syrup shack. I glanced out my bedroom window when I heard a whoop from the chess area. Milt was literally *in* the game, standing next to the king, a good spot for him since that piece wouldn't get a lot of action.

Kind of like me.

With that thought I climbed on the bed, settled back against the big pillows, and dialed Lawyer's number.

He sounded tired. "How are you?"

"Good. We just finished dinner. I'm getting ready for work tomorrow."

"Sorry, I had to leave dinner early…did you stay long after?"

"A little while." Just enough to learn I was in a contest for your affections. "Thanks for inviting me. It was great."

"Mom and Veronica really like you."

I stalled, not sure what I wanted to say. "They're very nice." It even sounded disingenuous to *my* ears.

He laughed. "But. You have something else to add?"

"You came back to town Friday night to be with Veronica at the hospital. Very noble. Really. But we talked that night and you acted like you were still out of town."

"Marleigh..." He said my name as if it were rolling around on his tongue, like tasting a new wine, causing a flutter inside of me. "Veronica is embarrassed by her situation. She asked that I not tell anyone she'd gone to the hospital."

I tried to decide if I'd been too harsh on Veronica. She must have a health condition. "Okay. I won't ask. Her medical stuff is private. But just know that I'm fine with you helping her like that, so you don't have to cover up what you're doing."

He was silent. "You're still not comfortable with my friendship with Veronica and I don't blame you."

I looked up from the bed, thinking I heard a footstep in the hallway. I crossed to the door and peeked outside but no one was there.

"You still there?" He sounded anxious.

"Right here. Yeah. I don't know about you two. It seems she wants to be more than friends."

"That's not going to happen."

"What if she turned on those original charms that won you over when you were dating...would that change your mind?" My impression was that Veronica was building up a full-on assault now that I had Lawyer's attention.

"We had only dated two months when I broke up with her." He sighed. "Here's the deal. My reasons for helping her are built on incredible guilt on my part."

"People break up all the time. I'm not sure guilt is the right emotion, is it?"

He was silent for a few moments. I sensed statements being considered and discarded. He finally said, "The night

I broke up with her, she left from my apartment before I could drive her home. She was mugged and spent a few days in the hospital. Traumatized to the point where she dropped out of *Once*, a Broadway play she had fought hard to get a part in." He sighed. "I know this isn't my fault but I still feel rotten about it."

He was a teacher in a high school outside of Philadelphia then. "Did you move back here just to get away from the city?"

"I was already packed and on my way back. One reason was that I was breaking up with her."

"Were there other reasons?" My jealousy came through even though I had tried to sound casual.

He laughed. "Yeah. Here's one. I didn't love her, and on most days I didn't even like her."

"Sorry for all of the distrust." I didn't like how carefully I said what I was thinking. I didn't want to constrict my feelings with him. "I'm working through this."

"You have captivated me. Seriously. I haven't felt this way in a long while. Maybe ever."

The smile that took over my face was huge. Glad he couldn't see it because it gave so much away. "I'm slightly taken with you, too. When can we get together and explore those feelings, without your mom and Veronica?"

"I leave in the morning for Philly. Veronica's moving back and I offered to drive."

My heart sank. I had barely seen him in the last four days and now he was leaving again. "Wow. Okay." This should feel like good news. The competition was going home, but I wasn't so sure this would be the end of her. "So possibly back by Tuesday? We could get together then."

"I should be. I'll call when I'm heading back."

Sitting in the large rocking chair, I swayed back and forth which matched my thought process. I should hang in there. I should forget about him. Stay in touch. Don't take any more calls. Back and forth. Nothing solved.

I moved to a small writing desk and pulled out the therapy plans for my three patients the next day. At that moment, I remembered I wanted to ask Lawyer about the abandoned mining town, West Trout Run. Just because this couple at the inn had said it was safe didn't mean I should take Sofie there. I was ambivalent about calling Lawyer back, but the only other person I knew to call was Jaxson, and I was more uncertain about that. He'd already announced that we had somehow moved beyond just running friends. Calling him could mean so much more than a phone call to him.

I settled on Elyk. Remote areas and the backwoods were rattlesnake havens, a must for my denim-clad, snake-wrangling friend.

Dottie answered the home phone; her childlike voice was always a surprise. Although she was a "little person," nothing stood in her way, and her happiness was infectious. "Marleigh. Thanks for hosting a Mary Kay party this Wednesday."

Oh, crap. I hadn't done a thing to plan for this. "Sure. But if there's another time, you know, to get more people there, we could change it."

"I think we're good. Elyk said you had quite a few coming." She sounded like a kid anticipating a birthday.

I was going to kill Elyk. How could he set up his girlfriend this way? Who would I ask? Veronica's face flashed in my mind and I was relieved she'd already be back in Philadelphia. No sense slathering expensive makeup on her flawless face unless we could ugly her up a little. Catty? Yes. Guilty about it? No. "Dottie, let's hope so. You know how people can flake on something like this." I drew in a long breath, processing the knowledge I was having a party. "What's a good time?"

We agreed on seven o'clock, then she put Elyk on the phone. He laughed when I chastised him for creating a situation for me. "What if no one comes, Elyk? Dottie will be angry or hurt."

"I knew you'd put together a good group, Marleigh."

"Dottie is standing right there, isn't she?" I groaned. "Stop this. I'm already pissed off at you."

"Well, I guess you can brag about your ability to attract people ... but remember, humility is good, too."

He loved playing this game. He'd done it to me before and I kept falling into his trap. Even if I asked to be put on speakerphone to include Dottie, he wouldn't have complied. "I hate you." Unfortunately, I was half smiling and no anger came from my words.

He laughed. "What did you call about then?"

"West Trout Run. Have you been there?"

"Are you saying you're ready to rattlesnake hunt again?"

"I'd rather oil my feet and stand on hot coals. So, no." I shifted positions at the writing desk. "I want to take a client there to nudge some old memories but I'm not sure it's safe."

There was no answer for a moment, then he spoke. "Good trout fishing out there. What're you planning on doing with him?"

"It's a her. Probably just drive around and park. Walk to a few buildings." I'd heard uncertainty in his voice. Maybe it was a bad idea. "Are there structures still standing?"

"Yeah. A barn, the church, the store, and part of the long house where the men slept. People go there and walk around, so you should be okay."

"Thanks." I wrote lumber camp into my day planner for Tuesday. "How's the puzzle contest going?"

"Sent off number thirty today. Halfway there."

"What're you going to buy with sixty thousand dollars?"

He hesitated. "Can't say."

"Dottie still there?"

"Yup." Then he hung up.

The word "goodbye" seemed to elude him. Maybe if it went backwards like his name, he'd be comfortable with it. I tried it out. "Eybdoog." Too hard on the tongue.

When my phone rang again, I had no idea whose number was on the screen. I almost let it go to voicemail when I thought of Marshal Schumer and the possibility of news about my parents. I punched the button. "Hello."

"Hi, Marleigh. Christian here."

Had I given him this cell number? I didn't think so. "How are you?"

"Good. Just wanted to say today was fun. Thanks for coming by."

"Thanks for inviting me." I realized I was smiling. I should feel bad, but I justified that if Lawyer could have a close female friend, I could have one, too, of the male variety.

"I put up the new saying on the marquee. We're a good team when we put our heads together."

"The wine helped. But, yeah. Anything involving words, I'm in."

"We'll do it again," he said. Then I heard something drop, like the sound of a pool ball hitting a wooden floor.

"Where are you?"

"In the church. I dropped a mallet."

I laughed. "And you need a mallet because?"

"Knocking sense into some people." He chuckled. "Actually, I just sealed a crate of bibles."

Lawyer's words came back to me. *"Like sending Bibles for Babies or some made-up shit like that."*

"Who gets the bibles?" I asked.

He was silent for a moment too long it seemed. "Inner city churches mostly. But often they go overseas."

"Nice." I wasn't sure what else to add. "I just learned that you could have chosen an even more remote spot to live than Beaver Hollow." *What a name.*

"I doubt it." I heard the smile in his words. "But where's that?"

"There's a Methodist church out in an abandoned town called West Trout Run. A fixer-upper."

He was silent and it felt like he was preoccupied. Then he said, "I'll have to check it out. I guess you have a busy day tomorrow. Back to helping everyone else with their words."

"Just three people. I'd take more but six clients are all I have right now."

He cleared his throat. "I got your cell number from Mrs. Tabbish. I hope that was okay."

I moved to the window and pulled aside the curtains. The sky was closing down. It was that time of the evening when all color fades, absorbed into an achromatic space that exists between night and morning. "I wondered about that. Thanks for letting me know."

We hung up. I wasn't sure what I thought about Christian, but I wasn't going to analyze it too much. My feelings for Lawyer were much different than those for Christian. It was like comparing being fully intoxicated to having just the slightest buzz. In this situation, I was sticking with feeling drunk around the fireman.

SEEING STRAIGHT

I jerked awake the next morning, running from something large. Trying to slow my pounding heart, I stayed snuggled under the down comforter, straining to remember any threads from the dream. The more I tried to pull parts together, the more it dissipated like fog. Present but impossible to grasp. In the dream, I'd been in the dark. Not just the shadiness of nighttime but like black syrup, an obscure drape which fell over the sun and oozed everywhere. That was all I had. Nothing else rose to my consciousness. It was rare that I ever remembered a dream. I pushed the darkness away and focused on what I'd be doing today, finally calming my nerves.

Out of the shower, I dressed and headed to the kitchen. Avoiding the guests, I met Rose in the kitchen. "What can I do to help you?"

She untied the green apron from her waist and draped it over a chair. "You can eat an extra big piece of this maple bacon pie I made." She pointed to the rectangular glass dish with half of the food gone. "Hand me a plate."

It smelled wonderful. Once she had a large square loaded on my dish, I took the first bite and chewed. Cupping my hand to shield my mouth, I said around the food, "What's in it?"

"Bacon, cheese, hash browns, eggs, and secret spices." She smiled.

She always said that. "Fairy Rose dust," I said and touched her arm. "That's the secret spice."

She blushed and dropped a muffin on my plate. "Orange, elderberry, and walnuts. Healthy enough to skip your vitamins today." She took the warm batch into the dining room.

It was gone before she returned. "You're going to make me so fat I'll need one of those cow waterbeds."

She laughed then snapped her fingers. "We have new people arriving tonight. Hopefully, they'll be teachers or nurses or librarians. I love the variety we get here but lately it has been a little too loony."

Perhaps all bed and breakfast owners would say the same thing. An idea flashed through my head. "You should write a book. Call it *Inn Difference. Or Differences INN Opinions.*"

Richard laughed, having heard my idea from the doorway. "That's not a bad idea. We'd change the location of our place and the people's names, but we've seen and heard some pretty interesting things, haven't we, Rose?"

She waggled her finger. "We will do no such thing. We'd never hear another crazy story in our lives and I'm not willing to make that trade."

Richard shrugged. "We'll publish it under Milt's name."

Rose touched my back. "Thank you for all that you're doing with Milt. He seems happier now that he's saying more."

"My pleasure. I hope the jokes kick loose the rest of his words...I can't help but think how trapped he must feel." *Trapped* made me think of Elyk and how he trapped me into this upcoming party. I had to bring it up eventually, well, now.

"Wednesday night, Elyk's girlfriend Dottie would like to have a few ladies over to try out the makeup she sells. If you want to say 'no' I'm fine with that."

Rose thought a moment. "That sounds like fun. Do you want to have it inside or out under the gazebo?"

She was too nice for my own good. Now I needed to find women to come. "Inside might be easier since we need good light. I'll set up everything and you won't have to worry."

Richard leaned closer. "Rose lives for the next entertainment event. You won't inconvenience her in any way." He pointed to his wife. "Look. She's already planning out the food."

Rose chuckled. "I might have been thinking ahead just a little. Oh, Richard. You do know me, sweetheart."

Richard winked at her and blew a kiss.

"Thank you, Rose. Thank you so much." I checked the kitchen clock. "I have to get going, but let's talk about what needs to happen for the party."

"Sure." Rose grabbed a pitcher of water. "How many people are coming?"

I sighed. "Right now, it's Dottie and me."

Rose straightened her shoulders. "I'll see what I can do about that."

"I'm so grateful, Rose."

Gathering all my supplies, I headed to the car and packed them inside. The sunrise had quit showing off its colors, and the sky was now clear and blue in all directions.

Ten minutes later, I passed through Wellsfield with its mandatory old courthouse on a long sloping green. A cannon and a memorial to veterans of four wars broke up the acre of grass. At the intersection, a white church held one corner while a small bookstore sat on the other.

A few blocks later, I was off into the wilds. Thick trees on each side of the road absorbed the light as I headed to Bear Hollow Road and Tinsel's house. Fifteen minutes later,

I passed The Little Church in the Pines. I smiled, seeing Christian had used one of my ideas on the marquee.

God wants full custody, not just weekends!

Accepting I'd had a fun time with him yesterday was easy. I could use more friends, and having someone with connections in a higher place couldn't hurt. As the church grew smaller in the rearview mirror, I realized I'd be back that day. I could have changed the schedule and seen Tinsel later in the day, but if Jake found out I'd manipulated my schedule for my own convenience, it wouldn't have gone over well. I had enough dings on my work record without adding any more.

Turning into the narrow lane toward Tinsel's house, I came to a halt. A large branch had fallen, blocking the road. Switching off the car, I got out and grabbed the thickest end of the branch and tugged. It barely moved. I planted my feet and pulled harder, stepping backward, slowly jerking and dragging it down. First into a grass-choked dry ditch and then into the shrubs at the edge of the forest. Yanking one last time, I tripped backward over a log, my outcry cutting into the sudden silence in the trees. I lay for a moment, staring up at the bits of blue through the upper foliage, cursing my clumsiness. I assessed if I was hurt or not. Getting to my feet, I brushed off the leaves and pine needles. I'd have a few bruises, nothing more. Making my way back to the car, my hair fell forward and I realized I lost my headband. I swore again, deleting all the points I earned in church yesterday. Staring at the thick woods, it seemed hopeless to go looking. I left the car where it was, grabbed my therapy bag, and breathed deeply while walking to Tinsel's front door. Arriving in a bad mood was not good.

She opened the door wearing the exact same clothes she had on yesterday. "In here." She smiled widely and grabbed my hand. "My church friend."

"I am." I closed the door behind me and we crossed to the dining table where we sat. "That was fun."

Her smile stuck as she studied me. "You with Pastor Betts at church for hours." She smoothed down her blouse. "Good man for boyfriend."

I held up my hand, waving away the thought. "No. We're just friends." I studied her for a moment. "How did you know I was there?" My car hadn't been visible from the road.

She stood and crossed to the counter, picked up the small box sitting there, and handed it my way. "I money a new Chia for Pastor Betts."

The box held an angel Chia Pet. Shouldn't it be considered sacrilegious to grow green weeds on a religious figure? "This company truly has an exhaustive inventory."

"You car it to him." She nodded like that had been settled.

I started to argue until I realized I could turn this into a therapy moment. "Okay. You will write him a note. We'll practice the verbs in the sentences before you write them and then you can read it to me when it's all done."

She disappeared down a hallway and came back with a few sheets of flowery stationery and a pen, and sat them on the table. She scowled at me, then reached over and plucked a leaf from the back of my scalp. "You in the trees?"

"Yes. For a minute, I was in the trees." I shrugged, then tapped the paper. "What will you write to Pastor Betts?"

"I money this for you because you good mouth and words at sermon."

I laughed. "Okay. We will start with saying that."

We worked for fifteen minutes, writing four paragraphs about how happy Tinsel was to have him here, how his sermons meant so much to her, and why she hoped he would stay for a very long time. Sentences full of verbs. She'd repeated them several times and was about to read the whole letter when her phone rang. She sprung from her chair to snatch the mobile handset from the charger, scaring Lovey out from under the table. She ignored the growling dog as he faced off against a table leg as if it were menacing. "Hello?"

Here was one thing I'd learned during my externship: Phone calls were never ignored by this age group. No matter what.

Tinsel listened for a full minute before speaking. "Yes. Dog in my house." She listened again.

Lovey wandered toward me, sniffing the air and I froze. Maybe like a T-Rex, if the dog sensed no movement, it wouldn't attack my leg.

Tinsel bobbed her head as if the caller could see her. "Okay. Mailbox two to my house."

Oh, no. This was not good. Anyone who would buy Chia Pets probably had a huge smiley face next to her number on telemarketing lists. This was a form of elder abuse, especially when she couldn't properly communicate. I needed to interfere, so I motioned that I wanted the handset. "May I talk to them?"

She looked confused but handed the handset to me. "Hi." I didn't wait for a response. "Whatever you are selling, this lady won't be needing any."

Lovey wandered toward the wall, stopping short of a plug in an outlet. Then she went crazy, barking and charging at the plug, spitting and choking on her own saliva.

The caller was saying something but the dog was making too much noise. I went ahead with my thoughts. "And put Mrs. Tabbish on your 'Do Not Call List.'"

Tinsel was trying to pick up the snarling dog, but he was launching himself from all angles at the perceived enemy.

The man was still talking in my handset. "They are particularly good for old dogs who have poor eyesight."

That stopped me. "Wait. What are you selling?"

"Dog spectacles. They're like goggles but with a slight amount of correction."

Tinsel finally had the dog pointed in the other direction. But Lovey staggered toward the kitchen doorway and stumbled right into the wall, missing the clearing on the first try.

I lingered on his last words, then said, "We'll take *one* pair." I handed the phone back to Tinsel. "It's worth a try."

After she hung up, Tinsel successfully read through her letter one more time. I slipped it into the Chia Angel box. "I'll let you know what the pastor says." I left her with lists of sentences to read aloud and confirmed our next visit.

I was processing Tinsel's speech progress about ten feet from my car when I heard the first growl. Low and menacing, I knew it was no lovely small dog this time. I froze. Tinsel's house was long out of sight behind me. My eyes moved to the woods on both sides of the road, searching for an animal. When silence returned, I wondered if I imagined it. I dug out my keys and had them ready in case I needed to run for the car.

The growl began again, and in that moment, I saw the bear. It slowly rose up on its hind legs, standing over my car trunk.

I screamed and dropped my bag but didn't move. I'd never outrun it if I tried to make it to Tinsel's porch. She'd call 911, yelling a cryptic message like, "girl no arm at my door!"

The bear made more noises. Weird high-pitched sounds and my heart pounded faster. I was not facing off with just any bear; this one was wounded. I had the tiny Mace® and mini fire extinguisher on my chain. Not exactly what I needed. My breath was coming in bursts and I knew it was bad to show fear, but that's all I had to display at the moment.

I slowly stepped toward the trees. I'd find a branch, or a rock, something with which to defend myself.

The animal rose taller and I noticed two things: my headband was around one arm, its chest and stomach appeared to be cut open with blue and red showing from its innards. How was it even alive with such horrible wounds?

Then a new noise, an incongruous noise, hit me. Laughter. A man's laughter.

The bear head crumbled into a pile of fur beside my car, and Frank, the roadkill specialist, stood there in a red and blue plaid shirt and filthy jeans. "Had you going, didn't I?"

My legs had jelled and I couldn't have moved even if a real bear had charged. The F- bomb flew from my mouth. I questioned Frank's sanity before but this removed all doubt. He had to be certifiable. Who draped a bear carcass over himself for a practical joke? And if he wasn't crazy, he was the biggest jerk on earth. I drew in a long breath as he dragged the bearskin with its attached head away from my car. I tested out my ability to walk and it seemed fine. As I headed to my car, I refused to make eye contact, and this seemed to humor him more. He guffawed now, wiping tears from his eyes.

My face felt so hot I thought I heard it sizzle. Words left my mouth, and I hardly recognized my voice. "You are not funny!"

He crossed his arms. "Well, I don't know about that. I was certainly entertained."

"Yeah." I stood by my front bumper unable to get to the driver's door without sliding by him. "That's what happens when no one wants to be around you."

His face changed from sunshine and lollipops to that of a clown with a cleaver. "It was a little joke. If you can't take a joke, maybe you shouldn't be working with patients *or* my mother."

And maybe you shouldn't be around other human beings. "Your mother and I get along great. And trying to scare someone to death is not a joke. It almost seems criminal."

When he squinted, all the skin on his forehead bunched together between his eyebrows, something I'd seen on a Star Trek episode.

Maybe I shouldn't have mentioned the criminal idea.

He stepped away from the car and swept his hand toward my door. "You know what's criminal?" He didn't want an answer. "You being such a tight ass. You and that preacher boy are perfect for each other."

Tinsel had obviously been talking. "We're friends. We don't try to make each other feel horrible, like *some* people I know."

"You're weirdos, that's what you are." He picked up the bear head and I noticed it took some effort with the hide still attached and hanging out of his arms. "Moving here from different parts of the country. That don't make you normal." He took a few side steps, dragging the hide along. "I've spent most of my days figuring how to get out of here. Not you." He pulled the animal a few more feet, its paws leaving marks in the dirt. "I'll come visit you one day after I've flown the coop." With that, he mustered enormous strength, turned, and dragged the bear hide away until he was out of sight.

With mixed feelings, I loaded the therapy bag in the car and slid behind the wheel, relishing an adrenaline-free moment. I wanted to hang on to how much I disliked him but with his parting words, now I felt sorry for him. I slowly backed out the car, then executed a twenty-eight-point turn, not wanting Tinsel to see me turn around in front of her house. She'd wonder where'd I'd been for ten minutes. I didn't want to explain how her son was a psycho most likely selling drugs. Christian had asked if I thought Tinsel was safe with Frank around and now I wondered. I'd seen a whole new side of him, a desperate side, and it didn't look good.

Farming It

"What happened to the goats?" Honey and I stood on her front porch, observing her once-green yard, now a moonscape with patches of sparse green, pushing up across its face.

She readjusted her hair in a clip at the back of her head. The day had turned hot and sultry, enhancing the scent of urine, dirt, and farm animals. "They're out in the woods." She pointed to the rolling hills of thick trees. "After they ate all of the damn grass, they just disappeared." She reached inside of her blue tank top and readjusted her bra. "I hear them in the trees so they haven't gone far."

"Traitors," I said, leaning against the chipped-paint railing, hoping Karl and Casey would be back soon. Honey had met me at the door, saying they'd gone to buy discarded vegetables from a grocer to lure the goats back into the yard. "They didn't like the newspaper diet?"

"About as much as I like ketchup on corn flakes."

I laughed. "How are you going to keep them here once the vegetables are gone?"

"Karl's gonna fence an area in."

Really? "Is he handy like that?"

She smiled and shrugged. "Not really." She pulled out her old cell phone from a bright pink bra and squinted at it. "If he stopped for a beer, I'm going to be mad."

"Well, yeah. Taking Casey into a bar isn't good."

She frowned. "I'd be pissed because he didn't take *me*. Casey's been in bars before."

"Good to know." I held back a parenting lecture—they never went over well—and turned the conversation to her. "How's your reading coming?" I asked, not wanting to know any more.

"Great. Just wonderful."

Her voice didn't match her words. I said, "What can I do to help you?"

She snorted. "Take me back to fifth grade when my brain was still fresh. I need a replacement now."

"How often do you practice?"

"That's the thing. With Karl home all of the mother-truckin' time now, my schedule for everything is thrown off."

By "everything," I knew she meant her daily dose of TV soaps and a tumbler of gin. "When does he go back to work?" I was anxious for that time, too. He made me nervous, and like today, I didn't have my little patient to work with.

"He's got scads of sick days left, but I hope to Christ he won't use them all."

"And he wouldn't like your idea of learning to read." She had said this before but it hadn't made sense. He should want her to improve herself.

Her face changed; she looked afraid. "I married a trucker for a reason. Karl is gone enough that he has no idea I can't read."

"Really?"

"Truly."

We both turned to the approaching sound of an engine. The black cab of Karl's big rig ground toward us. Casey was waving wildly, his face pressed up close to the windshield.

I hopped off the railing. "No seatbelt, huh?"

"Don't start."

"Just saying." I waited for the truck to stop and Casey to scramble down from the cab. I touched Honey's arm. "I'm bringing you some books on tape. Paired with the actual books, your reading will take off."

"I'm holding you to that, Marleigh." Within seconds Casey was wrapped around Honey's legs and our conversation shifted. She rubbed his thick hair. "What did you and daddy do?"

"I ee i-keem." He turned to me, grabbed my hand, and spun himself so he was wrapped up in my arm, snuggled close. The kid was high-energy cuteness.

I squeezed him to my side. "And we do know you like ice cream."

Karl yelled our way. "Honey. A little help here." He tugged black garbage bags from the cab area. When they hit the ground they flattened out, blasting the sound of rotten fruits and vegetables breaking open from inside.

Honey looked my way. "You two go work inside. I'll take care of Farmer Karl."

Once I had all the worksheets out, I focused on the early developing speech sounds Casey had never heard before getting his hearing aids. The /f/, /t/, /k/, and the /p/. All of these were voiceless sounds, meaning the vocal cords don't engage while these sounds are said. Their counterparts, /v/, /d/, /g/, and /b/, were made the exact same way but were voiced sounds. He'd learned these quickly.

After we practiced the "F" sound in pictures, I set out a deck of the picture cards face down. "Okay, Casey. We're going to make silly sentences. Say, 'In my pocket, I *found* a. ...' then choose one of these cards. I'll go first." I chose a card but didn't look at it, and said, "In my pocket, I found ..." then I showed him the card. "A foot."

He giggled. "A hoot," he said, still laughing.

"Say, 'ffffoot.'"

"Foot." He grabbed a card. "My hurn."

"Yes, your turn." We'd get to the /t/ sound soon enough. "Say the whole sentence first."

"In my pocket, I hound ..."

I tapped his arm. "Found. Make the mad cat sound at the beginning." I made my hands into claws in front of me and hissed with my top teeth on my bottom lip. "FFF."

"In my pocket, I fffound a ..." Then he held up the card and said, "A farm." He rolled off the chair onto the floor, giggling.

"A farm!" I played along. "You can't keep a farm in your pocket." I pulled him back into his chair and we finished saying thirty silly sentences. By the end of the session, he no longer needed the mad cat sound reminder. I packed up the therapy supplies as he chose a candy from my treat bag.

Glancing out of the large front window, I saw that Karl's solution was working. Goats had returned from the forest, gathering in small groups, eating from the piles of food randomly placed around the yard.

Casey and I walked out together, and stood by Karl and Honey on the porch. I broke the silence. "Casey did really well today."

Karl squinted my way, then turned to Casey. "What did you learn from your teacher?" He sounded annoyed to have to hear this.

I nudged Casey closer. "Tell your daddy one of the funny sentences we practiced."

Casey crammed his hand in his pocket and clearly enunciated, "I found a fishing pole in my pocket."

"The hell's he talking about?" Karl yanked his son's hand from his pocket then turned to me. "You teaching my kid to talk bad?"

His anger pushed me a step backward. "No. Um, we're working on the beginning F sound and 'fishing pole' was just one of the phrases we practiced." I hurried on. "We said lots of other words like 'frog,' 'fan,' and 'fence.'"

"Choose another sound." He pulled Casey behind him. "So far I am not impressed with anything you've done for this family."

Honey cleared her throat. "C'mon, Karl. Marleigh let us know about Casey's hearing loss. We had no clue."

He snorted. "She also let the law know about my collection of newspapers. Now we have this mess to deal with." He pointed to the garbage-strewn yard.

A warm breeze blew across the ground, ripe with the mixed scents of farm animals and decomposing food. And, yes, I had inadvertently led the police here two weeks ago. Then the Health Department got interested and Karl was told to clean out the stacks of newspapers or have the house condemned. "I'm sorry about that." I turned my attention to the yard and sighed. "And this, too." I picked up my bag and walked down a couple of sagging steps. "I'm excited about Casey's speech though. I hope you'll see the progress, too."

As I walked to the car, they debated behind my back whether or not I should be allowed to return. It sounded like Honey won as Karl shouted, "Fine, but if my kid says 'fuck' we'll know it's because of her."

Or maybe not.

I carefully drove around a cluster of goats, wondering what Karl would do once the garbage was gone. He'd made no attempt to add the newspapers to their lunch. It could be that I'd be seeing Casey in an entirely different location if things didn't change, although I hoped that wouldn't happen. I'd ask Lawyer if storing the papers away from the house, maybe in a steel shed, would solve the problem.

I didn't want to think of Lawyer. He and Veronica were on their drive to Philadelphia. Although I wanted to call him, I couldn't bring myself to do it. He had to *want* to talk to me. I needed him to call, not the other way around.

I drove by a vast farm. The barn and several outbuildings monopolized the center with a small farmhouse off to the side. Dirt roads formed tentacles, which like an octopus, extended out from the main barn, reaching up over the hills in all directions. Cutting through fields colored from dark green to mustard. Sleepy cows in one field, attentive horses in another. I could only imagine how hard being a farmer must be. I'd be terrible at that job. A couple of plants on my balcony in San Francisco kept me pretty busy, and I managed to kill a jade tree, a plant my neighbor said was extra hardy. Pretty sure I have a brown thumb.

The sprawling acreage seemed nothing short of optimistic. Farmers had to clutch onto a confidence that all the pieces would hold together, that the rains would come, that they'd remain devoted to the land.

When my phone rang, my heart skipped a beat and I smugly thought, *Lawyer.*

I glanced at the caller ID, and groaned while pulling the car to the side of the road because I couldn't drive and try to decipher butchered English at the same time. "Hi, Jaxson."

"What's the haps?"

"I'm working. One more stop to go." I thought I heard a chair squeak on his end. "What're you doing?"

"Just out in the world slaying it."

"You're not in your office?"

"At the moment I am. I ran that info you asked. About the taxidermist."

"Formalin Frank." The bearskin prankster. "Yeah. Anything interesting?"

"Shit the fuck yeah."

"Does that mean an extra big 'yes'?"

"Yuppers." He laughed. "The guy is elusive, doesn't have a lot of friends, and he drives hundreds of miles a week."

"I bet all that's true," I said. "But is there anything specific to drugs because I drive all over, too. Mileage wise, I probably get three quarters of a way to New York City each week."

"My girlfriend said he has a huge 'Keep Out' sign in front of his property."

Now this was shocking. Not the sign, but that Jaxson had a girlfriend. "Who's your girlfriend?"

He cleared his throat. "Ex-girlfriend. She threw shade at me in front of everyone…works over at the Bun and Brewster."

"Oh. I've never stopped in there but I've seen it."

"The squad's going running again tomorrow. Laying down a dozen if you're up to it."

I could use a long run, and I *was* friendly with some of the other members now so I wasn't just stuck with listening to him. "Tell me when and where."

After he told me, he said, "I'm hoping you can help us with Frank. You of all people have an excuse to get close to him, with seeing his mother ship and all."

"I'm not sure that will work. I'm not his favorite person."

"Look Marleigh. We have a problem here. We just busted a chicken coop house, heavy on the horse."

A large truck loaded with gravel blasted by and rocked my car. "What?" Suddenly I felt unsafe sitting along the road. I needed to get going.

"An apartment with drugs. Heroin."

"And what do you think I should do? Ask Frank to see his stash?"

"Not what I'm preaching. We need something to opinionate that he's a sus. See if he'll show you his taxidermy shop. Learn where the Formalin comes from."

Dare to see his little shop of horrors? "I'll see what I can learn but I'm not doing that." I checked the mirror and pulled onto the road.

"Just saying. You could help us stop the brown sugar express around here."

I sighed. Maybe I was wrong about Frank. "Jaxson, I mean it could be anyone, right? I met the preacher of The Little Church in the Pines. He's shipping bibles everywhere. I mean, c'mon. In movies, drugs always get shipped in bibles."

He was silent for a moment. "Too obvi but we can check him out for slag, too."

"See you tomorrow, Jaxson." I had no idea heroin had so many names. Or maybe it didn't. I should have gotten an assurance from Jaxson that he wouldn't mention Frank or Christian to the point where they might hear indirect buzz. I didn't want that to happen.

Thirty seconds later my phone rang again. Now I was annoyed with Jaxson and I didn't mind that it showed. I hit the answer button. "Look! You need to be chillaxing. The guy is totes cray, so I'll take my time getting to know him," I said.

"What?" Lawyer laughed but I also heard the concern there.

Crap. "I was just talking to the cop, Jaxson Mills. I thought it was him calling back and that's seriously how he talks."

"Yeah, I know that guy. Can't build a normal sentence to save his life. Who are you getting to know that's crazy?"

Lawyer knew everyone. "Frank Tabbish. The taxidermist."

"Because?" This was asked in that special tone of voice that implied anger.

"Jaxson said there was a heroin problem in the area, and something about it being cut with Formalin so I suggested looking at Frank."

"I suggest you stick to being a speech therapist and not getting involved." He drew in a long breath. "Especially if this guy is involved in drugs."

Lectures never sat well with me so I changed the subject. "What time will you be back tomorrow?"

"That's why I called. This could go a few more days than I thought."

Veronica. Working on her plan to win him back, no doubt. Might as well play along. Going for sexy, I said, "Oh, no. I was looking forward to alone time with you."

It sounded like he groaned. "I was looking forward to that, too. I need to make sure she's settled and then I'll be back. Hold those thoughts."

I smiled. "I'd rather hold you."

A car door slammed on his end of the line. I heard Veronica say, "Here's your drink."

To me, he said, "We'll talk soon," and then he hung up.

The feeling rising in my chest was jealousy, or *jelly* as Jaxson would say. And I didn't like it. I didn't want to miss people. I had enough people I already missed and one more seemed like one too many. I'd been focusing on the idea the worst was over in my life and better things were on the way. I was on a path of discovery, confident that I'd find relatives of my birthparents, that I'd belong to someone again.

I needed a lot of things, but not an emotional tug-of-war. My mood had soured. I had to whip my emotions back into shape before I got to Luella's house. They had enough problems without adding a grumpy therapist to their day.

A green Subaru sat in their usual parking spot when I arrived at Luella's. I pulled in next to it. A woman about forty sat in the driver's seat. When I turned off the car, she motioned for me to come around to her window. As I passed the back of her car, I read the bumper sticker—"Nurses can't fix stupid but they can sedate it." Rarely had I met my colleagues out at homes, so this was a nice surprise.

"Hi. I'm Marleigh." I stuck out my hand but she didn't reach for it. She wore her long hair in a braid, the auburn color shot through with blonde streaks. Around her neck was the same lanyard I wore, but she had several pens hooked onto the sides of it.

"I don't shake hands. MRSA and all that. I'm Maria Frederic. Welcome to our team."

"Thank you. I'm glad to meet another member. I know we also have a physical therapist, but I've never met him."

"Ray. You probably won't."

"Why's that?"

"He does what I call drive-by therapy. Barely spends five minutes with the patients. Not sure why they keep him."

"Wow. I couldn't rehab anyone in five minutes."

"Exactly." She lifted her chin toward Luella's house. "How are they doing?"

"Good. We've dropped down to one visit a week. Did you just finish with Luella?"

She said, "Nobody's home."

I looked at the house like it might explain why the homebound patient was not at home. "Any note?"

"Nope. I'm debating about reporting them."

They were already in trouble for having chickens inside. "Maybe we can give them a little wiggle room. Wait to see what happened."

She studied me with the kind of look that questioned a person's intentions. "We could. I was mainly checking back to see if they got rid of the chickens."

Now I remembered. This was the nurse who'd turned them in.

"They did," I said.

"Really?"

"Yup. Not in the house. They're out on the back porch now."

She nodded. "Well, good...you going to wait around and see if they get home?"

"I think I will." I pulled out my phone and looked at the time. "I've got a few more minutes."

She pulled a form from her bag, stuck it to a clipboard, and handed it out the window with a pen. "We just had a patient conference. If you'll sign here..." She stabbed the paper at the bottom with her index finger. "I can get paid."

I stalled. Was this legal? She seemed like a rule follower, but I hadn't heard we'd get paid for just talking to each other. I went for the joke. "Speaking of drive-by therapy."

She didn't laugh but pushed the clipboard closer. "I'll sign yours, too. No reason we can't help each other."

"I'll wait to see if I get my visit in." I'd ask Jake about charging for a patient conference when I got the chance, but for now I scribbled my name on her form.

"Thanks, Marleigh. I'll see you around."

I mumbled something about "the same here" as she pulled away.

Fifteen minutes passed, so I called Luella's phone and left a message. "Call me when you get home. I need to know you're okay." Luella had been in and out of the hospital for pneumonia. I really hoped that wasn't the reason they were gone, because that would mean I wasn't doing a very good job correcting her swallow.

On the drive home, I debated what to wear that afternoon when I met Elyk. Anticipating old buildings and hiking, I decided on running shoes with casual clothes.

EXPLORATION

"Have you eaten?" Elyk stood inside of his store, looking like a woodsman in his usual outfit of thick-soled boots, black jeans tucked inside, and a ratty olive-colored T-shirt that said, "Kiss me. I'm almost positive I'm not your cousin."

I rolled my eyes but smiled. "Nice message."

"Gotta keep up appearances."

"To answer your question. I ate at the Bed and Breakfast."

He handed me a white paper bag with a giant grease spot. "I want you to try this."

Inside lay a wedge of dark pie, wafting the warm scent of molasses and spice. "Mmmm. What is it?"

"I heard you tell someone you'd never had Shoo Fly Pie." He pulled a plate and fork from under the counter. "Now you can check that off your I'm-becoming-a-bumpkin list."

How thoughtful was this? I was touched, especially since I was usually the butt of his jokes. "Oh, yum. Thanks." I slowly ripped the bag until I could reach the heavy piece of pie and set it on the plate. "Split it with me?"

"Just a bite." He grabbed another fork and cut off the front of the wedge and popped it in his mouth. He opened his eyes wide as he chewed, then said, "Passable."

I'd be eating a lot more of this pie; it was that good. "Amazing."

He set a glass of water in front of me as I took the last piece. In the middle of the soft pie, I bit into something crunchy. I gagged and spit into a napkin; whatever it was had wings. A large black fly landed in the napkin. "What the hell, Elyk?"

His face brightened for just a second. "Don't blow lunch or anything. The fly's fake but this here's *real* Shoo Fly Pie."

"Um, that was mean."

"You mean it was funny. Had it been a real fly, now that would have been mean." He was packing up his wallet and grabbing car keys. "You need to stay alert. The fly was right there if you'd looked," he said, shaking his head.

"Any other surprises in store for me?"

He stopped, seeming to consider my words. "I was done for the day but now you have me thinking." He gave me a friendly pinch on the arm. "C'mon. Daylight's wasting."

"It's not dark for five hours." Surely, we wouldn't be in the camp that long.

"I gotta be back before six when people are *hangry* and need food." He flipped the sign on the door to 'Closed' and locked up.

I climbed into his pickup and fastened my seatbelt.

We rode in silence for a bit before I asked what he knew about Christian Betts.

"He's been here for a few months. He's popular because he's young, laid-back, not all that righteous attitude."

"I've met him. That's a good description...I heard the last minister just died in his sleep."

Elyk's brows bunched, like caterpillars running headlong into each other. "They figured a stroke. Took them months to find the next sucker who'd want to take over that job."

"But that's strange, right? Who'd want a job in a rural area, especially when they were from the city?"

"You sound suspicious of him."

"Don't you think Christian could possibly be the guy selling drugs?"

"Naw. The drugs just started showing up, but he's been here for three months." He flipped on the turn signal and pulled onto a smaller road that veered to the left. Trees pressed in, pushing out the sunlight. "He's ripping people off with that hefty tithing. Asks for twenty percent or some outrageous shit like that."

"He's sending bibles to Africa."

"What a great gift when you're starving and sick."

I laughed. "Good point."

Then I saw the sign: "West Trout Run 2 miles." The rutted, one-lane dirt road had us creeping downhill into three tight switchbacks. I had both hands on the dashboard to keep myself in the seat as we reached the bottom, crossing a narrow wooden bridge painted red, a stark contrast to the dark green tunnel of trees ahead. We bumped over the wooden slats, riding through the short tunnel before exiting the woods. A wide river on the left threw up white caps. A small gravel area on the right served as a parking lot. We got out of the car and crossed to another graying sign that read: West Trout Run, Lumberman's Camp, 1847–1932. I snapped a few photos of the sign, the river, and the town. A newer sign below showcased an official notice covered in Plexiglas. Despite the protection, the edges had yellowed and the words were blurred. This wasn't a national park.

A hundred yards past the sign, dangerously uninhabitable shacks presented sagging roofs and walls, decayed like some forest giant had been gnawing at them.

Elyk pointed to the Plexiglas notice. "Says there used to be sixty houses, a Methodist church, and even a hotel. A hopping place."

I moved closer to read the sign. A brief historical outline touted Pennsylvania as one of the largest producers of
lumber from colonial times to the early twentieth century.
What started with white ash and pine soon turned to hemlock. The name "woodhick" was given to the men working
in these lumber camps—from the log drivers and peelers to
the grabbers and sawyers.

I tapped the Plexiglas. "So saying 'he's a hick' isn't really
derogatory."

Elyk smiled. "Right. You should walk up to somebody
today and call 'em a hick." He pointed toward the abandoned structures. "Let's go see if we can find somebody for
you to insult."

The rushing river roared behind us while the gravel
crunch of our feet grew louder as we approached the ghost
town. The buildings on the outskirts had long ago succumbed
to the advancement of the forest, but the center of town still
maintained clear paths. I snapped a few more pictures.

"I sure as hell didn't come here to go to church," Elyk
said, referring to the church steeple rising behind a sunken
grocery store. "But I'm betting there's juicy rattlers in there.
Follow me."

"Crap. You know how much I love rattlers," I said.

"I do. As much as I love clothes shopping."

We circled several collapsed buildings.

"I mentioned my client. I'm not sure I should bring her
here tomorrow," I said, thinking out loud. "I mean. It's not
like this is the town she'd remember. Coming here might be
more traumatizing than helpful."

Elyk ignored me and charged ahead. "Whatever. You're
the speech whisperer." He headed toward the church.

In Methodist fashion, the church had a set of wide stairs
leading up to double doors. Above, rose the steeple with

a bell in the top of the tower and the narrow face of the church had a tall window on each side of the door. The exterior was spotted where worn, once-white paint allowed gray, rotted wood sections to peek through.

Expecting the door to squeal, I was surprised by how quietly it opened. We crossed the threshold and stood inside in the dimness. Soft amber light fell onto the wooden pews from five windows on each side.

I breathed deeply. The sluggish air was musty, full of mold, dust, and rodent droppings. "I like this smell, but I don't know why."

Elyk's face twisted into a smile. "You're weird," he said, then sniffed the air. "I'm getting a whiff of something dead."

We were whispering as the setting seemed to demand it. He continued, "Maybe not everyone left the camp all those years ago."

"Like there're catacombs filled with skulls in the basement?" I knocked my shoulder gently into his bicep.

A thrashing sound echoed off the back wall behind the altar and stopped us. Something was hitting the walls and scratching on the floor.

Elyk headed that way. I grabbed his arm to stop him.

"Wait. It could be a bear."

"Or a lion or tiger. Oh My! Dorothy... I'm thinking it's the rattler of the century eating his dinner, and my lucky day!"

"Be serious. This is bear country and that sounds like something big back there."

"K, you're as clueless as Stevie Wonder with an Etch-A-Sketch." He moved down the center aisle before I followed.

I kept trying to forget this town was listed in the book, *The Ghost Towns of Northern Pennsylvania.* Having a huge guy by my side and not on the other side of the church, no matter what was making that noise, seemed prudent.

We passed through a door, opening into a hallway. Small rooms were off to each side. At the end of the hallway, a portion of the back wall was missing, revealing a hole large enough for a man to slip through. The sounds got louder. Elyk seemed to really think it was his lucky day, which eased my anxiety. He snapped his fingers toward me. "Give me your phone."

"Why?" I slowly pulled it from my pocket.

He reached for it and illuminated the flashlight, shining it into the space. At first nothing happened, then a deer scrambled from the darkness and bolted out of the opening in the wall.

"Whoa!" I jumped backwards, grabbing my chest.

He cursed, then peered into the space and turned to me. "See how wrong you were?"

"Like you guessed right."

"There's probably a rattler down. But it stinks and I'm not interested."

I stood next to him. A set of wooden steps dropped down into complete darkness. "Yeah, count me out."

We turned to explore the rest of the church. One wall had a chiseled plaque inscribed with twenty-five Articles of Religion. We ducked into the minister's small sanctuary, which had been stripped of everything but a wooden altar and a few loosely placed candle stubs. Another room looked like it had been for storage, and another room at the end of the hallway was locked. Elyk cupped his hands to the beveled glass section in the center of the wooden door. "Can't go through here. Looks like a private room."

"I want to see." I stood on tiptoe and tried to peer through the dusty glass but all I saw was the ceiling. "Give me a boost," I said turning to him.

"Nope. Not touching anybody's ass except Dottie's."

"Yes, please don't, big guy. Make a sling with your hands."

He linked his hands together and I stepped into them as he said, "Why don't you get Lawyer to give you a *boost?* He seems willing."

I blushed as I stared down at him. "Yes, in fact, we're working on that." I looked back to the window to end the subject.

Inside the room were wooden racks along one wall with long strings hanging down and a wooden table, holding dozens of wooden molds and large vats. A small fireplace was at the other end. A candlemaking operation. "Funny, this is the only door actually locked."

"Weird." He lowered me and pointed toward the hallway. "And disappointing. Let's ditch the dungeon."

I was happy to "ditch the dungeon" having already become a little spooked. Then we explored the bunkhouse. Its long building must have slept dozens of men in bunks or on cots. Broken potbellied stoves sat in the center aisle every thirty feet, and crooked hooks hung along the walls for their clothes. Most of the houses had fallen in on themselves and only the front façade of the store remained, propped up from the back like a movie set in an old Western.

We'd fallen into a comfortable silence now, interested in our own details of discovery. On the way back to the car, he grabbed my shoulder to stop me, then pointed to the ground. "Dorothy! That's a red-spotted newt." Across the trail, skittered a bright orangish-red newt with darker red spots on its back outlined in black.

"Stop calling me Dorothy. I'm not even from Kansas. And you're no Wizard. But that is a beautiful newt, if you can call a newt beautiful." I slowly leaned a tiny bit closer to get a better look. I didn't want it leaping toward my throat; I'd seen documentaries.

"You should pick it up," he said. "It will change color in your hands."

"Really?" I bent down to reach for the tiny creature when he quickly yanked me back.

"Just shitting you. That thing is completely venomous."

"Next time remind me that I should never, ever go into the woods with you."

"No, I'm really done. I swear. It's really too easy with you."

"So it's my fault that you do this?"

His face said he was anxious not to have me upset with him. "Sorry, no. I'm just pissed we didn't find the holy grail of rattlers."

Once we were in the car, he backed out and we headed up the steep road and back across the bridge. I'd decided after all to bring Sofie here for a visit. We'd only go inside the bunkhouse building and church. She was healthy enough to walk the same paths Elyk and I walked today. I'd get Jon's permission and we could come together. I waited until we pulled onto the paved road once again before speaking. "Thanks Elyk. I'm glad you were with me."

"Glad you asked. Haven't thought of that place for a while. Imagine the crazy shit that happened there back in the day. Cutting down trees all day, dragging them down to the river. Living deep in the woods. No Internet or phones...Actually, I'm thinking I was born during the wrong era."

"They probably had crossword puzzles."

He shrugged. "But it only had synonyms for lumber."

Twenty minutes later, after Elyk rambled aloud the whole time about what it must have been like to live in West Trout

Run, I unbuckled my seatbelt in front of his store, grabbed my purse from under the seat, and said, "Thanks for the Shoo Fly Pie. Delicious, fly and all."

"You're welcome."

I opened the door and got out as he also exited his side. As he walked toward his store and I walked toward my car and dug out my keys, I said, "Tell Dottie 'hi.' "

I drove away, wondering why I counted him as a friend when he could be so infuriating. But I knew what it was. Deep down inside that big guy was a whole lot of kindness and caring. And there was no way he'd ever be boring.

I passed a billboard that hadn't meant much to me until just now. The Bark Peelers' Convention was ten days away. Held in Hummock, a small town that boasted a large lumber museum. The sign announced the dates of the July 4th weekend and listed out the events: greased pole climbing, log rolling, apple pie bake-off, and woodhick skills. Lawyer had teased me about learning these skills for the event. I'd replied that wasn't funny *haha* but no, thanks, I have no interest in going. Now, after seeing West Trout Run, I didn't know how I could refuse.

When I reached the B&B, Milt was relaxing in a lawn chair in a shady patch of lawn under the wide reach of the catalpa tree. He watched me as I crossed the yard, not waving or otherwise acknowledging me. As I got closer, I smiled. "How are you, handsome?"

He stared my way for a moment, but then his lips pinched together. He made a noise like a cough and said, "I joke again." He reached into his shirt pocket and pulled out a folded sheet of paper, his gnarled hand holding it my way.

I scanned the sheet. He had printed off a page of jokes.

"These are good. Which one do you want to learn first?" I asked.

I leaned down and let him study the page. He pointed to one in the middle. I read it aloud. "What do you get when you cross a pickle with a female deer? A dill d—" I shot a look his way. "Milt! We are *not* doing this joke."

If a wrinkled apple could look mischievous, that's what I saw on his face. He slowly reached for the paper, studied it again, and pointed to another line. I glanced at it. "Okay. That's better." I dropped down onto the grass next to his chair. "We can try this out tonight with the new guests. Have you met them?"

His intense stare said he had something to say. I waited. When nothing came out I probed. "They have a mean kid with them?"

He touched his mouth.

"They can't speak? They talk too much?"

He rubbed his hands on his legs. I was about to get an answer. "Woof woof."

I cocked my head. "They have a dog?"

He touched his mouth again.

"They talk like dogs?"

He sagged. I felt terrible.

"I'm sorry. I'm sure it will make sense when I meet them, Milt."

His gaze dropped to his hands, two claws hooked together in his lap.

I leaned toward him and cupped his hands in mine, the thin skin barely covering what felt like baby bird bodies. Frail bones with little tissue between them.

"Your joke. Let's get practicing."

When he straightened his posture, I was relieved. My job was to make people feel happy about their attempts to speak. I was a speech pathologist, not a speech *sadologist*. I needed to double my efforts in trying to understand Milt.

SEARCHING

It was an hour before dinner started and all the guests had returned from rafting Piney Creek and were showering. I passed them in the hallway as I headed to Richard's office, but got no "dog" hint from them as we introduced ourselves.

I had an idea. As I logged onto the Internet, I wondered why I had not thought of this before. I researched Witness Security Program and came up with the link I needed: How to drop off the face of the earth. I believed that seeing the process the Kingstons had gone through to change their location, their names, and jobs, I'd try to backtrack to the time before they had witnessed the "bad thing." Bad things were defined as observing a crime committed by organized crime or racketeering, drug trafficking offenses, or a federal felony in which the witness has been threatened with violence for speaking out. Daryl and Amber had seen one of those activities in Pittsburgh, and through an order by the U.S. Attorney General, they'd been turned over to the Marshals Service. It hadn't occurred to me, but Scott Schumer's service had screwed up, in the end offering no protection for them. And they must have seen danger heading their way, or they wouldn't have put me up for adoption just four days before they died.

Heaviness settled in my chest and I felt tears prick my eyes. If the Kingstons had been successful in starting over,

I wondered what my life would have been like. Raised in a rural town, in the east instead of the west, in the mountains instead of by the ocean. It was hard to know. I read more from the website. The Kingstons would have signed a Memorandum of Understanding, verifying they understood the rules of the program. Maybe Scott could find that form and the original agent assigned to my parents' case. One of the key objectives of the Witness Security Program is that the Marshals Service would help witnesses assimilate into their new communities and become self-sufficient. Among other things, this required assistance with securing employment, like obtaining one reasonable job opportunity for each witness. The Marshals also provided assistance in finding housing, provided subsistence payments on average of $60,000 per year, and made up new identity documents.

I read further and found an interesting comment. "Witnesses are advised to keep their current initials or same first name." What if the Kingstons had done just that, kept their first names or initials? I opened another website, The Seeker.com. Its slogan was, *"If you can't find your missing friends or relatives through The Seeker, they have left the planet."* This was the case with both sets of my parents, but maybe not with my birth grandparents. Daryl and Amber Kingston had died young, twenty-seven and twenty-five respectively. Fast-forward to now and their parents could be age sixty-five to seventy-five, and still alive.

After I created an account, I put in Daryl and Amber's birthdates and pushed, "Find."

"No results found" popped up and I shrugged. That was a long shot since those were their witness protection names, but I had to try. So I searched a Pittsburgh database for Daryl K. and Amber with their separate birthdates. Knowing my mother's maiden name would have been so helpful to me and to anyone looking for her. It would be a secret that the original agent would have in his file; it created total anonymity for my mother. The site spun and searched while I chewed my thumbnail down to nothing.

My heart skipped a beat when five names appeared for "Daryl K." All with his birthday, all within the Pittsburgh area. Nothing showed up for Amber. When I tried to click further on the names, the site blocked me. I began to imagine reunions again with Daryl's family because, although I couldn't search these names, I expected Marshal Schumer could get this information without much effort.

As I dialed his number, my hand trembled. Could it be this easy? I might be within days of having answers. The phone went to voicemail. My message said I wanted to meet him the next afternoon and that I had some new information about the Kingstons, and he should call me back as soon as possible.

I left the office and bounded down the back steps to the kitchen, looking for Rose and Richard. I followed the metallic clangs, coming from the backyard where Richard was tossing horseshoes. The metal shoes found their mark, toss after toss. I approached his side. "Do you ever miss?"

He wiped his hands on a gray cloth and stuck it in his back pocket. "If I close my eyes I'm not too good." He headed to the other end of the pit. "Want to throw a few?"

I'd toss boulders at the moment, I was so energized. "Sure."

He handed me two horseshoes and returned to the other end. "You go first."

I threw the first shoe, and it somersaulted through the air, a novice's toss, landing once and bouncing toward Richard's leg. He stepped back just in time. I flinched. "Sorry."

He laughed. "No harm, no foul. Keep your throw to one smooth movement and point your open hand toward the stake when you release."

My second pitch didn't tumble in the air this time, but it landed four feet short and slid across the sand. "Not bad." Richard retrieved them, then took a professional stance beside the stake and tossed his horseshoe. It sailed smoothly through an eight-foot-high arc before dropping open-end-first onto the stake. There was a sharp *clink* as the shoe encircled it. "A ringer!" he said as if this had never happened to him before. A few moments later, the second shoe landed on top of the first one.

I whined. "A double ringer...I should have asked for a few points, like in golf." I picked up the horseshoes and headed his way.

He snapped his fingers. "Hey. What did the drunk golfer say when he saw the results of his Breathalyzer test?"

I shrugged. "I don't know."

"I had no idea there was so much blood in my alcohol system."

I laughed. "Good one. If you have a second I wanted to tell you my good news. Well, I think it's good news."

He stopped cleaning the horseshoes and squinted my way. "And I thought you just wanted my company."

"Well. There was that, too." I didn't wait for him to answer. "I was searching the Internet and may have found my birthfather before he changed his name and moved to Butterfield."

Richard let out a low whistle. "That is the best news. Rose and I say all the time that we hope you find some part of your family."

"I know. I feel like I'm close now." The smile on my face wouldn't subside so I left it there.

Richard put his hand on my back. "Rose will want to hear this." He nudged me to the kitchen door. Inside, she was tying on a red apron, getting ready for the next wonderful meal. I explained what I'd told Richard and she stepped forward to hug me. "If you find relatives—"

I stopped her. "*When* I find relatives."

"We'll invite them here for the reunion."

I hugged her this time. "You're so nice. Thank you."

A guy rapped his knuckles on the open doorway. "Am I interrupting?"

Richard waved him in. "Marleigh, this is James Bangor. He and his wife Allegra will be here for the evening."

James was a small man, wiry with a black goatee but no mustache. An Amish look, except he wore bright blue pants and a pink golf shirt.

We shook hands and I asked him where they were from.

"Outside of Lincoln. Small town, farm area." He turned just as his wife stepped into the room. "Baby, this is Marleigh."

Allegra was taller than her husband by two inches, possibly five feet ten. Her turquoise-colored eyes and bright pink lipstick stood out against a great tan. Dressed fashionably in a skirt and strappy striped top, I got no *dog* vibe from either she or her husband. Maybe Milt had misunderstood who they were. "My pleasure. How was your river run today?"

"Amazing," James said. "The scenery here is astounding for flatlanders like us."

"It is beautiful, isn't it? I'm actually from San Francisco, staying the summer. I need to do that river run before I leave, though. I hear it's pretty spectacular."

Allegra pushed a strand of short brown hair behind her ear. Her silver earring had a small dangling dog at the bottom. "We even floated past two ghost towns."

Richard turned from the sink where he was washing his hands. "Tiaghmonda and West Trout Run, right?"

"Oh, wow," I said. Of course, the river along the town would be navigable. That's where the logs had been sent downriver. "I was at West Trout Run today."

All eyes turned my way but Richard spoke first. "You were?"

"Yes. I went with Elyk."

Richard studied me. "Why'd you go there?"

"I was intrigued because one of my patients has been talking about the old lumber towns. Elyk is always good company so we made the trip together."

Richard and Rose exchanged a look that was full of questions; probably, what about your fireman boyfriend?

"I had some free time since Lawyer drove his friend back to Philadelphia."

"Oh, okay." Rose opened the oven and peeked inside before closing it again.

Allegra's eyes brightened. "That was the first place we passed on the river. Did it seem haunted to you?"

"No." I laughed. "A deer running in one building startled us, but no ghosts."

"Was there a cemetery?" James pulled his wife closer. "We love exploring old ones."

Strange, there must have been one there. "We didn't see one. But we also didn't stay that long either."

Rose turned to Richard. "Why don't you walk the kids up to our cemetery? Marleigh and I can get dinner ready."

They left, Richard already explaining how their inn had been a mortuary in the late 1800s. I asked Rose how she was feeling and she said her hip was better.

While Rose prepared the pork medallions, I peeled and chopped parsnips, carrots, rutabagas, and turnips. I thought of my California mom. "I used to make parsnip and carrot fries with my mom when my dad was out of town."

Rose said, "I've never made those. What do you use?"

"Just olive oil, salt, pepper, and dill." I laughed. "My dad hated most vegetables so my mom and I cooked vegetarian when he left." Suddenly, my throat stuck on the thought we'd never cook together again. Letting the echo of those final words fall silent, I felt my chin quiver. I missed them terribly and having a buffer of two thousand miles from all that happened there had helped. But maybe, it was also that there was a limit to what the mind could or would absorb at any given time. I could recall so much from the week leading up to my parents' deaths, but after and for eight weeks until graduation, I had only fuzzy memories. Nothing specific I could force into focus. Their friends came and went, some awkward, some with too much to say. Others offered how time would heal the pain. Those were the worst visits. How did they know my pain? No one can tell another person how they will feel in a week, or in a month.

Rose had washed her hands and was at my side. "It must be hard, Marleigh. You've lost so much."

I swiped tears from my cheeks with the back of my hand. "It's weird. It hits me in waves." I pointed to the vegetables. "Over the simplest of things, like a stupid parsnip."

Rose smiled. "But just think. You are closer than ever to finding your first family."

"I am." I drew in a long breath. "I'm excited about that."

We melded our cooking efforts and put the large casserole dishes in the oven to bake and then turned our attention to setting the table. Rose said, "Your work with Milt is paying off. I heard him outside while I was hanging laundry and he said some phrases I hadn't heard before."

That made me smile. "Like what?"

"Well, he said he loved jokes, and wanted a drink and then there was some stuff that made no sense." She shrugged. "Something about pickles and deer."

I cleared my throat, hoping he hadn't spoken the punch line. "He's saying a lot more, isn't he? And, if it's okay, he's going to tell another joke at dinner."

"Perfect. He's happier these days."

Everyone returned and got washed up and seated for dinner. James and Allegra continued to discuss the history of the area with Richard as we passed the food around. Before clearing the table and preparing for dessert, I asked the couple what they did for a living.

Milt grabbed my leg and his eyes grew larger. I leaned closer assuming he was ready for his joke. "Right after this, okay?"

James wiped his mouth and dropped his napkin in his lap. He turned to Rose. "Do you mind if we discuss this at dinner?"

She waved the question away. "No topics are off limits in our home."

James smiled, directing his answer to me. "We test dog food."

I wasn't sure why this was a bad topic. "Like in a lab for bacteria and other bad ingredients?"

"No." Allegra laughed. "We taste-test dog food."

Something climbed to the back of my throat, and Milt touched my leg as if to say I told you so. Speechless, I let her go on.

"We're just like the people who are hired by companies to taste-test items produced and sold to grocery stores for humans, but we're paid to taste-test new formulas for pets before those products hit the market."

"Paid quite well," James added.

"I would think so." Rose's face held her usual agreeable look, but I noticed she'd pushed her plate away.

I looked back and forth from husband to wife. "Do you ever get sick?"

James chuckled. "We spit out the food before swallowing it. Well, most times we do. And, really after a few good chews of the food or treat, you get a nice idea about flavor, and if a dog will find it agreeable."

I was grossed out. "I have to hand it to you. You seem to like what you're doing."

Allegra said, "We met working in a lab, testing car safety. Now our job is fun, rooms full of dogs, and we really can see that what we are doing matters."

Richard cleared his throat. "That's what's important."

I helped clear the table and we brought in the vanilla bread pudding with cinnamon syrup. The spicy warm scent helped settle my stomach, and as soon as we finished eating, I addressed Milt. "Are you ready?"

He stared my way, saying nothing. I turned to the table. "We have a new joke for you. Did you hear about the guy who got his left arm cut off?"

I pointed toward Milt in a *take-it-away* motion but he said nothing. We all waited, smiles stuck on our faces. I knew the signs that he was about to speak and he wasn't making any of those movements either. When it became clear he wasn't going to answer, I said, "We're going to keep you in suspense until a later date."

My gaze caught Rose's and I lifted my eyebrows as if to say *I have no clue.*

The guests thanked Rose for dinner and headed out to the back porch to play card games. The east-facing screened-in porch was perfect this time of night, cooling down but offering a sweeping view of the backyard. A jigsaw puzzle was always in progress and the room had shelves full of games.

I turned to Milt. "What's wrong?"

He stared at me. Finally, he said, "Don't know."

"New words!" I patted his leg. "Milt, you are saying so much more now. What don't you know?"

"Not real." He dropped his eyes and studied his hands on the table.

What was he trying to tell me? "Can you explain?"

He rubbed his hands on the tablecloth, slowly pushing it together, then flattened it out. "Gratuitous laugh."

I rocked back in my chair and laughed. "Whoa! A million dollar word." He didn't look up so I hoped I hadn't hurt his feelings. "I think I know what you're saying. You think these jokes are just getting you gratuitous laughs and you don't like it."

He barely bobbed his head.

"The jokes are actually funny but let's not do them if that's how you feel."

"Family." He looked toward the kitchen.

Now that I thought about it, I'd trained him like a circus monkey to do a trick on command at the dinner table. "Want to go tell your joke to Rose and Richard?"

He slowly pushed himself upright, which I took as a "yes." I followed along beside him, slowly traversing the room. Once in the kitchen I got the innkeepers' attention. "Okay, guys. Did you hear about the guy who got his left arm cut off?"

In chorus, they said "no" at the same time and Rose rubbed her hands nervously.

Milt looked at them and said, "He's all right now."

Their laughter was genuine and I saw that this sincerity registered on Milt's face.

I left them alone in the kitchen, pleased that he was suddenly saying so much. I couldn't take all the credit for this. It just seemed like he was finally ready to start talking again. Back in Richard's office, I caught up on my neglected social media. I'd been off every site for weeks, not feeling all that social. Now I quickly looked at friends' posts, pictures, and chats but didn't respond. They were spread around the country, some in new jobs, some on internships but none of them looking for their dead parents' pasts. I couldn't relate at the moment.

I uploaded a few of the West Trout Run photos to Snapchat and Instagram with the title, Hauntingly Beautiful. Then I started a new board on Pinterest labeled "Pennsylvania." I moved landscape and countryside pins in there from a few other people's accounts and added a few of my recent pictures.

My cell rang, and although I hoped it was Lawyer, I was thrilled to see Scott Schumer's number. He got right to the point. "You've been doing some sleuthing?"

"I have. I read that people in the protection program will often keep their original initials or their first name. I ran the name Daryl K with his birthday in the Pittsburgh area and I got five matches with addresses. I was hoping you could get more information since I couldn't."

He was quiet for a moment. "Let's meet and talk. What time tomorrow?"

"How about two … do you want the addresses now?"

"Sure."

I read them off and he repeated them back, and we hung up. I was annoyed that he wasn't as excited as I was, although he had never been anything but neutral when we'd talked.

But I wanted someone to be excited. I dialed Lawyer's number. It occurred to me I hadn't asked where he'd be staying. Were they in a hotel room together? At Veronica's apartment? Maybe I didn't want to know. His phone went to voicemail. "Hey, handsome. I hope your trip is going as planned. Give me a call when you can. I have some good news to share."

I logged out of the computer and tidied up the desk. Just as I stood, Richard poked his head in the door. "Guess what?" He looked concerned.

"I have no idea."

"The Sheriff is bringing the Diffleys back. They should be here in an hour."

"Sounds like the experiment didn't go too well."

Richard paused, then said, "They're returning without Beers. He wandered off the second day and they haven't seen him since."

The Hair of the Dog

"You found nothing in the boxes?" Jaxson and I were on the long slope of a hill, six miles into the run, so my words came out in short phrases. The rest of the group—just five people—hung back because he had asked to speak with me alone. I hated that they might think we had a personal relationship.

"Bibles. The preacher's shipping bibles." Jaxson clapped his hands together. "My chief was pissed...we even went to the effort."

"I warned you I'm...no good at this." It took a few seconds to catch my breath. "I'm not...the person that you want...to check out Frank."

"We're interested in him." He drew in a long breath. "Show curiosity. Get out to his shop...and see what it's all about." He rolled his eyes. "Find locked doors. Things he gets squirrely about."

"Have you met this guy? Squirrelly's not only his occupation...it's probably his middle name."

We crested the hill and I was relieved to see a gentle grade sloping down into the next valley. Running downhill on a steep grade burned out your legs almost as fast as churning uphill. "If he's as big a drug runner as you suspect, I'm sure this is not a good idea."

"We're kind of despo here. We have another day blazer who's now dead. Some sus is selling pure skag to naïve locals and it's rockin' the cradle." He looked over his shoulder. "You ever feel like you're in danger, text 'Sunshine Superman' and I'll know you're in trouble."

I snorted. "I'd be dead before I get that typed ... and this just verifies that what you're asking IS too dangerous."

"Okay. Just text 'cake.' "

"Cake?" I laughed. "And you will know how and where to help me with that one word?" I slowed down to wait for the others. "Let's forget about this, okay? I'm no good at being sneaky."

He was interrupted from saying anything further as the group caught up to us. To stop all questions about our relationship, I turned to Jaxson but made sure everyone heard, "I'll ask my boyfriend about that when he gets back."

Jaxson scowled, picked up his pace, moving out of sight like a tennis ball swatted out of the court. No one tried to catch him, which I found interesting. By the time we'd finished, he'd calmed down, congratulating everyone on a successful twelve miles, or in his words a "fruitful ninety-six furlongs."

On my drive back to Tungston, my car's tires parted the shifting fog in the low-lying areas, and at times I lost sight of the road. Trees emerged upward from a wavering white blanket, their bases lost in the light murkiness.

Showered and back on the road toward Beryl's, the wind had picked up, and giant white clouds stampeded overhead. Richard warned there was rain on the way. No one had heard from Beers and the prediction of an approaching storm did nothing to calm his parents' worries. The Sheriff's Department and Search and Rescue had reached the Diffleys' camping spot at first light, confident they'd have him back by midday.

Beryl didn't answer the door when I knocked. I held my breath and listened. His voice, gruff and stern, came from the back of the house. I headed that way wondering who he was talking to.

Just before I turned the corner, he growled, "Stay there!" Was he talking to me? Alerting me to some danger? I peeked around the side of his house and then laughed. Beryl was seated on an upturned grate. He had one arm around The Dog who was trying to escape a set of buzzing electric shears. Half of his body was shaved; the pile of thick gray and white fur lay around Beryl's feet. He had explained how he shaved The Dog every year and gave the fur to Ivory. She spread it around her garden to keep the raccoons out of her corn.

The Other Dog sat patiently a few yards away, his head cocked toward me as I crossed the lawn. "Is it always this hard?" I approached The Other Dog and let him sniff my hand before petting him. He leaned into my leg so I could scratch the length of his back.

Holding the shears in front of him, he said, "Usually people help me instead of asking dumb questions." He dipped his head toward The Dog. "Come hold him a minute."

The man had two settings: demanding and bossy. "I'll be covered in hair. I have people to see all day."

"Well, I've got a lint roller you can use right after you help me." He made a hurry-up motion with the electric shears.

I let out a long breath, set my bag by The Other Dog, and walked a few steps toward him. Kneeling down, I held the shaved side of The Dog close to me as he sniffed my neck and face. I spoke baby talk to the animal. "Yes, I know. Your daddy is so mean."

"He can't hear you."

I could smell the faint aroma of scotch in the stream of Beryl's words. That worried me. He'd been drunk the night of his accident. Drinking during the day said something, but I wasn't going to bring it up.

Beryl shaved long paths down the side of the dog. Peels of fur fell away, curling to the ground.

"But *you* can." I smiled. "Actually, you're a good guy. I like teasing you."

He moved the shears around the dog's neck but left his face untouched.

"He'll look like a lion," I said.

Beryl set down the shaver and grabbed a brush, gently going over the areas he had cut, removing stray fur. "It grows back fast."

I tipped my head toward The Other Dog. "These two guys still getting along?"

"Best of friends." He finished the job and we let The Dog go.

The Dog threw himself on the grass, sliding around on his side and then stood and shook himself. Beryl's face softened, the affection for his dogs evident. The Other Dog carefully approached the new skinny creature. Once he'd sniffed him and recognized him as his friend, they took off running together.

Beryl handed me a large black lawn and leaf bag. "One more thing." I held it open while he stuffed the fur inside. He packed away the shears and brush in a barber kit. "You carry these and I'll get the bag."

I reached for the small box and my therapy bag. "Then we work, right?"

He grabbed the bag and I followed behind as he slowly dragged it to the front of the house, stopping beside the driveway near my car. "Pop the trunk," he said.

I huffed and planted my feet. "Why me? Just have Ivory come and get it."

"Because she said she's seeing you today."

I let my head drop back. No wonder the Kingstons got discovered hiding out in this area. There were no secrets anywhere. I clicked my key fob and the trunk opened. He stuffed the large bag inside and closed the lid. "See? That wasn't so hard." Then he gave me his crooked smile. "Let's go work."

He called the dogs using the vibrating device and we all trundled into the front door. The dogs headed to their water bowls and drank loudly before choosing the couch to settle on. Beryl washed his hands at the sink.

I pulled his chart from the bag. "Have you been doing your exercises?"

"Religiously."

He took the chair at the table and I sat across from him. "Okay. Show me your stuff."

He correctly ran through all ten sets of the swallowing and strengthening exercises. Twenty minutes of practice. "Nice." I made notes in the chart. "Have you choked on any liquids lately?"

"Nope."

I wrote more. "I think you are almost ready for whole foods again, but still, cut your food small, into tiny pieces, or grind up the meat first."

I added one more exercise to his list—a dry swallow. "Hold the tip of your tongue between your front teeth and swallow. The goal is to get three swallows in a row but it can be quite hard." I demonstrated. "You try."

He completed one, his throat muscles working extra hard before he quit. Gruffly, he said, "Don't like an audience. I'll do it later."

"Perfect." The man was ex-military tough, yet this simple exercise was too hard. I'd let him have his dignity.

We confirmed our next visit and stood. My clothes were covered in hair. "Oh, yeah. Could I borrow that lint brush?"

He left the room, hanging on to walls at first, then he steadied himself. His walker remained folded by the front door. Another statement of his dignity. If he could get around without it, he would. Cupboards opened and closed, a doorknob turned, muffled rummaging sounds came from a closet. He returned a moment later and shrugged. "Seems I don't have one."

"What?" I pointed to my black skinny pants and red top. "I can't go into other people's houses this way."

He thought for a moment, walked to a drawer, pulled out a dishcloth and ran it under the tap water. He handed it my way. "Rub it around in circles. It'll come off."

I sighed but accepted the cloth. The hair balled up into wads that were easy to pick off, but some errant fur refused to be lifted. I was going to be late for my appointment with Sofie if I picked off every hair. "Thanks." I handed back the cloth. "Next time warn me and I'll bring coveralls."

"You'll live," he said, dropping the cloth in the sink.

We said our goodbyes, and a few minutes later, I drove away.

The sky had lowered and layers of clouds—silver gray to a dark slate—obscured the sun. As I passed through the medium-sized town of Hanks Ford, the main hotel glowed purplish against the darkening sky. With no umbrella in the car, I hoped the rain would hold off. I had wanted to take Sofie to West Trout Run, but not only would that town be a muddy mess, I doubted I could navigate the steep road leading down to it.

My mind jumped to Beers; the alienated teenager lost somewhere in the wilds. I sent good thoughts his way, hoping he'd been found.

By the time I arrived at the Dougans' home, the rain did too. Along with the rain came thunder and lightning, a run-for-your-life kind of storm. I pulled as close to their front porch as possible and parked. Sofie and Jon were sitting on their porch swing, and through the blurriness of the rain, they looked like a happily married couple. Not one, combating loss and certainly not two people trying to connect across the evaporated memories they had built together.

Even though I dashed from the car, therapy bag in hand, my back was soaked by the time I reached the top steps. "Oh man!" I shivered, the water running down my back and arms. "It's crazy out."

Sofie studied me, then said, "Did you fall off a float?"

Jon approached me, quietly explaining, "She is stuck on that logging camp today. Her grandfather, the fireman, guys floating on logs to the processing plant in Williamsport." He crossed his arms. "The validation therapy is working most times, and she's been pretty happy, but it's hell on me."

"It's really hard to join her in the past, I know. You lose bits of yourself along the way." I placed my hand on his arm. "But, by doing this, you avoid completely alienating her. You stay together."

He sighed. "The hard part is I was never there so I'm not sure what to say to her."

"I wanted to take her to an old lumber town I visited just yesterday. West Trout Run. Do you know of it?"

He shrugged. "Never heard of it."

"About thirty miles from here. But with this going on..." I pointed to the sheet of thick water falling beyond the roofline. "It will have to wait. Maybe when I'm back on Thursday. We can all go."

"If you think it will help her." He held a list in his hand. "Do you mind if I run some errands while you two meet? I don't get much time away."

"You're going out in this?"

"I have no choice. But I will be back before you're done." Then he added, "And, I know you are aware of this already, but never leave her alone. She can get into mischief, can't you, my dear?" He leaned down and kissed Sofie's forehead.

"Dad!" She swatted him away. "Don't kiss me!"

He visibly flinched, then recovered and drew in a deep breath. "Okay, I won't." The words caught in his throat and he turned and quickly went into the house.

Sofie patted her perfectly styled hair. "He's a good dad."

I took the seat next to her on the swing. "How are you today?"

"Do I know you?" Her eyebrows pinched together, suspicion written all over her face.

"I'm Marleigh. We're friends. And I was told that you are just the person to explain what goes on in those lumber camps you visit."

"Oh, I am." She leaned closer to me and whispered, "And don't tell my dad but I sneak out at night to see my boyfriend." She waggled her drawn-on eyebrows and smiled.

"Your boyfriend, the fireman?"

"Yes. Roger. He catches a ride into town and we go to a movie, or kiss."

Little Miss Sneaky. Why are we always surprised to hear that all things sex were not created by our own generation?

Jon's car backed out of the driveway and we waved to him. Poor guy. He was trying to manage, but I've learned in my research and experience that when the wife is the one to fall prey to disease or loss, it's much harder on the husband, especially on people Jon's age.

The Dougan phone rang and I ignored it until Sofie struggled to get out of the swing, sending it swaying in all directions; the movement dropping her back into a seated position. "It's Roger," she said, panicked. "He got my message and he's trying to reach me." She locked her hands on the metal chain, and rocked the swing back and forth in what looked like an effort to eventually catapult herself out.

"I'll get it," I said, patting her leg. "Be right back." I jogged inside in search of the phone. The ringing was radiating from the kitchen, but when I found the phone base on the wall, the portable receiver wasn't in place. *Great.* I checked in their bedroom, but by then the phone had become silent. I peeked into the bathroom decorated in something I'd call *Very Bold, Very Gold.* The last door down that single hallway led to the laundry room but not to the handheld phone.

Retracing my steps down the hallway, I stopped by the wall of photos of Jon and Sofie. Alzheimer's was an interesting disease. Not only did it suck the memories out of a person's mind, it also sucked the life out of the person's facial expressions. The younger Sofie pictured there looked spunky, full of antics, like she had a good sense of humor. The woman sitting with me on the front porch couldn't joke and wore a flat expression, even when she was excited or upset. As the disease progresses, I learned her face would become more mask-like. Over time, moving the ninety-eight facial muscles around to create expressions would be forgotten.

When I came back out to the porch, ready to say I knew the person would call back, I saw that Sofie was no longer sitting in the swing. Oh, no. *"Never leave her alone."* Jon had been very clear about that today. I scanned the yard and street through the downpour but didn't see her there. He said she was fast, but how could she have gotten so far out of my eyesight in such a short time? She'd be soaked and there'd be no way for me to cover up the fact I left her alone. I had no choice but to go looking for her. I was on the bottom steps when I heard a clatter from *inside the house.* "Thank you," I muttered as I hurried inside.

I walked from room to room, calling Sofie's name but she didn't respond. Had what I heard been her falling? Panic rose in my chest. I turned in the other direction and walked through the kitchen and discovered a door ajar. I pulled it open, thinking it was a closet, but a set of steps led to the basement. I thumped down the stairs. The acrid scent of smoke hit my nose before I registered the flaming rags on a worktable.

Sofie stood in front of them. Her mouth formed a smile. She flapped her hands in front of her body, shifting her feet, excited. "Better call the fire department."

The flames reached orange and yellow fingers six inches into the air, but the fire was contained in that one area.

When Sofie moved toward a pile of newspapers, that set me in motion. I ran around to the corners of the dimly lit room, looking for something wet or smothering. I found cans of gasoline, kerosene, and lighter fluid all on one shelf. The house was an inferno waiting to happen.

"Sofie, don't do that." I reached her side and twisted the newspapers from her hands.

She slapped at me, much stronger than I imagined. "It has to be bigger!" she wailed before running off into a darker recess to find who-knew-what. A blowtorch, a couple sticks of dynamite, a little nitroglycerin?

With no water in sight, I walked to the canning shelf, realizing I had no choice. I cranked the lid off a large jar of pears and poured the juice and the soggy albino fruit onto the pile of rags. The juice flushed the sizzling mess off the table onto the floor with a heavy *fwop* sound, like a jellyfish dropping onto cement. I waited to see if it would burn any further, but the fire was out.

The sickening sweet smell of smoky pears filled the basement and Sofie walked toward me, waving her hand in front of her face. "Dad said no smoking in the house. You are in Double Dutch trouble."

I could almost bet on that. In my defense, Jon had said she could get into mischief, but didn't mention she was a pyromaniac. I didn't want to wonder whether this would work with Lawyer.

Locating some gardening gloves and a dustpan, I scooped the mess into a plastic bag that I enlisted Sofie to hold open. I couldn't let her out of my sight again. Nor could I leave the mess there without cleaning it up.

Twenty minutes later, we returned to the front porch. The rain had lightened to a drizzle. We were talking about the lumber camp photos in the book, *The Ghost Towns of Northern Pennsylvania*, when Jon returned. Sofie was calm now, and more than ever I felt a trip to West Trout Run would benefit her. We could take pictures of her and the buildings and make a memory book.

Jon got out of his car in the rain with a smile on his face. The drive having done him some good. I stood so he could sit next to his wife. I cleared my throat. "We had a bit of an incident."

He looked from his wife to me, and back. "What happened?"

"The phone rang," I said.

"It was Roger." Sofie sat up straighter. "He needs to meet me."

Jon looked sad for a moment.

"She was getting upset so I ran to answer the phone." I scanned the large yard. "I'm sorry. You told me not to leave her and I did."

"What'd she do?"

I explained the situation. The fire, the clean up, my assessment of no major damage, except for a singed work-table and the loss of a jar of pears.

The color drained from his cheeks, and he turned the pigment of old caulking.

I said, "I'm truly sorry—"

"Actually, I'm worried about something else." He seemed to debate how to say his next words. "We've had two recent fires in town." He glanced at his wife. "No one knows who started them, but they're being classified as arson."

Sofie pushed back and forth on the swing, a slight smile on her lips.

Could this be right? Sofie had set the fire that Lawyer and I had seen from the fire tower, then another one a few days later? I needed to tell Lawyer, didn't I?

"Please don't tell anyone about this," Jon said. The color hadn't returned to his face. "I'm going to handle it."

"What will you do?"

"I'm going to have to put locks on the inside of the doors." He pointed to the front door. "We promised years ago we would never put each other in a nursing home. I just can't do it."

He looked terrible.

"Okay. But only because no one was hurt in those fires and you're going to take care of it... I want to take her back to the time period she's stuck in. Would you mind if on Thursday I drive her out to West Trout Run? It's old and abandoned, but safe."

"If you think it will help her."

"I do." I picked up my bag.

I turned and there in the distance, against a far green hill where the sun had parted, a double rainbow arced across the land. I pointed. "See? Things are looking up." I smiled. "Get those locks and I'll see you Thursday."

I still had Tinsel's gift for Christian. When I saw that his SUV was at the church, I pulled in behind and parked. He was out the door and approaching my car, calling out a hearty hello before I could get the gift out.

"Hi. Sorry to come unannounced." I reached into the bag I'd brought, pulled out the Chia Angel, and handed it to him. "From Tinsel Tabbish."

He laughed. "Fantastic." He slowly turned it in his hands, shaking his head. "I will have to put it on the organ so she can see it." He tucked it under his arm.

I saw he had changed the marquee to read:

Church is like fudge—Sweet with a few nuts. Come to our ice cream social, Tues. 7 PM

I felt jilted. This wasn't one of the sayings we had come up with. "Clever. But won't you alienate people by calling them 'nuts'?"

He said, "Nope. There's a commonality in country churches. Every community has wonderful members alongside its church nuts, just like every family has a feuding family member or three."

A little snort escaped me. "Not me. I have no one to feud with." I'd wanted to make a joke, but the words hit me hard and I choked at the end of the sentence.

He looked my way. "Parents, grandparents, sisters?" He raised his eyebrows. "In-laws, outlaws? No one?"

"It's a bit complicated but my parents in San Francisco, who I thought were my birthparents, died in a plane accident in March. Later, I discovered I was adopted from this area. Last week, I learned my biological parents are dead. I never had siblings and my grandparents died. At this point, I'm looking for anyone, any family member." I cupped my parents' rings on my necklace.

"I'm sorry, Marleigh. Such a tragic turn of events for someone as young as yourself." He turned right and headed onto a narrower road.

"Watch who you're labeling young." I'd been curious about his age. "You aren't much older than I am."

He laughed. "I didn't just get out of college. I'm sure I have you by ten years."

Exactly ten years. I smiled, deciding to let him wonder. "I'm here to retrace my parents' lives, before they gave me up for adoption. I have a U.S. Marshal helping me."

He turned to study the view of his yard, seeming to think about those words. He said nothing.

I continued, "Anyone you need to search for? ... This guy seems to know his stuff."

He didn't laugh at first, and when he did, it seemed like an effort. "Every family has at least one black sheep and some families have more." He turned his gaze my way. "I'd be afraid of what he'd find if he dug around in mine." He rested his hand on my arm for a moment. "Tragedies and accidents will always occur even though we wish, with all our hearts, they wouldn't. But being proactive, like you are doing, can be the fastest way to heal."

He sounded like a preacher again. I wanted to ask more about his dark family secrets but the moment had moved on. He had closed down.

I returned the topic to a less stressful discussion. "Let me know if you need help with the ice cream social. It's another one of those things on my list." Lawyer wouldn't be back by tomorrow evening anyway. I had a right to keep busy.

He brightened. "I will. We'll be serving about one hundred and fifty people. I'll take all the help I can get."

"Which other saying are you thinking of posting on the sign this week?"

"How about, 'I asked God for a bike, but I know God doesn't work that way. So I stole a bike and asked for forgiveness'?"

I laughed. "Funny, but too long."

"You need to come up with something about food or ice cream."

"Me?"

"You're the clever one here."

He had returned to normal guy mode. The stiffness and distance I'd felt between us was gone. "Okay. I'm on it." I realized he would probably like seeing the old church in West Trout Run. I explained a little bit about the town and the church.

He smiled. "I'm going to have to find the time. It sounds like something I'd like to see."

Seeing is Believing

Melvin stood in the choir loft of the church, an open hymnal in his hands, a look of anticipation on his face. Sandy and I made up the total sum of his audience, sitting in the front row of pews. Ivory had been in their house earlier while Sandy got her hair done, but left before I arrived. The bag of dog fur in my trunk would have to wait until I could get to Ivory's house.

I held up my phone for Melvin to see, ready to push play on a YouTube video for the song Melvin was about to sing. "Are you ready?"

"I'm not," Sandy whispered, keeping a smile pasted on her lips.

He bobbed his head, then raised the hymnal to a reading position. "Belching bitches in heaven."

Sandy groaned. I touched her leg and leaned close. "Let's give him a minute." I started the song, and although he stumbled on several words at the beginning, he quickly fell in line with the music, his voice rich and deep.

"Through many dangers, toils and snares,
I have already come;
'Tis grace hath brought me safe thus far,
And grace will lead me home."

The knot inside of me loosened. This could have gone completely in the opposite direction, leaving the sanctity of the church forever reverberating with obscenities.

As he continued, his back straightened, he held his head high, and in that moment I noticed the moisture on his cheeks. My eyes stung and then blurred as I swiped my tears away.

"When we've been there ten thousand years,
Bright shining as the sun,
We've no less days to sing God's praise
Than when we'd first begun."

When he finished, we clapped and cheered. He smiled, equally as shocked as we were.

"Why does he do so well here?" Sandy asked.

"He associates being in that loft with singing. He's comfortable. The pressure is off and his mind can produce the song like he used to." I spun through YouTube to the next song we'd talked about. "Melvin. Ready for the next one? And don't talk this time. Just nod when you're ready."

He flipped through the book and stopped, smoothing the page flat with one hand. He met my gaze and nodded.

He performed this song even better than the first. I swelled with pride and almost forgot that one of my other patients tried to set her basement on fire just an hour earlier.

When he finished the song, he gently closed the songbook and set it on the stack on a table in the choir loft. He descended the carpeted stairs, wearing a huge smile on his face.

"Well..." I stood to meet him. "That must have felt pretty amazing."

"Puckered pig butts on earth." He raised his hands in a sign of exultation.

I laughed. "Don't hold back. Tell us what you really think."

"Angels." He touched his chest.

Sandy put an arm around his waist. "That's right, Mel. There must be angels."

As we walked back across the road to their house, I asked, "Sandy, would you ask the minister to let Melvin practice with the choir? He'll show them what he can do. Later, when he's back in front of a full house, we'll worry about his idle chitchat."

"Sure can."

We had no sooner entered the kitchen when Melvin grabbed the phone and handed it to his wife. "Beat the bastard." He made a hurry-up motion with his finger.

I left Sandy dialing the minister's number as I started my car. This visit had gone better than I'd hoped.

I drove the short distance to the small park to write my notes. In Sofie's file, I didn't mention the fire, but I had good things to say about Jon's use of validation therapy. And Beryl and Melvin's visits were both positive.

My phone rang and I dug it out of my purse.

"Marleigh. Marshal Schumer here. I'm in your area and I have some news about the Kingstons."

The hair on my arms rose, not from fear but from shock. He'd uttered words I didn't think I'd hear. All this talk about dead ends and sealed files, I'd started believing nothing would be uncovered or revealed. "That's great. I'm just finishing up in Blackout. Where are you?"

He agreed to meet me at The Gray Roof Inn in thirty minutes. The same place Beryl and I had picked up The Other Dog. As excitement raced through my bloodstream, I backed off the gas when my car caught air going over a hill. *What a time it would be to die in a car accident.* I wished

Lawyer were here to share this big moment since he had gotten Scott involved. This could be where I learn enough to feel satisfied. It was about resetting the clock back to a place where things turned that never should have turned. Before the Kingstons' deaths, before I moved to California. I'd call him the second we were done.

I slid to a stop, going too fast, embarrassed when I saw Scott standing by his car. Arms crossed. Wearing dark shades. So *Marshal*-looking.

His hand was thrust out to shake mine when I approached him. "You got here fast."

I shrugged. "Roads are mostly empty this time of day."

"Hunh," was all he said as he studied my clothes. "You have a dog?"

I looked down at my clothes and tried to brush off more embedded hair. "No. I just helped a patient shave his dog."

"Speech therapy must be different than I thought." He pointed to the bar and headed in that direction while I followed. Once inside, we found an open table. Country music played at a low enough decibel to allow conversation. Two guys in plaid shirts and Caterpillar caps shot pool under a garish light, and a middle-aged couple leaned over pints of beer at another table, loudly whispering. A telltale sign they'd been here awhile and the empty pitcher on the table wasn't their first.

A guy with a walrus mustache and ponytail left the bar and stopped at our table. He used a damp rag to smear the wet rings on the table, left from previous drinks while asking what we wanted. I ordered Coke, and Scott requested tonic water with lime. The bartender smelled like past-tense cigarette smoke and fuel oil.

When he left, Scott leaned back and studied me. "Did your adoption papers come with your birth certificate?"

"No." I remembered the embarrassing moments trying to sign up for soccer, getting a driver's license, enrolling in college without one. My parents had insisted they'd lost it. Because they always managed to get me what I needed, I never thought twice. "I've never had one." It was like I'd washed up onshore into my adoptive parents' arms, wearing a garbage bag, and carrying no documents with a date stamp signifying I had come into existence.

Scott waited a few moments before answering. "Thought so. Couldn't find one on you. The agencies were sloppy back then. The program was new and lots of things fell through the cracks."

"My birth certificate would have solved this fast. The Kingstons' real names would be listed there."

Our drinks arrived. Scott took a long pull then said, "WITSEC Marshals often either had to forge documents, or they simply failed to provide enough for everyone. I mean, you were a baby, just one year old at the time. The marshals were busy getting all new documentation for your parents...marriage certificates, licenses, their own birth certificates, jobs." He finished his drink and pushed it away on the small napkin.

"If they were that disorganized, they may have even left the loophole that pointed the criminals to the Kingstons' new home."

"Possibly." He shrugged. "The mob, however, has feelers everywhere."

"Wait. You know it was the mob?"

He pulled out the notebook I'd seen him use before. He flipped a few pages and read, "On August nineteen, nineteen ninety-one, Joey Naples was killed in a mob hit in Youngstown, Ohio, by a sniper. Shot from a long distance away with a high-powered rifle." He met my eyes and I saw accomplishment there. "The three Naples brothers were Pittsburgh mob lieutenants stationed in Youngstown. Joey was the last of his brothers to be killed in a ten-year period. He'd only been the hotshot capo for four years."

I was confused. "This was in Ohio then, not in Pittsburgh?"

"Youngstown, Ohio, used to be the nation's crime capital."

"I had no idea...So I was born in Ohio?"

Scott's smile was Government Issue—serious with a bit of irony, not a regular-guy smile. "No clue where you were born. Yet. All we know is your birthparents, now known as the Kingstons, saw Naples get shot in August of nineteen ninety-one, as he stood on construction property where he was building a house. Why they were there? Had they seen the sniper? That I don't know yet."

"But Ohio? Why did a local sheriff here say they were from Pittsburgh?"

"Pittsburgh and Youngstown are only an hour apart. They might have been there visiting...out pushing you, a seven-month-old in a stroller and then *ka-boom*, their lives changed forever."

I gave a shudder, involuntary, like I'd bitten into raw tuna. I thought about all of this. "They had to have seen the shooter, or why else would they get protection?"

"That's the thing. The FBI suspected the hit was engineered by Lenny Strollo, a bigger mob guy, already in prison at the time. Seems he was worried about losing his Youngstown businesses to Joey Naples. So they didn't see Strollo."

I sighed. "But they saw who Strollo hired."

He shrugged. "I am just getting started on this thing. I can't find their original names or *their* birth records either."

He did that stiff smile thing again. "You're just a bunch of aliens for all the government knows...Like outer space aliens."

I laughed. "Please don't write that we're from Uranus. I couldn't take the jokes."

He tipped an imaginary hat my way. "Saturn then. And things have changed these days with WITSEC. You'd be able to find your birthparents a whole lot easier now."

"Why's that?" *Cheated* was the word that jumped in my head. I felt cheated and swindled.

"The current protection program ends for witnesses three months after a convicted criminal is sentenced. Then, the witnesses are basically on their own."

"Are people even safe after three months?"

He reached in his back pocket for his wallet. "Not really. That's part of the reason witnesses are more reluctant to cooperate these days. They feel they're just being used, some say just chewed up and spit out."

I finished my drink and Scott motioned the bartender over. He dropped a slip of paper on the table. The $6.40 tab was in slanted handwriting. Scott laid a ten on top and we headed for the door.

Once outside, I stuck out my hand first and he took it. "I'm grateful for what you're doing. Things are in motion and I can see some sort of progress. I may get the answers I've wanted."

"Well, I'm all in now. I need to know why the mob tracked them down in rural Pennsylvania, thirteen months after they'd seen the crime and already testified. I'm assuming they testified. I don't know that for sure."

"Call me with anything, okay?"

He tossed his large set of keys a few inches in the air, caught them without taking his eyes off mine, smiled, and headed for his car. I watched him pull away and we both raised a hand.

My car was a hundred degrees inside and the scent of dog hair had worked its way in from the trunk. I started the engine, turned the A/C to high, and buzzed the windows lower and got out. Leaning against the side of the car, I dialed Lawyer, so excited to tell him my news.

Two rings and then Veronica's voice. "Hello, Marleigh." She drew my name out, making three comical syllables. Mar, eh, leigh.

"Uh...hi...Can you put Lawyer on?"

"He can't take the call while he's in the shower."

Bitch. I heard the smile in her voice. I should introduce her to Melvin. Let him rapid fire a few choice words her way. "Okay. Then could you ask him to call me when he's available?"

She chuckled, almost a purr. "He's not available. You need to remember that." Then she hung up.

Melvin had taught me a lot of swearing combinations and I ran through most of them in my next few breaths. I hated jealousy. Or loss. Had I lost him? More than anything, I wanted to walk with him, to touch him, to breathe his air, but now I wasn't sure where things stood between us. And how would I get an answer now that she had commandeered his phone?

I turned the car toward Tungs, trying to actively do something. To form an intention that took my mind off Lawyer, his mouth, and his arms around me.

I pushed Lawyer out of my head, realizing I had several things to plan. The most pressing being Dottie's makeup party tomorrow night. I had invited no one but Rose. And I'd told Christian I'd help with the ice cream social this evening. Oh, yeah. I had some very important things to do all right.

But for now, as I drove the back roads toward home, I imagined my unnamed birthparents, young, walking in Youngstown. *It's a humid day in August, but sunny, hopeful. They're laughing, no they're talking, discussing a move to this quiet neighborhood where new houses were popping up. Then, the gunshot. An unknown man falls, and they see something. They see the shooter, or his car, or hear someone say a name.* My heart pounded as I imagined myself as them, as I thought about what they went through in those moments—the fear, the uncertainty. Should they run or would that make them a target? Hide, trying to protect their baby? Needing to give up everything—friends, family, work connections—but mostly their identities. They were in the wrong place at the wrong time. Then the chaos of the following days and weeks. The sudden need to be recreated, reengineered, changed, to live a new life in their own prison of sorts. To escape meant possible death.

One of them or both must have peeked outside of those new prison walls. They'd been found in tiny town U.S.A.—killed, their deaths made to look like an accident. That thought held me by the throat for a moment. What if the sheriff who reported them dead was in on it? What if he had "family" ties outside of the area?

This was something else Scott needed to check out.

JUST BEING SOCIAL

The back lawn of the church was full of people, sitting at twenty tables of different shapes and sizes. Laughter and conversation pushed into the kitchen area where Christian and I filled platters with more desserts.

"More like a dessert social than ice cream, don't you think?" I tried to arrange the desserts in semi-artistic patterns, the pastries outnumbering the vanilla ice cream six to one.

"I got carried away shopping in Binghamton. Big city, you know?" He laughed. "I found the best German bakery. Did you try the funnel cake or the Montgomery Pie?"

I dropped a hand to my stomach. "Maybe too many times." I pointed to the square doughnuts I was stacking. "What did you call these again?"

"Fastnachts. If they're filled with jelly or crème, they're P czkis."

I'd taken German in college. "Fast nights, huh? Like the night before Lent?"

"Exactly." He pulled out three more liters of birch beer from the fridge and we headed out to the party. I'd arrived just in time to help put out tablecloths and set the tables. People arrived on time. The slamming of car doors out front seemed to have been synchronized with the hands on the clock as they neared the seven o'clock hour. I set the platters on the food table and made sure others were still filled. I wanted to see a church activity up close, and here I was. One more checkmark on my to-do list. Lifting the platter, I said, "Off to check on my date."

He smiled. "You know I'm jealous."

I really hoped he was kidding. He was a catch—good-looking, mannerly, fun—but a catch for someone else, not for me. I seemed to like pursuing guys I couldn't easily attain. I moved off to the gaming area.

Eggs in a Basket was in full swing as families ran back and forth carrying an egg balanced on a spoon, trying to get the most in a basket without breaking any. Isolated in my job, I didn't see many children, so the groups of children were a nice surprise. Casey and his mom needed this kind of socialization and I wished I'd invited them. I moved past the area where a round of blanket volleyball had ended, and approached the serious gaming tables.

Milt was seated at the poker table with three other men and two women, one of them Tinsel. An outsider would say he was half-dead, sunken in his chair, both of his gnarled hands clutching the seven cards. His head barely moving, tracking the plays; however, the stack of plastic chips beside him said he was not only in the game, but winning.

Milt needed an outing but more than anything, he didn't needed to sit through another dinner with human dog food testers. I brought him along, calling Christian ahead of time, asking if I could bring a date. He'd been silent then said, "Of course." I saw relief on his face as I led Milt from my car to the table.

I stood behind Milt. "Everything going okay over here?"

Tinsel spoke, looking toward Milt. "He cards very well." A blush filled her cheeks as Milt met her gaze. I kept my face neutral but I was smiling inside. Was Tinsel flirting? Perhaps

Milt *would* like a little female company after all these years without Mildred.

"I hear he's pretty sharp when it comes to cards." Another hand was dealt and Milt slowly reached for the cards. I knew him a little bit after these few weeks together. The look in his eyes, the tightness in his jawline—he was having a blast. "Anyone need a drink? Another round of funnel cake?"

They waved me off and I headed back to the kitchen. I checked my phone for messages like I'd already done several times, and to make sure I hadn't turned the ringer off. Why the heck hadn't Lawyer called back or texted?

I stacked some dishes in the dishwasher, wiped down the cutting boards, and looked around for trash bags. After I pulled open all the cupboards, I remembered I'd seen some in the basement.

I thumped down the stairs and pulled the string for the overhead light. I'd seen the trash bags by the cartons of beeswax so I headed there. He'd been busy with getting shipments of bibles ready. Cardboard boxes were now standing open, the bibles stacked in the bottoms, individually shrink-wrapped. He obviously took great care in getting them to their final destinations. I pulled the lid up on the box of trash bags and yanked out a few.

I tugged the string to shut off the light and climbed the steps. Just as I turned into the kitchen, I bumped into Christian.

"Where were you?" His eyes were demanding my attention.

I held up the bags. "I remembered you had these down there."

He looked down the steps behind me. "I keep some up here too, just for future reference."

I hesitated at his cool tone, then asked, "How many bibles do you get out a month?"

He slowly smiled. "A few hundred."

"It looks like a lot of careful work. All that wrapping."

His eyes softened. "The wrapping is to prevent moisture and insects from getting in."

"Did you finish the candles? The wax was gone."

"I did." He closed the door behind me. "I'm considering just buying them next time. Lots of work for only a few dozen candles."

I shrugged. "I said I'd help." I snapped my fingers. "That old church I told you about had a room with old-fashioned candlemaking stuff."

He stared at me, his face changing again. This time mask-like. "Sounds like you thoroughly explored that old town. Who'd you go with?"

"Just a friend." Why would he want to know that? I changed the subject. "Tomorrow night at the Bed and Breakfast, I need about ten ladies for a Mary Kay party. Do you mind if I ask around?"

"Sure." He set dishes in the sink. "Go ahead. Lots of the ladies will like that."

Within minutes, I had eleven women who said they would come! The church party wound down shortly after as the sun dropped behind the tall maples. I finished helping with cleanup, leaving Milt and Tinsel at the tiny table Christian and I had eaten at just a few days ago. It seemed like weeks. So much had happened since I'd first set foot in this church.

As I passed the table, I heard Milt say, "Alone."

And Tinsel's response, "Your wife death in ground?"

They were having a conversation in their own broken ways. I felt like crying. My "kids" were talking.

Dressed in nice clothes and looking like a human being, Frank Tabbish rounded the corner to pick up Tinsel.

I didn't want to get involved in the whole drug problem because I was no detective. But when I thought about all the young people dying in the last few weeks, there was the other side of this—that Formalin idea. If seeing Frank's place of work would lead to any valuable information, I decided I would do my small part.

I stopped him before he reached his mother, where we could talk alone. "You look nice."

He studied me, looking for a snide comment or insult. "I do clean up pretty well, don't I?'

I paused a minute. So many questions in my head. *So the drug trade, huh? Been moving heroin long?* I went with: "I'm interested in your job. In how you take something so dead and make it look alive."

He shrugged. "Just picked up a smashed rabbit one day, shoved cotton inside and said, hey, that's nice."

"Really?" I tipped my head to the side and narrowed my stare. "It's that simple?"

"You're that simple."

He had a stare that could burn rust off a fender. I took a step backwards and reassessed, yet again, how much I wanted to know about him.

He continued, "I got trained at the Pocono Institute of Taxidermy … one of the oldest, most respected schools in the business." He smiled. "My specialty is true-to-form mounts."

"I'd like to see that." I folded my arms. "Any chance I could come out in the morning? I could bring your mom, use the visit as therapy."

"Sure. She hasn't been out there in weeks, since I added some new sections onto the garage."

Like the heroin cutting table? "Okay. I'll do that. Thanks."

A few moments later, I thanked Christian for my first real down-home church picnic.

"Hope to see you around soon," he said. "I'll give you a call and maybe we can explore some other abandoned towns. If you have time, that is."

I smiled. "Sure. Sounds good." I walked Milt to the car. The pockmarked moon hung low in the sky. On the drive back to Tungs, we were both lost in our thoughts.

I was getting closer to the truth about the Kingstons; they'd been involved with the mob, so this could be dangerous. And I couldn't stop thinking about Lawyer, about Veronica spinning a web he might never leave.

FRANKLY SPEAKING

I texted Lawyer before I left to pick up Tinsel and take her to Frank's house. "Just checking to see if you'll be back tonight! Miss you."

When a text came back from him a few minutes later, before I arrived at Tinsel's, I was instantly angry. "This is V. Lawyer can't come to the phone right now." I had no other number to reach him and Veronica seemed to be thwarting all my attempts through his cell phone. I could call his mom, but I didn't want to involve her in this triangle. I'd try again in a few hours.

After I picked up Tinsel, we drove to Frank's place of operation. A small blue stucco house attached to a large, two-story building set back against a dark tree line with a massive yard in front. His truck was parked off to the side, so I knew he was home.

"Frank wood and nail the garage." Tinsel pointed to the big building.

"He built that?" I asked. Not knowing what to expect, I was still surprised to see that the property was neat and trash-free. No hanging animals, no scraps of hides, no blood trails. A curl of white smoke rose from a metal barrel in the center of the yard. Burning papers was legal here, something I hadn't yet gotten used to. You start a fire in a can in San Francisco and you get arrested.

I put the car in park and Tinsel poked me in the arm. "Good man to husband." She smiled as if to say, *What are you waiting for?*

Frank walked out the double doors of the garage and waited for us to approach him. "Hi, Mom." He made no move to hug her and she seemed fine with that. He stared my way. "Morning."

"Hi. Thanks for letting us come by." I kept my hands clasped behind my back, not about to shake his, knowing it had recently been inside some animal. "Let's see what you do."

He led us inside. The four walls were lined with shelves full of cans and instruments. A hoist hung over a table stained with brown smears. A giant ceiling fan slowly chopped the air as a mixture of chemicals cleared my sinus passages with each breath.

"Let's start here." He pulled open a giant freezer door. "I save the specimens in here until I get ready to skin them."

The floor space was ten feet wide and equally as deep. A congregation of animals filled the space from the back wall to halfway across the floor. They were all facing forward slumped against each other like a drunk, nearly conscious group of mishmash friends waiting for a concert.

He pointed to a table with butcher paper on top. A large industrial-sized roll hung on a dispenser off to the side. "Skinning them is where the skill comes in. The skin has to fit over a form I build creating the body."

"I assumed all stuffed animals kept their body... that it was just freeze-dried or something."

He snorted. "City girl." He pointed to a measuring area, stacks of wire, and bags of plaster of Paris. "The guts would stink. I take measurements of the remaining body, then chuck it out but I keep the skull and leg bones. I create a mannequin from them out of wood and galvanized wire."

Tinsel seemed enthralled. Maybe he had never shared this process with her before.

She said, "The eyes in face real ones?"

"I had the same question," I said. A boar's head above the table seemed to follow us with his eyes which looked so real.

"Nah. I buy the eyes, beaks, and claws." He flipped open a magazine on a beat-up wooden desk off to the side of the skinning table. It was full of artificial body parts—teeth, jaws, tongues—along with paints, forms, and display cases with optional plants, leaves, and backgrounds.

"So, basically you kill the animal, a thing of beauty, and then recreate it into the same thing it just was."

He glared at me. "That's where I differ from everyone else. I don't personally kill my subjects." His face had reddened and his attitude had soured.

Tinsel pressed her lips together. "Very kind."

I carefully formed my next words since I wasn't supposed to be antagonizing him. "You carry guns in your vehicle. But you don't hunt?"

"Only to put a wounded animal out of its misery."

"That's humane," I said, walking around the room looking for the embalming area. No canisters or bags were labeled Formalin or heroin, which was disappointing. I needed something. "Do you ever embalm the bodies?"

He pointed to a padlocked metal door next to a faucet over washtub-size sinks. On a big nail beside the door hung a set of tarnished keys. "The dangerous stuff is in there. I use a kind of Formaldehyde as a preservative. It evaporates the water and locks up the cells so a corpse won't rot as quickly." His faced cracked into a wry smile. "Go to a funeral home and touch a corpse ... it's solid, not soft." He waved at the door. "Also got tanning solutions, all kinds of salts and chemicals that you don't need to hear about."

Was Formalin used to set up heroin? It was found in the local victims who had overdosed. I couldn't think of a way to ask this question, and unless he opened the door, I wouldn't be looking inside. That's what warrants were for.

He was talking but I hadn't been listening. Something about what he does with the hide.

"... tanning salt removes the moisture and holds the cells open, then you relax the skin in a bath. The water is sucked up by the hide and it softens somewhat. Then I pickle the skin with acid."

I was getting a bit queasy from the smells, the partially built animals, all the glowering heads on the wall. I tried for a joke. "Sounds like a cooking class."

He studied me. "Sounds like you're asking to come to dinner."

I snorted just as Tinsel said, "Yes. We food here sometime."

Frank laughed and walked us back to the car. I'd work with Tinsel on her verbs on the ten-minute drive back to her house.

I knew no more about Frank and any drug connection than when I first arrived. I was happy to leave this to Jaxson.

A Picture is Worth a
Thousand Words

Casey was rolling around on the ground with his big dog, Chipper. It was a great scene. Unfortunately, Karl ruined it by sitting on the porch shirtless with a can of Pabst in his hand. The weather-beaten bench sagged under his weight. As I got closer, I noticed his body was covered in a sheen of sweat and he was out of breath. As unhealthy as he looked, he couldn't have gotten that overworked pulling the tab on that beer.

He filled in the blanks for me. "Been hauling papers to the cellar. Only way in is through the back." He tipped the beer and made guzzling sounds, perhaps to prove this was extra thirsty work.

"Hard stuff on a hot day," I said. His hands and forearms were smeared black with newsprint. I looked around. "Do you have a wheelbarrow?"

He held the cold beer can straight up against his forehead with his head tipped back, and looked at me with downcast eyes. "As if I'd put my newspapers in something dirty like that." He spoke his words with the patience of an iceberg.

In picturing his backyard, I didn't remember doors to a cellar. Assuming the cellar was under the house, I didn't see how he had solved his problem with the county. They'd still be a danger under there. "Is the cellar going to keep the county happy?"

He dropped his head back to level. "No idea since the locks I put on those damn doors *will* keep the county *out.*"

Casey ran up to my side and hugged my legs. "My Marleigh," he said clearly.

"Aw. That was nice, Casey." I rubbed his thick hair. "Are you ready to go inside and work?"

Karl stood and scratched his back, the ink on his fingers leaving marks there among the patches of black hair. "I gotta run into town. Get more feed for the goats."

The animals lay around the patchy lawn, the once-lush grass nibbled down to dirt, the piles of vegetables nearly gone. It occurred to me that Karl's hoarding problem had morphed into something new—collecting goats. "If they aren't eating the papers, are you going to take them back?"

"Nope." He studied his yard. "They've grown on me." He turned to Casey. "Work hard with your teacher. No fuckin' around, ya hear me?" He raised his hand in a high-five gesture.

Good Lord. Did he have to talk to Casey like that?

Casey high-fived Karl. "No, fuhhing aroun'."

Cringing, I took Casey's hand and pulled him inside. Honey joined us moments later while we worked on several phrases and sentences with the /k/ and /g/ sounds. She sighed, grabbing my attention. "We're going to be thrown out of here any day." She pointed to a wall, now bare, once hidden behind the newspapers. "Moving them under the house is stupid."

"And dangerous."

"That, too." She hung her head. "I don't know what to do."

Casey picked up my phone and was pretending to shoot with it. I had it out in case Lawyer texted. What was going on there? How hard would it be to get a minute away and call? I was losing patience. Then Casey pretended to take pictures, making a believable clicking sound. And then a thought hit me. My eyes went wide and I grabbed Honey's arm. "Are you on Pinterest?"

"Kind of. Why?"

"Think about it. You save your own pins, but you also collect pins from everyone else." I smiled widely. "It's a hoarder's dream!"

"Okay." She shrugged. "Calm down. I'll get back on."

I laughed. "No. Not you. Let's set up an account for Karl, take pictures of the front of every newspaper...you said he doesn't keep them for reading...and he can pin them all to his wall. He can even set his setting to private."

She froze, nothing on her moved, and I think she was holding her breath. Then she laid the next words out slowly, each one standing in front of the footprint of the last. "You. Are. A. Damn. Genius." She grabbed me by the arms and rattled a few of my back fillings loose.

I steadied myself as she disappeared around the corner into the kitchen. Her footfalls thumped up the stairs, and then seconds later, back down. She returned with an old iPhone. "Okay. You hold the paper open and I'll snap the pictures."

She moved to the first stack.

I looked from her to Casey. He waited at the table, his feet swinging back and forth, waiting for me. "Can you start without me? I need to work with Casey first, like for twenty minutes."

Her face said she didn't want to wait. She sighed and set the old iPhone on the table. "I'll open up all of the papers so we can see the fronts." She tipped her head toward her son. "He's doing better...just cut it short."

With those words, I stretched the session out for twenty-*five* minutes, and gave Casey a candy at the end. He scampered outside to find his dog as I joined her in the dining room. "Okay. I'll hold the papers up and you snap them." After each photo, she checked to see that the image was clear, then she set the paper in a new stack by the door. Would Karl throw these away was the real question.

I had a little wiggle room in my schedule before I had to leave for Luella's. Although it seemed like we were making good progress, when I announced I had to go, we'd only moved through four stacks of newsprint. Of course, they had been four feet high. "When will Karl be back?"

Honey looked to the '60s clock on the wall. Gold spikes in a starburst around the clock in the center. "I have about forty more minutes." She stretched her back. "I'll set up the account and get these photos up."

"Is he going to buy this idea?"

She rolled her eyes. "I'll let you know."

I ruffled Casey's hair as I walked past him on the porch. Two goats followed me to my car, nibbling on my shirt and therapy bag. I shooed them away but they stayed close. I slowly pulled away as they followed the car, looking in my windows, bleating about something. Maybe asking not to be left behind.

ACTORS

"What do you mean you were hiding?" My arms were crossed as I stared down Luella and Margritte, sitting side by side on their orange tweed couch, looking like guilty children. "The nurse and I assumed something had happened."

"Nope," Luella said. "She's the one that turned our babies in. Didn't want her nosing around anymore."

"We don't need her." Margritte petted a chicken on a towel on her lap. "We only need you."

I started to take in a calming breath, but then remembered the poor air quality in their house. "I think she would be fine. You moved the chickens out of the house, at least most of them." I pointed toward the one on Margritte's lap.

She shooed my words away. "We bring them in here one at a time and love on them. They've been traumatized by the changes." She stuck her face onto the chicken's head and kissed it, then cooed baby talk to the animal. "Haven't you, Bo Peep?"

My phone rang, buzzing in my back pocket on silent. "Excuse me." I reached for it but didn't recognize the number, so I didn't answer. I had a responsibility to report the sisters' actions, but I also understood how they felt about their chickens. "Will you promise that you'll let Maria in next time? You could get dropped from the agency if you don't."

They bobbed their heads in tandem.

"Let's get to work," I said. Margritte disappeared with Bo Peep while Luella practiced for the next thirty minutes with the swallowing exercises I'd given her. "You know. You're doing well enough that I think you'll only need a few more sessions."

She looked panicked. "Who'll help us take chickens to Burt?"

They made money selling off chickens to a small market near Ivory's home. I had helped them out once, but vowed I wouldn't do it again. "Maybe Burt can come here."

I set up our one visit for the next week just as a scream came from the back of the house. I hurried in that direction, thinking Margritte had fallen. Bursting through the back screen door and into the yard, I found Margritte crying, holding a chicken wrapped in the same green towel.

"What happened?" I reached her side. The chicken looked like it was sleeping, head draped over the side of her fleshy arm, swinging from side to side as the woman quaked with her weeping. "Is it dead?"

Through her sobs, I made out that this was Anastasia and something was wrong with her. "The vets," she said, pushing by me and heading back through the house.

I followed her but she was out the front door and making a beeline for my car. I turned to Luella. "I can't drive her to the vets."

"Why not?"

"I ... because, well ... I ..." I stopped. I was done seeing people today so I didn't have an excuse. I just didn't want more chickens in my car. Sighing, I headed outside, then opened the back door and set my therapy bag inside. Got in the driver's seat and slowly turned my head to Margritte. "Exactly where are we going?"

She flicked the tears from her face; the sobbing had passed and her face was splotched with red. Her eyes aged in fleshy folds. "I'll give you directions as you drive. Go left out of the drive."

I reined in my anger. The sisters didn't drive. I glanced at the bird in her arms. It stirred a little. "What do you think happened?"

She looked straight ahead. "Hard to say." She pointed to the right at the next crossroads and we continued on that way for five minutes. At that moment, the chicken perked up and squawked, looking around like it had been taking a nap.

"Maybe she's better." I slowed the car. "Do you want to go home?"

"Keep driving." Margritte tried to pet the bird back into a sleeping position, but its head was snaking around in all directions, its eyes startled, and it was squawking loudly. Then it squirmed from her grasp and took off flying, slamming its weight into the side of my head. Its feet, raking through my hair as it looked for purchase. I ducked away as the car swerved into the middle of the road and then back toward the ditch. I got it under control, narrowly missing the plunge into a swamp off to the side. "Oh my gosh! Get ahold of her."

Margritte reached for the chicken, but it slid from her grasp and escaped into the back seat. It beat itself against the rear window and then flew forward again. I pulled the car to the side of the road. "We can't do this! This bird's going to get us killed."

Margritte snapped, "It's because of your car! It smells like dogs and it's scaring Anastasia."

"It does not smell—" Then I remembered I had a garbage bag filled with dog fur in the trunk. I sighed. "What do you suggest then?"

She paused as the bird flapped around on the floor-boards in the back. "I'm going to give her another shot of ether, if you can hold her."

I scowled at her. "What do you mean *another* shot?" The truth started sinking in. "You doped her up so I'd take her with me?"

"Maybe."

I gripped the steering wheel and squeezed it with all my strength. "Dammit!" I got out of the car, slammed my door to tune out the squawking, and walked away. Following the side of the road, I stopped, staring into the forest as if answers might come from the trees. *How much trouble would I be in for leaving them beside the road?* I'd call someone to come. Jaxson would love to help me out of this *sitch.*

Margritte stepped from the car; the chicken was asleep, once again wrapped in a towel. She blurted, "Burt's is just up ahead. This ether stuff works good but as we now know, it doesn't last long."

I had no words. I got back in the car, hating that I'd been tricked. She started giving me directions. "I know where we are."

A few moments passed, then she said, "I'm sorry, Marleigh. We sure don't treat you very well."

I glanced her way then faced the road, still angry. "You don't. And where did you get ether? That's dangerous."

"We use it to start the old diesel truck out back." She held up a small brown vial. Backlit by the window, I saw liquid inside.

"The truck you never drive?"

"That's the one." Her voice was happy, upbeat. She'd gotten her way.

When we pulled in front of Burt's store, I said, "I'll be back to pick you up in fifteen minutes. I'm going to drop off this dog hair."

It only made sense while I was there and it would give me time to calm down.

Back in the car, I passed Christian's church. The sign read:

We have a guy that will love the hell out of you.

That was one of my ideas. I liked that I had a part in creating these. It gave me the sense that I belonged here, somehow.

Ivory wasn't home but I dragged the bag out of my car and headed around to her cornfield behind her house. She lived in a two-story log home with an attached garage. Acres and acres of grass surrounded the house, miniaturizing it. In the front flowerbeds stood colorful gnomes and whirligigs. I tugged and dragged the black bag to her field, a third acre of corn she called White Knight. According to her, it was her sole income and was sought out by locals once harvested. I'd last seen the garden a few weeks ago and it was filled with small, tender shoots. She'd said it would be knee-high by the Fourth of July and it looked like she'd been right. From somewhere in the center of the garden, a radio played rap music—something by Jay Z—completely incongruous to a meandering cornfield on a warm summer's day. The dog hair kept raccoons away and I supposed those lyrics did, too.

Back in my car, I had a few minutes to kill so I stopped at The Little Church in the Pines. I didn't see Christian's car; it could've been in the garage. He didn't answer the front door or the side door but it was unlocked. I pushed inside and listened. "Hello?" Nothing. I turned just as I noticed a dim light in the basement. I walked down the stairs and stopped. A new light stood on a table near the wine racks, pushing yellow hues into the darker spaces of the room. Slowly, I turned in the space, now much larger. All the evidence of bible packing was gone, and the area was swept clean. I returned to my car and called his number, getting his voicemail. It gave the times for church service and talked about the youth group meeting. All very professional. I left him a message. "Hey. I stopped by to thank you for last night. Sorry to miss you. Call me."

Before leaving, I saw that the unidentified caller had left a message earlier. I pulled onto the road and listened. My heart skipped a beat when I heard Lawyer's voice. "Marleigh. I'm sorry I haven't called. It's been crazy down here. First, the guy that was going to help testify in Veronica's assault case hasn't shown and somehow I lost my phone." Well, I could answer where his phone was—in Veronica's hands. He didn't leave a number, saying the one he called from was at the courthouse. "I'll be back tomorrow afternoon. Clear your schedule because I have some big plans for us."

I had no idea how he would shake Veronica and I didn't care. My earlier doubt evaporated. His voice said he was interested in one person—me. I still had a smile on my face when Margritte slipped into the front seat.

"You're not mad?" Her purse tipped off her lap as she tried to stuff folded bills in it.

I helped her scoop the items back in and placed it in her round lap. "Oh, I'm mad. I don't like being tricked. Let's discuss it next time before you put on a crying act."

"That was no act." She looked like a lost child for a moment. "I hate to see Anastasia go, but we need to make room for the forty new babies we're getting."

I silently groaned. "Outside ones, I hope."

"Of course. Why would we want forty chickens in our home?"

"Why indeed."

Half an hour later, I directed the car for home. I had a makeup party to throw.

I left a message for Jaxson, saying I'd seen nothing unusual or drug-like, but there was a locked closet in Frank's workshop.

On the outskirts of a tiny burg called Patience with an excruciating speed limit of ten, I had time to check out an elderly man, sitting on the stoop of a graying house with a pair of binoculars to his face pointed toward a neighbor's farm. A woman, wearing a floppy hat, trimmed bushes beside him.

A memory came crashing in from when I was about six. My mom and I were at the Heart of the City Farmers' Market. She'd bought a sunhat for me, but it was scratchy and I kept taking it off. She'd gotten impatient and angry, and insisted that if I took it off one more time, I couldn't watch Nickelodeon when I got home. She also made a big deal about how nice I looked in hats; my closet was full of them. The other memory was of my father with his binoculars, watching the shore while we fished. With perspective now, I realized my parents knew they had adopted a kid who should stay hidden. I saw my mom's face again and realized it wasn't impatience or anger; she had been consumed with fear. My childhood was untrustworthy. My memories even felt somewhat fabricated, full of events people narrated to me after the fact, and I went along with the stories.

I needed to call the CEO of my dad's company, Dean Kennedy. If my parents knew I was a kid whose birthparents had been killed, wouldn't my father have confided in his closest work associate? Dean and his wife Angela had no children, but they owned an avocado farm in Visalia, about two hundred miles south of San Francisco. We'd been there a few times. While my dad and Dean went over the company's books, and my mom and Angela discussed bridge club gossip, I got to ride horses or play with the newborn kittens in the hayloft. They sent the biggest flower arrangement to my parents' funeral with a note saying they were in Europe, but if I ever needed anything, to contact them. Well, I needed answers and something told me they might just have them.

BLUSHING

My Frisbee sailed through the long strips of lowering sunlight filtered by the branches of towering maple trees, but missed the basket Richard had set up at the end of the yard. Zero for four attempts. I was out with Rose and Richard and the new guests, a family of six. They were here for the weekend to explore the area and visit relatives. As far as we could tell they were straight-up normal. No weird jobs or eating habits. She was a teacher, he an accountant from Des Moines. Their children's ages ranged from fifteen down to five. The Diffleys had moved into a hotel to be closer to the sheriff's headquarters in Wellsfield. No sign of Beers. No one wanted to say it, but a city kid lost in bear country was never a good thing.

Richard threw the Frisbee, and it arched over our heads and dropped perfectly into the target. "Bingo!" he exclaimed. Everyone else groaned. He'd been hitting the basket all evening.

This was my chance to excuse myself. Dottie would be here any moment and then the makeup party could begin. I hoped the church ladies all showed; I wanted this to be a success for Dottie. And someone needed to buy makeup tonight. I was a lip gloss, one foundation type of girl—also on a budget.

Rose and I'd made hors d'oeuvres. Small crab quiches, cherry tomatoes, basil and fresh mozzarella on skewers, melon-wrapped prosciutto, and lemon tarts. Bowls of nuts and sweet potato chips completed the table. The dining room table was cleared and would serve as our makeup area.

When the front door bell rang, Dottie stood there—all four feet of her—dressed in black tights, a pink baby doll top, and pink Vans. "Hi, Marleigh." Her voice was high-pitched, and if you weren't looking, you'd assume a young girl was talking.

"Come in." I took the cases out of her hands and set them on the floor, and bent over to give her a hug. "This will be fun. I think we'll have quite the turnout tonight."

"You're so nice to offer this."

I smiled, knowing I'd been completely forced into it by Elyk. But I had so few friends here that I didn't want to lose two of them.

She followed me into the dining area. I set the cases on the table and obeyed her instructions for setting out twelve pink placemats, each with individual mirrors, disposable makeup brushes, and makeup removal pads. I checked my watch and noticed it was just past seven. People should be arriving.

We talked as we tried the food. Elyk's puzzle contest was halfway over and he was still in the running for the sixty grand. I asked, "What would you guys do with the money?"

"Get married and fix up our house." She blushed crimson. "And start a family."

Food stalled on its way to my mouth. I didn't want to visualize how that could even happen. Elyk and Dottie. The sizes of a buffalo and a small calf. I pushed the image away. Maybe she meant adopting. That made me remember I had news. "I'm getting closer to finding out about the Kingstons, my birthparents, and maybe some relatives. I have a U.S. Marshal looking into it." With all the evening preparations, I hadn't called Dean Kennedy. I had to get to him soon.

"Can you imagine? The relatives probably have wondered about you, too." Her face glowed with the statement.

A slow smile took over my face. "Oh my gosh. I hadn't even thought about the family's side of this." Family members and friends would have known the Kingstons had a daughter before they died. Maybe they've been looking for me.

I pondered that as we ate, neither of us wanting to mention the time. The clock behind me ticked away the seconds as we waited, the sound mocking, taunting me with doubt. Where was everyone?

Rose popped her head in the door, looking surprised. "Just seeing how it's all working out."

I forced a smile. "People seem to be running late."

"That happens." Rose studied the preparations on the makeup table. "And if they don't all come, we will just punt." She left.

I said, "Rose is so nice. She'll probably round up her friends."

Dottie opened and closed a makeup case, looking doubtful. "We'll give it a few more minutes."

I had no phone numbers for the ladies I'd invited. They all knew the Bed & Breakfast when I'd talked to them. I could call Christian and ask him for numbers, but that seemed like an imposition. As the time ticked toward seven thirty, I was pissed. Not one of the eleven ladies could remember to come? It seemed so unlikely.

When it seemed that the party was a bust, Rose entered with Evelyn, the teacher. "Dottie, we're ready when you are." I could have cried. We all took seats at one end of the table. Dottie started her talk; the background of the company, the quality of the products, and why they have a money-back guarantee. Just as we were dipping into a face cleanser, the swinging door from the kitchen creaked open and Milt walked in. He sat next to me and picked up the cleansing cloth. I laughed. "Well hello, Milt. You must realize that men need skin care, too."

He didn't answer but rubbed the cloth around his face, staring straight ahead. Rose was trying not to laugh, her face jittering with the effort.

"Okay, then." Dottie recovered and continued with the next steps of toning and moisturizing.

Milt followed along. "Nice," he said at one point.

We all laughed. He didn't seem to care.

An hour later, we all wore foundation, eyeliner, eye shadow, mascara, and lipstick. Milt had applied everything, studying himself in the mirror after each application. He looked clownish—his makeup applied with his imprecise hand—mascara on his eyebrow on one side, eyeliner drawn in the loose skin a half inch below his eyes. Thank goodness the lipstick he'd chosen—Almost Nude—was nearly the natural color of his lips.

Order sheets came out and everyone ordered, probably over-ordering to make up for the scarce amount of attendees. Dottie said she would ship to our Iowa guest for free.

Milt checked a face powder. When I leaned over and asked him if he was sure, he said, "Lady friend."

Tinsel! He *had* liked her. I was proud of my accidental matchmaking skills. He stood and shuffled off to his favorite chair in the library.

I helped Dottie clean up. "Thank you, Marleigh. I know you think this was a bad party, but it wasn't."

"I'm not sure what happened, Dottie. About a dozen women said they were coming, just last night."

I walked Dottie to her car and waited for her to climb into the adapted driver's seat. She said, "Are you going to the Bark Peelers' Convention next week?"

Lawyer's fire company was in charge of safety. He'd talked about it like we were going together. "I think I am."

She smiled. "It's not at all like the last festival. This will be a lot more fun."

"I certainly hope so." The last one with live rattlesnakes hadn't ended well for me.

I watched her drive away. She could teach me a lot. Confident and happy even though she could have felt the opposite.

Back inside I washed the dishes. When Rose walked through, I thanked her for rescuing me.

"It was fun. No thanks needed." She laughed, grabbed a towel, and started wiping the plates. "And I don't know what got into Dad. I've never seen him do something like that before."

"That was funny." I didn't want to give away his secret of a possible girlfriend just yet. "Is he still in drag?"

"Richard has him in the shower."

I said good night and headed to my room. I was beat.

It was too late to call Dean, even if he was back in California. He and Angela travelled a lot for the company, one reason they said they never had kids. "Too hard on a family to be living out of suitcases."

Grabbing my phone, I dialed Christian. I wanted to know what he thought might have happened with my invitations. Had I offended people last night? Because that was not my intention.

"Marleigh." His voice was serious, sober. "I've been meaning to call you back... You stopped by and I missed you."

"I did. The place looked like you'd left town." I laughed but he didn't join me.

"I'm not going anywhere. I needed to clean up that basement is all." His voice now sounded sad.

"Are you okay?"

"It's been a bad afternoon. And a longer evening. I called an emergency prayer meeting for the congregation."

"What's happened?" Had Tinsel died? I brushed the thought away. Why did I automatically think things like that?

"One of our youth, a seventeen-year-old girl, Samantha Hart? Her parents were there the other night. She overdosed this afternoon and passed away."

"Oh, my gosh, Christian!" My mind skipped to Frank. Did he get to the congregation through his mom? He had been there the other night. Did he already have a meeting set up to deliver to this girl? "That's just terrible." I had the answer as to why no one came to the party.

"I didn't expect anything like this to hit our church community, you know... It's usually just a story in the paper about some other kid, in some other town."

What is the proper response to a situation like this? I had to offer something to make him feel better. "I think the problem is that the dealer might actually be from our area."

The line went completely silent. Not even his breathing could be heard. "What are you saying?"

"You can't say anything, and I guess you won't since you've taken that oath and all. But the police suspect that Tinsel's son is using his taxidermy business to cover up being a drug dealer."

More silence, then he cleared his throat. "I've seen him. Why would they suspect a guy like that?"

"They found Formalin in the heroin at the scene of one of the kids who died. Not many people use Formalin... just undertakers and taxidermists."

"Interesting." He drew in a long breath. "Why are you involved, Miss Speech Therapist?" His voice was lighter again, more relaxed.

"I'm not that involved, but I have access to Frank through Tinsel. I stopped by his place this morning...There's one locked door in his shop that might be hiding something."

"You shouldn't be snooping like that. If he's dangerous, who knows what he might do." My phone beeped, meaning a call was coming in. He continued, "You might find yourself stuffed on a mantel somewhere."

I shivered. "Not funny." The phone beeped again and I pulled it away to check the ID. Lawyer. "Christian. I have to go. We'll talk soon."

I pushed the button to catch the call. "Hello?"

Veronica's voice purred from the other end of our connection. "You might think Lawyer is devoted to you. You know that night before he left for fire training? I think he told you he was fixing things around the house." She laughed. "Well, no. We went out to the quarry, to stargaze and *enjoy* our time together, if you know what I mean."

Lawyer and I had been to the quarry just two weeks earlier. And yes, I knew what she meant. Well, we half enjoyed our time there until she had called and insisted he come home. My blood pressure rose and a vein in my neck felt huge. I was angry with her, but I wouldn't let her know that though. "If you aren't worried about your relationship with him, why have you taken his phone?"

"He called you?" Her voice lost some confidence.

"Of course...and he's aware of your plan to try to win him back. He's not interested."

She snorted. "Thanks for the heads-up. I'll just try harder."

Then the phone clicked off.

Rose tapped on my door and handed me a note. "I should have given this to you earlier." I glanced at it and was instantly happy. Lawyer's mom, Ginny, had called the inn and wanted me to call her back.

"Actually, perfect timing," I said, then she left.

It occurred to me that Lawyer's mother had been home alone while he and Veronica were away. How did she get around without help? I debated, looking at the clock. Nine thirty wasn't that late, was it? If Milt was still up then Lawyer's mother, who was much younger, should be, too. I dialed his home number and she answered on the third ring.

"Ginny, it's Marleigh ... I wondered if I could do anything for you while Lawyer is away."

"Oh, aren't you sweet. My sister, Florence, is visiting from Ohio so I'm perfectly fine."

"That's good." I cleared my throat. "I wanted to make sure."

"Marleigh. I called to give you a message from Lawyer." I heard movement on her end, papers being flipped. "Let me get the information he gave me." More paper shuffling and then I heard her say to someone, "Can you read this to her?"

A woman came on the line. "This is Florence. She's told me nice things about you, Marleigh."

"Hi. That's kind." I waited for her to deliver the message. Did I want to know what Lawyer had told her, but hadn't called to tell me?

"Lawyer's lost his phone, but he got another one. Here's his number." She slowly read off ten digits. "He wants you to call tomorrow at two p.m."

"So specific."

"It sounded like he would be free to talk then," Florence said. "And I hope to meet you soon."

After I'd said goodbye to both of them, I headed into my closet. I had some sorting out to do and it wasn't going to happen in my wide-open room. I closed the door and slid down the wall, breathing deeply. Cotton was comforting; silk embodied wealth. I breathed in again, trying to hold in the scents. Leather was strengthening, enduring. And wool. It connected with the animal in me, the innate creature I needed in a struggle against discouragement. And I was discouraged. Who to believe? Veronica knew that Lawyer had told me he was going to fix things around his house. She knew about the quarry. But I trusted what I heard in Lawyer's voice when we talked. I trusted the way he had held me, kissed me. I'd have a chance to ask him tomorrow.

I awoke an hour later, unsure of where I was. The inn was quiet as I crept out of the closet and changed into my pajamas, and slid under the covers. I'd been dreaming—something pleasant—a woman's voice, someone stroking my hair. Could I possibly remember being two? Everything I'd read says memories are unreliable to ages three or four. But this felt like an earlier memory. I chased the tail of it and fell back to sleep.

A Peek at the Past

I was on my way to Sofie's when Scott Schumer phoned. "Nothing new on the Kingstons," he said. "But I'm looking up the sheriff who investigated their deaths. He must have known about them being in the WITSEC program since they were required to check in monthly. I'll let you know."

I had good feelings about this. Finding my Kingston relatives seemed closer than ever. A reunion would be about undoing the damage from loss, filling in the holes, repairing the rearview mirror.

With four hours to go until I'd call Lawyer, I parked in front of Sofie's house. There I would break every home-health rule and drive her to West Trout Run. A therapeutic idea, just forty minutes away, not a twelve-hour wild goose chase.

I had a question for Jon the moment I entered the foyer. "Where does she get the matches?" This was a question I'd wanted to ask the last time I was here.

Jon shrugged. "I'm a smoker. I have books lying around but even when I don't, she seems to get her hands on them."

I thought of Milt and how he had the obsession with rolling dice and rearranging the B&B. Richard said they hide all the dice, but he still seems to find them.

"If it ever comes out that she set the local fires, it will be important to show that you put a stop to it by hiding matches." That sounded harsh, even to my own ears.

His face contorted, then softened. "You're right." He seemed to be thinking through his next words. "I probably shouldn't tell you this but since you're helping us..." He motioned me to move away from Sofie where she sat in the living room chair, knitting, listening to the police scanner. "I think she's done this before."

"Really? When?"

"Before I met her." His voice became thin, then cluttered and he cleared his throat before continuing. "There was a rash of fires near her hometown about forty-five years ago." He raised his eyebrows. "About the time period she's stuck in right now."

He might be onto something. She said she was waiting for someone when she started the fire in her basement, for this fireman, Roger Kline. What if she had tried the same thing when she was younger and it had worked? "You could be right. She doesn't know that Roger is long gone, right? She's trying to get his attention."

He shrugged. "So you think taking her out to that abandoned town will help?"

I thought about that. What did I hope to achieve there? "If she sees that it's in ruins, that the place no longer exists, perhaps we can get her to accept that this time period, with Roger Kline in it, was in the past. And that he's not a current option."

We both turned to study Sofie. Her knitting needles had stopped clacking together. She looked our way. "Is Roger here for me?"

Nothing wrong with her hearing. "Sofie. Do you want to ride out to West Trout Run? You can show us around."

Jon touched my arm and whispered, "I'm not going. It hurts to have her this lost to me. I can't bear to hear about her exploits with this Roger character."

I agreed to be back within two hours. I gave him my cell phone number in case he wanted to see how it was going. Buckled in and ready to go, Sofie looked girlish, anticipating a chance to see her beau.

I allowed her to enjoy the scenery as we fell into a comfortable silence. We travelled deeper into the rural areas, the trees thickened, and the homesteads became scarce. I was surprised when she was the one to start the conversation. "I haven't made a suit in the longest time."

"How many do you think you have sewed?"

She thought for a few moments. "Forty. Could be fifty. My gramps and I come out here every week. This is our third year."

"Do you see Roger every week?"

"When he's here. He rides the logs sometimes, into Williamsport or he works at the tannery. But we pass letters back and forth." Her eyes lost focus as she returned to her youth, to the excitement of being young and wanted.

I signaled to make the turn leading downhill to the river and town. "Do you have any of his letters?"

"Of course, I do." She brushed her hair away from her face. "I keep them in a safe box." I watched the anxiety dart back and forth between Sofie's eyes. Her brow and forehead, creasing and relaxing as she tried to process what she'd just said, and what we were doing. Then her head whipped toward me, fear in her eyes. "You're not my grandfather. Where are you taking me?"

We were dropping down the narrow road into the town. Branches scraped the roof of the car and she flinched. I said, "I want you to tell me about this town. I think you know a lot about it."

She didn't answer. We crossed the narrow red bridge, the wooden slats clacking under the car's tires, then we headed through the last grouping of a thick tunnel of trees. When the river came into sight, she pointed. "We swim there. Oh. It's chilly."

I looked at the fast-moving water, splashing against rocks, deep blue with black undertones, stopping for no man. "Are you sure? That looks dangerous."

"At the end of summer, when it slows down. Right now it'll suck your knickers off."

I nodded. I cleared the last of the ruts in the dirt road and pulled into the parking space, the car's hood pointing into the forest next to two other cars. Off to our left was the town. I was unsure of what her reaction might be once she saw it was in ruins.

We got out and headed for the settlement. As if to put truth behind Sofie's words, the river made sucking and gurgling noises, eating at the edges of its banks. When West Trout Run came fully into view, Sofie stopped and drew in her breath. "What happened?"

I sent a question back to her. "What do you think is going on?"

She studied the town.

I took her picture with my phone, thinking we could discuss it when we were back in her home.

She started walking again, her eyes wide, taking in so much. "Someone let The Red Horse loose, but not just in the clearing this time."

"Hmm. I don't understand. Can you explain more of that?"

She pointed to the woods. "This is a big secret, but when the men don't get paid enough, they set a fire in the woods, to show the owners how important they are when they put it out."

"Did Roger talk about that?"

She smiled, possibly remembering the man behind the name. "Everybody knows this is how it works. If the bosses don't want to pay overtime, a nickel will buy the woodsman a book of matches." She raised her hands and fanned her fingers, symbolizing something blowing up. "*Whoosh.*"

"Do you carry matches?"

She patted her pants pocket. "I keep a few on hand."

As Jon suspected.

We drew near the old store. "Do you recognize this store? Maybe you bought things here?"

"I did buy things. I mean do." Her face constricted. "Just last week."

A rusty sign swung by one nail from the front window frame announcing, Old Gold Cigarettes and SpearHead Chewing Tobacco. Sofie slowly walked around the front of the decrepit store, muttering to herself.

A look inside revealed discarded gas cans, a lopsided counter, empty shelving. "You used to come here, didn't you? But it's been a longer time than you think."

Two separate universes must have brushed by each other in her mind, clear spheres of different eras she tried to make go together. A tear slid from one eye and her face flushed red. She staggered and I caught her under the arm.

"I know it's hard, Sofie. Are you okay?"

The struggle on her face said that these two polar worlds weren't meshing very well. "I don't know what happened here." She wrung her hands. "Do you think Roger is okay?"

"It's okay, Sofie." I reached for her hands. "The main thing is that you are safe and okay." Her hand was bony, the prominent tendons strung tight enough to strum.

Sofie squeezed back while more tears escaped her eyes. "I'm just confused," she said. "Why did you bring me here?" Her voice hit a panicked pitch.

That was a good question. I had hoped that by showing her the town, how it had fallen into ruin, she might move to the point in time when she'd met Jon and married him. Not such a big jump like Jon had been trying to make, all the way to having grown-up children. Having her recognize she was married to Jon would make their lives much easier at this point. "You grew up and didn't come here anymore. You graduated high school and married Jon Dougan." I looked into her eyes. "Do you remember that?"

Her face scrunched together, then I saw something cross her mind. "I remember a Jon. He was nice to me when he came back from the war."

"That's him." I had no idea when or how they'd met, but I went along with her memory. "And you got married."

She thought about that. "We did. I wore a pink dress." She leaned in close, and in a conspiratorial voice said, "I couldn't wear white after what we had done." She laughed.

"Sofie! You shouldn't tell me this." I had to face Jon soon. "But I'm glad you're remembering it."

"Oh, we had lots of navel engagements before we got married." She smiled. "Hard to forget a thing like that."

I laughed. "Navel engagements, huh? I can only imagine." I pointed to the church behind the store. "This whole place closed down when logging ended." We started walking again, and I steered her toward the church. "You came here a lot but then you grew up and got married."

She seemed sad again. Her shadow dragged along beside her, small and jittering on the dirt road. Maybe all that remained of her old self.

We climbed the stairs and entered the church. A young couple was sitting in the pews at the front, their heads together, whispering. We walked down the aisle and turned left to the back rooms. No deer startled us as we walked through the back hallways. "Did you ever help make candles?" I reached for the door to the little room Elyk had looked in. The small window in the door had cardboard up on the inside so I couldn't see in. "That's weird. We could see in here a few days ago."

"People steal things."

"Probably right." Maybe the visitor traffic out here was getting to be too much. People probably did pick up things to collect them.

We walked through the rest of the town and I took a few more pictures. The final one I snapped was of Sofie standing beside the sign to the town. She'd lost her distressed look. I think the trip had done her good.

We were silent almost the whole way home. When we reached her street, she said, "Thanks for taking me to visit."

"You're welcome." I eased out the next statement. "You can tell Jon all about it."

She paused, then said, "He'll be interested. He likes history and stuff like that."

I smiled. This is what I'd hoped for. Jon would be so relieved to have her living in the present.

She asked, "But did you know it was haunted?"

"What?" Had I mentioned I'd seen a book, listing these lumberyards as the haunted camps of Pennsylvania?

"There was someone in the woods when we were leaving." Her eyes widened. "A ghost was looking out at us."

Rejoicing

The sky held onto a bright blue day when I pulled into Melvin's. In their kitchen, Sandy pointed to the den. Melvin's voice carried through the house, strong and clear, as he sang a church hymn. "We shall come rejoicing, bringing in the sheaves."

"They've said he could practice with the choir, and if it goes well, they'll let him back in on Sundays."

I'd always felt like his church had been a little tough on him after he'd had his stroke. Foul-mouthed and all, yes, he had shocked most people, but where was the universal acceptance? "That's great news. He must be so happy."

"And he's using more real words now. Even without his word board."

The word board was to give him a way of talking without actually speaking, a place to communicate between his actual thoughts and his creative swearing. Once he saw the words he pointed to, he might also "hear" them in his mind and use them. And this was happening. So rewarding to know my technique was working with him.

"Is Ivory here today?" I asked.

"She called and asked to change her time to tomorrow. Said she had a big gardening project to finish." Her face looked doubtful. "Do you think she works in the garden?"

"She has a huge garden, all corn. Surprising as that is, she's quite the farmer."

Sandy shrugged.

I found Melvin standing at a short bookcase, one arm resting on the top, like he was casually addressing a crowd. Lying open in front of him on a table was a hymnal. His face broke into a smile when I walked in. "Hell's holy bells. I'm singing for tonight."

"I heard...You sound good. You're singing. And you aren't swearing as much."

"Elephant lady is good practice." He clasped his hands together in a prayerful manner and raised them toward the ceiling.

I thought about his words, thinking it was mean to keep commenting on Ivory's large size. Then I realized the elephant reference might be about her name. "Let's practice something." We said "Ivory" over and over until he could say her name when I asked. Once he was seated, we ran through half an hour of pictures, talking about what the people were doing. He performed at fifty percent proficiency, a bittersweet moment for me because I realized how much I would miss these patients once I left Tungs at the end of the summer. And I didn't like losing people I'd become attached to.

I set up our time for next week and left him with longer sentences to practice. "Break a leg," I said.

"Thanks." He smiled. "No more peckerwood."

I laughed and raised a hand for goodbye. Once in my car, I looked up the word *peckerwood*: "A nuisance or a bother," the reverse of the word woodpecker, thought to be a pesky bird. So his statement wasn't completely off track. He was saying he'd no longer be a bother. Probably not to me, nor a bother to the congregation at church.

Renewed Connection

I arrived at the inn with about thirty minutes to spare before the planned talk with Lawyer. I was flushed just thinking about it. And I fought to keep doubt away. Was this a call to say he couldn't see me anymore? That he and Veronica were working things out? My argument was that he wouldn't have set this up through his mother just to tell me those things.

Milt was asleep by the Koi pond when I went looking for him. He still had a little brown coloring in his eyebrows from the makeup party. I'd see Tinsel in therapy tomorrow and could find out what she was thinking about seeing Milt again.

I felt guilty spying on her son, Frank, setting up the ruse of wanting to know what he did for a living. If he were somehow involved in selling drugs, Tinsel would be crushed. But the visit did help me get past his aggressively odd behavior. With the visit, he seemed to have moved past it as well.

The inn was quiet so when my phone rang, I jumped. It was Jon, telling me Sofie had clear thoughts all day, was happy and talkative, and saying the trip to the camp had been good. "Do you think you could take her out there again?" he asked.

I thought about that. I wasn't scheduled to see her until next week, but I was intrigued by her "ghost in the woods" comment. And the visit seemed to help her stay grounded in the near present, recognizing Jon. That was a very good thing, probably for everyone around given her penchant for pyromania to attract now-deceased lovers. I could drive out tomorrow, not as her therapist but as a friend. "Maybe early afternoon. I have clients in the morning, then I could come by."

We agreed and hung up.

The clock said it was time to call Lawyer. I checked my makeup in the mirror and then laughed. This wasn't going to be a Skype call. He picked up on the fourth ring and sounded out of breath. "Hey," he said.

"Hi." How awkward. It seemed we had nothing to say to each other.

He cleared his throat. "You were right about Veronica. She may have had different plans for us than just remaining friends. I'm sorry."

An apology was good but I had to know if he had lied to me. "Last Thursday. I wanted to get together and you said you had to repair things around the house."

"Veronica wanted to go over her case, so she'd have it straight in her head."

"You lied."

He was quiet. "I did. Again, I'm sorry."

"And you took her to the quarry, to our quarry, to talk and make out?" I couldn't hide the annoyance in my tone.

"What?" He sputtered. "No. We sat on our back porch. Where did you get that idea?"

"Veronica has been calling me from your phone. She's told me a lot of things."

"Dammit! *She* has my phone? I cannot believe this." Then he swore again.

"You aren't trying to work things out with her?"

"Christ, no. Just the opposite." He let out an exasperated breath. "And, I had you call me at this number because I haven't had a free moment to talk without her nearby."

I wanted to believe him. Just hearing his voice, I was filled with that feeling, that thrill you get when you're around something potent—an amazing view, a powerfully arousing scent. At the moment, it was his voice in my ear. "I don't know. How does she know about the quarry?"

"Marleigh. We need to talk. In person."

"Any idea when that might happen?"

"Tonight. I'll be there no later than seven ... I'll explain everything over dinner."

I knew he was waiting for my reply. I needed to get this cleared up—one way or another.

He spoke again. "Marleigh?"

"See you at seven," I said and clicked off.

My insides quivered, like I'd drunk a cocktail of baby octopi. A mixture of excitement and pissed off. I should go for a run—a good hard one. There was a steep hill on the way into Wellsfield I'd been eyeing. It begged me to come and try to beat it. I wandered around my bedroom, feeling lost. I needed to feel like I'd accomplished something. There were just too many loose pieces floating around in my head—Lawyer, my parents, the Kingstons' lives and deaths. Too many loose ends to grab all at once.

I had five hours to kill before I met with Lawyer. There was something I needed to do since I arrived in Tungston, something I'd been putting off, a visit that could no longer wait.

A Place Gone By

The scenic valley that surrounded Butterfield was framed by miles of horse property. In the near distance, majestic mountains dazzled in the afternoon light. My hometown. At least for a year and a half it had been. I tried to feel a connection as I drove around. At the heart of the town was the park graced with tall leafy trees, metal benches, a bandstand at its center. Streets branched off in four directions from there full of specialty shops, cafes, and a historic hotel dating back to early settlers. Three buntings in red, white, and blue hung from the front of the turn-of-the-century brick bank, and the movie theatre's marquee outlined in white lights jutted out over the sidewalk. A movie from last year played. I got no vibes, saw no flashes of being pushed in a stroller, or sitting on a lap and hearing music.

But I was hopeful. Butterfield seemed like the kind of town where residents would rally around and help a young family like the Kingstons move in. They'd probably come home at some point and found a rhubarb pie on their kitchen table with a note. There would be answers here. Even though it had been twenty-two years, surely someone would remember this young couple with a baby.

It was a closed adoption so my papers had no address on them to search for. But the post office is an information hub for a town this small and might be able to help.

The building was single-story masonry with arched windows, flanking the wooden front door. The interior was small with combination lock mailboxes on the wall to the left. Straight ahead was another enclosed area with a Dutch door in the center, the bottom closed. Behind the opened top stood a woman in a white postal shirt, stamping envelopes with a handheld machine.

She looked up as I approached. "What can I do for you?"

"I used to live here, a long time ago, but I was quite small, until I was two years old. I'm wondering if you know which house my family lived in." I shrugged. "They passed away and I would like to see the house I lived in after I was born."

She cocked her head and then turned to her computer and clicked a few keys. "What were their names?"

"Daryl and Amber Kingston." My heart picked up a flutter. The Kingstons would have stood at this very counter to get stamps, to send mail.

She frowned. "You sure they lived here?"

"Yeah." I dug out the paper I jotted the number on. "They had a P.O. box. Number one three nine one."

Her hands stalled over the keys. "We don't go that high. Only have three hundred P.O. boxes here." She leaned on the countertop. "I'm going to call a friend who knows everyone. I'll be right back."

She disappeared through a spring-loaded door. As it swung back and forth on its hinges, I caught parts of her conversation—"young lady, looking for address, years ago"—until the door closed and then I couldn't make out any words.

She returned with an index card. Neatly printed on it was the address 451 Grant Street. "Here you go. Old man Fassbinder's house. Ernie. He remembers them. Lives on the same street."

My face flushed.

Here it was, after all this time—an answer. Someone who knew the Kingstons, who knew me. It felt like I was traveling in time, the years peeling away. Soon the emptiness would begin to fill. I thanked her, and on jittery legs, I made it to my car and followed her directions to Grant Street, no more than five blocks away. The houses were post World War II, small brick structures, neat lawns, American flags angled off most porches.

I knocked and stood back, glancing down the street, willing my child's mind to envision something.

Ernie Fassbinder answered the door. He was a big man, bald, with large hands. He wore olive green pants held halfway up his chest by black suspenders. Underneath, a buttoned-down blue shirt, something orange stained the front. After I introduced myself, he muttered, "C'mon," under his breath and turned his back on me, leaving the door open.

A fan on the entry floor pushed a hot, vinegary smell around. He walked to the living room off to the right. I had to step carefully over a sleeping dog, its muzzle grayed; one ear had a knick out of it. The room was trapped in decades-old decorations. Brown shag carpet, mint green sofa and chairs, dark wood coffee table with purple glass grapes in a bowl. His body sunk deep into the couch and a puff of dust and dog hair flew up from the space between the cushions, but he didn't seem to notice.

I had to clear away the clutter on the floor to move my chair next to him. "Thanks for seeing me. I know I'm completely unannounced."

With the TV remote, he lowered the volume of a bowling tournament he'd been watching. "Connie called from the post office."

"I mean, just to drop by like this." I waited for him to say something, but he sucked on a toothpick in the corner of his mouth. I continued, "I'm from California, but my parents and I lived here for a short while in nineteen ninety-one."

"Connie told me." He pulled out the toothpick and pointed it toward me. "I don't remember you but I heard they had a kid."

"You remember them?"

He cleared his throat, a wet sound. "Young, not friendly, kept to themselves."

Yeah. They were hiding out from criminals.

"Moved in, in the middle of the night. Your dad worked out at the Henderson's Salt Mining Company. Long hours out there."

Information about Daryl! This was amazing. They weren't just names. Scott Schumer said jobs were found for witnesses in their new towns. Here Daryl worked at a salt company, but what had he done before this in Pittsburgh? What if he'd been corporate, had worked in finance? Then he'd found himself working in a blue-collar job, maybe going down into a mine.

I sat on my hands to hide that they were shaking. "I'm here because I don't remember my parents. They died when I was two."

He made a grunting noise. "Bad car wreck, they say."

"Yes. That's right. They're buried in the Roseburg Cemetery." I fought a lump in my throat that threatened to block my speech. "I have no pictures of them, no contact with the rest of their families. I was adopted and raised by a couple in California before Daryl and Amber died ... I wonder about them. Do I look like my parents?"

He studied me, but didn't speak. The dog snored and rolled over. Then he said, "You do. You favor your mother."

I couldn't contain the smile spreading across my face. I looked like my mother. With the Kingstons being from Pittsburgh—a city founded by Hungarians, Bulgarians, and Italians—I'd wondered about my blonde hair. I let this new image of my mother sink in and Ernie didn't seem in any hurry to interrupt.

"What else can you tell me?"

He shrugged. "I could tell you they barbequed on the back deck, so what? They didn't go to our local festivals, didn't favor a church, and only went out at night."

I leaned closer. "All of those details are important to me. Just to learn anything about them ... that's why I'm here."

"Twenty years is a long time, but not that long when the mob is involved."

That comment left me dumb. I flinched. "Wait. You know they were killed by the mob?" Was this common knowledge?

He pointed a crooked finger in the air, stabbing out his next words. "A boat drives into the bank at a lake, motor running, no one's on board. Mob hit. A guy's found under thick ice in his pond and he's not an ice fisherman. Mob. A car with a young couple rolls on a back road, no other car in sight." He tipped his head down. "You tell me."

A chill ran up my back. Marshal Schumer had suggested they'd been found out by one of "the families," but this guy seemed so sure of it.

"Maybe it really was just what it looked like ... a terrible car accident."

"Maybe." He squinted my way. "But two hours after they died, their house burned down."

I gasped. No one *ever* mentioned this. Shouldn't Scott Schumer have known? "And no one was arrested?" If he was so clear about who did this, why hadn't the local law enforcement caught on and done something?

"These mob families are like cancer. They get into us or into our communities, act like regular families or common folk, until they strike... Whoever hit your family did it and got out like that." He snapped his fingers. "Scared the *bejeesus* out of everyone left behind. People get really *unnosy* when stuff like that happens."

Scott had asked why I wanted to stir up this old story, and now I wondered if twenty-two years were enough of a buffer between people wanting the Kingstons gone and me, looking into their deaths. "So, there's no house for me to see?"

"Empty lot. No one has ever done anything with it."

And probably never would. The Marshals Service would own it, just one of the three thousand locations they use across the country. I sunk back into my chair. I learned new information, met someone who knew the Kingstons. They were alive and we were a family until they were discovered. There was triumph in knowing I looked like my mother, but there was also crushing sadness. I stood and put out my hand. "Thanks for letting me talk to you, Mr. Fassbinder."

He didn't get up. "Always wondered where you got to." He scratched his arm. "Don't know if your parents got a tip or not, but they figured out what was about to happen. They saved your life."

I swallowed hard, only able to bob my head in agreement.

I slowly drove around Butterfield before I headed back to Tungs. Not imagining I'd ever return, I crisscrossed town, memorizing the feel of it, the smells, and the look. But there was nothing here for me, except desolation and dead ends. An empty lot.

A Natural High

"You've been busy." Lawyer stroked my hair, my head lay on his shoulder. We were lying on a large blanket spread on a hill, overlooking the town of Mansboro with the lights of the town blinking in the valley below. I was buzzed, I admit it, and almost on the brink of dizzy. We left the restaurant, Fifty Ways to Please Your Liver, a half hour earlier. They made dozens of martinis; I tried three and dubbed each the best. He'd had one.

"You don't know the half of it," I said. And he didn't. I skipped the part about going to West Trout Run with Elyk. About taking Sofie back there. At the moment, I liked the feel of his muscular leg thrown over me, nestling me along the length of his warm body, his breath in my hair.

A little surprised when he pulled into the Bed & Breakfast on time, I felt shy at first until we got to his truck and he pulled me into an embrace. When he kissed me, it shook me so hard I didn't know I wanted him like that, like this, a *need*. How could I have forgotten his effect on me? Here he was now, up close, his breath, his tongue. In the final throes of sunset, he looked into my eyes and I believed he saw things there no one else had bothered to look for. He saw *me*.

We cleared the air. He explained that Veronica's maneuvering was to get him to stay and that the assault was fabricated to make him feel guilty so he would stay. She had purposely slept with a guy she knew who liked it rough to make it look like she had been raped. Her lies affected him; he brought her home, coddled her, and came running when she called claiming she was having a flashback. She knew about the quarry because he had chewed her out after she had called him to come home when he and I were there together. His final assessment: "She's a damn good actress. Led me to believe there had been a crime, that there would even be a trial." He clenched his jaw and looked upward before continuing. "We were talking to her parents yesterday when they blew her cover, having never heard of any of this."

Deep inside I was celebrating.

"That's terrible," I said.

He changed the subject. "Did you learn anything new about your birthparents?"

I told him what I discovered in Butterfield and he said he was sorry he hadn't been with me.

"I may never find out who the Kingstons were before they came here," I said.

That grabbed his attention. "This doesn't mean you're heading back to California, does it?"

"No. You promised me a Bark Carni—"

"Bark Peelers' *Convention*," he corrected.

I whispered in his ear, "Don't say peel unless you mean it," and ground against his leg. He kissed me again.

"Scott is talking to the sheriff who was at the scene of their car wreck all those years ago. He might know something but I'm not expecting much."

We watched the sky change from deep blue to indigo to deeper shades of evening. Now a clear night sky connected the horizons studded in between with thousands of twinkling stars. That was the best thing about the rural sky. No light pollution, and now, no more Veronica.

He laughed. "Are you drunk?"

"Only a tiny bit." I kissed him. "Why don't you show me some of those woodhicking skills you're always talking about?"

"What do you want to learn first?" His voice was husky and we were both breathing fast. "Pole climbing, bark peeling, or log rolling?"

I rolled on top of him, and flattened my body onto his. He wrapped me tightly as we kissed. I pulled away and studied him in the starlight. "Why don't you tell me about log rolling?"

His face broke into a smirk. His dimples popped along the sides of his mouth. "Okay." He wrapped me back in his arms and rolled me over so he was on top. "The trick is to stay on top of the log." He leaned to the side and unbuttoned my shirt. "It's certain death under the water." He arched up and pulled my shirt out from under me and slid it off my arms over my head. He took his shirt off. My heartbeat had to be pushing up some vein under my skin because the drumming was all I could hear.

Dropping back down, his weight on me was pure pleasure. "Under the water is death, but on top, up here, that's pure heaven," he whispered.

We wiggled out of the rest of our clothes and explored each other, our urgency building the more we tested, the more we discovered. Under the immensity of the sky above us, we took in nothing but each other and the desire we had held for so long.

After, we lay in each other's arms, talking about nothing important, just content to be pressed together, whispering through each other's heartbeat.

Puzzle Pieces

All through breakfast preparation, my mind replayed our time together—our urgency, then tranquility, and another round of lovemaking. He had brought me home after midnight and I tiptoed to my room, his cologne lingering on my clothes; the feel of him alive in my mind and still on my skin. We agreed to see each other again that night. I know I was personally trying to make up for three months of no sex, so tonight couldn't come too soon. I had a busy day before I dropped off my paperwork at Therapy on Wheels, so I quickly dressed in black walking shorts, a black and blue Madras plaid shirt, and black sandals. It was going to be a hot one. Richard said, "It's the kind of day that when you get up, the chair comes with you."

I made a call to Scott Schumer while I was driving the back roads with virtually no other traffic. When he answered, I told him about my visit to Butterfield, about Ernie Fassbinder and what he'd told me. "The Kingstons had it worse than I thought. Someone burned their house down, and now I'm wondering if it really is too dangerous to keep looking."

"I warned you about that... Here's what I found. The Kingstons were on vacation in Pittsburgh when they saw Joey Naples take a hit. They weren't from there."

My world was upended again. "Where were they from?"

"I'm searching that. And I'm trying to get their records unsealed. This Strollo guy who they testified against was convicted of racketeering in ninety-seven and went to federal prison. In ninety-nine, Strollo went into government hiding, turning state's evidence against other mobsters. He's no longer a threat. Sonny Ciancutti, who runs Pittsburgh now, I'm sure would like to find Strollo long before he cared to look for the daughter of two dead witnesses from decades ago."

"It was nice to see the town they spent their last days in, although they didn't socialize much ... and their P.O. box number? Nonexistent. I felt kind of silly asking about it at the post office." I drove around a huge piece of farm equipment that hogged the right lane of the road. The farmer waved. I lifted my elbow in a greeting, having no free hands.

Scott laughed. "All of the P.O. boxes we create are bluffs. What number did they have?"

"Thirteen ninety-one."

"We code them all. The numbers correlate to letters in the alphabet. Thirteen ninety-one is MIA. M being thirteen."

"Missing in Action."

"Yup. Gotta love Marshal humor."

"Then how did they get their mail with no P.O. Box?"

"Well, WITSEC is lonely that way. There wouldn't have been much mail coming to them. Just government correspondence, bills, checks."

"They finalized my adoption just days before they died. That had to involve documents." A thought hit me. "Maybe the agency who set up the adoption wrote back, and maybe the Kingstons died before they read it. Where would that correspondence have gone?"

He was silent for several moments. "In storage. In your parents' file, the one I'm trying to get access to."

He seemed antsy to get going but I had one more question. "How did you find out about the mafia guys if you haven't seen the file?"

He laughed. "Google."

He told me he'd call as soon as he had more information.

I wanted to call Lawyer but he wouldn't be picking up his new phone until later today. He would text me the number. His "lost" cell was never recovered. He assumed it was at the bottom of the Schuylkill River, outside of Philadelphia, near Veronica's parents' home where he'd learned the truth about Veronica's long list of lies. He would be hiring a college student his family knew to be at the house part-time with his mother. There was no need for a Veronica in her life now.

I had time for one more call before reaching Tinsel's house. I dialed Dean Kennedy, feeling guilty I hadn't checked in with him or his wife, Angela, since I left San Francisco. I didn't have anything to do with running the storage company my parents had built, that Dean now runs, but he and his wife had been good friends of my parents. They traveled a lot together, played bridge, went to plays. When I said I was coming to rural Pennsylvania to follow up on something I found in my parents' safe, they seemed worried. I appeased them by saying I had a job and it was probably nothing, but they asked that I keep in touch. Now four weeks into summer, I probably should.

"Marleigh!" Dean seemed genuinely excited. "We wondered how everything was going, how you were liking life in the backwoods."

I laughed. "Let's say the first few weeks were rough...a learning curve for certain. But I've made friends. My clients are interesting, well more like challenging, but great. And, I can say I've tried Shoo Fly Pie."

He laughed. "It sounds like things are working out... How are you holding up? Emotionally, I mean."

He had a right to ask. I'd finished college like a zombie, lurching around, often forgetful, unable to process too much at once. That was until I got a new purpose—until I found my adoption papers—then I regained myself. "I've had sad moments. But, Dean, did you know I was adopted? From a small town back here."

He was quiet, then I heard him move the phone to his other ear. "Really? When you were a baby?"

"No, I was two."

"I started with the company when you were older than that... Wow. That had to have been quite a surprise. Is this the *thing* you were following up on? The information you found in your parents' safe?"

"Yes." Would telling him about the Kingstons and the WITSEC program put him in danger? I didn't know. "And they never mentioned my adoption to you? Because they seemed so protective, even when we came out to your ranch. Remember? They wouldn't let me play in the barn with those neighborhood kids."

"They were protective. I just accepted they had a cute little girl and they didn't want anything to happen to her." There was a second of silence and I heard a pen tapping on a desk. "Have you found your birthparents?"

"I have not. There've been roadblocks, but I'm still looking."

"Let us know when you do find something. We could use a little intrigue in our lives." He sounded genuinely happy for the possibility that I could gain new parents.

"I will."

"Marleigh. Seriously. We're here to listen."

I was taking the last turn on the road before heading down Tinsel's drive. "Give Angela a hug, Dean. I promise to call more often."

When I reached Tinsel's house, I was relieved to see that Frank wasn't visiting his mother. But I was barely on her top porch step when I heard crying coming from inside. I yanked the doors open and stepped in, letting my eyes adjust to the dark room. "Tinsel?"

She sat hunched over in an armchair in the corner. All the shades were drawn and pieces of broken Chia Pets were scattered across the carpet. "What's wrong?" I knelt down beside her.

"Frank in jail!" She moaned. She grabbed my hand and squeezed, her fingers ice cold. "Police and drugs in shop. Now arrest him."

She'd used a verb but it was no time to point out that accomplishment. "Oh, my gosh!" It had happened. That locked closet *did* have drugs in it. This was very bad for the guy who said he wanted to save up to leave this place. I'm sure going to prison wasn't Frank's plan. I wanted to say something comforting, to pull her into a hug, but that felt intrusive. I placed my hand on her back. "I'm sorry." The woman felt frail, like a broken bird. She shuddered and cried, unable to get ahold of herself. Since I'd been the one to tip off Jaxson, my words of comfort sounded hollow, even to my ears. "When did they arrest him?"

"Early this morning." She dropped her head and mopped at her face with a soggy Kleenex. "My son not take drugs." Lovey wandered out from behind her chair, and I froze to avoid getting bitten. Then I noticed the tiny dog spectacles on her face, her eyes magnified, blinking up at me like a miniature aviator.

Most dealers don't. "I'm sure this will get sorted out." Why was I lying to her? If he had heroin in his possession that could be traced to the local deaths, the only sorting out would be how soon before he'd be sentenced.

I stood and reached out to pet Lovey. "She's calm now."

"Glasses make Lovey not monster."

I moved to pick up part of a broken frog on the carpet and wasn't attacked by the dog. "Maybe we can glue these together."

She took the broken pottery in her hands and turned it over and over. "Mother and son. The dead things in our houses."

The correlation worked. He kept dead animals and she kept Chia Pets after they'd "died." "I hadn't thought of that. But don't break any more, okay? They're your special collection."

We gathered all the pieces from the floor while the dog staggered around snuffling. This activity seemed to help Tinsel rein in her sadness for a moment. I vacuumed and then we sat at the kitchen table. I wrapped a sweater around her shoulders to stop her from shaking. She was in no condition to work on her speech today. "Can I call someone for you?"

She picked at the edge of the plastic placemat. "Nobody left." Tears leaked from her eyes and she didn't bother to wipe them away. "Alone. Alone." I'd hate myself if it weren't for the fact that people had overdosed and died. Frank wasn't selling marijuana; he'd chosen heroin, and in this case, it was proving deadly.

"You know who else is alone?"

Her eyes studied mine, magnified through her tears. "You?"

My stomach jumped. That was true if I were judged in the parents department. "No. That cute man you met at the ice cream social. Milt."

A small smile touched her lips. "Nice man, but quiet."

I laughed. "A man of few words until you get to know him." I held her hand. "We'll have you over to dinner soon. And then play cards. He likes cards."

"Okay." She squeezed my hand. "You and Pastor Betts?"

No thanks. I was completely and thoroughly debunked by a fireman last night. I smiled. "We're just friends." I got an idea. "But, I'll call him. He's just up around the corner."

She smiled. "I make coffee for him."

"Tinsel. You're using verbs now. Did you notice that?"

She nodded. "I eyes that."

When Christian picked up, I moved into the front entryway to talk to him. "Frank Tabbish has been arrested for having drugs at his place."

"No way! That's what you thought might be going on." He sounded as shocked as I'd been.

"Could you come by and sit with Tinsel? She's pretty upset and I need to get to my next patient."

"You know. Today's not so good. I'm on my way to Harrisburg to our district ministerial association meeting... Let me talk to her for a few minutes."

"Thank you, Christian... And when you get a chance, call me. I've had some interesting news about my birthparents."

"From that Marshal friend of yours?" His voice held a sharpness. He always seemed to bristle when I mentioned Scott.

I laughed. "Yeah. From him and Google."

"Remember..." His voice mocked. "Google does not have all of life's answers."

"That should be your next church message."

He chuckled. "Good idea ... See you Sunday?"

"Yeah. I think so." Tinsel was beside me, anticipation etched on her face. "I'm going to hand you to Mrs. Tabbish now. Talk to you soon."

Lovey and I wandered around the kitchen, her *bespectacledness* making her adorable now. Who knew? A little clearer vision—anger issues solved. Sounded like a T-shirt.

Tinsel handed my phone back and shrugged. "Coming by tomorrow."

Fifteen minutes later, I left her wrapped up in an afghan in her comfy chair, her favorite game show on, Lovey snoring on her lap. I'd check in with her later.

In the car, I dialed Jaxson. "Was Frank shocked when you arrested him?"

"Hella shocked." He laughed. "He went totes cray, saying we had the wrong guy."

"Are you sure it's him?"

"Yeah, we found a bundle in that locked closet you told me about."

"A bundle of what?"

"A bundle is ten bags of H."

Part of me wondered why Frank would stoop to selling drugs, but then I'd seen his occupation. Scooping up and reengineering dead animals would depress me. "What happens next?"

"They set his bail high, because of the deaths, so he's going to sit in jail." He *tssked.* "He'll be canned meat for a long time. Too bad we don't have the chair anymore. He'd be tasting the electric cure."

"His mom's really upset."

"Should be. She raised a criminal."

Harsh words, but I hadn't dealt with the deaths he and his department had seen in the last few weeks. "I don't think we should blame our parents for who we become."

"You favor your mother." I still liked the sound of those words.

"This whole working-together-to-solve-crimes thing is giving me life ... I think we should look into a little mattress polo, you and I."

I snorted then covered it up. "We're friends. That's good enough."

"And we caught Frank so easily, you never had to flip me your safe word."

"Cake? Thank goodness." I sighed. "And if I were in trouble, how would I have fit that into a conversation about taxidermy?"

"There's a squirrel here that looks flatter than a *cake* in a pan."

I laughed. "Yeah. That wouldn't have been weird." The car rocked as a logging truck blew by. I fought the wheel one-handed. "Hey. Gotta go. But call me if you hear more."

I pointed my car toward Casey's and yawned widely. Last night was catching up to me, but I wasn't complaining. Lawyer's sensual mouth, his strong and sure touch. Those body parts were my favorite. Remembering more of the evening, I laughed, thinking, *Yeah, right. You're forgetting that one big thing.* So tonight I'd vowed not to drink. I wanted no buffer between my senses and this man who literally sets me on fire.

A New Interest

Karl's truck was gone when I reached Casey's, so that made me happy. What was bothering me was the new hesitation in my car's speed, like it was falling asleep and waking up seconds later. All the gauges looked fine, so I'd worry about it later. Once outside in the Lesters' yard, the heat of the day carried long scented ribbons of hot dung and rotting vegetables. The goats were getting fatter, lazily sleeping under the canopies of the trees, by the porch, anywhere there was a piece of shade.

The front door was open so I pushed inside. "Whoa," I said, looking around. The dining room was spacious, all the newspapers gone, the wooden table and antique hutch visible for the first time.

Honey peeked around the corner from the kitchen. "Un-fucking-believable, huh?"

"I have to know. Are the papers in the basement, or did he like my Pinterest idea?"

She stamped her barefoot on the worn floorboards. "Nothing under there, but mice and probably his old dead grandma."

I flinched.

"Just shitting you." Her laugh ended in a gurgle sound at the end. "We're pretty sure it's just mice."

I raised my eyebrows. "He actually threw the papers away and went for the pinning idea?" I shrugged. "Like he made an account in his name?"

"I suggested Karl's Klutter but he went with Lester's News Stand." She leaned close to me, her breath was minty—not a trace of alcohol. "When you see him next, you can't mention Pinterest was your idea."

"Why does it matter whose idea it was if it works?" Sheesh. I wanted some credit for them not having their house condemned.

"He thinks I'm smart. I like it that way."

"Deal. I won't say anything." I looked around again. "He won't buy more papers, will he?"

She laughed. "Says he'll just take pictures when he gets tempted."

Casey came charging in the front door, flinging himself on the floor, rolling like a guy on fire. "I'm Assroh Man!"

I scowled. *With all the bad language in the house, maybe getting his hearing back wasn't in Casey's best interest. How was I going to teach this boy not to swear?* "He's who?"

Honey helped him to his feet and brushed grass and dirt off his knees. "Asteroid Man. We watched a documentary about the end of the world this morning, didn't we baby?" She leaned over him, tucking his shirt into his shorts, nearly lifting him off the ground in the process.

I bit my tongue and slammed my lips together. The end of the world? He's five! *I will not lecture, I will not lecture.* One of Casey's hearing aids squealed and I twisted it back in place. "C'mon, Asteroid Man. Let's get to work."

Casey had improved his sound production at the phrase and sentence level to the point I could move onto picture books with him. I chose one with simple phrases about the owl that wasn't so wise. Together we told the story; first with me reading a short line, and then him repeating it. I'd forgotten to bring more books for Honey and this gave me an idea.

I pulled up Google on my phone and searched for bookmobiles in the area. One popped up in a town I recognized in the county. I jotted the phone number down, pleased. If Honey wouldn't take the time to go to the library, we'd bring the library to her.

A news story caught my eye. "Local man arrested for possession of heroin." There was Frank's mug shot. He looked bad, his face frozen with an angry stare, like he'd had a swig of Formalin before they hauled him in. I felt bad and then I didn't. He'd ruined people's lives.

We finished the owl story and were halfway through *The Dog Who Wanted To Be A Cat* when Honey came in and sat on the edge of the couch. She interrupted, "Don't let Karl catch you reading transgender crap to him."

"Wha—? No. That's not it." I showed her the book. "The dog wants to stay inside like the cat, and get carried around."

"Whatever." She flipped her hair off her neck and turned her head toward Casey. "He's doing pretty good, huh?"

Was I going to cry? She'd never recognized his progress before. "Doing great." I handed her the phone number and explained the bookmobile. "They even have books on tape like I suggested. You follow along and learn the words you didn't know before."

"Sometimes you're more smart than sass."

I gathered my things and winked. "I don't know about that. But thanks."

I confirmed our next appointment and tousled Casey's hair. "Off you go, buddy."

When I got to the porch, the goat stench hit hard.

My phone vibrated. Lawyer texted me his new number with the question, "Where to tonight? Your choice."

I replied, "I'm thinking, but be ready. Back to u soon."

I pulled out along Rutabaga Drive and my car was really protesting now. Something clicking, there was an occasional bang and it seemed to be hesitating more than ever. I was supposed to be taking Sofie out to West Trout Run. I dialed Jon Dougan's number to cancel.

A Big Production

"You can take our car." Jon solved my problem by letting me drive their 2010 Buick LaCrosse to the abandoned town. He was anxious to have Sofie visit there again because her thoughts had stayed grounded most of the day before, once we returned. "She remembers us and our kids," he said, his chin quivering when I arrived at their house. But he added that this morning she slipped back to thinking she was single and working with her grandfather.

The car windows were darker than I was used to but once I had the vehicle on the road, it was easy to handle. I had no idea what had happened to my car. My car had always been dependable, traveling a hundred miles a day, so why did it now have a major breakdown?

Sofie wore a bright pink lipstick today, spiking above her lip line in two places like she'd applied it while jumping rope.

Or maybe Jon had helped.

It *was* hard to put lipstick on someone's mouth. I'd helped a woman at a nursing home once and it was like moving the tube of color over two squirmy worms.

She'd been talking about Roger and his friends in the lumber camp. "Those boys work from dusk to dark. They get up before daylight and eat half a dozen fried eggs and bacon so's to get out into those woods at first light."

"They have to be pretty tough."

She smiled, but not at me. A long ago suitor had her attention for a moment. I let her enjoy that as I tried to come up with a place for Lawyer and me to go tonight. I hardly knew the area so I was at a disadvantage.

"Gramps and I get here around the noon meal, which the men eat in the woods. Usually just pork fatback and beans. Roger says you can judge a camp by the cookhouse."

"Why's that?"

"If there's a rocking chair in the kitchen, no good." She waved her arms like calling someone safe at home plate. "A good cook has no time to be sitting in any kind of chair."

"Good point... What did you say Roger does when there's no fire?"

"Everything. Logging and peeling bark in the summer, but in the fall, after the nettles died down, when you can see the ginseng leaves, he'd go *shanging* for about two months."

"I have no idea what that is." I took a right and saw that we were half a mile from the turnoff and the steep downhill trail.

Her face changed to surprise that I had never heard of something so obvious. "Digging up ginseng roots. For the Asians." She leaned toward me, whispering, "They think it's a healthy thing."

"Ginseng? Sure. It's sold everywhere near my place in San Francisco."

She dropped back in her seat. "What are you? A pioneer? A hobo? Nobody I know has been past the Mississippi." She was instantly agitated, two different time periods colliding in our car. She twisted her shirt, then wrung her hands.

She was back living in the 1930s.

"I saw it in National Geographic," I said.

That appeased her. She licked her lips with a dry tongue, and paused to gather her thoughts. "That's a nice magazine."

We reached the road down to the river and the town, but a log had been dropped across the entrance, blocking our passage. "What the heck?" No one was in sight—no forest ranger or county worker. Why would this be blocked off when it was open yesterday?

"This is disappointing." I turned to Sofie and shrugged.

Tears brimmed her eyes. "But Roger needs a noonday meal."

I debated what to do. "Wait here," I said. I put the car in park and got out. Grabbing the smaller end of the log, I tried to drag it to the side so I could drive past. It moved an inch before I dropped it; the muscles in my back and shoulders screamed. There was no other branch to lever it away. I walked back to the car and studied Sofie. She was in good shape physically. "Are you in the mood to walk to camp today?"

She was out of her seat and standing by the log before I knew it. I pulled off to the side of the road near the trees, so the car wouldn't be blocking the road if the log got moved.

The day was clear, still hot but tolerable under the awning of trees as we headed down the road. We went slowly, talking quietly as if the forest demanded this. Our feet hit the red wooden bridge and beat out a steady rhythm as we crossed toward thicker trees on the other side. I studied the thirty-foot drop to a smaller creek below. Clear water snaked through the lush, green growth, gurgling on a course it couldn't halt, framed by forest at the top of the ravine.

Sofie halted at the mouth of the tree tunnel. "There's ghosts in here."

I saw nothing. "It's okay, Sofie. Just dark because the trees are so thick." I walked a few steps out of the sunlight and reached my hand back for her to take. "See? It's fine."

Hesitantly, she took my hand and we followed the road. A thick silence surrounded us, muffling our footsteps. A hundred yards ahead, daylight waited. I encouraged her along, whispering that we were okay, that I could hear the roar from the river which was just up ahead.

We stepped out into the open space. A large bird took flight over our heads and I grabbed my heart. "Whoa," I said. "I guess I am a bit jumpy."

"That's because there's ghosts here," she whispered, and pointed toward the trees. "In there."

I hesitated and cocked my head, wondering at first what I heard. It sounded like a door flung open, hitting into a wall. Could it be another animal crashing around? I studied the settlement in front of us and nothing moved. There were no cars, and today it really felt like a ghost town. My gaze followed her finger toward the woods, relieved to see only thick shades of green. "But no ghosts today."

Side by side, we crunched along the road, not speaking. I let her enjoy her memories, understanding that sometimes there isn't enough time to relish the past, especially when one's past is lost to them.

We'd seen the store yesterday so this time I led her to the left, to what remained of a small building. The faded red cross on one wall suggested it had been the hospital. Most of the roof was missing, but we found a cleared path that let us look in the back windows. Beds once laid out along one wall were now just rusted metal springs. White porcelain washbowls sat on counters above cabinets. There was a hand pump in one sink. "Do you think many men died out here?"

"They still die." Her tone was angry. "Tom Wilkins got on the wrong side of a slide just a few weeks ago. Found him miles downriver, so broken up they couldn't show him to his mama."

I'd forgotten to use present tense. "That's terrible. So dangerous here."

She looked to the empty paths around the buildings. Weeds choked out the foundation walls. "Everyone's gone."

"Let's go through the church and out to the cookhouse." I helped her walk over some flat stones that had been a wall of a blacksmith's shop. Lost in our thoughts, we stepped into the church and headed to the rear. We cut down the next hallway and I stopped. The door to the candle room was open today and I leaned in. A light from the window illuminated the interior, but there was a lantern on a cement shelf, throwing light onto the new items inside: all the candlemaking supplies missing from Christian's church basement. What the hell? He had come here already? And why had he set up shop so far from his church? I looked down the hallway and no one was around. The air held the scent of recently warmed wax and now there were candle forms, packing cartons, Saran Wrap. Was Christian here? My heart thudded, remembering he'd told me he was in a conference near Harrisburg today. So if he hadn't brought this stuff from his basement, then who had? Sofie paced the floor in the hallway, looking at the old paintings on the walls.

I walked to a closed carton and pulled back the flaps. Below lay rows of four-inch thick round candles, side by side. I touched one of them. The wax layer was soft, warm, recently poured. This is what I had just smelled.

We should leave. I listened again but heard nothing, although clearly someone had just been here. I needed to show this to Jaxson. I had no idea what was going on, but something wasn't right. Digging out one of the candles, I held it up. Although the yellowish wax made it opaque, the candle had a white core.

My hands trembled as I pulled out my keys. Using the longest one, I cut through the wax and a long bag of white material fell out onto the floor. "Shit," I whispered. This was a drug shipment.

There was no way Christian was doing this, yet the evidence was right in front of me. Was he working with Frank? That would be so easy to have arranged with Tinsel as a connection. Or had Frank used Christian, setting up a lookalike shipping system, moving drugs in bibles instead of inside his stuffed animals? Either way, I knew now why the road was blocked and why we needed to leave immediately.

I took Sofie's arm and led her toward the front of the church. "We have to go."

She struggled out of my grasp. "Roger is waiting." She marched back the way we had just come.

"No! Sofie. We can't stay here now." I went after her, trying to keep my voice as quiet as possible. "We'll come back."

She headed into the little room with the drugs and started to close the door on me. "I'm waiting for Roger."

I pushed, wedging my body in the door so she couldn't close it. I said, "Seriously. There *is* a ghost here today and we're in danger."

Her eyes went wide. I assumed she was reacting to the word "ghost" until I noticed she was looking over my shoulder. A hand yanked me backward, and I hit the wall on the other side of the hall hard enough to yelp.

It was Christian, his face red with fury. He spoke to Sofie. "Come out here right now."

She obeyed without arguing and stood at my side.

"Out to the pews." He pointed toward the door, leading to the main area of the church, but not before he pulled the door closed and locked it.

He pushed me into a front row pew and Sofie sat next to me.

"Christian—"

"Shut up." He took a wooden chair and placed it a few feet away, facing us. "You have no fucking idea what you've done."

He hadn't seen *me* in his preparation room, so I pretended no knowledge of what we'd found. "This is one of my patients, Sofie. She has dementia."

"I do not." She scowled and scooted a few feet away. "I am perfectly fine."

"She does." I talked fast. "We were visiting the town because she used to work here years ago. I told you about her. Looks like you've had a chance to look around. Maybe you could—"

"Stop it." He leaned forward, rubbing his palms into his eyes, his fingers extended toward his hairline. Then he looked up, his eyes boring into mine. "The log across the road didn't tell you anything?"

"No, I just got out and moved it." I forced my voice to stay level but I heard a quaver there. Surely he wouldn't hurt us. He and I were friends. We'd laughed together. Put on an ice cream social.

"Really? Then where's your goddamn car?" His voice was soft and level, scary in that it held no affect.

"Okay. I didn't move the log. But we're done now, so we'll just walk back out." I held up my hands. "And I can see you are having an off day... no clue what's gotten into you."

His face twisted into something new, but it wasn't a smile. "You're telling me you weren't snooping in the rooms before I got there?"

"Sofie'd just walked in when you came along." He might believe that since that is what he saw. "We're just here for a few minutes to jog her memory before heading back." I searched his eyes for a bit of understanding and got none.

A sneer slowly spread across his mouth. "Here's why I know you're lying." He leaned forward again, his eyes hard like small green marbles. "You haven't asked what's in the room and that's because you already know."

I shrugged. "Doesn't matter to me what you do with your time. Candlemaking is cool." I fought to keep my hands from trembling by clasping them in front of me.

"It does though. You were helping the local cops, checking out Tinsel's son." He almost smiled this time. "By the way, once you told me about that locked room he has, it was easy to set Frank up...And I told you how one of my stupid parishioners OD'd? That will be linked to Frank, too. But again, my point is that you're lying." He cocked his head. "It's a sin, you know."

"She *is* a liar." Sofie slapped at my arm even though I wasn't looking her way. "Roger isn't here."

"Who's Roger?"

"Her boyfriend from forty years ago."

Sofie was agitated now. "He *is* my boyfriend but I don't know who *you* are."

I reached for Sofie but she pulled away. *Great. Now I have to fight her, too.* I started to stand, looking for a less submissive position from which to reason with him.

He sprung from the chair and grabbed my hair, shoving me to my seat, doubling me over on the pew, holding me there. My head was on fire where he twisted my hair tighter. He leaned close to my ear. "You have put me in such a bad position... and I really don't want to have to take care of you."

"Yeah, I don't want that either," I mumbled into my legs.

Sofie rose and headed toward the center aisle.

He gave my hair one last twist and went after her, grabbing her from behind, an arm across her neck, squeezing.

"Leave her alone!" I launched myself at him, pulled on his arms, trying to loosen them. Sofie's face was turning red. I scratched at his face, trying to remember any self-defense Beryl had tried to show me, but I couldn't get near Christian's throat to poke him there. I grabbed his ear, sinking my nails deep into his flesh.

"Bitch!" he screamed, pushing Sofie onto the pew where she sagged but remained upright.

Thank God.

I backed away from him. He faced me, wound up, ready to spring. I held up my hands. "Please let her go. She really won't remember any of this." I hurried on. "I'll show you." I slid onto the seat next to Sofie. "Why are we here, Sofie?"

When her eyes met mine, my heart broke. The fear and mistrust on her face shattered me. I was supposed to be helping her and instead I'd put her in danger. "I don't know," she said.

I pointed to the room we'd come from. "What was in that little room with the lantern?"

Her chin quivered and looked at both of us now. "Old chairs, I think."

"Sofie, how old are you?"

She didn't answer at first and I silently begged her not to say "seventy." She rubbed her neck where he had choked her. "I'm seventeen and I'm going to tell Gramps that you"—she pointed to Christian—"were rude."

Christian was thinking, pulling on the ear I'd scratched. "Big deal. So she can't remember shit. You should have thought of that before you got all nosy. I had the perfect place to work all of these months and now, you've ruined that, leaving me little choice."

"Yes, you do. Let her walk back to the car." The glimmer of hope gave me strength. "Or she can just stay in the old store. She wanted to look around longer but I didn't let her. Someone will come by once you move the log."

He paced, studied her, and then barked at her. "Get out of here."

I was relieved when she stood, but then she didn't leave. I said, "Sofie, go on now. Just walk to the store and wait there for your boyfriend."

Her face lit up. "Roger's there?"

I spoke soothingly. It wasn't lost on me that this might be the last conversation I'd ever have with a client. "He will be. You just need to think about seeing him. But don't follow me, okay?"

And just like that, she smoothed her hair back and smiled at both of us, turning and heading down the aisle and out the door.

The room got quiet, eerily so. I had to know. "What are you going to do with me?"

He sighed. "I'm going to eventually shoot you and then take you back and bury you behind the church, next to old Reverend McCallister."

My heart pounded and I tried not to black out. I needed to stall, to think of a way to run into the woods. And the truth hit me that he had killed before. "Let me guess. You were somehow involved in there being a job opening."

He smiled, a cruel thing. "He did die in his chair. But I was passing through this area and might have sped that up for him. At least that was what I told the family members."

Family members! *I'm from a big Italian family, New Jersey.* All the talk about the Kingstons and the mob. "Seriously?

You're from a crime family?" My voice was a little numb. I hadn't thought of this and I could see my plan starting to falter if he had those connections. A wave of anger passed through me. I was reliving the Kingstons' nightmare. Except there would be no witness protection for me. It didn't look like I'd live long enough to tell anyone anything. And, if by some miracle I got away, a long line of "relatives," not the kind I was hoping to meet, would come looking for me.

A board lay on the floor under the pews where I'd been bent over. I stood and took a step closer to him and stopped. "Just shoot and get it over with." I let my shoulders sag, going for a defeated look. My breath stopped when he pulled a pistol from his back, from under his shirt.

I cut my eyes to the doorway, widening them like I'd seen someone, and yelled, "Run! He's got a gun!" Christian spun and aimed the gun at the door and fired off a shot. The sound deafened my moves as I dove for the board, wrapped both hands around it, and once on my knees, I swung with all I had at his shins.

He yelled, dropped to his knees and the gun clattered to the floor and slid under the pews, skittering a few rows back.

I ran past him to the hallway, trying to judge if I'd make the cutout in the back wall the deer had jumped through. I wouldn't. He'd be there long before me and I'd take a bullet to the back. I threw the board down the hall and it made a noise that covered the sound of my steps when I descended into the basement.

The dark was complete, having all my attention as I tried to make my eyes bore through the blackness. I missed the last step but held a scream inside as I hit the dirt floor, knocking the air out of me. Crawling on the dirt floor, my hands fumbled around, taking inventory of my new surroundings.

Broken table, upturned single bed with metal springs on a frame. Wooden crates, a broken podium on its side, jars and bottles filled with liquids. I crawled behind the podium but the space in back wouldn't hide me. The smell of death was stronger as I moved farther into the room, and when I touched fur I knew why. I pulled out my phone and hit the flashlight. A large deer, long dead, lay flattened in the back corner; one leg caught in a drain, the limb twisted the wrong way. This was the stench Elyk and I smelled on our first visit.

The floor above creaked and I heard him in the hallway; it sounded like he was limping.

I turned off the light. I had my little can of Mace® and a tiny fire extinguisher—a child's joke of a weapon against a gun.

He called out, "Remember, Marleigh. God answers all knee mail. Or how about, 'Can't sleep? Don't count sheep, talk to the shepherd.'" He laughed, took another step.

I lifted the edge of the hide on the deer. Even though it was desiccated and down to skin and skeleton, it was heavy. I slowly pulled it over myself, gagging at the smell, a shiver of revulsion as the rib cage climbed my back. I moved under it, lying flat on the floor as it covered me. Now what? Stay here until I died?

I thumbed my phone to silent then texted Jaxson. I typed quickly, made an error, typed again. Finally I had, "Cake time! Not Frank. Black tar has a prayer." Then to Scott. I trusted him to find Sofie and get her out of this town. Heroin smuggling was a federal crime—his area of expertise. I recited the alphabet in my head to get the right numbers to their corresponding letters for "help." Then I quickly pulled up the picture of Sofie by the West Trout Run sign and typed "P.O. Box 851216!" beneath it and pushed send. The top step creaked. My guts felt like they were filled with nightcrawlers.

Lawyer was last. "Meet me in 15 at the top of OUR fire tower." Send.

Two more steps protested across the cellar. He said, "Let the Lord light up your life, not GE." He sounded crazy, a desperate raging tinge that wasn't there before.

Weak light appeared along the edges of the deer hide. I flattened myself lower until the inside cavity went dark again.

A kick caught the deer carcass in the side. I froze, willing him to move on. Seconds later, the carcass was ripped off me. I scrambled to my knees and my phone bounced away.

"You are one tough girl." He had the gun against the side of my head. "You'd make my family proud." He pushed the gun hard against my temple. "Up."

"Maybe I should meet them." I shrugged. "I'm free today."

He picked up my phone. "Too late." He thumbed through my messages, stopping on the last one to Lawyer. "Aw. That's cute. Unfortunately, you can't keep that appointment."

He read the one to Scott and I saw his eyebrows bunch. "What's this P.O. Box number?"

I needed to get the phone away before he saw the message to Jaxson. I stood and backed toward the steps. "That's to Sofie's husband so he can come get his wife and their car."

He followed me with the gun. "I was wondering how your car made it here with all the diesel fuel I put in your tank."

"When did you do that?"

"When you said you were at Tinsel's. A quick drive-by while I had her on the phone."

Any of those obstacles could have stopped me from being here—a car that didn't work, the barrier across the road—but I'd pressed on.

With a nudge from the gun, he pushed me up the stairs. I'd tried. I held little hope that any of the messages would make it in time to save me, but Sofie would be found. Maybe Jaxson would figure out my message and get to the church before I was buried in some unknown place on the grounds. And now that I no longer had the phone in my hand, I wished I'd told Lawyer I loved him.

We exited the front of the church and walked around the side of the store. His car was parked in the tunnel of trees, invisible from the angle Sofie and I had taken into the town. I hoped Sofie would be okay. We passed the store but I didn't see her there. As we neared the trees, I felt true panic. He would lead me to the woods and shoot me. I dragged my feet, making him push me along. Then, at our backs, the store blew up in a huge *whoosh*, fire and stones exploding into the sky from the interior. The windows blew out, sending the debris toward us. The explosion gave me the chance to run and I found a reserve of strength I didn't know I had. I'd never make it up the hill again before he caught me, so I headed for the churning river, the gun sounding at regular intervals behind me. Right before I dove in, something stung me in the thigh, a burning pain that would have dropped me to the ground had I not been airborne. But I had another worry. Had Sofie survived that blast? The thought ended when freezing water nearly knocked me unconscious. I fought to stay above the rolling waves.

Running the Rapids

I thrashed around in the strong current, then got a stroke going and tried to get closer to shore. I grabbed at a small branch hanging over the river. The fast moving water sucked me under. I let go and swam hard, heading for a rock up ahead. A whirlpool, spinning just before the rock, pulled me under again and I crashed into the boulder, which sent a shooting pain up my right forearm. Clawing at the waves with my good arm, I pushed off the rock with my foot and was spit out downstream, still in the center of the river. I was going to die. Not a good swimmer to start with, I stood no chance with one arm. Now I fought to regulate my breath, but between the freezing water and the pain raking my arm, my lungs felt like they were shriveling. Like an oxygen mask on a plane, but with no air flowing.

People flashed in my mind—milliseconds only—as I made one last attempt for the shore. Little Casey. I hoped they knew what a special kid they had. Melvin, Luella, Ivory. I learned from them. Elyk. I took in a mouthful of water and coughed, went under and fought my way to the surface, but my efforts led to diminished results. Elyk, my unconventional friend. Milt, my sounding board.

Slipping below the surface, I had the weirdest last thought: I pictured my closet, finding comfort, peace. Maybe death wouldn't be so terrible.

A hand grabbed the back of my shirt and hauled me out of the water. I lay face down on rough logs. I was rolled onto my back and a voice that seemed far away said, "You're okay now."

My last thought before everything went shiny white, then black was, "Why did God sound like Beers?"

The Devil's in the
Details

"**I**s the mob going to be looking for me?" The words scraped my sore throat as they came out. Scott Schumer scratched one cheek, pushing the rocker back and forth. We were all on the front porch of the inn. Rose had seen to lemonade and iced tea. Lawyer stood behind me, nudged out of a seat next to me on the swing by my wrinkled guard dog, Milt. He hadn't left my side since I came home from the hospital yesterday. Jaxson leaned against the railing.

Scott said, "Christian Betts, actually Christopher Baratta, was thrown out of his family's business. They'd gone straight years ago, turning from crime to honest businessmen. He unfortunately hadn't caught onto their new plan. Baratta has a rap sheet including gun violations, burglary, and drug possession. Jersey's been looking for him."

Jaxson said, "Weird that there was Formalin in the heroin."

Scott crossed his arms. "Found out it's also used in candlemaking. He knew what he was doing, but somehow the Formalin got into some of the dope. And, he'd been using that old church for months before you surprised him."

"Yeah, that's what he said. And I should have noticed he acted weird when I started talking about visiting it."

Jaxson chimed in, "He's up for murder one now. Solves that cold case on McCallister."

We all fell silent thinking of the events.

Then Milt vibrated, the signal he had something to say, and we all turned to him. "Made a fire?" he choked out.

I laughed. "Yes. Sofie sure did. A big fire. I was counting on her for this."

Lawyer squeezed my shoulder. "Big enough to be seen from the fire tower."

"You knew," Jaxson said. "You got me and the popo pointed to the church. You're *the* force. Nice work. Glad we didn't lose you."

"Thanks, Jaxson," I said.

We were all quiet again. Then I asked, "What's going to happen with Sofie?"

Lawyer said, "We've talked to Jon a lot. It was a hard decision but they're selling the house. It's too big anyway, he admitted. They'll be moving into the assisted living center out on Butler Road."

I sighed. They wouldn't charge her with each of the arson fires she set, so that was good. She saved my life. Well, she and someone else.

I tipped my head toward the front door. "Is Beers inside?"

Jaxson said, "Yeppers."

"I need to talk to him." I grabbed the chain to pull myself out of the swing and Lawyer lifted from behind, both hands gently around my waist. The bullet had only grazed my leg, and the wound was clean; nothing more drastic than four stitches to close it. The fact I'd been shot would take me a bit longer to get over.

Milt followed me inside and we found Beers at the table by himself, eating from a huge bowl of cereal.

I laughed, indicating the bowl. "Lunch, huh?"

He chewed and talked around the crunch. "Cereal is civilization."

"Indeed," I said, then asked, "where are your parents?"

He shrugged. "Packing, calling a taxi." He smiled. "Not bugging me."

I laughed, then grew serious. "Thanks for saving me."

"No problem." He scooped in another spoonful, watching me as he chewed.

"Just one question. Where have you been for six days?"

"Surviving. Walked about thirty miles, they said." He set down the spoon and smiled. "I saw you there with the old lady a few days ago."

"Ah." I crossed my arms. "You're the ghost in the woods."

He laughed. "She looked freaked…But mainly I was proving my parents wrong, that I could do something hard on my own."

"You built that raft?"

"Yup. Kinda shitty, but I hoped to make it to Maryland."

"Sorry I stopped you." I shrugged. "But not really."

"I'll be back." He pushed his chair away and took the bowl to the sink. "I'm thinking about going to the state college in Mansboro."

He let me hug him, popped on his headset, and smiled at me while turning up his music before leaving. Moments later, the Diffleys packed their bikes in the taxi and pulled away.

I sat with Milt. "You heard any good jokes lately?"

He slowly pointed to my wounded left leg. "You're all right now."

I laughed hard. The punch line fit me perfectly.

Scott Schumer popped his head in the kitchen and saw that Beers was gone. He stepped closer. "You okay with the stuff I told you about the Kingstons?"

I thought for a moment and raised my chin. "It's going to take a while to sink in." Off to my closet the second I got some time without my entourage. "Am I devastated? ... I was, before, but now I'm trying to see it as a positive thing."

He smiled, then saluted me.

I saluted back.

Lawyer came in. He enveloped me in a soft hug, all parts of our bodies touching. I felt a response in my girl parts even though I was sore almost everywhere else. He spoke, still holding me. "Jaxson left. Told me to remind you that you've always got the runs to look forward to. Whatever the hell that means."

I chuckled. "That's his running group." I pushed back a few inches and kissed him, long and slow, something I thought might never happen again. Then I studied his face, our eyes connecting in that deep way that unnerved me, but also made me delirious with trust. "You should know, I'm falling in love."

A crooked smile slowly spread across his face. "Well, you should know, I already beat you to it."

He would be back later tonight. We were going to his house to watch TV with his mom, to have pizza, to do normal things people who are still alive do. And for next weekend, he'd booked a weekend away in the Poconos.

My car would be fixed in another day; the Sheriff's Department was picking up the tab. Then I had to be back to work. I admit, I was ready for that, too.

A short while later, Milt and I sat next to each other in the closet. I hadn't shared what Scott told me earlier with anyone yet, although I'd tell people soon enough—definitely before we got to the Roseburg cemetery tomorrow.

"The Kingstons aren't buried in that cemetery I took you to." I pictured their headstone. "As a matter of fact, they aren't dead at all." My throat constricted. "They'd gone to the local sheriff's department when Daryl slipped up at his job at the salt mine. He trusted someone he shouldn't have, told them about missing football in Texas. You see, they lived in Dallas when they happened to be visiting Pittsburgh during the mob hit."

Milt cleared his throat, then said, "Religion there."

I laughed. "In Texas, football is." I patted his hand. "Daryl revealed accidentally that he and his family were in the witness protection program. A day later someone fired a shot at Amber while she was pushing me around the block, and that got everyone moving again."

It would be so hard to start over anonymously, to never mention a thing from your past. I couldn't blame him for slipping up.

"Things happened fast. I was put up for a closed adoption, which the Bennings jumped at. The sheriff at the time covered up their fake car accident, a quick burial ensued, and the Kingstons disappeared again."

"When you see them?"

Tears clouded my eyes. "I think I won't." I wiped the tears away.

A scan of the earth, using the same technology they used in King Tut's tomb, confirmed no organic matter inside the coffins below their gravesite. And when Scott Schumer investigated their last recorded relocation town in South Carolina, they had moved. Witnesses were supposed to check in with the government once a year, or more often if they relocated or had a life-changing event. But the Kingstons, over a decade ago when they would have been in their forties, dropped off the Marshal's radar.

The magnitude of the possibility that Daryl and Amber might still be alive was almost more than I could handle. I came here to find out about my dead birthparents, only to find out they weren't necessarily dead. And that I favored my mother.

"You favor your mother."

This, from the man who had lived next to my mother when she was a new mom. And I was a baby. This became the pillar around which I built my happiness. This was real. Everything else—that no one knew where my parents had gone, or if they were even still alive—remained a mystery I had no choice but to accept.

ACKNOWLEDGEMENTS

Thank you to all of my beta readers, Karen Nickell, Kristy Pappas, Rick Christensen, Jeff Lowder, Bill Chabala, Kate Chabala, John Hardy, and Brittani Jay who gave me invaluable feedback on the first draft of this manuscript and let me bounce ideas off of them. To my critique group for your monthly feedback: Bill Dennis, Linda Orvis, Sherri Curtis, Ericka Prechtel, Rich Casper and David Tippetts. To Faith Mayo, thank you for your amazing attention to detail, to finding plot deviations and for your editing ability. You are a rare find. To Hedgehog & Fox for your promotional skills. Thank you to Sarah Warner for your friendship and enthusiasm for this series. And as always, my biggest cheerleader has been by husband, John Hardy. My dream of publication is because you made it your dream for me, too.

Interview with the Author

INTERVIEWER: Your characters are so believable, yet quite unique. How do you come up with them?

KARLA: My goal is to avoid stereotypical characters. I create someone and then give them characteristics one would not suspect: Dottie is a skeet shooting champion; Elyk solves crosswords; and Beryl, who can seem so coarse, is a softy when it comes to less-than-perfect pets.

INTERVIEWER: How hard was it to write a sequel?

KARLA: A lot harder than I thought! It took me months to get traction. I needed to introduce Marleigh, her family situation, and all of the main characters without saying what had happened in the first book.

INTERVIEWER: Do you consider yourself a mystery writer?

KARLA: I wouldn't have said my goal was to write mysteries, but since I've based each book around one, I guess I am. My book has a little bit of everything in it, so let's just say I'm an everything writer.

INTERVIEWER: What are your greatest challenges as an author with an ever-increasing and avid fan base of readers?

KARLA: I love the connection I have with my readers through social media so I gravitate toward sharing time with them there when I'm not at work. I own a company and work there full-time. Sometimes it can take hours to check all of the websites, answer questions, and send out new notices to interested readers. I try to balance that time with sitting down and doing what I should be doing more often, which is writing.

INTERVIEWER: What have you learned about yourself as a writer?

KARLA: I can't sit down to write unless I know I have at least a two-hour block of time. I also have a hard time staying completely focused on my current project and will find myself doing research for a war idea or a noir screenplay! So many ideas—so little time! This has taught me to set deadlines.

CPSIA information can be obtained
at www.ICGtesting.com
Printed in the USA
FSOW01n0803021216
28077FS